Jeff Dawson is a journalist and author. He has been a long-standing contributor to *The Sunday Times* Culture section, writing regular A-list interview-led arts features (interviewees including the likes of Robert De Niro, George Clooney, Dustin Hoffman, Hugh Grant, Angelina Jolie, Jerry Seinfeld and Nicole Kidman). He is also a former US Editor of *Empire* magazine.

Jeff is the author of three non-fiction books – *Tarantino/Quentin Tarantino: The Cinema of Cool*, *Back Home: England And The 1970 World Cup*, which *The Times* rated 'Truly outstanding', and *Dead Reckoning: The Dunedin Star Disaster*, the latter nominated for the Mountbatten Maritime Prize.

Also by Jeff Dawson

An Ingo Finch Mystery

No Ordinary Killing
The Cold North Sea
Hell Gate

— NO —
ORDINARY
KILLING

JEFF DAWSON

CANELO

First published in the United Kingdom in 2017 by Endeavour Press Ltd

This edition published in the United Kingdom in 2021 by

Canelo
31 Helen Road
Oxford OX2 0DF
United Kingdom

A CIP catalogue record for this book is available from the British Library.

Print ISBN 978 1 78863 559 2
Ebook ISBN 978 1 78863 190 7

Look for more great books at www.canelo.co

Printed and bound in Great Britain by Clays Ltd, Elcograf S.p.A.

In memory of my dear Dad, who gave me my love of history.

Part One

Chapter One

Finch had heard that the dead could dance. Strung along the length of the wire, the vanguard of the Black Watch conspired for one final, macabre reel – their loose limbs jerked by the lashing rain and the *thud-thud-thud* of the artillery shells, which still shook the living to their core.

Ahead, on the rim of the Boer trench, a Highlander had been ensnared in an upright stance, kilt apron flapping, arms flung up at the moment of heroic sacrifice. The poor bastard's feet hovered inches off the ground, as if frozen at the start of his heavenly ascent.

In the pale moonlight, against the interminable rumble, the potshots came – the crack of Mauser accompanied by a heart-stopping *zing* off the rocks. The marksmen, sensing movement, still sought to thwart the spectral Caledonian advance.

"Miles, are you there?"

Finch's voice broke out of its whisper – a yelp of frustration at the sloth of his accomplice.

"Miles?"

The bile, the fear, was acrid in his throat. He hugged the hard African ground, took a handful of the red surface run-off and smeared it on his face, his hands, anything that might catch the light. His heart beat so loudly it tattooed in his ears.

"*Miles*," he hissed, raising himself on his elbows. It was hard to control the tremors.

He twisted to his left, scanning the terrain behind, the direction from whence they'd come. He was soaked, exhausted, achingly cold. His bloodied knees, protruding through the rips in his britches, were numb to sensation.

"Miles. Where are—?"

3

"Doctor, here. Over *here*."

Finch turned right. Private Miles crept over, dragging the stretcher behind him.

"Get down! For God's sake. Get down!"

The private complied, way too casually.

Crack-*zing*. Crack-*zing*. Crack-*zing*.

The shots were coming close.

Finch cast a sideways glance. The skinny, spotty, adolescent was unfathomably blasé about the death that circled them.

On the horizon, ten miles away, the blade of the Kimberley arc light stabbed vertically, flashing coded Morse off the scattered clouds. It was broadcasting its defiant message, no doubt – that it held fast, its citizens unbowed. Though the truth, Finch knew, was probably very different.

"Sir. Any Boojers?"

"Miles. Shut up."

His voice nearly snapped again. He was pretty sure they had found what they were looking for.

"There," he said, the wonder being that he'd discovered it at all.

The doctor propelled his 6ft frame by his forearms, dragging his own body alongside that of the casualty. He rubbed the dirt off the embroidered shoulder badge. The mounted St George of the Northumberland Fusiliers was just discernible. It was the lieutenant they'd been looking for, lying face-up, moaning faintly.

So sodden and battered, so caked in battlefield grime was he, there was no time for a diagnosis. That he was still breathing, after all these hours, was all that mattered – still wheezing, no rattle yet in the back of his throat.

The lieutenant saw the canteen attached to Finch's webbing belt and made a faint gesture. Finch unhooked it. Clumsily he unscrewed the cap. His hand shook so much that it clattered. He pressed it to the wounded man's lips.

"Easy, chum," he soothed. "Small sips."

They would have to drag him, pulling the stretcher along like a litter. It would require a big physical effort, keeping low all the way. Their own lines were half a mile back – half a mile over rocks, craters and cadavers. And with Boer bullets pinging at them.

Finch's legs were jelly, almost paralysed, like they used to be before the starter's gun in his days as a youth steeplechaser. Only worse. Much, much worse.

Finch motioned towards the stretcher, towards Miles. Jesus, did he have to spell everything out?

Miles pondered, then scraped it along the ground, nonchalant. They took the man between them – Finch's hands under the armpits, Miles grabbing the legs – and heaved him onto the canvas. He groaned again.

The increasing *boom-boom-boom* was stirring the Afrikaners now. Finch could hear murmurs, the shuttle of rifle bolts not 50 yards away.

According to military convention, artillery fire was a softening-up exercise, prelude to an advance – another pointless advance.

More visceral than the thunder of a tropical storm, the sheer volume of a barrage could break a spirit as much as a body. But they knew Brother Boojer now. Brother Boojer would simply dig in and bear it.

Zing, zing, zing.

They could feel the heat of the bullets, the lead ricocheting around them. The clang of Finch's canteen was no different to the rattle of the tin cans that the Boers had hung on the tripwires. There would be other Tommies out there, Finch guessed – scouts probing, snipping the wire. The Boers were laying on their customary hospitality.

"Over there…! Miles. Move it!"

The stretcher was abandoned as they hauled the casualty off it and into the lee of a fallen cavalry charger – bloated, capsized, its rancid grey entrails spewed across the veld.

The *wap-wap-wap* of bullets into the horse's hide confirmed that they'd been spotted. They pulled themselves in tight. At some point they'd have to make a dash – the sooner the better.

The beating in Finch's ears was deafening now, his breathing so fast, so shallow, he thought he would suffocate. The top of the carcass was being sheared off. Chunks of putrefied flesh rained down. If the Boers kept this up…

"Miles. Listen to me."

Crack-*zing*, crack-*zing*.

Miles was elsewhere.

"Miles!"

"Sir."

They were huddled together, knees pulled in under their chins, the wounded lieutenant folded around their shins.

"*Miles!*"

Finch put his palms to the infantryman's cheeks and yanked his face round. He looked him straight in the eye.

Crack-*zing*, crack-*zing*, crack-*zing*.

"We've got to get out of here. See there…"

Thirty yards back, an upturned ox cart.

"We go. Keep low. Zig-zag. You got that?"

"Sir."

He nodded.

"And him…"

Finch patted the lieutenant.

"…He comes with us. You hear? Absolutely imperative."

There was no disguising Miles' disdain.

"Orders!" Finch stressed.

The doctor reached inside his tunic and pulled out a small hip flask. He took a deep, deep breath and steadied his hand. He offered it to Miles.

"Talisker… Special occasions."

Miles wrinkled his brow.

"Whisky," Finch spelt out.

"Don't like whisky, sir."

Finch swigged and passed it over.

"You do now."

Miles complied, then pursed his lips. Finch could feel the boy shaking too. And a smell. He'd voided his bowels. He was scared, human, after all.

"Don't make no sense, doc."

The flat accent – northern mill town – made him seem lost, alone. His bottom lip was trembling.

"What?"

"All this."

"Miles. We're hiding inside a dead horse with a bunch of mad Dutchmen trying to kill us. We're in Africa in summer and it's freezing. None of this makes any bloody sense."

The private issued a nervous chuckle.

Crack-*zing*, crack-*zing*, crack—

In an instant, Miles was jolted forward, thrown face down into the dirt.

"*Miles!*"

The soldier moaned and rolled over. He hugged his left shoulder.

"Fuck, sir."

There was pain in his voice. He began hyperventilating.

"He nicked me. The fucking…"

Finch hauled him in. He put the flask to Miles' lips again.

"This hooch is older than you, Miles. You'll be cultivating quite a palate."

Finch fumbled for his penknife, slit the soldier's sleeve and did his best, in the dark, to examine his young charge, gently feeling around for the black hole of a wound. There was blood, but, mercifully, no sign of entry – no damage to bone or artery. The slug had just grazed.

"One to tell the grandchildren about, Miles. You're a lucky chap. And so is the future Mrs Miles."

Miles grimaced.

"Don't tell me there's no sweetheart…"

He helped the private up into a sitting position, the suffering etched deep into his young face. Finch wrestled his small medical pack over his shoulder and rummaged for a patch of gauze. He motioned for Miles to press it to the wound.

"Lucy, sir."

"Pretty name."

The lad was fighting it. He was doing well.

"And you, sir?"

He bound the gauze with a length of bandage, deftly ripping it with his teeth and tying off the ends, a handful of dirt applied to darken the white.

"That would be a long tale, private. Too long to hang about here for."

He nodded to Miles to drink again.

"One for the road, then heave-ho. Think you can manage?"

Miles passed the whisky back. He wriggled up onto his haunches, trying not to let Finch catch him wince as his weight fell on his wounded arm.

"On your count, sir. On your count."

A remote *pop*, way on high, changed everything. For a brief moment, time stood still, the battlefield frozen, its combatants rooted to the spot. For just a fleeting second, their world was illuminated – they, themselves, lit up like music hall stars.

Ahead, so close you could almost touch them, in blinding, eye-straining detail were the bearded features of the Boers 'neath their floppy bush hats, the bristle of rifles along the lip of their rough-hewn trench, running between the rounded, rubbled kops. Amid both parties lay the mess of corpses.

Off to the west, Finch saw a knot of crawling infantrymen. He was right. They had not been alone.

The flare went out; the darkness resumed, pitch black in an instant. And then came the screech and whistle overhead as a volley of shells flew towards their foe, the roar of the howitzers dispatching them riding in sonic delay from some way behind the Front.

To an almighty din that surpassed all else, so loud that your eyeballs vibrated, the ground warped and buckled and earth was thrown up, great geysers of soil vomited into the air, the gravel showering down.

Digging deep within himself, Finch scooped up the lieutenant and swung him over his shoulder in a fireman's lift.

Miles couldn't hear the doctor, but Finch yelled out anyway.

"Run, damnit. *Run!*"

Chapter Two

The black shape of the field hospital eventually hove into view. Outside, two Indian porters – Hindus, skinny, barefoot – were waiting with a stretcher.

Finch eased himself over the splintered tailboard.

"I'm afraid you wouldn't pass muster at the officers' mess," boomed a voice behind him.

"What the hell, sir? We went out there under a truce," Finch spluttered. "A medical mission. White flag—"

Major Cox gave a discreet cough and bade Finch follow, his immaculate brown boots crunching a path across the gravelly dirt.

The Afrikaner cattle ranch had been stranded the wrong side of the border, a few miles west of the Free State. Requisitioned by the Royal Army Medical Corps, it was serving well in its new guise – modest but solid, preferable to canvas.

Finch hobbled after his superior, making heavy weather of catching up. From the barn, with its corrugated iron roof, he could hear the lowing – not of beasts but of men, casualties from the afternoon assault, their pain a constant, ambient dirge.

Cox ducked after the major under a dewy awning. In a jerry-rigged ante-chamber, an adjutant sat at an upturned orange crate, prodding at a battered typewriter in the halo of a hurricane lamp, a Morse tapper set to one side.

In the outhouse behind it, Cox stooped through a doorway, lit his own lantern and hung it from a hook in the beam of the low ceiling. A worn green baize card table served as his desk. A canvas cot, with regulation blanket neatly folded, ran under the window.

"Brandy?" he offered.

Finch shrugged, feigning nonchalance.

Cox set two enamel mugs on the table all the same and, from somewhere, produced a dusty bottle of Santhagens.

"Transvaal armagnac."

He uncorked it, poured two generous measures, and tapped the side of his nose conspiratorially as to its provenance.

In one letter home, Finch had recorded his first impression – that on civvy street Cox would have made a slick businessman. He looked the part – the belly, the shining leather, the sleek hair, the oiled moustache.

Cox was going to make him wait – the theatre of superiority. There were two canvas chairs. Cox took the one behind the desk and gestured for Finch to sit before it.

There was a low distant rumble, like far-off thunder – the Royal Navy guns wheeled up from the south. The biggest, 'Joe Chamberlain', could send a shell five miles, or so they said.

Cox's cup vibrated against the bottle, a high-pitched rasp that sounded like a bumble bee.

"Spent a whole day pounding the hills only to discover the blighters have dug themselves into the ground."

"I'm no strategist, sir, but sending neat squares of men to march at a heavily armed trench in the middle of the day does not appear the most prudent fighting tactic."

Some of the Highlanders he'd tended in the field were still clutching lengths of knotted rope, tied off at 6ft intervals, the means by which they could maintain perfect formation, right up to the last.

"You're right," came the touché. "You're not a strategist."

Until recently, medical personnel had not been given leave to dress up in khaki, still less trusted with a corps formed in their honour. That Cox, a cavalryman, had been seconded to oversee a bunch of fey medics seemed a lingering source of resentment.

"What the hell were the brass thinking, sir? Us, the Boers. We were treating the wounded. Together. They were *helping* us for God's sake. Then the bloody artillery start shelling, right in the middle of it. We're stuck out there. No provisions, no weapons, nothing. Sitting ducks."

"It was unfortunate."

"Unfortunate? I was there for five hours. Shot at for *five hours*…"

Finch slumped back. It was hard not to drift away. He ran his hands through his hair. It was thick for a man of 40, at least his Italian barber flattered him. He was in decent shape too, if maybe half a stone for the worse. But he was no soldier. That was for the kids; the obedient, unthinking kids – kids like Miles.

"The private… Lancashires. I'll see that he gets commended. And you—"

"I'm not after a bloody medal."

Cox shot Finch a look, then softened.

"Ingo," he said. "I'm grateful."

There followed a perfunctory raising of mugs, a clink and a silent, savouring sip.

Finch had never known tiredness like it. It gnawed at the muscles round his eyes and scrambled his thoughts such that the words that slurred out of his mouth did not necessarily correlate to the ones forming in his head.

"Your casualty… the lieutenant?" asked Cox.

"Bruised, battered. He'll be okay."

"Did he talk?" Cox added.

"Talk?"

"You know, say anything?"

Laid out on the sacking on the floor of the cart, the lieutenant had groaned periodically, then began muttering in a delirium.

"A day's worth of African sun can do terrible things to a man."

"Nothing coherent? No names, orders?"

Finch shrugged. Logic had ceased to have any place in war.

"If he does…" said Cox.

There was a knock on the door – the adjutant brandishing a chit. He handed it to Cox and took a pace back. Cox absorbed the information. He held up an apologetic palm while he did so.

"Right away. Right away," he muttered, then gave the slip back to the adjutant and dismissed him.

The major rose. Finch had had his moment.

"Good work, Captain. That will be all… Staff will arrange for a hot drink and some grub."

Finch was about to protest that he was required in surgery.

"They'll send it over."

And, with that, the major was gone.

Finch took a minute or two to finish his drink. The guns rumbled on. He stood up and stretched his aching body. His left knee, in particular, would need disinfecting, patching up.

Outside, feathers of sleet swirled in the air. On the wind came the *pop-pop-pop* of small arms fire. The infantry assault was underway. At this distance it sounded so ineffectual, so childish. He thought he heard the skirl of pipes.

The barefoot Indian stretcher bearers were congregating, hunched together. Very soon, the first of what would be an endless stream of ambulances would come rattling into the yard.

An RAMC sergeant with a clipboard and two staff nurses emerged and huddled under an overhang, ready to direct the wounded to the correct area – dressing, theatre or to be laid on the straw in the far end of the barn where the only attention they'd receive would come in the form of some trite ministrations from the chaplain.

Finch asked an orderly to fetch him the strongest mug of tea he could brew, with enough sugar in it to make a spoon stand up.

Chapter Three

Jenkins looked up from the scrum.

"Jesus, Finch," he cooed, in the lilting Welsh of the Marches. "What the hell happened to you?"

In the stable block, which had been hung with tarpaulins, three tables were arrayed, each with a coterie of doctors, nurses and orderlies gathered round a forlorn and groaning individual.

On a tea chest was a wind-up gramophone player. The scratchy sound of Chopin's Nocturnes issuing through the dented trumpet was fighting a losing battle with the hail now drumming hard on the corrugated roof and the shrieks of the wounded in the passageway.

The whitewashed walls were spattered with viscera. The air was rank with human flesh. Sluiced blood ran into a gully that crossed the cobbled floor. Bits of tissue had blocked the drain. A shallow crimson lake had begun forming, reflecting the pale light of the paraffin lamps which swung with every random boom.

"Don't ask," replied Finch, scrubbing up over a bowl in his grimy undershirt.

A fair-haired nurse tied Finch's gown at the back while he sipped at his mug of sweet, scalding tea.

At table two lay a Highlander shivering in shock. A nurse held his guts in place while another sewed up the bayonet slash down his side.

At three, Richards, another in their fraternity of RAMC captains, merely uttered a perfunctory 'Lost him' as the final squelch and gurgle of life was expelled from some other charred mass barely recognisable as a human being.

Finch stepped over to enter the huddle alongside Jenkins.

"So what have we here?"

"Allow me to present Private Hamish Urquhart of the Seaforths," said the Welshman. "A chap who's had a spot of bother."

He turned to address his patient directly.

"Mr Urquhart? My colleague, Captain Ingo Finch."

Finch nodded a cursory greeting to the forlorn warrior. A muffled, weak voice floated up.

"Harold," he croaked. "Not Hamish... Harold."

Said Jenkins: "Right then. Let's have another look."

Wearing a kilt had at least spared Urquhart the indignity of having his trews snipped off. A bouncy, red-faced nurse simply rolled the thick, grubby blue/green tartan up around the soldier's thighs. A phlegm-tinged sigh signalled the young man's resignation to his fate.

While the soldier's foot and ankle seemed perfectly healthy, as did his knee, what lay between them amounted to nothing more than a bloody pulp, flecked with white shards of bone.

"Dum-dum bullet," said the fair-haired nurse.

A rubber tourniquet pulled tightly had quelled the spurting, but there was not an orthopaedic surgeon anywhere – and Jenkins was one of the very best – who could have salvaged this limb.

"Captain Finch, a second opinion?"

"Sorry Harold," said Finch.

"First class ticket to Cape Town and a luxury cruise home," said Jenkins. "How does that sound? Fit you with a peg, you'll be doing the Gay Gordon come Hogmanay."

The bouncy nurse placed a gauze mask over the soldier's mouth and cradled his head in her ample bosom. She poured on a few drops of chloroform.

"Right then. Counting back from 20," said Finch as he felt for the patient's pulse and timed its weak flutter against his pocket watch.

With a nod from Finch, Jenkins reached for the trolley. He raised his chosen tools and made a show of clanging them together, like an overly-lubricated father about to carve the Christmas turkey.

Moments later the rasping of the saw had stopped, the job was done. Jenkins blew away the dust like a gunslinger puffing satisfied on his muzzle. He gave a nod to Finch, then yelled an ironic 'Next!', at which a Hindu porter carried off a foot-shaped bundle to be plopped in a bucket.

It was the signal for Finch to perform his part of the sombre ritual – clamping things off, performing his needlework. At least at night, in the cool, the overhead lamps were a distraction for the horseflies.

As a family doctor back home, he had never before cut into anything more than a lab rat. In just a few short weeks he had been raised from a lancer of boils to some kind of surgeon. Truthfully, he felt more like a tradesman – a carpenter or plumber – removing bits, stemming flows, procedures far too gruesome for even the most cast iron of stomachs to bear.

Christ, he was tired. So tired he almost didn't care.

–

With dawn breaking, Finch stepped outside. He had passed through the pull of slumber into a fuzzy altered state. He felt like an undead character he had read about in a story by Edgar Allan Poe.

His own raw knees had been bandaged, but the left one was causing him particular difficulty. He could hardly bend it. He rubbed his chin. Bristles rasped. He needed a shave. He needed a bath to purge the sweat, blood and grime – his and others'. More than anything, he needed his bed.

It had been more than 72 hours since Finch had had any sustained sleep – before Lord Methuen had moved the 1st Division up over the Modder River, trying to beat a path to relieve besieged Kimberley. Extrapolating from the volume of casualties that had passed through their own hands during the night – 200 or more – Finch deduced that the army had failed.

Against a wall, an Indian orderly sorted through a mound of bloody odd boots, which had grown considerably. That he was barefoot made for an altogether bizarre spectacle.

Finch crossed the courtyard. He passed the horse paddock – the animals now stirring – and limped up the small hillock, the highest point on the farmstead. The ground was covered with a coarse and patchy grass.

He leaned on the splintered wooden fence and gazed off into the distance. The eastern horizon, deep in the Boer heartland, was being kissed by a crimson glow. In every direction, the black veld stretched away endlessly, pock-marked by the low, flat-topped kops and, to the north, the twin scars of the Magersfontein and Spytfontein ridges.

He didn't ordinarily smoke. As a doctor, he still harboured suspicion that inhaling hot tobacco fumes might not be as providential for one's lungs as the advertisers liked to boast. But he needed to balm his shredded nerves before retiring.

He sparked a lucifer and lit a cigarette from an overpriced packet of Navy Cut he had purchased at the Mess Co-operative. A slippery slope, he conceded. The match fizzed. The cigarette crackled. The embers glowed. Finch drew the vapours in deep and willed the relaxation. Wisps curled up into the lightening sky.

Away from the groans, all that could be heard now was the chirping of the dawn chorus in a cluster of jacaranda trees, as familiar a sound as the one back home. The windmill on the water tower creaked, turning slowly in the light breeze. It was blowing from the north this time. It already felt warmer. It smelled different... of baked earth. This weather was insane.

Before Finch retired to his billet, he checked in on the young lieutenant they had rescued. An orderly revealed that he was being kept in a wooden hut behind the main living quarters.

'Kept' seemed the operative word, for when Finch arrived, he found two muscling soldiers on the door, standing at ease, hands at the throats of their Lee-Metford rifles, their caps adorned with a scarlet crown, the red letters 'MFP' – Military Foot Police – on dark blue bands around their left biceps.

They seemed far more suited to the parade ground than battle, their webbing blancoed to a brilliant white rather than drabbed down and camouflaged with battlefield dirt.

They sprang to attention as Finch approached. The shorter of the two, a lance corporal, peered up sharply from beneath his peaked cap.

"Five minutes, sir. Orders."

Finch had never, in his entire career, had a time-limit placed on a bedside visit, but had no intention of lingering. Plus he was too tired to kick up a fuss. He pushed hard at the stiff door – warped in its frame – and went in.

From the single window, the room was bathed in the burgeoning dawn light. A nurse was tending to the man, who lay peacefully asleep, barely recognisable from the traumatised soul they had hauled back from the abyss.

He had been well cared for at any rate – a camp bed, fresh bandages around the crown of his head and right forearm, a horse blanket that seemed almost 50 per cent clean.

The hut was the farm's workshop, smelling of creosote and oil. Above a workbench with a vice bolted to it hung a rack of chisels, hammers and saws – a home-from-home to surgery, Finch mused.

The brisk nurse gave Finch the vitals – bruising, lacerations, two broken ribs, a fractured collarbone, but he would be okay with rest; he was severely dehydrated, drifting in and out of consciousness. When Finch asked why on earth the man should be under armed guard, she shrugged, excused herself and bustled out.

He stood over the man. There was still no name. What was he, about 27…28? Red hair. Eyes? Unknown at present, they were closed. Athletic build. About 5ft 10ins… 5ft 11ins? He had around three days' worth of beard and, judging by the dense carpet of freckles, had probably been up-country since the get-go.

Finch tried hard to recall the specifics of the events of the previous night, which seemed now like a lifetime ago. He had been ordered to attend to a man fitting the description given to him by Cox. Said individual was alive. It was all that had seemed to matter.

But that was in broad daylight, when both British and Boers had downed arms to lay out the wounded together. The Boers had come out of their trenches to a man. Someone said that their general, De La Rey, was amongst them, working alongside his men.

And then the bloody artillery had started up…

He cast an eye up. The shorter of the two guards was looking in on him. He nudged his colleague.

Surreptitiously, under the guise of taking the man's pulse, Finch sat down and started feeling around in the lieutenant's belongings.

There was nothing in his jacket pockets or his trousers. No identity card. The holster on the Sam Brown belt no longer housed a pistol.

A sudden yelp. He began to stir, a twitching seizing his face, his lower lip starting to quiver. He rolled his head to his left, opened his lids and with bright blue eyes fixed Finch.

The lieutenant's left hand gripped Finch's. Tight. Had he recognised him?

"*Ssshhh-ssshh!* Don't excite yourself."

"You must…"

There was fear. Real fear.

"Don't let them…"

He raised his right arm weakly, a finger pointed towards the door.

"Moriarty."

"Moriarty? You mean…" Finch asked with incredulity, "…like *Sherlock Holmes*?"

In a flash, both MFPs were into the room.

"I'm sorry, sir. I must ask you to leave," said the short one, curtly.

"This man has just come round. I'm his physician."

"Please don't force our hand, sir. We did say five minutes. You've had your time."

"On whose authority?"

"The Military Foot Police, sir."

"Why has this man been placed under arrest?"

The big one said nothing still. The little one cut across.

"Please, sir. Orders."

Though dog tired, Finch was not yet fully spent.

"Well I've got an order for you, the pair of you. You'll salute an officer. You understand!"

Neither had on his arrival. Both men now complied. There was a hint of sarcasm. Then the bigger, mute MFP positioned himself behind Finch, as if to march him out.

The lieutenant had lapsed back into unconsciousness again. There was a glance exchanged between the two military policemen.

"This is absurd," Finch huffed, but exited anyway.

The sun was on the up now, its long, low shadows striping the land. Steam was rising from the rich earth. On his way back to his billet, Finch stopped by Cox's office. The lights were out. The major would be asleep.

Curious as he was to this whole business, it would be a cruel man to drag another from his bed.

Finch's own one was calling to him. The matter could wait.

Chapter Four

The day before

In the main square, across from the great, deep hole of the Kimberley Mine, the regimental band of the Royal Garrison Artillery gave its matinee recital.

Mbutu recognised the tune. He had heard it many times – *Rule Britannia*. It was a highlight of the repertoire, whites discreetly clapping along while the cheery conductor waved his baton, throwing a smile of appreciation over his shoulder.

In the lull between church and Sunday lunch, this weekly turn by the musicians in their scarlet tunics and polished brass buttons seemed to lift spirits. Clinging to normality was an obsession – a stoic, civic duty amid all the strangeness.

Gathered around the bandstand they were a fine sight, these masters and mistresses. You could not deny it. Silks, satins, bows, white gloves. Servants to hoist frilled parasols. Men preening in their well-cut morning suits.

Such cumbersome garments – thick, stiff, awkward. No good in the sun. A sign that one didn't contend with the daily indignity of manual labour.

As he knew from his days down the mines – as everybody knew who toiled down the mines – 90 per cent of the world's diamonds came from Kimberley… and 90 per cent of Kimberley's diamonds were mined by De Beers. The company owned the town; the company owned you.

What was certain to Mbutu was that 90 per cent of the world's folk were not a fraction as wealthy as the folk gathered here – and that 90 per cent of *them* had never been underground.

The smashing of the rocks, the chipping of the stone, that was left to black men, the 'mine boys' – Basutos like himself; men from Bechuanaland, from Matabeleland; men who trekked hundreds of miles to this scorching hell where the wind blew off the Kalahari.

Here, they worked for a pittance and lived in the compounds – enclosures surrounded by fences with chicken wire roofs. Such quarters were situated outside the town so that blacks could not offend white eyes – or steal their precious stones.

For all the riches, for all the diamonds mined in the last 30 years, their entire quantity would barely fill a bucket. Such was their value. They were small, these stones, tiny, just shimmering motes in the mud and clay – easy to conceal, which meant stripping and searching and keeping the workers under lock and key.

The British in the Colony said that the Boers were bad, un-Christian – that they had no respect for their African brother; did not fulfil their obligation to raise him up, to treat him as one of God's children. It was true, the Afrikaners he had worked for had treated him like a dog. But they had never locked him in a cage...

...Or wedged a wooden block between a man's ankles and shattered his bones with a sledgehammer. That was what you got for stealing those motes of shiny dust. Let that be your Christian lesson.

Mbutu was lucky. Very lucky. Fortunate enough, now, to be out from behind the wire and living in a shack. To hell with those who spat upon him, calling him a traitor. He was looking after his wife and child. It was his duty.

Mbutu's talent was that he could run. Run fast. A gift, to him, as priceless as any stone. No one could cover the town and its surrounds like Mbutu – the British called him 'Johnny'. Johnny/Mbutu, Mbutu/Johnny, both could run like the wind.

He knew the terrain intimately. He carried messages and telegrams – to the villages of Beaconsfield and Kenilworth; along the redoubts and earthworks; from the Kimberley Club, where the men with purple, pitted noses sipped gin and tonics; to the great Sanatorium, the palatial health spa, where Cecil Rhodes himself had taken up residence.

Mr Rhodes, the man who ran De Beers. To the north, he even had a country named after him. A man more powerful and rich than an emperor. Mr Rhodes stayed put when he could have fled, crowed the masters. What loyalty!

But it was to ensure a British rescue, Mbutu knew. To save Kimberley... To save De Beers... To save his diamonds.

They thought he was mute, this Johnny. Johnny-with-the-fleet-foot – a man to stand quietly in the shadows and wait for the envelope.

But this Johnny had heard with his own ears what the General had said.

Being able to 'take it' was all bluff. The food was running out. They would need to start slaughtering the horses. The blacks' rations were to be halved. The Boers had severed the water main on the first day. The town's most valuable commodity was its wells, not its jewels. And if those same wells turned septic...

It was Mr Rhodes who was the problem, raged Colonel Kekewich to his subalterns. Mr Rhodes who was stirring up trouble. And now the relief, the army, was shuddering to a halt.

Three sudden blasts on the steam hooter.

Toot-toot-toot.

They had 30 seconds.

Way up high, on a gantry on the main mine's headgear, the spotter was waving and pointing. Pointing west. There was a whirl of bodies. Parisian finery was sent scuttling for the shelters. The band played on.

The bunkers that had been constructed on every street had been reserved for white folk. Mbutu took his chance in a ditch.

Someone complained about the Boers shelling on a Sunday. They had never done so before. Was there no decency left in warfare?

They could say all they liked about Long Tom, the Boers' siege gun. At least it was predictable. It announced itself without fail.

Six, five, four...

The incoming whistle grew louder.

Three, two, one...

Silence. An explosion. A muffled crump from the other side of town.

More likely the shell had landed in the soft slag heaps. It often did. He was sure the Boers were pulling their punches – fostering fear. Kimberley's value was as a hostage, not a conquest.

Sheet music had been scattered. Pages were gathered up. The audience re-appeared, straightening neckties, smoothing down voluminous skirts, brushing off the dust. African servants rushed to attend.

In the distance, the bell clanged on the fire engine. People craned their necks to see the pall of smoke. There was none yet. Maybe a dud.

Then the conductor tapped his baton. There was polite clapping. And they began again, this time with the audience joining in, heartily.

"Rule Britannia," they sang, "Britannia rules the waves."

On the shaded verandas of the stores – closed on the Sabbath – men in cloth caps and waistcoats leaned on the rail and smoked. A Coloured vendor wheeled a handcart selling 'siege soup', a penny a pint. It was Rhodes' personal idea, people had marvelled. What genius!

And then a boy weaved through, a white boy, little more than an urchin, passing out handbills. A man was hammering one to a telegraph pole.

Mbutu retrieved one from the dirt. There was to be a public meeting in the Town Hall, it said. Tonight. Seven o'clock. It would be addressed by Mr Rhodes himself. All were welcome.

Not all. In Kimberley… in South Africa… all were definitely not welcome.

–

There was a buzz of expectation. Though the blackout was in force, light seeped round the door's thick crepe curtain.

The Boers had had two months to find their range, mused Mbutu. Did it really make any difference?

In their droves they had come – the men, the ladies, their servants, clopping up in their gigs and buggies or strolling through the dusk from the Kimberley Club.

The servants and drivers took their place on the steps, milling about with the others – the blacks, Coloureds, Indians, Cape Malays and the Chinese, the 'coolies' who ran the laundry, the fortunate non-whites not locked up in the compounds.

There came clapping from inside. A man was speaking from the stage, making an introduction. Tumultuous applause and then a hush. A black man on the door waved his arms. On the steps everyone was shushing.

"He's coming. He's coming!"

And then they could hear him in full flow, castigating the army for its failure to break through and relieve the town.

For a big man, a powerful man – such a high voice. Rhodes sounded like a girl.

Was it really that hard to smite this rag-tag of Boer peasants? The people of Kimberley were his personal responsibility. At night, he was going to make the mines available for shelter.

Mbutu laughed. *So the white man was going underground after all.*

Amid the cheers there came a tap on the shoulder and Mbutu turned round. There were two men, two white men.

One – older, fatter, bespectacled – had a tweed suit and a walrus moustache; a watch chain hung on his waistcoat. His bowler hat seemed too small for his head. The other – younger, leaner – had a better milliner.

They flashed badges. "Agents," they said. "Of the Crown." Would he kindly come with them?

Were they sure?

"Don't argue."

Had they discovered that Mbutu had stolen milk from the Kimberley Club kitchen? Milk for his son. He didn't see how anyone could know. No one was there.

They were leading him now, away from the hall, across the street. He didn't like it. They took him behind the general store, away from the crowd. It was rough ground – gravel and clumped scrub. Crickets chirped. Rats scrabbled in the rubbish. On the perimeter, the searchlights were on. Great white cones of light swept the land.

"Johnny Fleetfoot?" asked the younger one, his voice not from the Colony but from England.

"My name is Mbutu," he said, proudly. "Mbutu Kefaleze."

"Says here Johnny Fleetfoot," the man queried, passing a piece of paper to his colleague.

That was what they called him, Mbutu explained. It was a nick-name. He was a runner. He was fast.

He was contemplating giving them a demonstration right now.

"And that's why we need your help," said the older one.

Help? An unusual request. A white man seeking a black man's assistance.

"We have it on good authority that you're a reliable man."

"And loyal to the Cape," added the younger one. "To the Empire."

Mbutu sighed. In a white man's war, the black man would lose either way. But he knew better than to say it.

From behind a sage bush stepped another man, a man in khaki – an army officer. A lieutenant. Mbutu recognised the insignia. On his shoulders the badge said 'Northumberland'. He had red hair, looked strong, and, even in the orange twilight Mbutu could see he had blue eyes, piercing blue eyes. He remained five yards away.

"How well do you know this country?" the older man was asking him now.

"Well," said Mbutu. "Better than any."

Was this the right answer?

He had worked in the survey gangs he told them. He had covered the ground right up the to the Free State border.

"Can you get this man through?" asked the younger one, pointing to the army officer – the officer who still said nothing.

Delivering a man?

"To the Free State?" asked Mbutu, puzzled.

"To the British lines," said the older man. "Just north of the Modder. Absolutely imperative."

"Imperative?"

"Important."

"I know what the word means."

Mbutu scratched his head. The lieutenant watched him intently.

It was eight miles at least, Mbutu explained. They would have to run the gauntlet of the Boer positions, the Boer sharpshooters. They would have to skirt the two big ridges. It was dangerous. And if they hadn't made it by sun-up—

"And that's why you must leave right now," said the young man. "This instant."

"And if I don't?"

There was silence.

The young man pressed a small cloth bag into his hand. Coins.

"Ten shillings…" he said. "Five here. The rest when you return."

He shook hands formally.

"Agent Rutherford," said the younger.

"Soames," added the elder, keeping his hands firmly in pocket.

The silent, nameless, red-haired officer swung a pigskin of water over his shoulder, approached, and thrust another at Mbutu.

"Here."

He had biltong, dried meat, he gestured. And a map.

The British and their maps.

He had a rifle, a Lee-Metford, as well as a revolver. Though, Mbutu noted, he wasn't sharing out the hardware.

From the heliograph station, the arc light was switched on, its beam fizzing high into the sky, about to commence its nightly flashing of coded Morse messages.

"Ten shillings," reiterated Rutherford.

"Come on," said the lieutenant, and strode off into the brush.

Chapter Five

Save for the removal of his boots, Finch fell onto his bed in the very clothes he had stood up in. Though at the point of exhaustion, the sleep was frustratingly fitful, his mind too active. Vivid images and noises flashed through his head.

Once more Finch writhed in fear. His sweat seeped through his shirt. And then the artillery barrage boomed, the monstrous shells raining in. The explosions grew louder... louder... louder... till suddenly, Finch realised, the sound was an intrusion from the outside world. Someone was knocking on his door.

He squinted up. Through bleary eyes, his batman was looming over him. He was proffering a mug of tea.

"Sir?"

"What the devil time is it?" Finch croaked.

"Half past nine, sir."

Barely three hours. His head was spinning.

"Sorry sir. An order."

Bloody orders.

"A retreat."

"Retreat?"

"Whole shebang. Pulling back to the Modder."

Finch hauled his weary body into a sitting position. He rubbed his eyes. He took the tea.

"You sure?"

Jesus, he was tired. Please God, let this be the last of it.

"Absolutely. Down to the last hobnail."

Not two weeks previously, significant carnage had ensued in ousting the Boers, their soldiers having dug themselves into the Modder's banks.

There were weeping willows, Finch remembered from crossing it, bobbing mallards. There was an elegant hotel with tethered rowing boats, a curious anomaly amid a killing field.

Traversing the river had been trumpeted as a great stride to the symbolic relief of Kimberley. To return 15,000 men back there was a hell of an undertaking, a hell of a capitulation.

"No sugar, sir. Spoonful of Golden Syrup. Thought you could use it."

"Thank you."

"Major's been told to get us rolling by 1100 hours."

Finch could hear it now: the shouting of men in the yard; the scrape of hooves and cartwheels; the crunch of boots; equipment being loaded.

"Very good, Clough."

The batman left.

He hobbled to the first-floor window. Awkwardly, he pulled back the heavy horse blanket he had rigged up as a curtain. He raised a hand to shield his blinking eyes, then yanked up the stiff and squeaking sash panel. The heat, the noise, the smell smacked his senses.

Down below, orderlies stripped to their grey, collarless undershirts, sleeves rolled up, were rushing about, great dark stains on their backs and underarms. The lightest of the casualties were being helped across the yard, blankets or tunics round their shoulders. Crates were being stacked. Cox was barking instructions.

The sky was blue, cloudless. Across the plain to the south, amid a cloud of dust, a train of ox carts was plodding towards the farmstead, the black African drivers swishing their whips.

Finch afforded himself some rudimentary ablutions, hitched his braces and, with difficulty, descended the creaking stairs. He limped out into the yard. Already it was hot. By noon it would be roasting. He was dripping sweat again. Annoying black flies danced around his face. He swiped at them to no avail.

"Morning Captain," boomed the major.

Cox explained the situation – Methuen feared the 1st Division being cut off; they simply hadn't got the manpower; too many officers lost; General Wauchope had bought it. Better to pull back and consolidate.

The conclusion did not have to be spelt out. It was a military disaster.

"And the men in our care?" asked Finch.

"Those that can stand it, come. The most critical cases will be handed over under a white flag. Taken in as POWs."

Usually, the morning after battle, up to a quarter of those who'd survived the bullets wouldn't have lasted the night. The early morning shift had taken care of business. On the hillock, the one on which Finch had stood not four hours earlier, a team of squaddies, stripped to their waists, was hacking into the earth with pickaxes and shovels.

The cogs were whirring in Finch's head. To move an entire army was a huge undertaking. Such a decision was not a snap one. It must have been made hours ago… yesterday. How on earth would a train of ox carts have lumbered up here?

The 'redeployment' would surely have been commanded well before the second wave of the assault went in – in which case what a pathetic, gratuitous waste.

Was that what Cox's telegraph message had been about?

"Sir, if I might ask—?"

"Morning Jenkins," Cox was bellowing now, turning away to Finch's comrade, similarly dishevelled, squinting under the sun.

"Finch will fill you in," said Cox and turned on his heel. "1100 hours, gentlemen. 1100 hours."

Finch and Jenkins looked at each other. In near symmetry they raised eyebrows and exhaled.

"C'mon," the Welshman beckoned, dark, narrow eyes flicking towards the mobile canteen, a mule-drawn wagon, which appeared to be shutting up shop. The urn was still steaming. They requisitioned bacon sandwiches, more tea, eating as they walked. It was the first food Finch had had in the best part of a day – last night's grub had never materialised.

Their 'butcher's shop' had been sloshed down, its whitewashed walls scrubbed, the drainage channels sluiced. In the middle of the room, at a lone trestle table, the RAMC sergeant and the staff sister were poring over paperwork.

Their reliable staff had already taken inventory of their supplies, tallying the wounded, identifying which ones could survive the journey and which, they estimated, could probably not.

Thirty-two had not survived the night, the ones the burial detail were now interring. The sergeant chimed in with details about the field ambulances at their disposal, the number of mules and carts and how the casualties were going to be arranged.

Finch understood the thinking behind the evacuation – get as many wounded back and rehabilitated, ready for action again. But the journey would be no picnic – a long, slow, slog in an un-sprung wagon over stony ground. No cover from the harsh noonday sun. Little water. There would be an uncomfortable, improvised overnight bivouac once south of the Modder. But it was still a further 50 miles to the railhead at Hopetown, from where the wounded would be transported on to Cape Town, 500 miles away. Not all of them would make it.

"Captain Jenkins. If I might have a word?" asked Finch.

The two men rose, went to the corner and conferred. Finch reasoned it out – it was surely better to leave, rather than take, as many wounded as they possibly could. He had been impressed by the Boers' attitude. They had good doctors. There was a modern hospital in Bloemfontein, a fraction of the distance to the Cape. As physicians, they would be acting in the best interests of their patients.

"The major wouldn't like it," Jenkins added.

"But how would he know?" whispered Finch.

Jenkins nodded.

"And another thing," said Finch. "I'd like to be the one to effect the transfer... the one left behind. Someone will have to do it. An officer."

"After all that happened yesterday?"

"*Because* of what happened yesterday."

"Whatever you say, Ingo. Whatever you say."

They shook hands.

"See you at the river," said Finch.

"And watch that knee."

A volley of gunfire cracked through the air. The dead were receiving their final salute.

Finch shambled out into the sun again. The pace had picked up. Men were running now. A bugle was sounding. Two dithering privates were being screamed at by a red-faced corporal.

The army observation balloon, which had hovered behind the British lines – requisitioned from a carnival and slopped over in olive paint – was being winched in on a great sagging cable, its nervous occupant gesturing emphatically to those down below.

The familiar rumble resumed. The naval guns. Across the veld, starbursts of dust began crowning the hills, the kops, even though every last soldier knew that the Boers had not taken refuge in them.

Finch rounded the farmhouse and lurched his way past rushing bodies up to the wooden hut. The MFPs on the door had gone. So too had the young lieutenant within.

Chapter Six

Annie stood on the so-called recreation deck – a small chained-off area ahead of the rear funnel that afforded an unbroken stroll of a paltry ten paces – and gazed off to the port side. Given the position of the sun, they must have changed course.

She was sure of it. Looking towards the stern, she saw the churning wash now arcing away.

They had been at sea for over two weeks – 16 days to be precise. Word aboard was that today was the day. Someone, one of the stewards, a kindly older man who'd been at sea since he was 14 he told her, had tipped her off about the swing to the northwest. When that happened, you could be sure you would be putting in to Cape Town.

No one had told them anything officially. There was a war on, didn't they know? There was secrecy. A ship must not betray its position to the enemy.

"But the Boers don't have a navy," someone pointed out.

No matter, came the reply. They have friends and allies at sea, spies in the ports. The movement of troops and transports was something of vital intelligence. And don't think that this thing might not escalate. What if the Germans decided to lend Kruger a hand? What then?

In the middle part of the passage, amid the dark foreboding hillocks of the Indian Ocean, they had gone days without seeing another vessel. To glimpse one was an incident of great excitement.

But, in the last two or three, there had been a marked increase in traffic, the other boats now of largely yawning irrelevance. Yesterday, though, they had been passed by a Royal Navy warship – a great, grey, ugly brute, turrets bristling with guns, its upright funnels like industrial chimney stacks, belching black filth into the azure sky.

Now, all around them, spread over miles, were the black, rocking shapes of vessels, some merchant, some naval, all heading to or from the same place.

The ship was slowing. Annie was sure of that too. The hum of the engines had dropped in tone, just marginally. She could now hear the hiss of the water in their wake and the squawks of the gulls that hovered on the breeze, scanning the frothing ocean for silvery titbits.

She had already learned that, when a ship slowed, it ceased riding high. Sure enough it began to pitch, the bow rising and falling as it crashed through the rollers. And the wind had changed. The spray slapped up and caught her mischievously in the face, raising an involuntary chuckle.

This was it.

It had all happened so remarkably quickly. Within days of the declaration of war, there was a rush of young Australian men to volunteer for service, supplementing the regulars being mustered for departure.

Women too. The New South Wales Army Medical Corps had wasted no time in posting advertisements around the Sydney Hospital requesting the service of nurses.

Annie had simply gone to the recruiting desk set up in the main hallway and expressed her interest – initially by way of enquiry, but transformed by a sudden flourish of enthusiasm that had been seized upon by her canny enlisters, into a confirmed act of volunteering.

The cheery, flattering sergeant and staff nurse from the Corps had applauded her patriotism, asked questions about her skills, whether she was single ('yes') and enquired as to whether or not Annie had any dependents. (None, she had replied. Parents both dead; a brother, two years younger, who was more than capable of looking after himself.) In which case, she was just the kind of young woman they were looking for.

They also warned her, in sombre terms, that it would be demanding work in a completely alien environment. She would be required to sign up for a minimum of 12 months and, even then, might spend most of that time stationed right there in New South Wales. She would be unlikely to depart for South Africa until January at the earliest, by which time the fighting most probably would be over.

It was fine, she said. She was sure. She had thought about it deeply (she hadn't). And when they blotted the ink on her signature, she knew her life had changed forever.

Within a week she was summoned by the ward sister, who called her into the office and informed her that her request to serve in South Africa had been accepted.

The very next day, Annie reported for duty at Corps headquarters, was fitted with a coarse uniform and thrust into a classroom with 11 other girls. There, an enthusiastic lecturer extolled the virtues of the new anaesthetics they would be using in the field hospitals and of the scientific wonder that was the X-Ray machine, a futuristic contraption that they would be operating to locate bullets in a wounded soldier's body.

The training did not last long. Five days later, the new army nurses were informed that they were to set sail imminently, prompting a great deal of soul-searching on Annie's part and the penning of her epic, terminal epistle to fiancé Edward.

To a military band, an explosion of coloured streamers and the cheers and tears of thousands – including her brother, who embraced her so tightly she thought she would crack a rib – the 12 New South Wales nurses, along with a contingent of the NSW Mounted Rifles, boarded the steamer SS *Melbourne* at the Woolloomooloo docks.

The voyage was calm at first. But, a week out, the Indian Ocean cut up rough, the ship pitching, rolling and yawing in a way that several thousand tons of steel would not, according to the laws of physics, have seemed possible. Annie did not suffer from sea-sickness, but plenty did.

It was the first time the nurses had been let out of their quarters. There, they had been quarantined from the four hundred men on board, making their pathetically small recreation deck, up high, an object of immense fascination for those men below, who, while performing their daily PT routines, would strain their necks for the merest glimpse of petticoat, the wolf-whistlers dealt with harshly by the drill sergeants.

With the outbreak of sea-sickness, the nurses were dispatched below decks to tend to the men. In Sydney, Annie had been seconded, for a while, to the Darlinghurst Gaol. The sights, the sounds, the smells, were not dissimilar to that of a prison. Nor were the men much different. There were polite men, rude men, smooth men, coarse men, patient men, angry men, naked men, priapic men.

–

Now, on the main deck, those same men, in their grey undershirts, were conducting their physical jerks. Arrayed in ranks, swinging their arms and touching their toes at the barking of the sergeant.

"*Land!*"

The cry came from somewhere up the front, the bows.

She saw the sudden swivelling of heads, felt the electric thrill of excitement.

"Stand to bloody attention the lot of you!" screamed the instructor. "You miserable shower of shit!"

"Can you see it? Is it true?" squealed Nurse Sullivan as the others gathered, one hand shielding their straining eyes, the other clamped reflexively onto their wind-blown boaters.

There, on the horizon, was a thin smudge of brown.

"Africa," yelped Sullivan.

"How exciting," chimed in ApThomas. "Lions and tigers!"

Sullivan rolled her eyes. Annie smiled.

The same old steward, the kindly one, appeared. He bore a tray with mugs of tea. He'd never seen this many ships, he said. Be warned, docking would be hours away. They might have to remain at anchor for a day or two.

The bell was rung. The sister appeared to usher the nurses back below. They groaned. But the decks must be cleared, they were told. Annie was in no rush. She lingered.

"Might I remind you, Nurse Jones, this is a working ship," snapped the sister, "not a pleasure cruise."

Chapter Seven

Finch stood alone in the courtyard. Save for the odd cough or groan from the barn, the farm seemed as empty and quiet as it would ever be – eerily so. Bandages trailed through the dirt.

In Finch's hand was a walking stick that he'd found – a birch staff with a crook handle. A ripped square of white sheeting hung from it, tied with two large knots.

Finch patted his left shoulder and ensured that his armband – white with a red cross upon it – was clearly visible. His head was bare and he had removed his belt, lest it be perceived to hold a holstered weapon – there was still debate about whether medical officers should exercise their right to bear defensive arms.

Behind him, a hundred yards away at the southern gate, an ox cart waited with its twin beasts of burden and an African driver sitting patiently. A hastily-made white flag fluttered over it, too. On board were three wounded, bewildered Tommies.

The strange calm did not last for long. On the plain to the north, a dust cloud was forming – a broad brown streak of air was advancing towards the farm, travelling at some speed.

And then Finch felt it… a visceral thunder – hooves, hundreds of hooves. The rumble grew louder, louder. His stomach lurched. He raised his makeshift flag and spread his arms wide, unambiguously. He braced himself.

The Boers were into the farmyard in a flash, a great whirlwind of man and steed that rendered the air thick with dirt, as if an earthen smokescreen had been laid down. The wall of grit hit like a sandstorm and stung Finch's eyes. He reflexively turned his back, coughing and spluttering. About him now, men were shouting in a guttural tongue, springing from their mounts, cocking rifle bolts, rushing from building to building.

How alien their soldiering was – men who were as comfortable with a gun on horseback as they were on the ground; no identifiable regiments or rank; an egalitarian force in which officers, even generals, were said to perform the most menial of duties alongside the men.

Finch had also heard of something unthinkable to Her Majesty's armed forces – strategic decisions taken by the men themselves on a simple show of hands.

The dust began to settle and he wheeled round to face his foe. Two burghers approached him, skin leathered, eyes bright, Mausers raised. They snapped at him to drop his flag and keep his hands high. One crept close. He began patting him down. The man smelled of soil, of leather, of days-old sweat.

The broad-brimmed slouch hats were practical, so were the bandoliers, the belts of cartridges that crisscrossed their torsos. But there was something unnervingly Biblical… Old Testament… about these men, too. All but the young ones had full, untrimmed beards, not unlike the Hassidic Jews he had seen in the East End of London. They wore not uniforms nor farm-wear but three-piece suits, as if donning their Sunday best was a way of giving thanks to the Lord for deliverance from bullets.

The Boer turned to his colleague. He seemed satisfied that Finch had no weapon.

A strong voice barked in Afrikaans and the two men stood back. A man with an uncharacteristic clipped beard swung his leg off his well-groomed palomino gelding. He was aged around 30. His mid-blue suit was of a fine corduroy. The brim of his hat had been pinned up on one side, like that of an Australian, adorned with the stub of a bright red feather. A gold watch chain hung on his waistcoat. There were links in his shirt cuffs. Unusually, he wore riding boots.

"Good day to you, Captain," he said, striding forward, confidently.

He thrust out his hand. Finch shook it. On either flank Finch could see horsemen charging across the veld still. Disconcertingly, he could hear distant gunfire.

"Pieter Swanepoel, Kroonstad Commando," the man announced.

His English was impeccable. His accent light. He pulled out a silver case, finely engraved.

"Cigarette?"

Finch nodded. The Boer officer flipped the lid. They were British smokes. Capstans.

There was a commotion from within the barn. Finch could hear sick men protesting. He did not like it.

"*Hier*," a Boer was yelling. "*Hier binne*."

"My men—" Finch protested.

"…will not be harmed," Swanepoel cut across. "You have my word."

Without looking up, the Boer commander uttered another order. The shouting stopped.

He seemed in no hurry. He struck a match, cupped his hands round the flame and lit first Finch's cigarette, then his own. He exhaled casually. He looked up at the sky.

"Warmer today, is it not?"

Finch didn't know what to say. He simply nodded. The strength of the cigarette caught him unawares. His head spun.

"It is high ground here," he continued. "Very flat. The weather can change…" he clicked his fingers "…like that."

He had got the measure of the British, thought Finch, opening with a meteorological meditation.

"It does take some getting used to."

Swanepoel smiled.

"So… Captain…?"

"Finch. Ingo Finch. Royal Army Medical Corps."

Finch saluted. There was no return. He felt stupid.

"…back to the Modder, eh?"

He was not prepared for discussion of military strategy. It was beyond his remit.

"By the terms of Geneva Convention, I'm not obliged…"

Swanepoel gave a mildly contemptuous snort.

"Come, come… Please, Captain. Relax. It's hardly a secret. This is open country. Natural barriers are few and far between. Little cover. You can't hide… plus, we have good intelligence. Eyes in your camp."

It would be no surprise, thought Finch. The army moved so ponderously and with so many hangers-on, its dealings were an open book.

Finch explained about the casualties. There were 63 men to be handed over. He gave a brief synopsis of the range of injuries.

"They will be well cared for," Swanepoel promised. "We have doctors with us. As soon as the Front is secure, they will be transported by rail back to Bloemfontein. The track is open behind our lines."

"Thank you."

Never before had armies been so dependent on railway lines, or so vulnerable to derailment. The Boers had thwarted the entire British advance by the simple act of dynamiting a set of points.

Finch gestured to the small hillock, the mass grave. He handed Swanepoel an envelope.

"The particulars. I would be grateful if you could erect some kind of marker. Then, when this is over—"

"Our presbyter will take care of it."

The commander tucked the envelope into his breast pocket.

There was shouting, an altercation. At the south gate, a small knot of Boers had surrounded the ox cart. They had demanded raised hands from the wounded Tommies, who were struggling to comply. A Boer had climbed onto the tailgate.

"Three casualties plus a driver. All unarmed," declared Finch. "You have *my* word."

Swanepoel shouted. The men stopped immediately. He exhaled more smoke.

"Two of my men will escort you to within a mile of your rear-guard."

Finch nodded at the barn. Swanepoel gave permission for him to explain the situation to his men. He hobbled to the building and went in. A Boer soldier accompanied him.

The first thing to hit him was the smell – of bodies, misery, sweat, excrement and the unmistakable tinge of rotting flesh. There was a constant drone – the damned flies. He tried not to gag.

They were a sorry sight – a row of men along each wall huddled in filthy horse blankets; no beds, just stained tarpaulins over the straw. Some men were without an arm, others a leg or both, some blinded. Amid the greying bandages and festering wounds he thought he recognised Urquhart, but was not sure. Several were unconscious. What use was operating on them if they ended up like this?

The Boer soldier spoke, his accent heavy.

"Doctors. Good. They come," he told Finch.

There was not a single objection from the men as Finch informed them of their situation, their sad eyes acknowledging.

Back outside, Swanepoel was holding two enamel mugs.

"Tea, Captain Finch? Your custom."

Finch took the mug and sipped the milk-less brew. It was unfamiliar but pleasant to taste.

"*Rooibos*. Redbush," said Swanepoel. "Come…"

The Boer commander led the way. The two men ambled up the hillock where the earth was dark and fresh, Finch using his walking stick now in the way it was intended. They stood for a moment in silence.

"You know I lived in England," he said. "Cambridge… Trinity. Passed the bar, then on to Kaapstad… Cape Town. Moved back home to Bloemfontein when the lines were being drawn."

"It is a beautiful country you have here," Finch mumbled, then regretted such a trite offering.

He reached inside his tunic to share his hip flask. It was empty.

He sighed. "It was a good one. Sorry."

"Next time," said Swanepoel, patting Finch's forearm. "Next time."

One of Swanepoel's men was calling him. The Boer officer shook his dregs onto the ground. He nodded towards the ox cart.

"Captain. Your carriage awaits… Here."

He passed Finch a small wax bag. Loose tea leaves. The *rooibos*.

"When you drink it, you will think of me."

Finch smiled. They shook hands. The commander strode off.

–

At the gate, Finch did his best to climb onto the ox cart. It was a painful exercise.

The three men on board were all Argylls – one had his hands bandaged, the second had a dressing over his left eye, the third lay shivering under a blanket. All were filthy. A curiosity of yesterday's battle was that a substantial number of the wounds had come in the form of sunstroke.

Pinned down by the enemy guns, many of the Highlanders had been forced to lie absolutely still, face down for hours in the heat of the African sun, unable to make the merest movement which would have attracted the Boer marksmen who could shoot a man dead at a thousand yards. The sun had roasted the backs of necks and bare white legs.

At Finch's signal, the African driver smacked his stick on the rear of the two oxen and, slowly, the cart trundled off up the dirt road.

Behind, two Boers followed – one middle-aged, with a full beard, the other young, notably clean-shaven. They were treating the slow pace as rest for their horses, which were encouraged to stop and chew on vegetation whenever they felt like it. The Boer horses were small, more like ponies, but they were lean and muscular, skew and piebald – working animals, cattle wranglers. The riders rode with a long stirrup.

A while later, as they came to the brow of a low hill, the Boer with the beard rode up and instructed the African ox driver to stop. There was contempt in his tone. The cart halted. The younger, smooth one, with a ruddy complexion, trotted ahead, dismounted and crept forward, ducking behind some acacia scrub. He extended a small telescope and viewed what Finch assumed to be the retreating British column.

Finch could see in the distance a huge swirling cloud, not just the dust of an army on the move but the smoke of a vast encampment, the huge tent city that would have started forming beyond the thin line of trees that marked the banks of the Modder. There would be an endless line of wagons waiting, queued up to cross the lone, rickety pontoon bridge the Royal Engineers had built to replace the one the Boers had blown up.

The young man rode part of the way back down. His companion sauntered up to confer. When they had spoken, Finch was invited to step down and join them. He made heavy weather of it. Fifty yards away a male ostrich bounded along with its loping stride.

"It is safe to proceed," faltered the bearded one, pressing tobacco into a clay pipe.

The added, more fluid announcement by his colleague that 'They're at least two miles ahead' was remarkable less for the information than that it was delivered in an unmistakable southern Irish brogue.

The man saw Finch startle and relished his confusion.

"MacBride's Brigade. Volunteers," he said.

"But—"

"But what, Captain?"

Finch shrugged and hobbled back to the wagon. The Highlander with the eye patch helped him up.

It was then that they heard it, blowing on the stiff northerly breeze – a volley, then a second, of rifle fire. They had been travelling half an hour but there was no mistaking where it came from – the farmstead.

Finch pushed himself to his feet, apoplectic.

"But what, Captain?"

Finch was shouting now.

"Your officer gave me his word! You have no right!"

The two Boer escorts turned and galloped away.

Tears came to Finch's eyes, his body racked by violent tremors. He screamed it till his voice was hoarse.

"YOU HAVE NO RIGHT...! YOU HAVE NO RIGHT...! YOU HAVE NO RIGHT!"

Part Two

Chapter Eight

Mbutu could feel the stare of the youth sitting opposite. The sinewy adolescent was reclining on the floor of the goods wagon, propped against the side-board, rocking to the rhythm with an unnerving nonchalance.

He had kept his gaze trained on Mbutu the whole time. Even now, in the gloom, Mbutu could sense the eyes fixed upon him. The light of the full moon that flashed between the slats glinted on the blade of a hunting knife. The youth turned it compulsively. It was clean, well-oiled, an object of affection.

Probably well used.

The young man was not with the others – this desperate ragtag of displaced souls. Not in spirit. When Mbutu had scrambled aboard the trundling wagon, south of the halt at Hopetown, he had just sat there.

He had barely moved since – not even when Mbutu secured his passage by sharing his last shards of indestructible chicken biltong. It was twilight then. Mbutu had noted the glassiness in his eyes, the dull reddened whites of someone high on *dagga*.

Coyly, Mbutu touched the cloth bag containing the five shillings tucked into his waistband.

The wooden boxcar was noisy, bare and uncomfortable. There was a thin scattering of straw. Save for some crates stacked at one end, stamped with the letters 'A.K.C.', it was empty. One box had been prised open. It contained flat tin drums, nothing of sustenance. Having disgorged its wares at the Front, the train was creaking south on the long return to Cape Town.

Turning his head, Mbutu could see the stars and smell the baked earth of the Karoo, an antidote to the stench of unwashed male within. The air was warm and dusty, an almost physical presence that coated everything with a fine sheen of wilderness dirt.

Mbutu was thirsty, starving, aching, tired, filthy. But he dare not sleep, dare not close his eyes.

Not with the youth.

There had been eight men in the wagon at first, only seven now. When they picked up speed beyond Hopetown, a gaunt Xhosa man had tried to rouse his sleeping friend only to discover that the slumber was now permanent.

Someone said a prayer for him, not much past 20 years of age, a sad bag of bones. The Xhosa mumbled something that got translated as lungs, 'weak lungs'. Then they engaged the lever and slid back the heavy door, just enough to heave the body out into the void.

The oldest man in the wagon was a Basuto like Mbutu. Samuel had a white-flecked beard and tight greying curls that looked as if they had been dusted with powder. He was 55, maybe 60? But stocky, still strong. Samuel assumed that common ethnicity would make Mbutu a suitable audience for a detailed narration of his life story.

The old talk. The old always talk.

He gave resumés of their travelling companions – the bereaved Xhosa and three Baralong – mine boys from Johannesburg.

"A long way from home."

They were all a long way from home. All a long way from home.

The staring youth was fleeing the fighting, too, he whispered.

"Zulu. Be careful, my friend. Be careful…"

Samuel trusted Mbutu but Mbutu trusted no one.

Trust made you vulnerable. Trust made you weak.

–

It had been 13 nights now but it seemed like a lifetime. Mbutu had done as was asked by the two agents and ushered the British officer beyond the city's perimeter. The initial danger had come from the city's defences, the searchlights sweeping the land. But the shafts of light were regular in their movement, easy to predict, and Mbutu knew of the depressions, how to keep low.

Skirting the Boer's vantage points, where snipers would have lodged, they had climbed, eventually, up to the narrow gully in the Spytfontein ridge, a deep crack that Mbutu knew – as much as 20ft down in places, barely a shoulder's width at times.

Not a word was exchanged between the men over four hours as they picked their way across boulders, stopping only to sip water.

Snakes. Do not turn the rocks.

Descending toward the plain, the gully opened outwards. The temperature began to plummet. It was Mbutu who spoke first.

"See there," he said, his hand tracing a barely visible zig-zag scar – the Boer trenches.

On the horizon he pointed out the flickers.

"Fires. British fires."

Careless fires.

And, on the brow of the gentle rise, the low outline of a farmstead.

It was as far as Mbutu could go. He had fulfilled his mission, he said.

Mbutu knew from the position of the Southern Cross that it must be around one o'clock. He would have to move fast to sneak back into Kimberley by sun-up, move fast to keep warm. He nodded at the lieutenant and turned to go.

Suddenly it came… the thin twine tight round his neck and the jolt of being yanked upwards off his feet while the searing hot pain shot up his jugular veins. The blood pounded in his head, his tongue launched outwards. His eyes bulged near out of their sockets, his left hand clawing at the cord.

But, instinctively, as the garrote was whipped over, Mbutu had raised his right arm, meaning that the twine had failed to make clean contact with his neck, trapping his wrist to his throat, incompletely blocking the airway or pinching off the blood-flow.

Realising his miscalculation, and with a great strain, the lieutenant sought to rectify his error by crossing his hands to tighten the strangle-hold, jerking Mbutu upwards onto the tips of his toes, walking backwards to negate the struggle, the killer's hot breath raging in Mbutu's ear.

Strong, unnaturally strong.

And then the man stumbled, staggering backwards, releasing his grip.

Mbutu was not a man of violence but a survival instinct found him reaching for a stone, a jagged rock the size of a house brick, which he swung at the man's head, missed, connecting instead – accompanied by a sharp crack – with the man's collarbone.

The man disappeared. Had he fallen?

Mbutu thought he saw a black shape tumbling down the rubbled slope.

And then Mbutu ran.

And ran. And ran.

—

Imperceptibly at first, the gaps began to lengthen between the clacking of the sleepers. Then they all felt it, the slackening of the rhythm – the train was slowing.

It was inevitable. The railway was single track. There was no means of passing. When trains met travelling in opposite directions, one had to yield, shunted into a siding. The northbound trains, loaded with troops and munitions, had priority.

The British were arriving in force now, said someone, offloaded in their thousands at the docks, flooding north. Indeed, Mbutu had heard of enlistment at Beaufort West – way down the line to Cape Town – of natives being mustered to help supply the big push on Kimberley. It was why he was here.

Sure enough, they could hear the distant toots. They were growing louder. Growing nearer. With a bellow and belch of steam, their own transport was creaking and clanking out of the way.

The only question now was when the stowaways were going to make their exit, at what speed it would be safe to jump.

But it was too late. They had been caught unawares. With a huge hiss they had jolted to a halt.

The Cape Government Railways were staffed by military personnel. Mbutu could hear the guards advancing up the line, banging on the side of the goods wagons and yanking back the doors.

He heard the smack of a rifle butt and a man yell out, then other protestations of mercy as the interlopers were ejected.

They must get out. Now!

Behind them, across the carriage, the other door lever sprang back.

They did not wait. As the heavy panel began to slide, eight bodies cascaded out, knocking over a soldier and spilling onto the gravel.

There were shouts, struggles. The weak Xhosa was easy meat, going down under a succession of gleefully sadistic blows. Others had wrestled free from the soldiers' clutches. Mbutu saw Samuel succumb and grabbed his arm, shirking off the attacker and hauling him towards the bush.

The Zulu youth's blade would have consequences for Mbutu after all. As the young man was assailed by one Tommy, he swung it upwards, forcefully and with lethal precision, under the soldier's ribs.

And then came the retribution.

Rifles were unslung, raised. Bolts shuttled.

An order: "Fire at will."

There were yelps as running men were felled.

Twenty yards from the advancing troops was waist-high scrub. Mbutu tried to grab Samuel, to pull him down into cover, but the older man crumpled.

All but one had crumpled.

And Johnny Fleetfoot was on his own again.

Running. Running. Running.

–

The train had long gone. There was nothing but the great expanse of the Karoo in every direction. Mbutu had no water, no food, he was exhausted. He could not begin to orientate himself till first light.

It was inevitable but, once his ears adjusted, Mbutu heard it – a throaty snarl, the sound of a predator. They would be able to smell him for miles.

He had no weapon, no fire, no hiding place, no means of defence whatsoever. What good was five shillings now?

Mbutu said a silent prayer and wished a good life for his wife and child and a merciful death for himself.

Please, oh Lord – a quick, painless death.

And then, in the middle of nowhere, came another sound.

He could just make out the words.

"*Aan die Koningseun gebied.*"

Glory to the newborn king.

Chapter Nine

Finch had had his fill of the other man in the railway carriage. Not that he wasn't of interest, but that he had conspired to arrive in Finch's life at absolutely the wrong moment.

He was irrepressibly chipper, possessed of a compulsive need to fill dead air with noise.

"Say Finch?" he nudged.

Finch twisted awkwardly. A 12-hour, overnight train journey on a slatted wooden seat was insufferable enough without the aural assault from this diminutive American, one dressed in a garish yellow check suit, bow tie and oversized bowler.

"Say Finch?" he pursued, polishing thick, horn-rim spectacles.

There had been a brief lull in Lloyd's verbal onslaught as the locomotive of the Cape Government Railways juddered to a halt, easing into yet another siding to allow one of the countless troop trains to pass in the opposite direction. At one stop there had been shots to ward off the vagabonds.

But as the train picked up speed, so did Lloyd.

"Say Finch. Did I tell you that I rode with Teddy Roosevelt in the Spanish-American?"

Finch said nothing.

"Finch…? Say Finch?"

"You did, Mr Lloyd," he sighed.

"Well, we'd bust out of Havana, see. In the jungle. Hot as hell. Like here, but not like here, if you know what I'm saying?"

Finch shrugged.

"Green, real green. Humid with it."

The heat of the Karoo was dry, absolutely. Even at dawn you could feel it blasting through the open window, leaching the last bit of moisture out of your throat.

Finch rested his head on his rolled-up jacket pressed against the glass, at one with the ambient *clickety-clack*. In the orange glow of daybreak the squat baobab trees were rising from the mist, exuding an other-worldly aura.

It was no good. He could feel Lloyd champing at the bit again. Finch lit himself a Navy Cut. He was getting a craving. His offer of one to Lloyd only increased the illusion of conviviality.

"Well anyways," went Lloyd, "we were in the jungle see…"

Still, second class was comparative luxury. He shouldn't complain. In third, the troops and the rag-tag of hangers-on were packed in like sardines. Behind them came the cars for the wounded. God knows the journey wasn't being kind. Finch imagined that the unloaded freight wagons at the rear would now be largely empty. What a waste.

Here in their six-seater carriage there were just the two of them, Lloyd having seen off the interlopers who'd entered at the stops en route – De Aar, then Beaufort West.

The compartment still seemed claustrophobic, the narrow-gauge railways of the Cape – built to allow engineers easier penetration of the solid rock of the northerly mining areas – lending a certain sense of Toy Town miniaturisation.

Up front, in first class, rode the senior officers. Second had been almost excessively reserved for the gentlemen of the press, of which Lloyd was one. Though to give Lloyd credit, mused Finch, he was not like the others – swilling the booze and playing cards, exuding a certain schadenfreude at the British Army's bloody nose.

A day-old *Cape Argus* lay folded haphazardly on Finch's lap. A hat-trick of British military defeats had been dubbed the 'Black Week' – annihilations at Stormberg, Colenso and, as the engagement he himself had been involved in had been anointed, the Battle of Magersfontein.

'Margaret's Spring', such a quaint name for a killing field.

And then there were the sieges – the border cities of Kimberley and Mafeking were cut off. So too was Ladysmith, over in Natal.

"Something the matter, Finch?" asked Lloyd.

Finch shook his head. It was difficult to explain. For all the horror, the fighting was still described in terms of 'good sport', as if the engagements were a Test match at the Kennington Oval. In the House of Commons, it was reported, Irish Nationalist MPs had stood and cheered at news of the defeats. The Liberals could barely suppress a smirk.

Though it had not been stated officially, it was hinted that the commander of the Imperial forces, Sir Redvers Buller – or 'Reverse' Buller – was to be sidelined. Currently at sea, holding fast for the Cape, were the popular General, Lord 'Bobs' Roberts and his number two, Lord Kitchener.

On the Natal Front, where Buller had taken personal command, it was rumoured he had forbidden his men to dig trenches, dismissing such a thing as 'dishonourable'. They said Buller had proscribed shooting from a prone position lest his men dirty their uniforms. Finch thought about the Highlanders and their pathetic knotted rope.

After all that had happened, Finch had not expected to be granted leave and, given the slaughter, felt guilty enough about taking it.

That he should be arriving in Cape Town on Christmas Eve was a happy coincidence. He might as well enjoy it. He would be back among the carnage in five days.

Two months from the outbreak of hostilities and the troop surge was finally on, at least, soldiers disembarking en masse from Britain and the Empire – men from the Dominions of Canada, Newfoundland, New South Wales, New Zealand; loyal subjects from India, Ceylon, Queensland, Victoria, even tiny Mauritius.

The great khaki flood had included plenty of RAMC, enough for Finch's own medical contingent to be relieved.

"We were with Teddy, right. Hell of a guy," Lloyd was going again. "Let me tell you, when McKinley's had his chips, Teddy's your man. The real deal. Oh boy, I tell ya. The real deal."

Finch studied the terrain, the only movement the bound and leap of the occasional springbok or the comedic gambol of an ostrich as the driver blew the whistle.

"And of course film, acetate, perishes in the humidity. Did I tell you that Cuba was humid? Hot like here but not like here?"

Finch nodded.

"So, anyways, Teddy, he commandeers a refrigerator from this navy vessel at Guantanamo and they lug it all the ways up by mule. Say, you guys have refrigerators…? Well let me tell you Finch, every kitchen in America's gonna have one within ten years. Make that every kitchen in the world."

Lloyd puffed out his chest.

"And they're gonna be made in the USA, Finch. Made in the US of A… You wanna make yourself a buck. Buy stock in Frigidaire."

The door slid open from the corridor, letting in a ripe gust of bawdy singing from the infantrymen in the rear. An officer, a lieutenant-colonel, entered and closed the door behind him. He nodded at both men and took the seat opposite Finch. He looked as weary as Finch felt.

"Hi," said Lloyd, thrusting out a hand. "Hal Lloyd… of the Cincinnati Lloyds. Director and Producer for the American Kinematograph Company."

Lloyd explained that he and his crew had been 'filming' the action, taking 'moving pictures' of the battlefield, to be projected on a screen in the music halls of Europe and the Americas. They had seven crates of equipment in the goods wagon.

Lloyd whipped out, for the officer's assumed delectation, a postcard-sized illustration of his kinematograph machine – a box on legs with a handle for cranking the reel of film past a lens, twenty-four frames a second.

It was 'the future' Lloyd assured.

The officer threw Finch a smile.

"Say, I was just telling Finch here how I rode with Teddy Roosevelt in the Spanish-American."

Chapter Ten

It was late afternoon when they pulled into Cape Town. As the train skirted the city, Finch once again drew an intake of breath at the majesty of Table Mountain, cloaked as ever with a mist on its summit which seemed to spill down its slopes.

There were few ports in the world to match Cape Town for spectacle, the sailors on the passage had told him – New York, Sydney, Hong Kong, Rio. He hoped one day to form a personal opinion.

Finch leaned out of the window. The authorities at King's Cross would surely never tolerate such laxity – onlookers ambling about the yards, the black workers of the rail gangs casually walking across the tracks. But never had the sounds of a city, that vibrant hum of activity, seemed more welcoming.

Even at noon in high summer it was considerably cooler than the north. And, beyond the steam and the oil and the coal, he could smell it – the sea.

As the train squeaked and shuddered to a halt under the vaulted roof, the locomotive yielded a great 'job-done' hiss and they were enveloped in a cacophony of noise.

Through the clouds of steam, Coloured porters rushed along the platform to the carriages. Handcarts were wheeled by shoeless blacks. Indians toted urns of tea. Everyone seemed to be screaming either for business or at each other.

Keeping a respectful distance, army personnel waited to part the khaki tide. RAMC orderlies congregated near the hospital cars, a line of ambulance wagons pulled right up alongside.

Beyond, on the far platform, infantry were arrayed in full kit, ready to embark. The neat puttees and shiny boots seemed ridiculously fastidious to one who'd been two months in the field. A sergeant major was barking at the men to present arms. Gleaming Lee-Metford rifles swung with precision.

Finch slid back the compartment door, stepped into the corridor and was carried on a human wave that swept him onto the platform and out towards the concourse. He managed to procure a porter who, somehow, emerged beaming with his kit bag.

Ahead Finch could see Lloyd with his crew, remonstrating with a team of porters, urging to them to handle his precious kinematograph boxes with care. One of them had been opened, he was complaining.

Beneath the glass of the atrium, gaily coloured birds flitted, tweeting and screeching on high.

Finch tipped the porter generously, swung his bag over his shoulder and emerged into the glorious sunshine, his eyes bombarded with colour – advertising hoardings, familiar ones for Horlicks, Lyons Tea and Guinness Stout; the enormous oranges, grapefruit and pineapples piled high on the stands of street vendors; the bright shirts of the black Africans.

On the pavement, city gents jostled their way through a knot of turbaned Sikh infantrymen. Behind, down Adderley Street, trams clanged by, cutting through a sea of carts. A traffic policeman with white gloves, standing on a box, blowing a shrill whistle, was trying to inflict order.

Finch made his way to the cab stand. The queue snaked round the side of the building.

"Very busy, sir," a black orderly informed. "Christmas Eve."

Finch had no map and tried to fathom from him a way to his backstreet hotel, which he deduced to be a couple of miles distant but whose route by a combination of trams – trams stuffed to the gunnels – seemed overly complicated.

He was about to set off by foot, the last thing he really wanted, when he heard a familiar voice.

"Finch. Say, Finch."

At the kerb, sitting up beside the African driver of a flatbed mule cart was Lloyd, his crew and precious crates in the rear.

"Room for one more."

Finch gave a wry smile.

–

Finch's hotel, The Belvedere, was a modest converted town house. Lloyd had dropped Finch off before continuing inland to his more sumptuous quarters at the Mount Nelson.

As he had alighted on the cobbles, Finch had found it impossible to resist Lloyd's invitation to join him there later for dinner. And, secretly, he was grateful for the offer. He knew no one to pass the evening with and, much as he could have crawled into bed right there and then, it seemed wrong not to mark Christmas Eve in some fashion.

Finch had a shave, took a quick dip in the bathtub across the corridor, put on his dress uniform and brushed his hair. No matter how hard he blew his nose, the dust of the Karoo seemed to have entered the very fibres of his being.

Kissed by the pink glow reflecting back off Table Mountain, the Mount Nelson Hotel was exquisite, its red-tiled drive lined with protea flowers. A waft of night-blooming jasmine scented the air. The white wooden building's verandas had been set with tiny candles.

You could hear the sounds of genteel society from within – polite chatter, the clinking of glasses and a string quartet playing Vivaldi. A general exited, his chest a wash of medals, a woman on his arm in an ivory evening gown and an ostrich feather in her hair.

It was here that Redvers Buller had stayed, Finch understood; where he had planned the early days of the campaign. Such an incongruous setting for the scheduling of death.

Finch soon found Lloyd in the elegant restaurant, a fat cigar clenched between his teeth. Lloyd greeted him like a long-lost brother and bade him sit at a large round table for 12 beneath a huge chandelier.

Finch instantly forgot the names of his dinner companions, male and female, none of whom were military, save for two captains, French and German, there as international observers. They seemed undiplomatically exuberant over the Empire's current misfortune.

Finch was too tired to argue with them. He bit his lip, laughed at Lloyd's jokes, especially once Lloyd insisted the American Kinematograph Company would be picking up the bill, and listened in earnest while Lloyd told of two 'buddies' of his in North Carolina, brothers, who were building a flying machine. He had no doubt about Lloyd's assertion, that the impending century would be an American one.

After some magnificent sea bass, washed down with a Chenin Blanc, Finch ordered a triple Talisker and lingered till midnight so that he might wish his company Merry Christmas.

He had now gone through tiredness and out the other side, so chose to walk home in the fresh air, hoping that it might sink his supper and wear him out, the alcohol an anaesthetic for his stiff leg, which he trusted would loosen up with exercise.

The main thoroughfare of Adderley was still a riot of noise. Nearby, on Long Street, with its ornate, overhanging wrought iron balconies, the drinkers, largely military, were spilling beyond the taverns onto the pavement. The atmosphere had gone beyond festive, the cobbles now a carpet of crunching glass, urine and vomit.

From one throng, a group of Military Foot Police was dragging away a drunken private. A volley of angry abuse came from his pals.

Further along, on a corner, Finch watched men gathered round a street hustler, a white South African playing Chase the Lady on an upturned tea chest. The man, doubtless operating with stooges, was fleecing his drunken audience.

Off the main drag, up an alleyway, Finch saw men, soldiers, buying *dagga*, the powerful South African marijuana, from a dealer who was letting them take a sample puff on his own reefer of superior quality.

In the background Finch heard glasses smashing, shouting and whistles blowing. He hastened on his way. From a doorway, a black woman in a tattered approximation of an evening dress offered him sexual favours.

Back in his hotel Finch climbed the tight winding stairs, undressed, crawled into bed and tried to sleep. The raucous merriment and the fiddler from the pub a few doors along put paid to that.

But, eventually, the exhaustion washed over him and he tipped into the blackness of the abyss.

–

He had no idea of the hour when a loud pounding on his door resulted in him groggily pulling on his shirt and trousers and finding himself face to face with a bellboy brandishing a paraffin lamp who urged that he come quickly. Half-thinking that he had overslept and was late for something, Finch tugged on untied boots, shrugged on his jacket and followed down the narrow staircase.

Standing in the lobby was a man in a Homburg hat, a grey suit and black necktie. He was an impressive figure – in his late 50s, Finch guessed, on the tall side, darkly handsome, with silver hair visible at the sides and back. He extended his hand and wished Finch a cursory 'Happy Christmas'.

Finch had quite forgotten what day it now was but mumbled a seasonal pleasantry in return.

"Detective Inspector Brookman, Cape Constabulary," he announced. "Sorry to wake you so early, sir, but I'm afraid we need your assistance."

His eyes were deep brown, almost black.

"Assistance?"

"Yes, sir. There's been a murder."

Chapter Eleven

The singing seemed to be coming from behind a low mound of rocks some hundred or more yards distant. Mbutu trod his way towards them. Closer, he could discern a glow emanating from within, and the sound, now clear – voices, male and female.

"*Hoor die blye eng'lelied.*"

Hark the herald angels sing. Dutch... Afrikaans, but not the Afrikaans of a native speaker – of those who had learned the hymn parrot fashion.

The snarling was closer, too. Short, sharp bursts. The creature had moved position. No, there was more than one. They were circling, communicating. There were jackal and hyena out here but this sounded like a big cat. There were no lions in the Karoo, but leopard... Didn't leopard hunt alone? Not always. It had been known...

"*Vrede opaard, aan God die eer.*"

Peace on earth and mercy mild.

Mbutu's eyes were long used to the dark. He was aided by a full moon, the stars a giddying splash across the black of the heavens. But his vision could not remotely match that of a feline.

He calculated the distance – ten, twelve seconds to the rocks if he ran full pelt; less than that for the animals to be upon him. His best bet was to ease his way over slowly, let the leopards circle, then sprint the last few yards before they closed in. But he would still have to scramble up the boulders...

"*God daal tot die sondaar neer.*"

God and sinners reconciled.

He edged on, his attuned senses recording his own painfully amplified footfalls. He could hear the breath and padding of feet – one animal to each side and, now, ominously, one straight ahead.

He stopped, absolutely frozen. He held his breath. He had become a pounding human heartbeat.

The cats stopped, too. All of them… silent.

He hadn't noticed but the carolling had also been suspended, as if the choristers were now aware of the fatal drama about to play out beyond their walls.

Then came the signal. An almighty primal roar that shook Mbutu to his core.

Attack!

He had 30 yards to reach cover. At an angle, away from the predators, he ran for his life.

Mbutu's feet kicked stones and were slowed by clumps of grass. He tripped, plunging forward, but just kept his footing. He could feel the thuds of padded paws pounding in.

He made it to the boulders and jumped up on one, almost as high as himself, and clung for dear life. It was smooth with no handholds. His fingers clawed but he slid back.

Join the triumph of the skies.

To his right he saw a streak of spots and then, suddenly, brightness…

Above him a flaming torch arced over the rocks and landed, fizzing, 6ft away. For an instant there were not three, but five leopard in tableau – paralysed, mesmerised, their retina reflecting back the bright yellow tongue of fire.

"Torch… Pick up! Wave!" someone was yelling.

Mbutu scrambled to it. The flame was dulling in the dirt, the rags unravelling. He grabbed the stick and swung it wildly above his head. The air fed the fire.

Then they were gone…

"Come! Quick! Will be back."

A tattered rope had been thrown down. No, not a rope, a vine, some sort of twisted, knotted fibre. Mbutu eased himself up. Hands reached out and grabbed his forearms. Never had he been so grateful for human contact.

Over the edge and he was in a natural corral, almost perfectly circular, about 30 yards across, sunken in the centre and with a fire burning, around which sat some 20 or so men and women, plus a smattering of infants.

In the torchlight he could see that the men who had pulled him to safety were short and slender. Their faces were flat with high cheekbones, eyes slanted, their hair matted, their beards thin and wispy like those of an adolescent. In daylight Mbutu knew that their skin would be paler than his – apricot, almost yellow.

They were not Bantu, like him, but Khoikhoi, descendants of the bushmen who once hunted across Southern Africa unchallenged. Before the white man and the black man moved in.

He'd encountered them before, west of Kimberley. The Nama people. They had been looked down upon, subsistence farmers scratching a living, exiled to this semi-desert.

Scratching a living but free. Not down a mine. Not in a cage.

Around the rim of the rocks, men stood on lookout. There were several with spears. One, he saw, had a rifle… if you could call it that, a cumbersome, weighty contraption with a flared muzzle – an ancient, flintlock blunderbuss.

"Thank you," panted Mbutu.

The one who had shouted to him, a fit-looking man of about 30, had a battered revolver tucked into his waistband. He seemed to be the leader.

He gave a nod and the man with the blunderbuss came over, though not by way of greeting but to thrust the barrel into the small of Mbutu's back. Spears were lowered either side. They pushed him down the slope.

The men and women sitting round the fire looked up at the interloper. The women appeared out of place in the wilds, in thick long dresses of the British Victorian style and wound headscarves.

The man, the leader, addressed them in a rapid tongue with a volley of clicking noises.

Mbutu knew nothing of the language but could hear the leader's name repeated – Hendrik – as they each took turns to put over their viewpoint to him.

It was a thorough hearing and seemed to take forever, some assailing Hendrik with lengthy diatribes, bringing gasps, mutterings or nods of condemnation; others with pithy utterances causing the audience to giggle.

An old lady, hunched, toothless, was helped to her feet. She raged for ages, wagging her finger in Mbutu's face amid a great tutting and general head-shaking.

Hendrik turned to him.

"Want to know where you come from," he summarised. "Want to know if can trust. Want to know if have seen…" he said it nervously, "…the devil soldiers?"

There was agitation, hand-wringing and a sudden burst of shrill ululation from the women.

Mbutu had heard enough superstitious native claptrap about the war to last him a lifetime, but now was not the time or place to tell these people that they were talking nonsense.

He waited for silence. He felt the great coercive blunderbuss.

"My name is Mbutu, Mbutu Kefaleze," he began. Hendrik translated. "I am a Basuto and I have spent the last ten years working for the diamond mines in Kimberley."

And he told them his story.

In the hours after his escape, Mbutu kept hidden at the western end of the Spytfontein ridge, placing himself high, tucked behind boulders just below the summit. He had a scrap or two of biltong but barely any water, his pigskin having split during the struggle.

At home, in the bush of Basutoland, he would have known how to survive – which plants to squeeze to make moisture, which sap to drink. But here? Mother Nature was mischievous. There were spiky pods in the scrub – horned cucumber – of which some varieties were toxic, others not. How to tell? There were no springbok, no gemsbok to guide him. The animals seemed to have fled. A sixth sense.

Down below, at first light, Mbutu could see the landscape shifting under great dark masses – troops on the move. And then he heard it, a great screech – like the Kimberley siege guns but multiplied a hundredfold – that penetrated his very being. The hills around him began exploding in great clouds of lethal rubble.

He lay in the lee of a boulder, fingers in ears, curled up like a baby for what seemed an eternity. And then, suddenly, with a silence that seemed even more deafening, the artillery stopped, the dust settled.

The gunfire after that seemed pathetic – small pops that carried on the wind. From his grandstand perch Mbutu watched as wave after wave of soldier ants marched casually towards their deaths, mown down at will.

The gully through the ridge was now cut off, blocked by the Boer horsemen that had mustered.

Mbutu had two choices when it came to getting back to Kimberley: circumvent the mountains – a journey that could take days across inhospitable terrain, without guarantee of food and water and without knowledge of troop movements; or move amongst the Boer army and access the pass from within the *laager* – their encampment.

Be smart, Mbutu. Your heart screams but you must go with your head.

That afternoon, Mbutu seized his chance. There appeared to be an amnesty or truce of sorts, a means for both sides to tend to their wounded. The Boers, like the British, moved with a whole army-within-an-army of black attendants – drivers, porters, carriers, runners, cooks.

With a lack of any apparent structure within the Boer brigades, it was easy to infiltrate. Mbutu simply walked down onto the plain and attached himself to a burial detail, tying his kerchief round his mouth, retrieving bodies, throwing stones at the vultures, hauling mashed remains onto ox carts. There were British there too now, tending to their own. Enemies one minute, friends the next. They were the same tribe after all.

And then the screeching began again. British shells. The truce was abandoned and they dived for cover.

That night, Mbutu ate pumpkin soup and rough dark bread, *boere-beskuit*. Never had food tasted so good. He sat round a fire with black farm boys from the Free State and the Transvaal, their heads filled with tales of the demonic British and their necromancy. Mbutu said nothing.

In darkness, Mbutu tried to make his way back to the gully to no avail. He would try again, he vowed, and again. But the next day he was moved further from the mountains, following the cavalry to the farmstead on the hill, unloading boxes of ammunition in the wake of the British retreat.

A Boer soldier whistled to him. He and several others were summoned to the cowshed. The stench was so great he thought he would vomit – worse than that of the corpses he had gathered up on the battlefield.

Here, in an airless room, lay a sorry mess of British injured – forlorn wretches whose greatest misfortune was having been allowed to live.

He and his black brethren had helped carry the rank and bleeding victims to waiting carts which would transport them on to the railway line and the hospital in Bloemfontein.

The Boers were not like the British. It was hard to tell who was in charge. No obvious ranks, no deference. Although there was a younger officer – smart, well-dressed, horse well-groomed – who was clearly taking umbrage with the command of a revered greybeard, a man Mbutu had heard whisper who was close to Oom Kruger himself.

The greybeard ordered his men to fire volleys of their rifles into the air in order, it appeared, to simulate an execution of the British wounded.

The British, he assured, would rise to the bait. They would seek revenge; they would make accusations of atrocity without proof and then conduct slaughter of their own in reprisal – bringing international condemnation, galvanising further the Boer Republics.

The younger officer, a captain, argued, and with some force, that such an act was immoral; that he, himself, had given his word to the British that their wounded would be cared for; that to employ such dishonourable tactics would only give licence to barbarity, endangering the lives of their own women and children. But the greybeard won out, and the charade began.

Soon after the wounded had been packed off, one of the blacks gave out a shriek of horror. Boers came running. Blacks came running. Behind a woodpile, placed there in hiding, were two bodies – the corpses of British soldiers, their faces leering, their throats crudely slit. One, a large individual, had been stripped of his uniform. The other, smaller, was a lance corporal, denoted by a single chevron on his sleeve. But these were not battle troops. They were too neat, too clean. Around the arm of the smaller man was a dark blue band, the red letters 'MFP'.

By the evening, Mbutu was becoming conspicuous. Questions were being asked by his own black brothers. Where was he at the battle on the Modder River? Why did no one recall him digging the defensive trenches? A lone Basuto with no Boer master? One who spoke fluent English?

The Boer army was fragmenting as it pushed south after the British rearguard. Mbutu's duty was to his wife and child. Once more he ran.

–

There was a murmur as the information was picked over. Mbutu did not tell them about the lieutenant he had escorted into the wild, certainly not about the money, and was careful not to betray any overt sympathy to the British cause in case their loyalties lay the other way – though he suspected indifference.

He simply told them of his displacement, moreover of his burning desire to be reunited with his family – a fact, once translated, that brought sympathy from the women.

A middle-aged man asked something.

"Does not explain how you came to be here," repeated Hendrik.

Mbutu enlightened them. They knew of the railway. They seemed to believe him. He expressed his gratitude. He owed them his life.

It was not over.

"And… the devil soldiers?" asked Hendrik. "You have not seen them?"

"Devil soldiers?"

He had not, he said.

A whisper went around.

"Could he ask *them* a question?" Mbutu added.

It was translated. More murmuring. Hendrik shrugged a 'go ahead'.

"What has led *you* here? Out in the middle of the Karoo… the middle of nowhere?"

Hendrik took it upon himself to answer, as if it were too painful for general discussion.

"We come. Villages. Northwest," he faltered. "We are peaceful people."

He cast his eyes down.

"But then war came."

The words hung.

"Men, women, children…"

Even with no direct understanding, it was obvious to the audience what was being said. Some of the women began to wail, a horrible, visceral animal outpouring of grief. A baby started to cry.

"It is the season of Christmas," added Hendrik.

It was. He had forgotten.

"We sing to Jesus."

There was more murmuring. Then the crone was on her feet again, screeching, pointing, jabbing at Mbutu. The rabble was roused, rising to add its abuse to hers.

Hendrik nodded to the men holding Mbutu. He felt the barrel hard against his back and, for the first time, the cold sharp blade of a spear at his side – just like the Lord.

The end, after all.

But then Hendrik smiled.

"The old woman… she says you can stay."

Thank you Lord. Thank you Jesus.

"You sleep. Rest. In the morning, you work."

Chapter Twelve

The detective allowed Finch to return to his room to dress properly. When he came downstairs again, the bellboy was waiting with black coffee, performing a fawning quasi-bow as he proffered the cup and saucer.

Finch took a few sips of the bitter brew. In the Cape they drank their coffee like nowhere else. He went through the charade of patting empty pockets to indicate that the tip would have to be deferred.

He stepped outside. It was cool but the sun was rising. After the tumult of the night, the only sound now was the squawk of seagulls.

Inspector Brookman stood on the pavement, gaze fixed on nothing in particular, hands clasped behind his back.

Finch gave a courteous cough and Brookman turned around. He had a kind, avuncular face, though his penetrating stare gave the sensation that he was privy to one's innermost thoughts.

After a cursory enquiry as to Finch's well-being and the comfort of his lodgings, he got to the matter in hand, his speech, a calm, softly-accented South African English, belying his decisiveness. The police mortuary was half a mile away, he said, a few blocks off Strand Street and around the corner from the police station proper. They must go there. At this hour, the quickest way was to walk.

Finch's knee was giving him gyp again. Last night's hike had been undertaken without the clarity of sound judgement. But Brookman had already turned on his heel, striding purposefully. Finch tried to keep up.

"A British officer has been killed," he began. "Killed, it would appear, unlawfully... Body deposited on the stoep of the victim's guest house. Was discovered by the maid just after four – about two hours ago – as she was getting up to start the chores, preparing breakfast."

Finch was still trying to process the fact that he was in Cape Town, that it was Christmas Day, he was hungover and not in the filth of a battlefield.

"You said unlawful killing?"

"Yes sir," said Brookman. "Foul play, no question. This wasn't a drunk choking on his own vomit, a stroke, a heart attack or anything like that. Not that we haven't had a few of those in our time amongst gentlemen revellers..."

He cast Finch a glance.

"...and in some unfortunate establishments."

Christ, his knee hurt.

"Foul play?"

"The police surgeon will tell you more."

Finch hobbled on.

"I don't mean to be rude, but if you have a police surgeon, why do you need me? I assumed—"

They were crossing Adderley Street again. A lone horse cart clopped along, the African driver hunched, almost asleep.

"Assumption is our enemy, Captain Finch," said Brookman. "Be vigilant. Regard only the facts. The fact is the Cape Constabulary is hard pushed to maintain law and order."

He gestured, without breaking stride, to the smashed plate glass window of a hardware store.

"Fifty thousand troops passing through Cape Town in the last week alone. The *uitlanders* flooding in from Jo'burg. To make things worse, units of the Cape Police are now being seconded on a paramilitary basis."

It was true. Police had been in the ranks at Magersfontein. They were de facto soldiers, right down to the khaki uniforms.

"Few us left to actually beat the streets. On top of that we've got the Cape Dutch. Two-thirds of the Cape Colony are Afrikaner, don't forget. Old Kruger's been rattling the cage. Personally, I think it'd only be a minority who'd revolt. The living's been good. But we're not equipped to put down an insurrection... And then there's the Coloureds."

"The Coloureds?"

"Talk of arms being passed around, bought on the black market. Fearing civil breakdown."

Brookman came to his point.

"Special orders have come into play. It's the Cape Constabulary's prerogative to hand any case involving military personnel over to the army authorities. Given this is a British officer we're talking about..."

the deceased… we're passing him over to the jurisdiction of the Military Foot Police. There's an MFP officer on his way over now. Here we are…"

Across the street stood a two-storey stone building with high gables and steps up to the entrance. A Union Jack hung over them. There was a constable outside.

"And me?" said Finch.

Brookman nodded at the policeman who held open the door.

"For us to wrap this up, to hand over the authority, the coroner requires the signature of an officer from the Royal Army Medical Corps."

Finch gave a snort. This was a pretty swift piece of hand-washing.

"Believe me, 35 years a copper, the last thing I want to do is to pass up a collar. But it's the most prudent allocation of resources. We'll co-operate with any leads. Do all we can to bring the perpetrators to book who – if my instincts serve – stand a good chance of being military anyway."

The interior was cool. They stood in the hallway while a policeman on the desk was dispatched through double doors. Finch did not know what to make of Brookman's last point.

"Got your name off the passenger manifests at the railway station," the detective added.

On the desk stood a candlestick telephone. The speed with which information could now be transmitted was perplexing to all but the young. In shiny mahogany with a brass dial and cradle, the earpiece hooked onto it, the wood of the contraption was waxed to a healthy sheen.

"They're up to their necks at the Military Hospital. Was sheer chance that you were the one closest to the police station."

Brookman threw Finch a knowing smirk.

"Well, the one closest to us that had the misfortune to answer his door at dawn on Christmas Day."

Finch cursed to himself.

"Shan't keep you long, sir."

The desk officer reappeared.

"He's just coming, sir."

Behind the constable followed a small, thin, stooped bald man wearing a waxed apron, his shirtsleeves rolled up, trailing a waft of chemicals.

"Stephen Krajicek, Deputy Coroner," he declared, briskly and cheerily, almost birdlike, pronouncing his name 'Cry-Check'.

He shook hands with Finch. Finch worried that he'd snap his fingers.

"Right you are, sir. If you wouldn't mind coming this way."

Judging by his enthusiasm, Finch got the impression that a cadaver on Christmas morning was the best kind of present Krajicek could have wished for.

Through the doors they entered a tiled room with narrow vented windows up high, the space brightly lit by an electric ceiling bulb which exuded a low hum. The stone floor had gullies crossing it and a drain cut into the middle, into which gurgled a slow whirlpool of blood.

There were two stainless steel tables. On each lay a body completely covered with a sheet, the nearest one stained a dark red about the abdomen, the farthest unmarked. Sad, cold feet poked out. Each corpse had a paper label tied around a big toe.

A young assistant fiddling with a tray of gleaming medical implements turned and nodded a hello. Krajicek motioned for the assistant to bring over a clipboard.

"Formality, sir. What we'll need is a signature… here, here and here," he pointed. "All you need to do is to confirm the description given – male, forties, colouring, approximate weight…"

The assistant moved to the head of the furthest table.

"If you wouldn't mind, sir," said the young man to Finch, extending a palm to direct him.

Finch moved past the first table and its bloodied corpse – "Knife fight," chirruped Krajicek – and took his place at the second, while the assistant did the honours, pulling the sheet back slowly and delicately to reveal a head and bare shoulders.

Finch had seen enough corpses, enough mangled bodies over the previous two months for one more not to bother him. But this one did. Not for its appearance – a purple hue to the face, blue around encrusted lips – but because of its identity; its brown hair, waxed moustache and round, chubby features…

Major Cox.

Chapter Thirteen

The red light of dawn had just begun to seep over the eastern horizon when Mbutu was woken by Hendrik shaking his shoulder.

Mbutu was uncomfortable and aching. He had no blanket or cover, merely his jacket to pull round him; his pillow was a clump of coarse grass. His hips hurt from the hard ground, his sleep fitful. And he was cold.

"Come," said Hendrik. Mbutu was handed a rough earthenware bowl containing a few sips of a thin, rank, meaty broth.

One of the women signalled to a pot of water and he drank a rationed draught straight from the ladle. It tasted fresh. There must be a source.

Others were stirring. There was a small knot of men – five or six – who sat cross-legged and motionless while one of the women went between them, dabbing their eyes with a damp cloth. Their gazes were fixed, unreactive… apparently sightless.

Hendrik gathered Mbutu and four of the fittest men.

"What happened to…?" Mbutu began, pointing back.

But Hendrik had no time. He said it again: "Come." They scrambled over the rocks down onto the plain. It no longer carried the menace of night.

There was a dot out in the sea of sagebrush that grew larger. Another man was running back towards them, bounding through the scrub. When he reached them, his words flowed in an excited, furious torrent of clicks.

The men entered into hurried discussion.

"Eland," Hendrik translated.

"*Vleis*… Flesh," one of the others added for Mbutu's benefit, his face scrunched, searching for the words.

His name, he learned, was Stefaan.

Mbutu was handed a spear, as if all men of colour would be familiar with its usage.

71

The shaft was made from an extremely light wood. The long, thin tip bound to it was a piece of chiselled flint. He flicked the edge with his thumb. It was razor sharp. It was a precision instrument, even if improvised.

Stefaan turned and they followed. Mbutu went to speak but Hendrik pressed a finger to his own lips.

Mbutu had earned a living as a runner, but even he was having trouble keeping pace as these slight men seemingly glided across the desert scrub with long, loping strides. Unlike Mbutu they were shoeless, the hard, stony ground no inconvenience.

The Nama had long ceased to be pure hunter-gatherers but there was something innate, instinctive, about their survivalist efficiency.

Ahead lay a cluster of aloes... quiver trees. Crouched behind one was another man. He pointed. Up ahead was a small herd of eland – large antelopes – nibbling on thorn scrub.

The man made some hand signals and the others fanned out, ducking down, keeping low. There was a light breeze. Slowly, from downwind, they closed in, spears raised.

With the sun now rising, bathing everything a brilliant orange, they were close enough for Mbutu to see the detail – the fine, light-brown coats; the spiralled antlers; the big brown, almost liquid eyes; the languorously swishing tails. They were beautiful creatures. Six of them. You could hear their jaws chomping.

Though the men had moved with incredible stealth, it had not been enough. One of the beasts stopped, raised its head and pricked its ears. The others stood still, senses primed.

Another signal and, suddenly, Stefaan was sprinting towards the closest eland, his arm pulled back ready to throw.

But it was too late. With a scramble of hooves, the eland bounded away. The spear, though launched an impressive distance and with some force, crashed harmlessly short. The others committed a hasty, ineffective follow-up volley.

There was chatter, the men dissecting their failure as they wandered out to retrieve their weapons.

Mbutu asked Hendrik why they didn't use their guns. They had limited ammunition, he replied. It was reserved for their own protection. Plus the spears had served them well thus far.

Mbutu. You bring bad luck wherever you go.

As the sun's rays kissed the land, a fine mist began swirling between the scrub and the aloes. For Mbutu it was strange, unearthly. It looked as if the ground were smoking after a fire.

"Come," said Hendrik again, and they retreated to the trees.

—

They were in the bush for several hours, chasing shadows, having advanced maybe three or four miles beyond their camp. At night, Mbutu had still been able to hear the faint and periodic blast of a train's whistle, but out here he was beyond civilisation. His civilisation.

Mbutu, you must get to Beaufort West.

When the sun was up fully, the ground became a carpet of yellow from the opening flowers of the wild pomegranate. The mist burnt away to be replaced by a shimmering haze.

Through it, they could see more buck – springbok and gemsbok; later, a herd of zebra – but the haze played tricks, distorting the distance. It was not going to be their day.

The breeze eased off. By mid-morning, the land grew unbearably hot and they had roamed far enough. They rested in the shade of more quiver trees, then turned their attention to snaring rabbits, which they did far more successfully, though without a big kill to sate their pride. A small pouch of biltong was passed around and water sipped from containers made from ostrich eggs. Taking turns on watch, they slept through midday.

Later, as the sun began its descent and they were walking in file back towards their camp, the lead man raised his hand, a sign for them to stop.

The light breeze had returned. Sure enough, on it, there came a mewing, a whimpering. They could all hear it now. Something sizeable, something in distress. Finally, their trophy.

They fanned out and homed in, spears ready. As they closed there came another sound, a frenzied snarling and yipping… The scavengers had arrived.

They were crouched on the ground, half crawling, mindful of the snakes. Round a low boulder pile they could see jackals biting and clawing at a hole under a rock, its entrance not much bigger than a large dinner plate.

A hail of stones sent the ragged dogs scampering.

Slowly they edged to the rock. The whimpering still came from within. The men displayed signs of puzzlement. A bushpig? It was unfamiliar.

That is not the sound of an animal.

Slowly, while the others stood ready to slay the beast when it charged out in a panic, one of their party crept forward and gently probed his spear into the hole.

There was a sharp yelp and he withdrew it. He went for a second attempt.

That is not the sound of an animal.

Before they could stop him, Mbutu had sprung forward and shoved the man out of the way. Against a clatter of protest, he thrust his own arm into the hole and pulled.

That is not the sound of an animal.

Standing before them now was a young girl, a white girl, of about seven years of age, her blonde hair matted, round blue eyes startled, her face, hands and white pinafore dress filthy with red desert dust.

Further scrambling and out climbed a woman, a white woman, equally dirty. Confronted by spear points, her expression was a picture of unbridled terror.

Chapter Fourteen

Finch must have uttered Cox's name because chirpy Krajicek confirmed: "That's right, sir..."

He read off from his notes.

"...Major Leonard Armstrong St John Cox."

The cold sweat trickled down off Finch's scalp. He took his desert-stained handkerchief and dabbed his forehead. The last thing he'd expected to see was the major silently scowling up at him. And on Christmas morning of all mornings.

"But how—?"

"That's what we're here to establish," said Brookman.

Krajicek flipped through his papers.

"Cox, Cox, Cox... Yes. Long way from home, too, by the looks of things."

Home? Was the Front now considered home?

"India, sir."

Now Finch understood.

"Have his domestic residence listed as a villa in Sialkot... the Punjab... Alas, wife and three children."

The little man tutted, as if Cox, by his own volition, had failed them.

A corporal appeared. He came and stood by Brookman. The detective nodded and he undid a button on the top pocket of his tunic to remove a notebook.

The sweat was streaming off Finch now. He could feel it beading on his forehead. A drip meandered down his nose.

"You all right, sir?" asked Brookman. "I'd have thought, as a medical man..."

"Glass of water?" added Krajicek.

"No, no. Good God, no. Nothing like that gentlemen," Finch dismissed, embarrassed. "It's just that it's... a bit of a shock."

"A *shock*, sir?"

Brookman raised an eyebrow.

"You see…" said Finch.

"Sir?"

"He's my commanding officer… My CO."

"Your CO?"

He studied the stony face again.

"Or rather *was*…"

Silence. Glances were exchanged between the detective and the deputy coroner.

"My, my, now *I'm* confused," chimed in Krajicek, a little too theatrically for Finch's liking.

He rifled through his paperwork again, making a great show of it.

"It says here…"

He proffered the clipboard to Finch so that he might examine the evidence for himself.

"…that the deceased was an officer with the 9th Queen's Royal Lancers."

The corporal ceremonially licked the stub of a pencil and recorded this detail.

"That's how he'd registered his regimental affiliation… what his papers stated."

The assistant brandished Cox's cap, showing the crossed-spears brass badge. He replaced it on the pile of khaki sitting on the counter.

Brookman, overlooking the corporal's shoulder, jabbed a finger at an apparent error in the note-taking.

"His serial number confirms it," added Krajicek. "We've already cross-referenced, of course. Wonderful device, the telephone."

All in the room bar Finch exhaled and shook their heads in enthusiastic and communal awe, as if a deity had been evoked.

Finch suddenly found himself on the defensive. The more he explained things, the more the sweat seemed to gush.

The Royal Army Medical Corps was brand new, he informed them. Doctors, surgeons… they had never before served in uniform. Many were civilian volunteers, like himself. For the time being, field units were being placed under the nominal charge of regular army officers, senior ones seconded specifically for the purpose.

"Believe me, it wasn't Cox's choice," he quipped.

He studied the lifeless face again. Poor bastard. No honour for this soldier.

"How so, sir?" asked Brookman.

"Beg your pardon?"

"You said it wasn't his choice."

"I mean I'm sure he felt… I don't know, inadequate… emasculated by the appointment… Not proper soldiering and all that… Especially when his regiment was actively engaged elsewhere."

"You say you were sure he felt that way?"

Good God, was he to deconstruct every sentence?

"I'm *guessing* he felt that way."

Brookman looked over the corporal's shoulder and mumbled something, pointing out further additions. He didn't look up.

"He told you this, sir?"

"Not directly."

"So he *didn't* tell you this?"

"I said not directly."

Now Brookman raised his gaze.

"So, *indirectly*, he *didn't* tell you that he that he felt his duties were not, as you say…"

He referred to the corporal's pad again. He squinted hard.

"…'Proper soldiering', sir," clarified the corporal.

"I spent a lot of hours with the man. It was an—"

"'Assumption'? Our old friend."

"…an *impression* I formed."

Finch mopped at his brow and neck.

"When did you last see the major?" asked Brookman.

Finch paused to work it out. The building was lit electrically. The ceiling lightbulb began buzzing. It flickered off then on again, as if responding to his thinking.

"A couple of days… *three* days ago, it would have been… the, what… 22nd? We were camped at the Modder River after the pull-back. Relief had arrived. He went on to Hopetown ahead of me… the train south."

"How did he appear?"

"I'm sorry… How do you mean?"

"His demeanour, his manner—"

"What a bizarre question," snapped Finch.

"Bizarre? Why do you think it bizarre?"

Brookman pointed at the notepad, ensuring that his underling had logged this apparently salient detail.

"Inspector, the entire army had just retreated... been *redeployed*... at a moment's notice. Our unit – *his* unit – was scattered to the four winds. Major Cox was not exactly singing and dancing."

"Come, come, sir. No need for sarcasm. If you could stick to the facts."

Finch tried to recount it: the initial withdrawal – thousands of men, soldiers milling aimlessly while marshals steered queues over the bridge, the pack mules fording the shallows, steam tractors shovelling earth, the burning thorn scrub wafting across a makeshift tented city; the utter shambles over following days as they gathered together an ad hoc field hospital to cope with it all.

"Cox has been described as an easy-going fellow. Jovial."

"Inspector. If you've had any experience of battle you'll know that men do not necessarily behave as one might expect..."

Brookman said nothing.

"There was not the usual relaxed assuredness he was given to exude, to be sure."

"And that was the last time you spoke to him?"

"Yes... I mean *no*."

"Which is it, sir?"

Finch picked his words carefully.

"I didn't *speak* to him on that occasion. He was 20, 30 yards away. He nodded at me. Acknowledged me. That was it. The last time I *spoke* to him, if we are to make a distinction, was... well, a day or two before... routine stuff, evacuating the wounded and all that... He'd barely been around. Had been off all over the place, up and down the lines."

There still was no reaction. Did they not believe him?

"We'd shipped nearly all remaining casualties south by then. Job done. He was going on to Cape Town ahead of me. 'Business to attend to' or something of that order."

"Business to attend to?"

"Of that origin, yes. He was a resourceful man. Enterprising."

"A black marketeer?"

"I never said that. Look Inspector, I just want to know how on earth... I mean, how the major ended up... dead?"

Brookman took his time. He recapped the basics – the body on the stoep… the maid…

The clipboard was passed to Finch again and, in a daze, he signed where Krajicek had scrawled 'X's.

One entry remained blank.

"Cause of death?" Finch asked.

"Well therein lies the question," Krajicek replied. "It's impossible to tell without a proper post mortem, of course, but we know that he'd not been dead long when we found him. With no onset of rigor mortis and in summer temperatures, it narrows time of death to between midnight and 2am I'd say."

Finch checked his pocket watch. It had stopped at just after three – an ongoing fault in the winding mechanism daresay worsened by the blood and mud of Magersfontein.

He looked instead to the clock on the wall. It was just gone seven. Possibly only five hours ago, then.

"Yes, but *how* did he die?"

Krajicek hovered his capped fountain pen over Cox's strangely lifeless mouth.

"See the discoloration around the lips?"

Finch nodded. They were bluish.

"Asphyxiation most probably."

The assistant passed Krajicek a typed sheet of paper. He studied it.

"Yes, yes. There was vomit in the lungs and internal trauma to the windpipe, suggesting something had been forced into his mouth."

"Into his mouth…?"

"Not difficult with a drunk, sir," said Brookman.

"A drunk?"

Krajicek leaned toward Finch and lowered his voice.

"I don't think there's any doubt that the deceased had consumed rather a lot of alcohol."

Half the army was drunk. Did one more officer really matter?

"Did they take anything?" asked Finch.

Everything stopped. For Brookman, this statement was so ripe with meaning that he chewed and savoured it like a rare filet mignon.

He repeated it slowly, for the delectation of all.

"You know, the thieves," spluttered Finch.

Brookman paused, letting Finch wriggle on the hook.

"Thieves?"

"I just assumed…"

Damn.

Brookman showed mercy this time.

"His wallet was still on him," he said. "Ten shillings in cash, his identity papers, plus a Zeiss wristwatch."

"Oh."

Krajicek seemed ridiculously perky.

"Unless the consequence of an extraordinary misfortune, the odds of which are hugely against, it appears this was no ordinary killing."

"Ordinary killing?"

"You see, beyond the alcohol, the tobacco and the vomit, there's another faintly discernible odour on the man," enthused the deputy coroner.

"There is?"

"Yes, Captain. Some kind of chemical. Chloroform I'd wager?"

The shelves lining the walls were crammed with glass jars and bottles containing liquid of every hue. The entire atmosphere of the room was a pungent cocktail of cleansers and preservatives.

Snorted Finch: "How can you possibly tell?"

"Trust me, Captain. When you've been in the game as long as I have…"

He pointed at Cox again.

"You're a doctor. See the purplish hue to the skin, the yellowing when you apply pressure."

Krajicek wrestled off a glove. He pressed a thumb to the fleshy mound of Cox's left shoulder. When he removed it, it left a creamy impression.

"Compatible with some kind of toxicity?" Finch ventured.

"Just a hunch," said Krajicek. "An interesting turn of events, I'm sure you'll agree."

Finch chose his words carefully.

"You mean he was poisoned?"

Brookman came closer.

"Thieves in Cape Town are not so sophisticated," he said.

Finch could feel his shirt collar now soaking.

"But I still don't understand. Who the hell would do such a thing?"

Brookman gave a sniff, as if enjoying a private joke.

"The law of averages would dictate that either the body was deposited at the guest house by the person who killed him," he said. "In which case the murderer was known to the deceased. He'd only stayed there one night, after all… Or—"

"Or?"

"Or it was dumped there in a panic. Most likely by a cabbie, I'd say… And, in either instance, said depositor would have known where to take him."

There was nothing smug about Brookman's pronouncement. Just the logical deduction of a seasoned professional.

"In my estimation, Major Cox died just before or even en route to his lodgings."

With a sudden rush, Finch went to interject. Brookman cut him off.

"Not an assumption, Captain, a likelihood according to the criminal law of probability."

Krajicek nodded at the assistant, who pulled the sheet back over.

"Logically, finding who deposited Major Cox's body is the place to begin our investigation," said Brookman. "We will do all we can to help, of course. But, like I say, after that, it's over to the Military Foot Police."

He pointedly took the clipboard from Finch.

"Thank you, sir."

Krajicek rubbed his hands together in expectation. Brookman handed it to him, like a parent rewarding an excitable child.

"We can schedule a post mortem for this afternoon," trilled the little man. "Quiet day. Shouldn't take too long, sir."

"All we ask, Captain," added Brookman, "is that you don't stray too far. Your hotel's fine. City centre, too. But if you do go for a wander, be sure to advise of your whereabouts."

"Why?" bristled Finch.

Brookman looked him straight in the eye.

"Just how well did you know Major Cox, sir?"

This was crazy.

"Quite well… I mean I'd worked with him, had dealings with him, in some capacity, every day for the past sixty or so…"

"Well then, there's your answer, Captain."

"Begging your pardon?"

"You're now an important part of our investigation."

"Surely you don't think… *I*… ?" Finch spluttered.

"Can your account for your movements between midnight and two o'clock this morning, sir?"

Finch felt his cheeks flush. Christ, why was he sweating so?

"I had Christmas Eve dinner with company at the Mount Nelson. I arrived back at my hotel at about, I don't know, half past one or thereabouts…"

He was racing through his answer. Too hasty.

"Front desk at the Belvedere can confirm my return."

"With whom?"

"I'm sorry?"

"With whom did you have dinner, sir?"

"It was a mixed party. There were a French and German officer there. What, nine or ten well-to-do civilians…? Businessmen, some wives. Damned if I can remember the names. But it was hosted by a Mr Hal Lloyd, I can tell you that… a resident of the hotel… an American. Correspondent of sorts."

The corporal was scribbling furiously.

Finch remembered something. He reached into an inside jacket pocket and pulled out his wallet. He handed a card to Brookman.

"The American Kinematograph Company?" read the inspector.

Finch couldn't resist it.

"It's the future."

"The future?"

"Nothing."

Brookman gave a harrumph. The corporal scratched out the last remark.

"What time did you leave?"

"I don't know. Half past midnight? Quarter to one?"

"And after that?"

"Walking… coming back through town."

Brookman pointed to Finch's knee. He arched an eyebrow.

"On that leg, sir?"

"I was trying to…"

"I'm sensing from your tone that you weren't overly enamoured of the deceased. Had you had any recent altercations with the major? Anything that—?"

Finch raised his voice.

"Look, I'm telling you…"

Brookman took his time. He nodded to the corporal who snapped shut his notebook and buttoned it back in his pocket. And then Brookman smiled.

"Don't worry, Captain. I can read a man like a book. You're not the killing type. But you see my point. At this present moment, we should rule out nothing."

He turned on his heel, the signal for Finch to follow.

"Find the person who dropped the body and we'll find the killer."

Finch walked to the door.

"Oh, and sir?" Krajicek called after him. "Merry Christmas."

Chapter Fifteen

The café had a high, tin-plated ceiling with floral patterns stamped into the metal. Around half of the rattan-backed chairs were occupied, largely by elderly couples in their church finery, white hair bobbing amid the palm fronds. Above them a slow, whirring fan sliced through the haze of cigar smoke.

Annie and her party took a seat by the window. It had fake Christmassy shapes gummed onto it – snowflakes, stars and angels, hand-cut from crisp white paper. Outside, a busker played carols on an out-of-tune accordion. A burly red-haired man in a dark blue suit sat at a pavement table, smoking, folding open his copy of the *Argus*.

The aroma of roasted coffee beans and cigars was invigorating – a reminder of more carefree days back home; an antidote to the carbolic and disinfectant and damaged flesh and cloistered men of the Cape Town Military Hospital.

From the waiter, Annie ordered a medium-strength coffee – an "espresso" she was informed, to be delivered from the great steaming contraption behind the counter – with warm milk on the side. And, for the hell of it, and at random, a sugary almond pastry. It was Christmas Day, after all.

"Fatten you up, girl," cackled Doris Hanwell, way too loudly, reaching over to pinch Annie's hip. "A man likes something to grab hold of."

The waiter, a skinny youth below military age, blushed visibly.

"Ain't that right, sweetheart?" Hanwell added, throwing him a wink.

"Doris," said Annie. "Leave the poor—"

"Aw, it's all right, Jones," she cut off. "This feller's but one thought on his mind."

There were six of them altogether, all nurses. Though the function of two of them – Chapel and ApThomas – seemed to be to act as a personal chorus to Hanwell's bawdiness, tittering at every utterance.

They were doing so again. The waiter skittered off, nearly knocking over some potted pampas grass.

Sullivan rolled her eyes.

"Shut it, Hanwell."

She nodded towards the overloaded pastry counter where the owner – a portly Italian man with pomaded hair and waxed moustache – appeared to be getting rather hot under his bow-tie and starched collar.

Hissed Hanwell: "It's bloody Christmas, remember?"

The coffee and cake arrived. The waiter deposited the crockery and cutlery amid much clatter and scuttled away again as fast as he could.

"*I* hadn't forgotten," chimed in McGregor.

Petite, fragile McGregor, reached into the pocket of her skirts and, furtively, pulled out a silver hip flask.

"Rum," she added, and proceeded to pour a generous tot into each of their drinks.

"You little beauty," went Hanwell.

Chapel and ApThomas tittered some more.

Annie still couldn't quite believe it. She was halfway round the world, sitting in a café in Cape Town. She felt a huge pang of guilt. Her absence would spell humiliation for Edward. It was a cruel thing for him to have had to suffer. Male pride was easily bruised, Edward's more than most. Annie prayed that he did not still hold a candle for her – that he might misconstrue all this as her blowing off steam; some little adventure to get it all out of her system.

McGregor was shaking Annie's shoulder.

"What?"

"Another tot?"

"Jesus, girl where were you?" asked Hanwell.

"Nowhere."

"Dreaming about a bloke, more like."

"Just leave it, Doris!" scolded McGregor, furtively pouring more rum.

Hanwell pulled a face. Her chorus tittered.

They were making a spectacle of themselves, knew Annie. Heads were turning. McGregor urged for hush. The acoustics were such that they were raising their voices unnaturally.

"C'mon, ladies. *Sssshhhhhhh.*"

The owner, all forced nervous grin, was flitting towards them now across the black and white tiles of the floor, weaving between the tables, light on his feet for someone so rotund.

"Good morning, *signorine*. Merry Christmas," he fawned. "I'm so glad you are enjoying yourself. But please, if I may ask…"

He gestured towards the others in his establishment. He had fine, engraved silver clips around his shirtsleeves. His waistcoat was fashioned from gaily swirling crimson silk.

"…my customers."

"All right. All right," shrugged off Hanwell.

Annie shot her a look.

"We're very sorry, sir" she cut in. "It's our first day off for two months. Truthfully, half-day… It's a lovely place you have here."

The man nodded his thanks.

"And Merry Christmas to you too," added Sullivan.

He retreated to the counter. More customers were entering.

Sullivan turned to Hanwell.

"Jesus, Doris. We're not even meant to be out unchaperoned,"

The door jangled. An RAMC officer entered. A captain.

"Christ, that's all we need."

The man seemed lost in thought. He nodded his own half-hearted festive greeting at the beaming owner and limped over to take his place at a single table in the far corner. Annie watched as he removed a leather-bound notebook and fountain pen from his jacket pocket and tapped out a cigarette.

"Where the bloody hell is Irwin, that trollop?" snapped Hanwell, too loudly again.

The RAMC captain was alone with his musing, staring dolefully out of the window. Though others were casting black looks in their direction.

"Sit tight. She'll be here," assured McGregor.

"That lieutenant again?"

"Victoria Rifles," said Chapel.

"I heard they're engaged," offered ApThomas.

"C'mon, let's go for a stroll," urged Hanwell.

"She said to wait," said Sullivan. "She'll be back."

"She'd better be," said Hanwell. "Or we're royally fucked."

"HANWELL!"

There was no tittering this time. The room fell deathly silent.

"A bit like she's being right now, I imagine."

This time the RAMC officer was glaring at them.

"Jesus, Hanwell," said McGregor.

Muttered Sullivan: "You've gone and down it now, girl…"

The RAMC captain scraped his chair back across the tiles, made a great theatrical show of getting to his feet and limped over towards them. He was middle-age handsome, dark-haired, blue-eyed, slightly haggard.

He cleared his throat.

"Might I remind you, you are in the service of the Royal Army Medical Corps," he began. "You are to conduct yourself as nurses… as ladies… at all times."

Hanwell merely sneered up at him.

"Lighten up, mate," she scoffed. "It's Christmas for Chrissakes."

That was it.

"STAND UP NOW! ALL OF YOU!"

The café's patrons watched agog. Slowly the nurses got to their feet. Aware that he was the centre of attention, the captain strained to keep his voice down.

"Don't think I don't appreciate what you've been doing here in the Cape," he growled. "I do. But this reprimand is for your benefit. Drunk, disorderly and insubordinate? I could have you all up on a charge… And without a chaperone…?"

Annie uttered a private 'Thank God' as, at that very moment, the door jangled again and Irwin bustled in, blustering in their direction, scattering empty chairs, red-cheeked, hair dishevelled beneath her straw boater, red cape askew.

"Merry Christmas, Captain," she said, all feigned doe-eyed innocence, as if butting in on a friendly tête-à-tête. "Staff Nurse Irwin, New South Wales Army Nursing Service Reserve. How can I help you?"

The captain dragged her aside for a quiet word out of their earshot. They remained standing.

He said nothing as he limped out, but Annie did, quietly.

"Bastard."

Chapter Sixteen

Finch exited Bettega's café and limped out through its doors. For one who'd never experienced Christmas in the Southern Hemisphere, a dishevelled street musician playing error-strewn carols on an accordion, and in glaring summer sunshine, seemed wildly out of place.

Everything at this present moment in time was topsy-turvy to Finch – Yuletide in summer; that he had gone from the carnage of the Front to genteel civility in the space of a train ride. Most of all, there was the fact that Cox was dead – *murdered* – and in what seemed the most bizarre of circumstances.

Those blasted colonial nurses hadn't helped his mood. In their grey dresses and boaters they looked like school governesses. Though they weren't behaving like them. He had been right to admonish them. He was saving their bloody bacon.

In private they could have done as they pleased. These were young women, thousands of miles from home. In the Cape Town Military Hospital they had already seen things no person, not even a nurse, should ever have to. If they got to the Front, they would face horrors to surpass even that. He, more than any, knew how hard nurses worked and how undervalued they were. Hal Lloyd was wrong. It wasn't going to be the American Century, it was going to be the Female Century.

The streets were still. There was little traffic. No trams. Turning the corner off the main drag, the only other pedestrian about was the well-built man with the red hair who had sat at a pavement table of the café.

Finch rounded the corner onto Empire Street and made for the Belvedere before doubling back to the tobacconist's to procure two new packets of Navy Cut. The old man behind the counter, with a face like leather and bushy white moustache tainted yellow, bade him Happy Christmas and told him that the British Army had nearly cleaned him out of supplies. This war was good for business.

When Finch stepped outside into the bright sun, the red-haired man, who was wearing a dark blue suit, was loitering on the street corner some 20 yards away, standing on the edge of the kerb as if to hail a cab. He would have little joy this morning.

Damn. Amid the chatter from the tobacconist, Finch had left his change on the counter. He turned on his heel and limped back to recover it. When he exited, the man was still there, this time staring into the window of an obviously closed haberdasher's shop.

At distance and wearing a bowler, the man was not close enough for Finch to identify facially.

But was he seriously being *followed*?

When Finch tested his theory by ducking into an alleyway, only for three men of similar attire to pass over the ensuing five minutes, he scolded himself for his paranoia. He shouldn't have allowed Brookman to get to him.

Back at the hotel, a maid was hauling a basket of sheets upstairs, about to make up his room, but he told her not to bother. Inside, he wrestled his boots off, rubbed his overheated feet, plumped his pillows and propped himself up on the bed. He pulled out the calfskin-bound notebook and his steel fountain pen, lit himself a cigarette – four smokes already today – and inhaled deeply.

Quite what he was going to write, he didn't know. It was what he had been trying to do in the café. With all that had happened over the previous hours, he felt compelled to put his observations in writing. To which end, he simply wrote down a name, '*Major L Cox*' followed by a subtitle: '*Death Of…*'

Finch did this not because of any attempt to solve the riddle of Cox's death – there were professional law officers there to do that – but because he knew, once he returned to duty, he would be asked questions about what had happened.

His jotting did not amount to much – Cox had arrived in Cape Town on December 23rd and had checked in at his guest house. He had, one assumed – that word again – spent just one night there, for the next evening he went out never to return, at least not alive, his body being dumped on the stoep in the early hours of this morning, the 25th, discovered by the maid. His valuables were intact. It did not appear to be a robbery. Cox had, according to the deputy coroner, consumed a lot of alcohol, but had been killed by something toxic…

poisoned… in conjunction with asphyxiation caused by an object forced into his throat.

Finch hadn't liked the inspector's playful suggestion that he himself might have been somehow involved. He knew why Brookman had said it. It was a clever way of announcing both his own powers of perception and his simultaneous power over Finch… should he choose to wield it.

He had been impressed with Brookman up till that point, but now wasn't so sure that he liked him. Maybe it wasn't his job to like him. Maybe it was Brookman signalling to Finch that he wasn't there to be liked.

Soon a letter would be dispatched to India informing Cox's next of kin of his unfortunate demise. All the more reason to get the details down while they were still fresh.

Having spent half an hour scrawling the basics, a muffled gong was sounded in the lobby. Finch had entirely forgotten his appointment for luncheon. Reluctantly, he hauled himself off his bed, wrestled his boots on, smartened himself and went downstairs.

In the dining room, a Christmas meal of roast beef had been prepared by the manageress, which would have been fine had Finch not been forced to share the repast with two other guests – an army chaplain and a sullen lieutenant commander of the Royal Navy, whose cruiser, HMS *Sybille*, had been performing picket duty off the Cape.

The latter was deeply sceptical of any military operation conducted on dry land and had a low opinion of the army in general, to which the chaplain, an army man himself, merely turned the other cheek, nodding along politely while the lieutenant commander unburdened himself.

Clearly, though both were in uniform, the naval officer took neither Finch nor the chaplain as soldiers. Finch's days in service had inured him to pomposity. He allowed his thoughts to drift elsewhere – in this case a wistful reminiscence of Christmases of his childhood.

Overjoyed that her guests were fostering an illusion of social discourse, the manageress, a small bustling dynamo of a woman whose skirts swished furiously, uncorked an acidic but potent plum brandy that emboldened the chaplain to lead them all in an improvised and half-baked prayer, a natural conclusion to their festivities.

In the lobby, Finch grabbed yesterday's *Argus*, retired to his room again and poured himself a generous measure from his dwindling whisky flask. He tried to keep his eyes open while he entertained the full scope of the British disaster that was unfolding in South Africa, more or less as the naval officer had outlined.

Finch could barely absorb the information, such was the heaviness of his eyelids. His body jerked in a reflexive spasm as his own snoring suddenly caught him unawares. Then he surrendered to it.

Some hours later, he did not know how many, he awoke with a start. It was daytime. He could see thin stripes of light through the shutters. But as he familiarised himself in the semi-darkness, his surroundings now included an additional item – a man standing over him.

Chapter Seventeen

The woman and child stood before the Nama men, the girl absolutely motionless, the woman's whole body racked with tremors. They were not only grubby but thin, weak, their lips dry and encrusted, scabbed, split open in places. Their exposed skin peeled from sunburn.

It was the little girl who spoke, hesitantly, quietly, her eyes fixed on the ostrich egg slung from the shoulder of one of the Nama. She pointed at it then cupped her hands.

"Please... water."

Hendrik nodded, the spears were lowered and the egg was passed forward. It was poured alternately between the mouths of the two females who drank as hard and as fast as their throats would allow, the liquid sloshing joyously over their faces.

"Not too much," cautioned Hendrik. "Too much... not good."

He patted his stomach to indicate pain.

The sated woman and child slumped to the ground. After her momentary rapture, the woman started shaking again. She began to cough, violently, squatting forward. The child rubbed her back.

There were furious clicks of discussion. Hendrik stood solemnly and listened. Mbutu, mindful of his own part in this drama, felt uncomfortable, standing apart.

Discussion turned to argument. The man Mbutu had pushed out of the way was the most animated, seemingly the spokesman for one of two opposing factions. He glowered at Mbutu between a babble of unintelligible invective. Eventually they ceased. Hendrik stepped forward.

"The men are div—?"

"Divided?"

"Yes, divided... Some want to take the woman, the girl, back, to look after them, care for them."

Mbutu nodded approval.

"The others…" Hendrik continued.

There was more clicking.

"…want to kill them."

"*Kill* them?"

"It is survival," explained Hendrik, matter of fact. "These people… Others will come looking… Brown men, white women…"

He made a display of interlocking his fingers.

"…Not good."

There was a warning shout from one of the men. They spun round. The woman had clearly heard, for she had grabbed the girl's hand and started to run, stumbling over her skirts.

They had barely gone ten yards when their path was blocked by the spears of the effortlessly bounding Nama. They were swiftly encircled, like unbroken colts forced into a pen.

The spears. Stay back.

"Please!" urged Mbutu. "Can't you see they're scared?"

The woman looked to him. Her eyes pleaded.

"Let us at least find out who they are," he added.

The Nama had been singing carols.

"Brothers. It is our Christian duty… *Christelike plig!*"

The men paused. Mbutu pushed his way into the circle. Hendrik translated for his men.

"You are mother and child?" he asked of the woman.

She nodded. She clutched her daughter to her. She began coughing again.

"White man come," shouted Stefaan in rough English. "Devil soldiers."

There were nods of agreement.

An eye for an eye. Your Christian Bible.

"Please," said Mbutu, palms up. "Have mercy."

He tried a new tack. He nodded to Hendrik to decode.

"Perhaps they have information… which can be of use to us."

There were a few shrugs. Mbutu had at least made them think. Subtly, he had included himself in their number.

Thanks be to God.

Mbutu faced the woman. He waited for calm.

"Please, do not be afraid," he soothed. "Your presence has unsettled some of the men. They have suffered great misfortune. They too are fugitives."

There was no reaction from her.

"For them to help you, we need to know how you came to be here… to be certain that you do not pose a threat."

A threat? How could they pose a threat?

"So… please… tell us. Who are you? Where have you come from?"

There was no answer, just a stony silence, the woman's eyes locked on his.

"Take your time. How long…?"

Nothing.

"What is your—?"

The coughing fit returned. When it had passed, Mbutu asked the same questions in Afrikaans. There was still no response.

Please. Speak. Your life depends on it.

Some of the men yelled at the woman, frustration building.

A small voice cut in.

"She can't talk."

It was the child.

"She can't talk?"

"No… not since…"

Mbutu squatted down so that he was at the girl's level. She had beautiful pale blue eyes with a dark line around the rim of the iris. He looked straight into them. There were no tears. Whatever she had witnessed, she was beyond them. And then she fell into his arms and clung tightly to his neck.

Hendrik took control.

"Wait," he said.

He walked towards his men and spread his arms wide, ushering them into a huddle.

"Child. What is your name?" Mbutu whispered.

"Emily."

"Emily. I will look after you. You and your mother."

After a minute, Hendrik walked back over. He spoke to the interlopers directly.

"Come," he said. "You are safe with us."

With great relief, the girl squeezed Mbutu's neck, then he released her to fling her arms around her mother's skirts.

Mbutu stood. He touched Hendrik's arm.

"Thank you."

Hendrik smiled.

"It is you who are lucky also," he said.

Lucky?

"Habobe... the man you pushed?"

Mbutu nodded.

"He wanted to kill you too."

–

The girl and her mother were taken in by the Nama women and given mealies and milk. The Nama may have fled their village but they were resourceful enough to have grabbed essential supplies, including a goat.

One of the women made a poultice from pulped leaves and laid it on the worst of the sunburn. The girl, in particular, was treated with tenderness. Some of the younger Nama children, wide-eyed and curious, loitered.

With the sun going down, the now shivering pair were gently warmed before the fire, though their frequent bouts of coughing did not abate.

Riding on Mbutu's shoulders on the walk back, the girl had said little, but it was apparent she and her mother had been party to something awful... so awful it had robbed the woman of the power of speech.

Hendrik was of a like mind to Mbutu. There was no point in a forced, rushed interrogation. Tend to them, make them comfortable. The information would come much easier.

The Nama made swift work of the rabbits, which were now crackling on a spit; the others were diced and added to another bubbling broth.

With all that had happened, Mbutu had forgotten – but there they were, in the midst of the refugees, that small group of blind men sitting together, a pair of the Nama women tending to them. These were not men sightless from birth but ones familiarising themselves with their new condition.

Mbutu pulled Hendrik to one side.

"The men over there. What happened to them?"

Hendrik looked at the ground, mournful.

"It is better you hear from their own lips."

He indicated that Mbutu should pick up a large earthenware vessel of the rabbit stew and led him over to the blind men. Mbutu helped pass a bowl between them. They appreciated his help. Hendrik then sat cross-legged before them.

There were five of them, their eyes unfocused, a wetness around their tear ducts – pus, mucus glistening in the firelight.

The Nama, Mbutu already understood, respected directness. In his translation for Mbutu, Hendrik was typically forthright.

"Our new friend wants to know how you came to be this way," he said.

It was the oldest of the men who began, probably in his 40s, the whites of his eyes an inflamed red, the pupils cloudy. He dabbed at them with a large wet leaf.

"One day the soldiers arrived," Hendrik translated. "Not ordinary soldiers but devil soldiers. Monsters. Faceless. Round eyes. Big round eyes…"

"Devil soldiers?" shrugged Mbutu, his scepticism a little too obvious, even to a blind man.

"Demons!" shouted another. "Demons!"

"They surrounded our village," the older man continued. "No way in. No way out. They unleashed a terrible green spirit upon the people."

A green spirit?

"Men, women, children… Only a few surv—"

"Survived?"

"Survived."

Hendrik spoke in his own voice now.

"These men… They had been out hunting. But the green spirit…"

The green spirit?

"…It took their sight."

A blind man got to his feet. He was young, muscular, angry.

"Kill all!" he yelled in English. "Green spirit kill all!"

There were arms round him, comforting him, pulling him back down.

Devil soldiers?

Mbutu could not tell them that he did not believe such superstition. He offered his sympathy. He thanked the men for speaking to him.

"It's true," came a small voice.

They turned. Standing there with a horse blanket round her shoulders was the young white girl, Emily.

"What the men said. It's true."

The girl had a preternatural world-weariness, as if recent events had simply sucked the innocence out of her. She began coughing.

"Come, child," said Mbutu. "Do not be afraid."

Hendrik poured her some water and she sat with them. Mbutu looked over. The mother was asleep. They probed the girl with gentle questions.

"My name is Emily Sutton," she said. "I am seven-and-a-half years old."

"Do you have brothers, sisters, Emily?" asked Mbutu.

"No."

"Where are you from? From England?"

"Yes. The county of Staffordshire. My father... we lived in a rectory."

"A rectory?" asked Hendrik.

"Her father, a vicar... a preacher. Is that right, Emily?"

"Yes. We had chickens. I had to collect the eggs. My friend Louisa from school. She came to play. I dropped the basket. The eggs broke. Papa wasn't happy."

"Eggs?" asked Hendrik.

"It doesn't matter," said Mbutu. "Go on."

"Papa is a missionary. He wanted to spread the gospel. To come to Africa. We came to build a chapel... for the natives."

"When? How long ago?"

"After my birthday."

"When is your birthday?"

"March. March the 8th."

"Nine months ago," said Mbutu to Hendrik.

"It was very hot at first," Emily continued. "Much hotter than England. But the people were nice. Nama, like you..."

She pointed at Hendrik.

"And some Orlom... Orlum?"

"Oorlaam," Hendrik corrected.

Oorlaam. Good horsemen. Cattle raiders. Nama but with mixed slave blood.

"There was fighting?" asked Hendrik.

She shook her head. She fiddled with the hem of her pinafore dress.

"Papa told us of the war. It was far away. God would protect us."

God was protecting no one.

She looked up at them.

"And then…"

"Take your time. Let the words come," said Mbutu.

"A few days ago—"

"How many days?"

"I don't know… Soldiers. British soldiers—"

She stopped, unsure whether to continue. She tugged at her hem again.

"Please," said Mbutu. "It is safe. If you tell us we can help you. What about the soldiers?"

"They marched into the village. They had men in the middle… between them… in a line, a column. They had chains."

"White men? Black men?"

"White."

"A lot of men?"

"Quite a lot. Yes…"

"How many do you think?"

Mbutu cast his arm around.

"More than here?"

"Yes."

"How many more? A guess."

"I don't know. Lots more."

"You say they had chains?"

She indicated that they were bound around their ankles and wrists.

"Chained together, to each other. They made them stop, come to attention."

Convicts. No, prisoners of war.

"They put on hoods," she said. "Made of cloth."

"Cloth?"

"Like sacks, the cloth you make sacks with."

"The men in chains put on hoods?" asked Hendrik, confused.

"No, the soldiers."

"The soldiers put the hoods on the men in chains."

She threw an incongruous and momentary chuckle, as if Hendrik had been duped by some riddle.

"No, silly," she corrected in faux frustration. "The *soldiers*. They put the sacks… the hoods on *themselves*."

"The soldiers?"

Devil soldiers?

"There was smoke."

The green mist?

"It is as our sightless brothers have said," said Hendrik.

"The soldiers, they had guns. Anyone who tried to leave, to escape... One man ran, his friends told him not to, and they shot him. He fell over. Didn't move. He had his eyes closed like he was asleep. His wife, Kefane, she was upset. She cried. But then the smoke... Everyone in the village and the men in chains. People were coughing, being sick..., They started falling asleep too."

"My poor child," soothed Mbutu.

"It burnt their eyes and their mouths. They coughed and there was foam. People were screaming, begging, running. But anyone who tried to fight the soldiers or tried to escape, the soldiers hit them. Hard. Or shot them. Like Kefane's husband."

"Your father?" asked Mbutu. "Is he...?"

For the first time, the girl allowed herself a tiny sob.

"I don't know..."

"And your mother?"

"That's when she... That's why she—"

"You saw all this with your own eyes?" asked Hendrik.

She nodded.

"Then how did you escape?"

"Papa... The Oorlaam. They warned him. They said there would be trouble. They said the war would come. They told Papa to make plans. He didn't want to. But, when the soldiers came, he took us into the chapel. Mama, myself... under the floorboards."

"You hid?"

"Yes... Later we came out. Ran. The soldiers with the round eyes could not run too well. They fired at us. Missed. We've been hiding in the bush for, I don't know... Mama thinks three days. Men on horseback... a patrol... have been searching."

There was a sudden sense of purpose about Hendrik.

"Where is this village?" he asked.

The girl shrugged.

"You must wake the mother," Hendrik urged Mbutu. "Now!"

He couldn't fathom Hendrik's angst but Mbutu went over and gently shook the woman. When she came to, she immediately went into panic mode, shaking again.

"*Sh-Shhhhhh*," calmed Mbutu. "Please, your daughter, Emily, has been telling us of your plight... We need your assistance. Details."

When Mbutu returned with his arm around the mother, the girl was trying to pronounce the village's name but failing.

"Vanka... Vankalik-something...?"

It made little difference to Hendrik. The question was of its geography.

"Please," he told the woman. "You must show us where."

He took a stick and set to work on the blank canvas of the red dirt.

"Our camp," he said, drawing an 'X'.

He drew a long line. "Railway... Cape Town to Kimberley."

The last word filled Mbutu with a pang of heartache.

You will get there.

"Please."

Hendrik handed the stick to the mother. She tentatively made a mark out to the west of the X.

"How many hours from here?" asked Hendrik, impatiently. "By foot. How many hours?"

The woman shrugged. Hendrik suddenly seized her by the shoulders.

"You must tell us!"

The woman was shaking again. She turned her head away. Mbutu urged Hendrik to be gentle. It seemed unnecessarily forceful.

Mbutu put his hand gently on her arm.

"Please. The information is important. How many hours? Three, four, five, six...?"

She nodded at five.

"Five hours, you think?"

Yes.

Hendrik uttered an oath. No sooner had he done so than one of the Nama on sentry duty up on the edge of the rocky corral gave a shout. Hendrik scrambled up to him. Mbutu followed. Now he understood.

Dirt was kicked over the fire. The men on guard turned inward and urged the camp to be silent, for the mothers to quiet the infants.

In the twilight, you could see the silhouettes. Cantering across the bush was a cavalry patrol.

Chapter Eighteen

"Sir?"

Someone was shaking Finch's shoulder.

"Sir?"

He opened an eye. A Cape policeman was standing over him.

"Merry Christmas, sir."

Finch felt horrible, groggy.

"You came to my room and woke me up," he croaked, "just to wish me Merry Christmas?"

"No sir. I mean, I was just—"

"It's all right, Constable."

Finch hauled himself up slowly and sat on the edge of the bed. Not only was he dazed, he now had a throbbing head from the whisky. He felt parched, dehydrated.

It was daylight outside.

"What time is it?"

"Five o'clock, sir."

"AM or PM?"

The constable, quite young, laughed, thinking Finch to be joking. He then realised he wasn't.

"PM, sir."

"Then to what do I owe the honour?"

The constable cleared his throat, as if making an announcement.

"Detective Inspector Brookman, sir, kindly requests your presence. If you wouldn't mind…"

The policeman gestured to Finch's jacket on the back of the chair.

"Is he going to arrest me?"

"What, sir?"

"Never mind."

The young copper tried to help Finch to his feet.

"Damnit man, I'm not a cripple."

Finch stood up. He gulped some water from the jug by the wash-stand, rinsed his face and hoisted his braces.

"Police cab outside, sir."

–

When Finch arrived at the Wale Street police station, he understood right away what Brookman had meant by the city police being hard pushed to cope.

In contrast to the mortuary, the station proper was a riot of human activity. There were several handcuffed and boisterous drunks and pub brawlers, some with battered faces, being booked in. There was blood splattered over the parquet floor and up the whitewashed walls. The desk sergeant was having to yell to maintain order.

One man, with several front teeth knocked out, writhed and kicked at his captors like a snared animal. He was wrestled to the ground by three policemen. A truncheon was held fast across his throat.

As Finch was led down the corridor, he could hear more shouting. To the back of the station were the cells. He could see hands grabbing at the bars, rattling them.

Finch walked on past a pair of battered doors, which had the names 'Interview Room 1' and 'Interview Room 2' stencilled upon them.

The young policeman showed Finch into the room opposite, which turned out to be Brookman's office. It was somewhat tatty, airless and with the desk piled high with papers. Though it had a window, it backed onto an alleyway. Dust danced in the few beams of sunlight that crept in from on high. The cork pin-board on the wall was an explosion of notices.

"Come in, Captain," gestured Brookman, breaking off a discussion with the corporal from the mortuary. "Come in."

The corporal promptly exited. Finch noticed a red-crowned peaked cap on the hat stand. An army NCO appeared. His khaki uniform was adorned with white webbing and an MFP armband.

Brookman introduced him as Staff Sergeant Harmison of the Military Foot Police. He was a well-built man of about 35 years of age whose bent nose and close-cropped hair lent him the air of a boxer.

Unexpectedly, the sergeant saluted, with an emphatic: "Sah!"

"Sergeant Harmison has been briefed on the particulars of the Cox case and will be carrying it forward."

"Hear you were a friend of the deceased. My condolences, *sah*!" barked Harmison.

His accent was London. North, Finch thought. He nodded his acceptance. It was too complicated to redefine 'friend'.

"You've got the post mortem results?" asked Finch of Brookman.

"Not yet. Krajicek will be over in a while. But I thought you'd be interested to know there's been a development."

"A development?"

"A witness has come forward."

Harmison jabbed a thumb back over his shoulder.

"The cabbie… a darkie."

Harmison led Finch across the corridor and through the door marked 'Interview Room 2'. It was a miserable, stale, windowless pit, lit only by a dim bulb. The man sitting at the table was equally forlorn. He was Cape Coloured, that mélange of black, white, even Malay – legacy of the Dutch East India company's imported slaves – that had come to constitute a race of its very own.

The man's arms were folded on the scuffed and battered surface, his head buried in them such that only the back of his tight greying curls was visible. He wore a ripped and grubby white shirt. And he stank.

"Local force tracked him down quick enough," said Harmison. "Turns out a couple of officers had stopped him in the street and taken his licence number shortly before presumed time of death, around 2.30am. Had been acting suspiciously. Major Cox was drunk and dozing in the back of the trap at the time. The cabbie was on his way to drop the major at his guest house, just a hundred yards away."

He beamed a smile of pride.

"Had a right good go on him, sir."

"Who?" asked Finch.

"*Him*," he pointed.

The cabbie looked up. He was a man around 50, Finch guessed. Alarmingly, his left eye was swollen shut. He had a split lip. Blood trickled from his nostrils. He groaned. The smell was of urine.

"Bastard claims the officer was still alive when he dumped him at the guest house. My guess is he offed him soon after. Or—"

"Or?" asked Finch, sarcastically.

"Or it was one of his mates lying in wait."

Finch reached into his pocket and pulled out a clean white folded handkerchief and handed it to the man. He dabbed it to his left cheek.

"Sergeant?"

"Sah."

"Can you see to it that someone brings this man some water?"

The sergeant shrugged. He nodded at the police corporal loitering in the doorway.

Finch crouched down next to the man.

"Do you mind?" he asked, and gently cupped his hands under the man's cheekbones. He gently probed the sides of his nose with his thumbs, then felt around the man's jaw.

"Nothing broken."

The sergeant harrumphed. The police corporal returned, bearing an enamel jug. Finch dipped the handkerchief in it and instructed his patient to press it to his swollen eye.

"Hurts like hell I'm sure," said Finch.

The man nodded.

"But it's superficial. Lip'll heal in time. The swelling around the eye will come down."

The man looked up at him. He spoke weakly.

"Thank you."

Finch turned to Brookman.

"Inspector, if I might have a word."

Finch walked outside and beckoned Brookman back into his office. He closed the door. He strained to keep his voice down.

"What the hell are you doing beating up an innocent man?"

Brookman didn't react. He walked behind his desk, sat down and went through the charade of organising some papers. Only when Finch had calmed did he speak.

"Two things, Captain. One, I have beaten up nobody, nor do I condone it in the slightest. Two, why do you presume the cabbie to be innocent?"

"Isn't he?"

"Beyond your Florence Nightingale ministrations, you know nothing about him. How can you possibly form a judgement?"

Brookman was correct, knew Finch.

"I just assumed—"

Brookman shook his head and exhaled a mocking whistle.

"Please."

He bade Finch sit down too.

"The facts, Captain… Always the facts."

He pointed towards the door.

"For your information, the man in the other room is named Pinkie Coetzee, age 54. Lives in District Six. Wife and seven children. A licensed driver with the Cape Town Hansom Cab Company. An employee of five years standing. Clean record. He is the man, as you have heard, who drove Cox home. Claims to have placed him on the stoep of the guest house in the early hours of this morning."

It was turning out to be a very long day, mused Finch. Once upon a time he used to wish that Christmas Day would go on forever. Not this one.

"'Claims'?" he asked.

"I never deal in absolutes until such things are a hundred per cent certain."

"Go on," said Finch.

"According to Mr Coetzee's testimony, he picked up the fare… Cox… at around 2am outside the Officers' Club on the waterfront. Also claims that the officer was drunk and incapable. Had to be helped aboard."

He saw Finch wrinkle his brow.

"Such a thing isn't unusual, Doctor."

"I suppose not."

Finch reached for his Navy Cut cigarettes and offered one to Brookman, who admired the packet with its lifebelt emblem and the caricature of a bearded sailor within, whose cap band read 'Hero'.

"Thank you."

Finch lit a match and cupped his hand for the detective.

"Mr Coetzee claims he was instructed to take Cox to…"

He consulted his notes.

"…the Esperanza guest house on Atlantic View Drive. As you know, it was the maid there who discovered the dead body on the stoep some two, maybe three hours later."

Finch rubbed his chin.

"So he died in the cab? Is that what you're now saying?"

"Well here's where it gets interesting," said Brookman. "You see, two police officers were out on mounted patrol in the Green Point area last night, as you just heard Harmison mention…"

Brookman checked the names on a report.

"…Sergeant Hett and Private McDonald… They spotted Coetzee's cab parked, only a hundred yards or so from the lodgings as it turned out. Now here's the thing – the driver was, quote 'observed acting strangely, climbing in and out of the cabin.'"

"How odd," said Finch.

"They put the frighteners on Coetzee, thinking he had perhaps been going through his passenger's pockets – such things happen – but they were satisfied on speaking with Coetzee that Cox was merely drunk and that the cabbie, who had lost his way, was just ensuring his well-being."

Finch sighed. Bloody Cox.

"They directed him to the guest house and continued on their way. Ordinarily an incident like this wouldn't get written up, but, given that this has now turned into a murder investigation, we brought the two officers in to put it down on paper."

"Hang on a minute," cut in Finch. "They said Cox was dozing in the back? At what, two-thirty? I thought the time of death had been established earlier than that."

"There's always a degree of leeway."

Brookman held up his cigarette and gave a nod of approval.

"Tell me. What the hell's going on, Inspector?"

"Well, if Cox was certified to have been alive, within yards of his lodgings at 2.30am and was found dead on the stoep two hours later, you can hardly blame anyone for concluding that Coetzee had something to do with it."

Finch shook his head.

"You've already established that Cox was poisoned," he tutted.

"Not yet officially."

"All the same, an unorthodox method for a murder on the public highway. You said as much earlier. Moreover, you yourself stated that Cox was probably either already dead when put in the cab or died en route."

"I hypothesised, yes. Yet two of my officers have since filed a signed report declaring that Cox was alive – dead drunk, yes, but alive – at two-thirty."

He handed the typed report to Finch. Finch did not doubt what it said and waved it away.

"But that contradicts—"

"Captain, like I say, you must never rule out any possibility."

He tapped his temple with his index finger.

"The mind must always be open."

"Come on. What motive could the cabbie possibly have?" Finch snapped.

"There are any number of possible motives," Brookman responded. "Sometimes none is needed at all."

"It wasn't theft," said Finch. "His valuables were still on him. You said so."

"The ones that we found... Maybe Cox was knocking off the cabbie's wife. Who knows?" said Brookman.

"You don't seriously mean that?"

"I never 'mean'. I merely postulate."

"And anyway," went Finch. "why would a man, who has just been stopped by the police, kill his passenger via a complicated method, then dump the body at the deceased's own residence but yards away? He might as well have had a commemorative photograph taken."

Brookman spluttered a laugh.

"The history of crime is littered with some pretty stupid villains."

"You also said... *suggested*... that the killer was known to the victim. Cox had only been in town one day. How could the cabbie possibly know him?"

"Cox, I understand, was a pretty gregarious fellow."

Finch sighed again. He knew Brookman was playing with him. He gestured to the closed door and the MFP sergeant across the corridor.

"And anyway, you're not seriously going to hand the investigation to *that* Neanderthal?"

"It would not be my choice, I grant you. But why do you call him a Neanderthal?"

"Beating up a suspect like that."

"Why do you assume it was he who beat up Coetzee?"

"Because he said so."

Brookman's black eyes burned right into him.

"The trick is to listen to what is said," Brookman explained. "The choice of words, the tense, the syntax. Harmison appeared to express some perverse pleasure, I admit, at the alleged beating. But never once did he claim that it was he who had done it. Check his knuckles."

Brookman paused.

"Let me ask *you* a question, Captain. If Harmison didn't beat up Coetzee, then who did?"

"Judging by what I've seen today, could be any of your crew out there."

Brookman didn't rise to the jibe. He leaned forward.

"Very well, I shall tell you. It was Sergeant Hett and Private McDonald who roughed him over. Officers, I might add, who have now been temporarily suspended as a consequence of their actions."

Finch was beginning to feel like a prize trout being reeled in then let out, flapping on the line.

"Ask yourself Captain, why would they do that?"

"I don't know... To obtain a confession?"

"It's not their business to do so. Other than the report they filed, officers Hett and McDonald are not involved in the case."

"To get to the truth, then?"

"Beat a man long enough and he will tell you he wears ladies' undergarments... or whatever else he believes you want to hear. It is an ineffective method for extracting information."

"Then I don't know... Sadism?"

"In McDonald's case, perhaps. But no."

Finch shrugged.

"Try frustration... anger," said Brookman. "Bear in mind they both burst in to have a pop at Coetzee shortly after he was brought in, when my back was turned. They were furious with him."

"Why would Hett and McDonald be frustrated or angry with Coetzee?" asked Finch.

"Think."

The penny suddenly dropped.

"Because he had made fools of them?"

Brookman smiled. The pupil was doing well.

"Because, quite possibly, he had made fools of them, Captain... The last thing a copper wants is to be made a fool of. Believe me."

Finch exhaled a huge puff of smoke. He was starting to enjoy this. He didn't know if he should be feeling guilty for doing so.

"So, they were mistaken," Finch sighed. "Cox wasn't drunk at all, he was already dead when they stopped Coetzee's cab."

"Seems Hett has a pal round the corner at the mortuary. Got wind that Cox was most likely killed before their encounter and was feeling rather embarrassed about letting a dead body slip through their fingers. Coppers are worse than women for gossiping, sir."

"A case of what we call 'egg on the face', Inspector."

"Actually we say that too."

Brookman stood up. Finch did the same.

"Look, I'm not stating anything," said Brookman. "Far from me to impugn fellow officers of the law—"

"So," said Finch. "The cabbie was just *pretending* that Cox was still alive when the police stopped him, going through a charade."

"Exactly, Captain. He probably panicked, like I'd suggested earlier, if I might say so. Which means…?"

He let Finch finish it.

"…that he isn't telling us the whole story."

Brookman went to the door and opened it.

"Come on."

Across the corridor, Pinkiè Coetzee sat there, eyes fixed on an imaginary spot on the wall. His demeanour was one of non-cooperation.

Brookman reminded Coetzee that this was a murder investigation at its most critical juncture, the first 12 hours. Deceit, withholding evidence – they were serious offences. That said, he went through the rigmarole of apologising for Coetzee's treatment. The officers were being disciplined, he assured. He should no longer be afraid of telling the truth.

The corporal entered with a mug of rooibos tea and a hunk of bread with some dark meat pressed into a rough incision carved into it. Ostrich it looked like. He dumped it on the table before Coetzee. No plate.

Coetzee remained motionless. Brookman rubbed his chin, mulling over the next move.

Harmison, clearly unimpressed with the niceties of civil policing, was gearing up for more coercive action but Brookman raised a hand and stayed him. Again, Brookman urged Coetzee that he need be absolutely truthful. This was his chance to redeem himself.

Eventually Coetzee spoke. The words were slow and pained.

"*Ja*, I will tell you everything," he said. "But on one condition…"

The lingua franca of the Cape Coloureds was Afrikaans, a revelation for Finch on arrival in the colony. But nearly all spoke English equally fluently.

"You're not in any position to bloody negotiate," barked Harmison.

Brookman raised his hand again.

Coetzee's eyes turned to Finch.

"…that the doctor stays."

Finch thought he detected the faintest trace of a smile on Coetzee's lips. He reciprocated.

"Mr. Coetzee… Pinkie," said Finch, "as someone who isn't an officer of the law, I'm not sure if that's permissible."

He turned to Brookman. The inspector raised an eyebrow but did not demur.

"Very well," he consented.

Harmison gave a derisory snort.

The inspector nodded at the corporal, who unlocked Coetzee's handcuffs. The cabbie rubbed his wrists then devoured the bread and meat.

Sated, he wiped his hands on his trousers, swigged his tea and leant back in his chair.

"All right then Pinkie old chum, you've got your wish" said Brookman. "Now tell us everything… And I bloody well mean *everything.*"

Chapter Nineteen

Sixteen hours earlier...

Pinkie Coetzee twitched the reins and his bony mule clopped to a casual halt. Tattered palms rustled overhead, buffeted by the night breeze. A municipal gas lamp hissed. In its pale amber glow he re-examined the oblong of expensive vellum, the words upon it etched in a stylish, looped italic, the paper scored by a sharp, crisp fold.

The error was not his own. Having sauntered up and down the winding dirt path, peering hard at the clapboard dwellings, it seemed perfectly evident there was no guest house named 'Esperanza'.

(*Es-per-anza* it had been mouthed to him, like a parent to a child.)

He sighed.

Nie goed nie.

The man in his charge would now have to be roused. He would have to ascertain just where, exactly, to deposit him. He spat out his wad of tobacco. It arced out onto the ground.

Dit is nie goed nie.

There was a three-quarter moon, the light bright, though diffused by the low cloud. Below, on the headland of Green Point, lamps winked on the army encampment sprawling across the grassland. Silver flecks danced on the waves beyond, right out to the low black mass of Robben Island. The distant pound of the breakers that carried uphill was punctuated only by the clank of chains from the warships at anchor. Their silhouettes could just be traced.

The war had been good for business, he knew. No doubt about that. The private clubs near the waterfront disgorged free-spending officers throughout the night. There was no question either that the one lolling in his gig was as drunk as the proverbial lord, as the same British liked to say.

"*Baas?*"

No response.

Coetzee jumped down from his perch, his action too athletic for his bow legs to accommodate. He winced, took pause, then yanked back the canopy.

"*Baas?* Mister?"

Not even his horsewhip would stir this dozing beast.

Kak.

Beyond the battery on Signal Hill, Lion's Head loomed, behind it the sheet wall of Table Mountain. He buttoned up his hessian jacket. There were shillings and tickeys stuffed in his belt. Cutthroats lurked in the rubble of the uplands.

His battered watch told him it was just after half past two. He was finished for the night. *Should* be finished. A warm bed... a warm wife... were waiting.

He pushed back his straw hat and wiped the beads that were forming, despite the cool. Then he shook the officer roughly by the shoulder...

Nothing.

...before grabbing the serge of his lapels for a more emphatic rousing.

Kak!

It happened so quickly he barely had time to react. With a great and panicked heave, he struggled to bundle the officer back on board. The man landed with a thud, face up on the deck. Coetzee climbed up after him. Springs creaked. The mule snorted and scraped her hooves.

A shiver of fear shot down his back. The sweat became a trickle, cold between the shoulder blades.

"*Baas.* Please, *baas!*"

The fumes were strong. Coetzee's eyes were drawn to a flash of white at the mouth. Not saliva, not foam, but cloth – the protrusion of white silk... a *handkerchief*?

Slowly he extracted it, feeling momentarily and incongruously like a street magician – one he remembered from his childhood, pulling yards of bright material from a seemingly limitless sleeve.

There was no splutter, no gagging, the breath long since gone. Neither the man's chest nor his wrist yielded the faintest throb of life.

But... a Coloured man... a dead white. A white *officer*?

Coetzee's hands shook. For now, around him, the windows remain shuttered.

Dank God.

He took a deep breath, threw his arms around the man's soft midriff and hauled him up onto the worn leather seat. He wedged the body upright in the corner. Though it was a pointless gesture, he loosened the officer's tie.

Clip-clop.

Somewhere down below came the sound of another buggy. Momentarily, Coetzee's breath was a still as the officer's. But the vehicle was streets away. The sound soon faded. Slowly he exhaled…

Nie goed nie. Dit is nie goed nie.

"YOU!"

The word shot him through.

Out of the blackness, two mounted constables began to form. They were trotting downhill towards him. The onshore wind had muffled their approach.

"Stop what you're doing!"

He did.

"Step back!"

Their horses clopped alongside. The men wore khaki tunics, their slouch hats secured against the wind by chinstraps. The one who shouted was young, cocky, straight-backed.

"What were you up to?"

"What do you mean, sir?"

The second officer, older, extended his crop and flipped back the canvas flap. His arm displayed three stripes, a sergeant. He pulled a face to his underling.

"Behold your British officer."

They laughed. Should he laugh too? Coetzee smiled instead.

"Something funny?"

"No, sir."

The young one was down now, out of his saddle. He thrust his own crop under Pinkie's chin.

"You're sweating. It's not hot."

"They say Coloureds have been arming themselves," the sergeant cut in. "Got to be on our guard."

"That wouldn't be you, cabbie?" went the young one again, the other hand flitting to the revolver at his hip.

"No, sir. No."

"You sure?"

"Yes, *baas*."

"Louder!"

"Yes, *baas*!"

Fok jou, baas.

The sergeant wheeled his horse round. The constable moved his hand from his gun to seek out a pencil. He took out a pad and noted the number above the fender.

"Name?"

"Coetzee."

"Coetzee?"

"Pinkie Coetzee."

"Pinkie?"

"P–I–N–K–I–E."

He wrote it with disdain.

"You people…"

The mule, spooked by a male horse moving at her rear, whinnied and shuffled. Pinkie Coetzee willed his handbrake to hold.

The sergeant nodded. He had noticed something.

"Constable McDonald."

The underling followed up: "What's that in your hand?"

He had forgotten – the address.

The younger one – McDonald – snatched it.

"You take this from the officer?"

"No… I… It was…"

In a deft swipe his pistol was whipped up and rammed hard into Coetzee's cheek. He could smell the oil. The hammer was cocked.

"You go through his pockets?"

The barrel pinched his skin. He could feel the circle of the muzzle against his gum. His knees began to buckle.

"N-n-no!"

"I can't hear you!"

His voice cracked like an adolescent.

"NO!"

The constable grinned and passed the paper up. The sergeant studied it. He mused for a moment then bade his junior holster his weapon.

"You're headed the wrong way," said the sergeant.

"What?"

He pointed uphill.

"The Esperanza is at the top… Round the bend."

Dank God.

The sergeant trotted off. The constable put a foot in his stirrup and swung a leg over the saddle. He gave a 'click'. His horse followed.

Twenty yards away, one of them, Coetzee didn't know which, threw back a 'Merry Christmas'.

"Thank you, sir."

The young one. The bastard.

"I was talking to your mule."

Pinkie Coetzee spat again.

Fok… Fok, fok, fok!

—

Coetzee's audience listened intently. When he had finished, he swigged more tea then slumped back again.

"Could you describe the dead officer?" asked Brookman.

"*Ach*, man… medium height, round face, moustache… Like every officer in the British Army."

Brookman opened a cardboard folder and thrust a charcoal sketch in front of Coetzee – a hasty artist's impression of the man now lying on Krajicek's slab. Finch peered over Brookman's shoulder. It looked nothing like Cox. Not the Cox he had known.

"Could be him. I couldn't say. I'm not disputing the identity if that's who you say it is."

"If Cox was as drunk as you've described, how did he manage to climb into your cab? How was he capable of writing the address for the guest house?"

"He didn't."

"Explain."

"It was someone else, a passer-by. *He* helped the man into my cab."

Brookman threw Finch a glance.

"Tell us about this Good Samaritan," he continued.

"How you say… a well-dressed gent, a civilian. Chucked the officer's overcoat onto the seat then helped him aboard. He was a handful, all right. Then hopped out halfway."

"Quite the gentleman," remarked Brookman.

"Yes, *baas*. Paid up the full fare with a half-crown extra for me to escort the officer home. Half a crown. Shit man."

"Hold it, hold it, you miserable vermin," cut in Harmison. "You're telling us that a mysterious gent, a 'Good Samaritan', suddenly lines your pockets with silver and then disappears into thin air. You sure you didn't just nick it off the deceased?"

Coetzee rolled his eyes.

"There was not a tickey on my person, not a farthing that I did not earn… You can check my log… And I expect to get it all back."

"And you will, Mr Coetzee, you will," said Brookman, shooting Harmison a look. "It has all been inventoried. Corporal?"

The corporal rifled through some papers and handed Coetzee a chit.

"Can you describe him then, this Good Samaritan?" asked Harmison, less aggressively this time.

"A long coat. How you say, frock?"

"A frock coat, yes," said Brookman.

"*Ja*, and a top hat. A soft one… made from felt or something. He had a cane. Silver-topped."

"What about his face?"

"It was dark, difficult to tell. I carry hundreds of people every week. I'm sitting up high, they're low. Last night, wind, drizzle, the hood was up. My fares were under cover."

"A silver-topped cane? That's pretty specific," said Brookman. "You had good enough eyesight for that."

"It was metal, ornate. A bird's head, an eagle, I think. Yes, man, it was unusual. Glinted under the streetlight. That's why I remember."

"But you don't remember his face."

"Honestly, man, no. Believe me."

"The clothes, the cane. Sounds like a gent with particular taste."

"Now you mention it, he had a ring. A precious stone. A diamond? On the little finger of his left hand."

"Seems like you've become overly familiar with this man's jewellery," said Harmison.

"Like the cane, I noticed it because I had climbed down. I stood next to him while he wrote the officer's address."

"You mean *this*?"

Brookman reached inside his jacket pocket and produced a piece of folded vellum with a tear down one side. The words '*Esperanza, Atlantic View Drive*' were written upon it.

"Yes, *baas*. That's it."

Brookman turned to Finch.

"Captain, would you recognise Major Cox's handwriting?"

"I believe so."

He handed the thick piece of paper to Finch.

"This it?"

It was elegant and looped. Practised.

"No it's not."

"Wrote the address in a bound notebook," said Coetzee. "Looked like crocodile skin, the pattern…"

"Our Good Samaritan's shaping up to be quite the Fancy Dan," said Brookman.

There was a sudden and inappropriate burst of laughter around the room at Brookman's dubbing. Even Coetzee raised a smile.

"Inspector, may I ask something?" ventured Finch.

Brookman glared.

"If you must, Captain."

"When was this?" asked Finch.

"When?" said Coetzee. "Around two o'clock in the morning, Mister Doctor. It was my final fare. But I've already told the police this."

"Forgive me," said Finch. "I mean, when did the Good Samaritan… Fancy Dan…"

More chuckles.

"…hand you the address? As he jumped off?"

"No. At the start," said Coetzee. "As he helped the officer on board. Outside the club."

"So you mean to tell us you stood there, right next to him while he wrote the address," growled Harmison. "You noticed his clothes, his cane, his ring, but not his bleeding face?"

"I do not recall any blood."

"It's an expression, Mr Coetzee," Brookman enlightened.

"I mean I couldn't be certain. He was clean-shaven. In his 30s maybe. But anything more…?"

He shrugged.

"Funny, I don't think he was too fond of the dead man. Seemed to help him… how do you say…? reluctantly. After he'd pushed the officer into my cab he stormed off, only to return a moment later. Change of heart."

Brookman signalled for a pause. He took the lined ledger the corporal had been writing on and examined it.

"That's 'silver-topped cane'," he corrected. "Shaped like an 'eagle's head.'"

"That's what it says, sir."

"Damn it, Pienaar, your handwriting's like a five-year-old's."

Brookman stood, cleared his throat and began pacing, slowly.

"So let's get this straight… At around two o'clock you pick up the officer at the docks. He is drunk and incapable and is helped on board by our Fancy Dan. You can't identify Fancy Dan but he has on a frock coat, a felt topper and carries a cane."

He turned to the corporal like a teacher testing an inattentive student before the class.

"What kind of cane, Pienaar?"

"A silver-topped cane shaped like an eagle, sir."

"Thank you. You jump down. He produces a notebook upon which he writes the address of the officer's lodgings and rips out the page for you. You notice his diamond ring. You can't positively identify him but think he was in his 30s, clean-shaven… His build?"

"Build?"

"Height, weight."

"I don't know."

He looked up at the two standing men.

"Shorter than Mister Doctor. About the same as the sergeant."

"Your height, Sergeant Harmison?" asked Brookman.

"Five ten, sir."

"Not fat, not thin," said Coetzee. "Just normal."

"But otherwise what I have just outlined is correct?" said Brookman.

Coetzee nodded.

"The man has second thoughts about escorting the officer personally but then changes his mind and climbs in."

"One other thing," said Coetzee. "He asked me to take a back route. Not to use Strand Street."

"Why, do you think?"

"I thought to avoid embarrassment for the officer."

"And then, some minutes later, he jumps out and pays you the full fare plus half a crown tip for the officer's safe passage."

"No."

"No?"

"He paid me that upfront, too, when he gave me the address. At the club. When he hopped out, he just hopped out. Vanished."

"And where did he hop out?"

"The Somerset Road Cemetery. By the wall that runs along from the main gate."

"Very good," said Brookman. "So then what happened?"

Coetzee repeated that, on arrival in the neighbourhood, although he had found the road, he couldn't find the house. He was becoming uneasy in the uplands late at night. It was then that he decided he would have to rouse his slumbering passenger.

"And again, this was at what time?" asked Brookman.

"Just after half past two. I had a pocket watch."

"It too will be returned."

There was a slight flicker of remembrance on Coetzee's face.

"What is it? Come on."

"Remember how I said the officer fell out onto me? How I held him?"

"Yes."

"The smell. Not just drink. Something else?"

"Another odour?"

"More like… like a chemical one."

Brookman and Finch exchanged a look.

"I once worked in a photographer's laboratory, sweeping the floor. The smell… it reminded me."

"And then, after all that, after your little bit of play-acting, you just dump him on the stoep like a sack of potatoes."

Coetzee hung his head.

"I panicked—"

"You mean when Hett and McDonald came by."

"Who?" he asked.

"Your two police chums," said Finch. He nodded at Coetzee's swollen eye.

"Yes."

His tone turned more pleading.

"I knocked on the door before I ran back to the buggy, I swear. I wanted someone to take him in… He was already dead… Man, what could I do?"

"You could have told the truth."

"Come. You know how it is."

"You lied before. You said the officer was drunk. Now you say he was dead. Why the hell should we believe you?"

Coetzee reached into his pocket.

"Because of this."

With a flourish he pulled at his pocket and laid on the table a white silk men's handkerchief. It was monogrammed with the initials "L.C."

Chapter Twenty

The desert sun was setting, bathing the land a blood red. It was huge, bigger than anything Mbutu had ever seen, sinking rapidly now through the shimmering haze. Its descent on the horizon was a primal signal for the wildlife. A flock of long-legged birds flapped over, their wings making a whooping sound. A herd of bok stopped grazing and were suddenly on the move. From the bush came strange yips and yelps.

"There," said Hendrik. "See?"

Mbutu shielded his eyes. Sure enough there they were, not far from the first line of quiver trees they had stopped at on their morning hunt – horses with riders. They were line astern, about eight to ten of them, the horses walking. They were too far away for any detail. As the light began to fade, they too seemed to react and picked up speed. They were travelling away from the rocky corral, probably heading back to where they'd come from, pondered Hendrik.

The man with the blunderbuss gave clicking commentary.

"West," said Hendrik. "He says they are heading west."

"Thank God," said Mbutu.

"West means nothing!" Hendrik snapped.

Another of the men muttered something.

"He says it is a mistake… sheltering the mother and child."

"So what do we do?"

"Tonight. No fire," said Hendrik. "Must organise defence. In the morning we decide."

There were eight men on the rim of the rocks, including Hendrik and himself.

Hendrik had his battered revolver tucked in his waistband. There was the man with the blunderbuss. The others, though, had no firearms, no weapons that could be used in anything other than close combat. Now Mbutu understood why they had been conserving their ammunition.

The corral was roughly circular. Hendrik conferred with the men, and six of them posted themselves equidistantly around the rim, either squatting or lying prone, each scanning the landscape.

There was no sense of ego or the individual, observed Mbutu. The Nama's actions always seemed selfless, each man acting for the greater good.

Hendrik led Mbutu down to the others. He explained what was happening.

Inevitably there were questions. Though Mbutu understood not a word of it, he got the impression that Hendrik was doing his best not to let the blame fall too heavily on the white females.

Mbutu had positioned himself near them. The little girl looked up. He did not want to scare her but explained that they all needed to be cautious tonight.

The poor creatures have suffered enough.

With no fire to warm them, the Nama began huddling together. Emily and her mother were encouraged to join them. The rabbit broth was still hot, one of the women said. It was best that they eat it now.

Hendrik called for four more men. They, plus himself and Mbutu, would take the second watch. They would swap over in four hours.

None of them had a pocket watch. How would they know the time?

Hendrik merely pointed upwards. The stars.

A man returned with a bundle of spears. They took one each.

"Here," said Hendrik, and handed Mbutu what appeared to be a crooked wooden club but was in fact an ancient flintlock pistol.

"Me?"

It was heavy, the metalwork fussily ornate.

"None of these men feels comfortable."

Mbutu was not sure he was at ease either.

"Why not give it to one of the men on sentry duty now?"

"We must keep something in reserve," said Hendrik. "If those on the rocks are overwhelmed, the fight is not lost."

"You really think we're in that much danger?"

Hendrik put his finger to his lips. They had to act quickly, the light was nearly gone. They must show Mbutu how to use the gun while they still could.

Loading the pistol was a complicated procedure, made even more so from the explanation by committee, during which each of the men prodded and poked the device to a chorus of their unintelligible language.

A small leather pouch was produced. In it were what looked like wrapped paper sticks. Cartridges. They were passed around for inspection. A ramrod was pulled out of the slotted holder beneath the barrel. Evidently it was an important part of the loading ritual.

Mbutu had never seen such a weapon but thought he understood. It was a crude contraption, but worked on the same principle as a modern firearm.

The cartridge, about four inches long, contained gunpowder and a ball of shot. To load, the pistol was held vertically while the top was bitten off the paper cartridge and the black, pungent powder poured straight down the barrel. The shot was removed from the cartridge, the paper was chewed up as wadding, which was then rammed down on top of the gunpowder. Last came the shot, squashed down on top.

To fire the gun, the sculpted hammer had to be cocked. It had been oiled in recent times but was difficult to click back in position – a spring or catch was faulty. When it cocked, the trigger nudged forward into the firing position. To fire it required a good pull. The hammer had a piece of flint held in place, screwed in position between clamps, like a small vice. Pressing the trigger released the hammer, which sprang forward, sparked against a plate and, through a small hole, ignited the gunpowder within.

"Use two hands. Hold steady. It kicks," warned Hendrik. "Aim at the body."

"Do you think I'll need to?"

Hendrik looked him in the eye.

"Let us hope that none of us has to fight."

Hendrik scrambled up the rocks and conversed with the man with the blunderbuss. He came back down.

"The cavalry continued west until they could no longer be seen. Now all is quiet."

The four Nama of the second watch prepared to bed down. Mbutu studied them as they each dug a tiny pit to relieve pressure on their hip bones. Why had he never thought of that?

"Tonight will be cold," said Hendrik. He made a sleeping gesture, palms pressed together, his cheek laid against them. "But you must try."

Mbutu nodded.

"If anything happens, someone will wake us. But be ready."

He raised his revolver.

This time Mbutu loaded his pistol for real. It was fiddly. Reloading it in combat – were it to come to that – would be tricky. One cocked the hammer only prior to firing, he understood. He laid it on the ground next to him.

Mbutu pulled his jacket around him. It was not the cold that kept him from sleeping but his racing mind.

All was deathly still in the camp, but beyond it the Karoo was alive with noise – the squeaks and squawks and shrieks, the odd howl of a carnivore. And then he heard it again, the sound that had nearly chorused his departure from God's earth – the growl of a leopard.

He suddenly felt something at his side, but it was warm and human. The little girl.

"Don't be frightened child… See there, around the rocks."

She looked up.

"Men to protect us through the night."

He tucked his jacket around her. She snuggled in closer.

With the girl's head on his shoulder, Mbutu looked up at the stars, the unbelievable, magical spray across the heavens.

Thanks be to God.

He felt her breathing lapse into a gentle rasp. Though she could not hear, he whispered to her.

"Back home in Kimberley, I have a little boy, the same age. I cannot look after him so I will look after you."

–

He didn't know how long he had been asleep, but he awoke with a start.

Emily had gone. But he looked over and saw that she had returned to curl up with her mother.

No, that was not it.

He heard bird noises. A coo and a whistle.

That is not a bird.

He glanced up. Against the silver moon he saw the silhouette of a man moving around the rim of the rocks.

A man in uniform.

Chapter Twenty-One

Brookman, Finch and Harmison entered the inspector's office. Brookman shut his door behind them. He brought the monogrammed handkerchief to his nose and inhaled.

"Chloroform?" he asked.

"Maybe. Maybe not… I'm not sure," said Finch.

Harmison looked confused.

"Chloroform?"

"An anaesthetic."

Finch sniffed again. The odour was still discernible. Unfortunately so was Cox's bile.

"Has a hint of cough medicine about it. Codeine or something similar."

"Codeine?" asked Harmison.

"Sergeant," said Brookman. "I need to apprise you of a little more detail. I just require a moment with the doctor. Will you kindly inform the suspect that he is released on his own recognisance. Ask Pienaar to run the handkerchief over to the deputy coroner."

"You sure?"

"Sure, Sergeant?"

"About letting the darkie go?"

"I am."

Harmison took the handkerchief and exited. The door was closed more forcefully than it ought to have been. Brookman rolled his eyes, then went and stood behind his cluttered desk.

"So, Cox was killed with his own kerchief," said Finch.

"Unless the killer has the same initials and takes to leaving a souvenir."

The detective nodded towards the door.

"Do you trust him?"

"Harmison?"

"No, Doctor… Coetzee."

"Oh… I believe so."

"Lifetime on this job you can tell within seconds whether a man is lying. Or a woman for that matter. Though not quite so easily."

Finch smiled.

"That, in there, seemed to be the truth," agreed Brookman. "About 80 per cent truth anyhow."

"He's holding something back?"

"I'm convinced enough he's told us the main facts pertaining to Cox, which is what matters here."

The inspector produced a silver cigarette case and offered one to Finch. He took it. Brookman popped one between his own lips, took out a flint lighter and sparked them both up.

"And anyway," said Brookman. "Why would Coetzee make it up? Way too elaborate."

"You're happy for him to be released, though?"

"I have a sneaking feeling there's some small detail he's neglected. Something he's embarrassed about maybe. But he needs reassurance from us, a sense that we trust him. What better demonstration of that than letting him go? If Coetzee's up to mischief, and my hunch is he isn't, he's of better use to us back in play… Short-staffed as we are, we'll keep tabs on him. It's Christmas, he's not going far. If he behaves out of the ordinary, has a mysterious rendezvous with someone or starts splashing the cash, we'll bring him in."

The tobacco was coarser than Navy Cut. It was rough on Finch's throat. He coughed.

Brookman bent to unlock his desk drawer. As he did so a small medallion on a silver chain dangled out between his upper shirt buttons. A Star of David.

"Plus, I have this…"

He pulled out a typed sheet of paper and slid it across to Finch. He tucked his star back in. The document was headed 'Witness Statement'.

"The sworn testimony of a Mr Julius Januarie."

He pointed it out at the bottom.

"A work colleague of Coetzee's… fellow cabbie. Neither has any idea that the other has been in for questioning so they haven't been able to confer."

The first couple of paragraphs was in Afrikaans, with an English translation underneath.

"To save you the pain of Pienaar's illiteracy – although give him credit, he's unintelligible in *two* languages – the statement declares that Mr Januarie also picked up a gentleman broadly matching the description given by Coetzee…"

"Our Fancy Dan?"

Brookman nodded.

"…at the same location, the Somerset Road Cemetery, about an hour later. Around half past three. This time Fancy Dan was heading back into Cape Town."

"How did you get this information?"

"Quite simple. Telephoned the description of our man down to the taxi controller this afternoon… Wonderful device, the telephone. Wonderful…"

He was lost for an instant in admiration.

"…The controller asked every cabbie who passed through the depot whether they recognised the man. Mr Januarie did right away."

"Are you sure he got the time right? Not just a case of Fancy Dan hopping out from Coetzee's cab and hailing the next one back down to the waterfront? Didn't Januarie mean two-thirty not three-thirty?"

"Januarie was absolutely positive. Didn't clock on until three. And anyway, there's another interesting detail."

"There is?"

"This time our Fancy Dan wasn't quite so fancy. He was dishevelled, dirty."

"This could be easily explained."

"Of course it could. And in my experience the law of Ockham's Razor will out."

"That the simplest explanation is usually the most likely?"

Brookman beamed with the wide-eyed pride of a father whose toddler had just taken his first steps.

"I'm impressed… But until such time—"

"We must not make assumptions?"

"Captain, you have the makings of a true detective."

Finch grinned.

Brookman locked the statement back in his drawer.

"Does Harmison know about this?" enquired Finch.

Brookman shook his head. There was a mischievous glint in his eye.

"Seems Coetzee wasn't the only one withholding information," Finch quipped.

Brookman looked at his pocket watch.

"Which is why I need to have a chat with our esteemed MFP sergeant right away. He *will* be taking over the case after all."

Finch extinguished his cigarette and stood. He put his hand out to shake.

"Glad to have been of service…"

The inspector remained seated. He gestured for Finch to return to his chair. He came right to the point.

"How well did you know Cox? Really."

"Not again… You're not seriously—"

"As I've told you already, Captain. You're in the clear… clear as you're ever likely to be."

"Then—?"

"Then it's like this."

He took a moment to find the right words.

"The way I see it, dead or alive, in this town, you're the best friend Cox has got."

"I am?"

"We've itemised his particulars so no need to keep anything, which means there's a cardboard box lodged with the desk sergeant containing his possessions. Would you be a good fellow and take care of them for us?"

"I don't have a lot of room in my kit… I'm back at the Front in four days."

Brookman ignored him.

"There are a few things also at the guest house."

He began filling out a form. He handed it to Finch – a requisition order.

"It's not much altogether. A few items of clothing really. It's just that here it'll get swallowed up, end up stuffed in a municipal warehouse. You, you're better placed to return it to the RAMC, send it on to his family or whatever needs to be done. You can post on anything you need to before you leave town."

The family. Despite his earlier intentions, Finch had been losing sight of them. Brookman hadn't.

"And another thing. I'm guessing the army will be writing a letter or sending a telegram to the bereaved. I'm guessing too that it will curt, impersonal."

He handed Finch a business card. It contained Brookman's own police contact details. On the reverse, in pen, was written the name and Punjabi address of Mrs Isadora Cox.

"It would be comforting for them to receive something from someone who served with him."

This time Brookman stood. He thrust out his hand. Finch shook it.

"Thank you, Captain."

Mindful of Brookman's religious proclivities, he tempered his festive adieu.

"Season's cheer, Inspector."

Finch walked back to the front desk, past the chaos of the cells and the interview rooms. There, the desk sergeant retrieved a cardboard box, about the size of a fish tank, which he dumped on the counter. It had 'Cox dcsd.' scrawled on the lid. The sergeant handed him a clipboard with a pencil attached to it by a piece of string. On it was an itemisation of what was within:

> *Dress tunic, serge*
> *Dress trousers, serge*
> *Cotton shirt (khaki)*
> *Knitted tie (khaki)*
> *Riding boots, one pair (brown)*
> *Leather gloves, one pair (brown)*
> *Peaked cap*
> *Sam Brown belt w/holster*
> *Wristwatch*
> *Leather wallet*

Finch flipped open the flaps.

"Browning pistol and clip of ammunition were removed, sir. Quartermaster's orders. Deceased's identity card was retained. Undergarments were destroyed in the post mortem."

The clothes hadn't been folded, just stuffed in. But on first glance all seemed in order.

"Thank you, Sergeant."

Finch reached for the clipboard but stopped. He checked again.

"Something wrong, sir?"

"Yes Sergeant. Says here 'leather gloves, one pair.'"

He held up a single right-hand one.

The sergeant rummaged around.

"Someone's obviously made a mistake."

"Or lost the left one."

"Unlikely, sir."

"Even so..."

The sergeant corrected the entry. He would ask Inspector Brookman to initial the adjustment, he said.

Wait a minute, Finch thought. Wasn't there an overcoat? Didn't Pinkie Coetzee say something about the Fancy Dan throwing Cox's coat onto the cab seat?

"No overcoat?"

"None listed, sir."

"Sergeant, will you excuse me for a moment?"

He turned and headed back up the corridor. The door was closed. He could hear Brookman and Harmison in deep discussion. He felt sorry for Brookman. He was just getting stuck into this case. Now he was going to have to relinquish it. And to Harmison.

Finch returned to the desk and wrote a note explaining about the glove and the coat.

"Please, will you ensure that the inspector gets this the minute he comes out?" he asked the sergeant.

"Yes, sir."

–

It was dark outside. Christmas Day had practically been written off. He hadn't even been to church, his annual ritual, though he had had lunch with a cleric who had uttered a drunken prayer. Finch supposed it counted.

Back at the Belvedere, Finch was about to loft Cox's box upstairs when the bellboy called to him. While Finch was out, he'd had a visitor.

"Yes, sir. A gentleman. Left you this."

It was another calling card, printed with the name and Wynberg address of someone called 'Albert Rideau'.

"Did he say what it was concerning?"

"No, sir."

The bellboy lingered. Damn, he must keep more small change about his person. Finch rooted in his pocket and came up with some pennies.

The bellboy uttered a sarcastic: "Thank you, sir."

Finch felt embarrassed to ask for assistance and struggled upstairs alone. Inside his room he put the box on the table and lit the gas lamp. Once again, he went through the ritual of removing his boots and pouring himself a generous tot of Talisker. Christ, his knee was hurting.

He took out Cox's items one by one, hanging the clothes on the back of the chair and placing the boots next to each other on the floor. It somehow seemed more respectful.

The watch was a quality timepiece. Zeiss, German. It had fine black roman numerals on a white dial. The casing was silver, shiny, barely scratched. The crocodile strap, a dark greenish-brown, was still rather stiff, rather new.

Finch flipped it over. On the reverse, it had an engraved inscription: '*All my love, V.*'

'V?'

Finch reached inside his breast pocket and pulled out the two business cards he had acquired. He set the one from Albert Rideau aside and turned over the one from Brookman. Cox's wife was named Isadora. Though 'V' may have been her middle name or a pet one.

He prised open the popper on the battered, scuffed wallet. Inside was ten shillings in cash, just as Brookman had said. There was, too, a receipt from a chemist's shop printed on pale green paper, around a shilling's worth of postage stamps and a scrap of paper, ripped from a lined sheet, on which was scrawled, in pencil, the word '*Shawcroft*'.

Finch sipped his scotch and lit a Navy Cut.

He changed his mind about Cox's clothes. It was too unnerving to have them hung out like that. Plus there was a hint of Cox's cologne in the air. He put the boots back in the box and went to fold the garments away on top of them.

On a whim, he examined them. He started with the pockets. As he expected, the police had emptied them. But there was something odd about the jacket. On the inside, on the right, below the interior pocket, was a rip in the dark green silk, about ten inches long, running horizontally.

No, not a rip, an incision, a cut, a slash, made by something very sharp. A few inches above it, parallel, was a more ragged gash of about the same length, which had been sewn up, rather crudely by hand with black cotton thread.

When he held the jacket up he could see it was stretched out, a little misshapen on the right-hand side above the belt loop. Had Cox sewn something into the lining? Was the slash underneath the work of someone intent on removing it?

Whatever it was, it was no longer there.

Chapter Twenty-Two

Mbutu rolled over. The man next to him was curled in a foetal position, snoring lightly. Mbutu pressed his hand over the man's mouth and shook his shoulder. He spluttered hot breath and saliva into Mbutu's palm. Mbutu gestured up to the rocks, then pressed a finger to his own lips.

Mbutu's heart pounded at a rate he did not know it was possible to reach. He grabbed the flintlock pistol and the leather pouch. The other man wakened his neighbour who, in turn, roused the man next to him. The first man picked up his spear. Within seconds the six had been raised.

Hendrik brandished his revolver. He signalled for Mbutu and the first man to ascend the rocks either side of where Mbutu had seen the intruder. Mbutu nodded. He gestured for them to drive the interloper down in his direction.

The pair silently scrambled up, keeping low, forming a pincer movement to converge behind the intruder. On the rim of the corral, the sentry was still crouched, looking out across the desert.

Mbutu went to alert him. He lay his flintlock pistol aside, but when he went to touch the man's arm, he simply slumped over. Mbutu pulled his hand away. It was warm and sticky. The man rolled onto his back. A sliver of moonlight flashed on lifeless eyes. There was a dark mess under the chin. His throat had been slit.

Cold fear gripped Mbutu. His own lungs seemed to have shrunken. His breath came in short shallow gasps, like a man surfacing from too long under water.

Ahead, in the distance, came a whinny. Maybe 200 yards away, Mbutu could just make it out. The moonlight was enough for him to see horses tethered.

Get a hold of yourself.

To his colleague he signalled an exaggerated count, a finger at a time. One… two… three…

The Nama man acknowledged and turned to relay the information back down the slope. But as he did so there was the dart of a black mass. In a wild and instant blur a body was on top of him. There was a muffled yelp and the Nama man crumpled.

Now, Mbutu! Now!

He reached for his flintlock pistol on the ground but caught his foot as he picked it up. He staggered, fumbled and dropped it. The gun clanged and bounced down the rocks. Alerted, the intruder turned towards him. The moonlight glinted on the blade of a knife.

I cannot move.

BANG!

An ear-splitting roar and a burst of sparks came from somewhere behind and to the left. It shook him to his senses. The blunderbuss. Its blast reverberated around the rocks. But the weapon's discharge was haphazard, the gun aimed up into nowhere. It was the last desperate reflex of a man already mortally wounded. He too tumbled over.

Mbutu swivelled back. The intruder was bounding between the boulders towards him just yards away. Mbutu leapt down the rocks. There was a swishing sound, like that of a whip, and a soft thud. His pursuer dropped to the ground, squealing and writhing in agony. Mbutu could see him clawing desperately at the shaft of a spear now protruding vertically from his abdomen.

The weapon. Find it. Now!

Mbutu scrambled to where he guessed the gun had landed. The camp was a now a frenzy of screams and panic, Nama women running this way and that, grabbing their children, huddling with the blind men behind scattered boulders in the centre. Hendrik and the others stood on the outside, backs to them, facing outwards, trying to protect them. The light was bright enough to discern more shapes among the rocks on the far side.

Mbutu was on his hands and knees clawing fruitlessly.

Where did it go? Somewhere here.

From down low, amid the swirl of bodies, Mbutu saw Hendrik raise his revolver, take aim at another intruder and miss. Against the bright muzzle flash of a rifle, Mbutu watched as another man – it looked like Stefaan – fall. The gunfire laid everybody low, crouching. This intruder was now down in the middle, carbine raised, aiming it into the huddled wretches before him who cowered and flinched. He was looking for something... *someone.*

Then he saw them, the white females.

"Down here," he yelled to a comrade.

Mbutu was now on his belly, only feet from the soldier. The man had not seen him.

There. Was that it?

The flintlock pistol had fallen between two rocks. The light reflected on the engraved finery of the stock. He reached his hand into the gap and willed his arm an extra two inches in length. He could feel it. Somehow he manipulated it with his fingers. He got his full hand on the ornate metal knob screwed to the end of the butt. He pulled. He freed it.

The soldier caught Mbutu in the corner of his eye and spun to his right. Mbutu's hands shook. The gun felt like lead. He seemed to have no control over his body. He was on his knees, trembling.

Was this how it was to be? That he would die a coward?

Time seemed to slow down, as if in a dream, as if out of his own body watching himself. He held the stock tight with his left hand while cocking the hammer with his right. It was stiff, awkward. It failed to lock in position.

The soldier's rifle was aimed from the hip.

Mbutu tried again. It clicked. He raised the heavy weapon with trembling hands.

Aim for the body.

And with another great 'crack!', an explosion of smoke and fire and a recoil that knocked him onto his own backside, Mbutu shot a man stone dead.

There was still a third intruder. Mbutu heard more spears clatter against the rocks. There were more shots. More screams. Frantically Mbutu scuttled over to the white mother and child. And then he saw the third soldier charge down the rocks at the far end, running towards them.

A Nama man flung himself at the soldier, his knife at the ready, but the slight African was no match, pushed aside and shot clinically through the head.

There seemed to be no more protectors. How many had fallen?

The leather pouch was slung over Mbutu's shoulder. He fumbled and pulled out a cartridge. The white woman clung to his arm. He had to shrug her off. He was on his knees again, the pistol now held between his thighs, pointing upwards, the acrid smoke from the red hot barrel wafting straight into his face.

He grabbed a cartridge, bit off the end, poured the powder down.

The soldier had spotted the women hunched behind Mbutu. He shuttled the bolt, the gun was raised, he was ten yards away.

Mbutu spat a wad of paper and pressed the shot on top. He withdrew the ramrod from the holder but his hands were shaking so much he dropped it. Emily handed it to him. He tried to insert it in the barrel. He was trembling uncontrollably. It was hopeless.

The man aimed first at the quaking mother, the little girl squealing and clinging to her skirt. An execution.

Mbutu rammed the shot home. There was a sneer on the man's face. Contempt for Mbutu. The pathetic black man with his pathetic, useless gun.

But this time the hammer was cocked more easily. Mbutu knew what he had to do. He raised the pistol and shot into the guts. At close range it lifted the man off his feet. He smacked onto his back, lifeless.

It was the final act – the last resounding blast to reverberate around the rocks. Through the ringing in his ears, Mbutu could discern no more fighting. He sat there for a moment, the mother and child sobbing. To the east, the sun had begun to creep over the horizon. The first shafts of daylight were skimming the rim of the corral. There was clicking chatter from around and about him. Someone was shouting down. Their attackers were no more.

The few Nama men remaining checked the bodies of the soldiers. The two Mbutu had shot were most certainly dead. The one up on the rocks, the one with the spear sticking out of him, was still whimpering. A Nama man approached him. He twisted the spear and the man screamed. He casually sought out a rock the size of a cannon ball and wielded it above the man's head. He brought it down. The noise stopped.

And then there was a shriek. The crone, the one who had berated Mbutu on arrival, was waving her arms, signalling across the corral.

There, the white woman and child were huddled together still, and, standing over them, was a fourth soldier. He had his revolver trained on them.

Mbutu yelled at the man: "STOP! NO!"

But he was powerless. The pistol was raised, pointed at the child this time. And then came the agony of the shot.

It happened way too quickly to comprehend but the soldier staggered back, knees bent, shoulders sagging, like a drunk stumbling for the barroom door. He was clutching his eye. Another shot. He collapsed.

In the hands of the mute woman, wrestled from under her skirts, was a tiny, smoking Derringer pistol.

—

The sun was up. The goat started bleating. The Nama dead were laid out, the bodies tended to lovingly by the women. Thwarting the enemy had come at the price of five Nama dead, including Stefaan and Habobe.

The corpses of the four soldiers were dragged down far less tenderly and deposited at the far end of the corral.

Mbutu, Hendrik and a couple of the others went to examine the bodies. They were white men – young white men. Mbutu had been cooped up long enough in Kimberley to recognise the khaki uniforms of the British Army. One of the them – the executioner that the white woman had felled – had been an officer. His epaulettes bore the pips of a second lieutenant. Mbutu thought for a moment of the other lieutenant, the red-haired one, the one responsible for him being here.

Curiously, though they carried badges of rank – the others being two being privates and a lance corporal – Mbutu noticed that none bore any regimental insignia on their tunics. On their shoulders were darker patches of material and rings of thread where badges had been removed. They were bare-headed, without hats. Probably discarded before the assault to minimise their profile.

Mbutu gestured to the remaining Nama men. He could not speak their tongue but there must be words that they understood.

"Horses… *Perde*."

He made a whinnying sound and flapped his hands above his ears. Hendrik translated.

They must move the horses fast. They were evidence. Others would come to look for them. The beasts would also be useful. Transport or meat.

They climbed out of the rocky corral and jogged over. With predators about, the soldiers had taken a risk leaving their steeds there.

They had clearly not intended to linger, their mission an intended short, sharp killing.

But there were *four* horses, not three. Mbutu's miscalculation had had near tragic consequences.

One horse, a bay mare, had been tethered away from the others. Mbutu had missed it.

The British officer. Must not fraternise with his men.

Even the man's peaked cap, had been cast down separately, away from the three slouch hats.

The men let the horses get used to their own smell. They did not panic. They were untied from the branches of the thick thorn scrub and gently led back to the rocks. They could not be taken within, but behind the corral was a depression overhung with acacia. They could be hidden there.

Mbutu noticed a borehole. So that was where the Nama had drawn their water. The horses would be thirsty too. He hoped they did not drain their resources, though they seemed to know which grass to chew on, which leaves to nibble. Moisture came in many forms.

Once secure, they removed the saddlebags and brought them inside. There was another revolver amongst the lieutenant's things, and clips of ammunition for both it and the rifles, which were gathered up.

They were short firearms, smaller than ordinary rifles, intended for use by horsemen – carbines. From the bodies were retrieved four good army knives. Small consolation, but the Nama were now far better armed than they were before.

There were water canteens, enamel mugs, some basic army cooking utensils, tea, biltong, no personal information or identity cards. There were waterproof capes which doubled as groundsheets. Rolls of bedding. There were compasses. There were maps.

The British and their maps.

There was also a dirty piece of linen that looked as if it had been ripped from a petticoat. The white women had not been difficult to stalk. Had they known they were being pursued, Mbutu was sure Hendrik would have covered their tracks.

And there was something else. In each saddlebag was what looked like a piece of sackcloth. Unrolled, the sackcloth became a hood. Each had two round glass eyeholes in brass sockets and a curious red rubber pipe at the mouth – actually two rubber reeds that pinched against each other, giving the impression of a bird's beak.

The Nama recoiled. There was agitated chatter.

Round eyes.

The devil soldiers.

Hendrik pointed to the bodies of the soldiers. They must dispose of them quickly, ahead of their own dead.

They were dragged out beyond the depression. They smelled – not yet of death, but of soldiering, of leather kit, of stale sweat. They smelled of white men, of the white man's food.

The ground was hard to dig. They found flat stones to carve as much of a hollow as they could – no man felt like expending much effort on the dead soldiers' behalf – then lay the men next to each other and covered them with a cairn of stones.

Their boots were of no use to the barefooted Nama. They wondered whether they should keep some of the clothing. Hendrik relayed that is was essential they keep nothing whatsoever. If the bodies were found, there should be nothing that could link their deaths to them. Conceivably, as British soldiers, they could have been ambushed by a party of Boers.

When they returned to the rocks, the fire had been re-lit. Some of the Nama women were cooking. Others were preparing a more fitting burial for their own fallen.

Mbutu went and sat with the white woman and child.

He asked if they were all right. The woman nodded.

"Please, sir," asked the girl.

"What is it, Emily?"

"Will you help me find my father?"

"Your father? I thought he was… I thought he—"

Said Emily: "We don't know."

Chapter Twenty-Three

After leaving another message for the evidently busy Brookman, Finch took the tram to Green Point. He found Atlantic View Drive easily enough. Not far from the stop, it wound up into the hills. As he climbed, the view grew more impressive. The city sprawled before him. Below, the Point itself, formerly grassland, was now a tented city of khaki.

The wind was blowing onshore. Beyond the hum and clatter of the trams, you could hear the barks of drill instructors. In the distance, on the white-flecked bay, sat the anchored grey warships.

Turning inland, before Table Mountain, loomed Signal Hill with its artillery battery, and, between them, the conical hump of Lion's Head.

The streets crawled upwards, doubling back on each other to follow the contours. Atlantic View Drive had a sharp switchback, the reason, he now understood, why Pinkie Coetzee had become disorientated.

With his knee hurting as ever, Finch hobbled up round the bend. The Esperanza guest house was a modest two-storey clapboard affair, set back from the dusty trail behind a small, well-tended rose garden, trimmed by a white picket fence – certainly better tended than the house's paintwork which peeled and cracked.

Finch lifted the catch on the stiff gate and walked up the terracotta path. On the veranda, a young African maid in a headscarf swept the boards with a birch-twig broom.

"Good day, sir," she smiled and gave a slight curtsy.

Give Coetzee credit, he thought. He had hauled Cox's ample body all the way up.

The maid pulled back the fly screen and opened the solid wooden front door. It had a stained glass panel with a romanticised version of a sailing ship – all billowing white sails – set into it. She scurried through to find her master.

On the main drag below, the electric tram clanged lazily along its tracks. A Cape sugarbird flitted around a protea flower winding up the balustrade.

Finch removed his pith helmet and tucked it in the crook of his left arm. He stepped across the threshold. Inside, the hallway was dark and cool. From the sitting room, a carriage clock ticked with exaggerated loudness.

Presently, a woman appeared from the kitchen at the rear, wiping floury hands on her apron, fiddling with the bow behind her back, then wresting it off over her head. She was in her early 40s, Finch guessed, but looked older, her face betraying a life of toil – tanned and lined, her greying hair pulled back in a tight bun, her plain and faded blue dress fastened up to the throat. She was sinewy, her features handsome but unadorned save for a smudge of flour on her cheek. No jewellery except a modest wedding band. Keen hazel eyes fixed him. Guarded.

"Good morning," Finch began. "I was wondering if I might speak with the landlord."

At home he'd paid a thousand house calls, priding himself on his social skills. A military uniform changed everything.

The woman threw a quick glance through the doorway to the sitting room. Above the mantelpiece, hovering over a wooden crucifix, hung a framed lithograph draped with black crepe. A stern-looking man in his Sunday finery gazed back over a full-set beard.

"You can talk to me," replied the woman in the heavy accented English of the Afrikaner.

"Ingo Finch, Royal Army Medical Corps," he announced.

"Du Plessis. Ans Du Plessis."

She eyed him up and down. He extended a hand. She did not take it.

"What can I do for you, Captain...?"

He had not declared his rank but she had determined it.

"...You are not here for a room."

She had determined that too.

The woman barked something guttural over her shoulder, towards the kitchen. He caught the name of the maid, Mathilda.

"You would like tea," she said, a statement more than an offer.

He nodded.

This time her hand met his. The grip was firm, the skin as rough as any Tommy's.

"*Mevrouw* Du Plessis, I am here to enquire—"

"You are here about Major Cox."

He nodded.

"You are part of the enquiry?"

"No, not exactly—"

"A friend?"

Finch could never describe himself as such. It was politic to leave it there.

"We served together. He was my CO… commanding officer. The police thought it would be useful if I gathered the major's things. I can ship them on to wherever they need to go."

He reached into his tunic and brought out the requisition order. It contained a short paragraph, 'To whom it may concern…'

Du Plessis read it. She beckoned Finch through the cool, dark wood hallway into the front parlour. She bade him sit. The room was on the chintzy side, a little cluttered. A potted palm sprouted behind a baby grand piano, the small portraits ranged upon it suggesting it rarely saw much use. The carpet, at the doorway, was threadbare, a sign of regular traffic.

He perched on the scuffed maroon velvet of an antique divan. Du Plessis sat opposite on a high-backed wicker armchair. Only then was she ready to engage him. Her gaze remained intent, cautious.

"The unfortunate Major Cox has caused me great inconvenience," she sniped.

"I'm sure it's been very difficult. I am terribly sorry."

"The police, the questioning, the paperwork, not to mention the loss of rent. And no good for business. Word gets out."

She was honest, thought Finch.

"I'll be frank with you Captain… Doctor…"

More frank?

"…I didn't like Major Cox particularly."

Her description came in staccato bursts.

"He had weaknesses… A good customer, yes… Pleasant enough… He stayed here at my house three, four occasions over the past eight, nine months… But each time, trouble… Even before all *this*…"

She raised her hands in exasperation, meaning the war, his murder, both.

Mathilda entered bearing a tray. She set it upon the low coffee table between them – a pewter teapot, strainer, willow pattern cups and saucers, silver spoons, a cut lemon.

"I say, sorry to be a spoilsport," chirruped Finch. "Would you happen to have any milk?"

Du Plessis rolled her eyes.

"The British and milk. Milk in tea, milk in coffee…"

Mathilda stifled a little chuckle before scuttling off again. The landlady looked up at the picture above the mantelpiece.

"My Louis. We ran a farm. Three hundred head of cattle. Up in the north… on the Orange River. Dead eight years, God rest his soul. Typhoid."

Finch mumbled a further apology. He thought of the farm at Magersfontein and fiddled awkwardly with Cox's wristwatch, now strapped to his own arm and which, in lieu of his own defunct timepiece and his dependency on tram and railway schedules, he had decided to borrow. He hoped that Cox wouldn't have minded.

"*Ach*… God makes his plans," said Du Plessis. "We had no sons. No children. Became too much work. The Karoo. It is harsh country. Sold the place and moved down here. A fresh start."

Finch's milk arrived in a ridiculously large jug. Du Plessis poured the tea. He thought he caught the flicker of an ironic smile.

"You say Cox was in trouble. What do you mean?"

"If you knew him well, you wouldn't be asking such a question. I note you didn't confirm your friendship."

She was sharp, he thought.

"Often back late and drunk. For a married man, he was very fond of female company… the wrong kind of female company. He knew I was aware of what was going on. But he was a charmer. Could talk his way out of anything."

"You could be describing half of the entire British officer corps," quipped Finch. "Not reason enough to get a man killed."

"That was only the half of it," she continued. "He was a gambler. I'm sure of it. The second time he stayed. Was here for a week or so in the Winter. Before the fighting started. Two men turned up looking for him. Luckily for Cox, he wasn't in. These men weren't on a social visit."

Finch sipped his tea – rooibos. He was acquiring a taste for it. He wondered whether he could get it in England.

"A few days afterwards, they came around again. Same thing, no Cox. Wanted to come in and wait for him but I said no. Told them he could be hours. They returned later that night, too late, and I told them so. Cox kept quiet. Checked out first thing."

"You think he owed them money?"

"Who knows. They warned him to 'stay away'."

"Stay away from what?"

She shrugged.

"Anyway, just two days ago, Christmas Eve, another man came knocking at my door. Early morning. You could hear the slosh of water, Cox singing to himself while he was shaving. There was no way for me to pretend that he wasn't in. Cox appeared on the landing in his undershirt with soap on his face and a towel round his shoulders. He looked embarrassed. He said it was all right to let the visitor in."

"The visitor?"

"A gentleman. I do not know his name."

"What happened?"

"Invited him up like a long-lost friend. All smiles. Charm itself. Though it was just for public show."

"How so?"

"Inside there were raised voices. Shouting."

"You heard it?"

"The whole street would have heard it. I banged on the door and warned them I would call the police."

"What were they arguing about?"

"I don't know… Something… Someone…?"

The man had then stormed out of the house, Du Plessis explained. Cox had asked her to tip him off if he showed up again.

"Did he?"

"Yes, about two hours later. He burst right in… right there in the hallway… yelling up the stairs, calling Major Cox a liar. He said he would kill him."

"He threatened he would *kill* Cox?"

She nodded. She shrugged.

"One of my other officer guests, the Hampshires, didn't like his tone. Came down to speak with him. Gave enough time for Cox to run. He climbed out of his window and shinned down the drainpipe. There…"

She turned and pointed out through the rear sash window, beneath the burgundy festoon blind, towards the back garden.

"Disappeared over the back wall in his undershirt. The man—"

"The gent?"

"*Ja*. He burst right in, charged straight through the kitchen and out of the back door. Gave Mathilda a fright. Went over the wall after him."

Finch was leaning forward now, elbows on knees, listening with intent.

"Can you describe the man, the gent?"

"I've told all this to the police."

"Please. Indulge me."

"Why?"

"Because…" he faltered.

"I have told you all that I need to tell. Everything is a matter of record."

He placed his cup and saucer back on the table, a small theatrical gesture while he gathered his thoughts.

"Are you really here to collect his things?" she asked.

"Actually I *am* here to do that. I also thought it would help to have someone here to bat for Cox…"

No, too British, too damn colloquial.

"…to show a face on his behalf."

Her eyes didn't move from his.

"Captain, I have been running this boarding house for eight years. When you let strangers sleep under your roof you become a good judge of character."

She gazed some more – the master fisherman, fisher*woman*, playing him on the line. She gave a light cough and put her hand to her mouth.

"I believe that you are genuine."

"Thank you."

She sipped some tea – the ritual slow, methodical.

"The gentleman…? Top hat. Cane. A rich man. Or one who liked to give the impression of being a rich man. Oh yes. Diamond ring. Very showy. Pin-stripes. Silk cravat. How do you say…? white gaiter on the shoe?"

"Spats?"

"*Ja*. Spats."

"The officer from the Hampshires. He can confirm this?"

"Lieutenant Compton gave evidence to the police. He returned to the Front that afternoon."

So the police have this description?

"Of course. The detective. The Jew—"

"Brookman."

"*Ja*, Brookman. I told him myself when they turned up to remove Cox's body."

You crafty beggar, Brookman. Pinkie Coetzee was merely confirming a description you already held.

"You said there were two men on a previous occasion. They came to warn him off about something?"

"That was a while ago now. Back in, let me think… June, maybe July. One was young, 20s. Decent clothes. Suit. Bowler. Lean. It is hard to remember."

"His face?"

She thought for a moment.

"Sort of long nose is all I can say. How would you say it in English? Sneery. No whiskers."

"And the other?"

"You could not forget him. No. Not at all. A big man. Huge. Like a bear. Older. Dark hair. Clipped beard. Looked strong. Very strong."

"How about Mathilda? Can she add anything? About the gent in particular?"

"You may speak with her if you wish…"

Mathilda was summoned. Finch stood and asked her to take his place on the divan. It was probably the first time she had ever sat in her mistress' front parlour, he guessed. Her discomfort was palpable. It was obvious she believed she was in trouble and he tried to allay her fears. He thought it cruel to ask her to recount the discovery of Cox's body – that would have been recorded in great detail by the police – so he asked her, instead, a few questions about the men chasing Cox.

She corroborated the accounts given by Du Plessis. Finch thanked her sincerely but she couldn't wriggle away fast enough.

He turned back to Du Plessis.

"Was that the last time you saw Cox?"

"No, he returned that night, the 24th. Crept in quietly. Kept the lights off. I was in bed reading. Heard him move around in his room for about ten minutes or so before he slipped out again. Next day. Christmas morning…"

She let out a sigh.

"Well, you know the rest."

Finch absorbed the information. He mulled over the details.

"Did you actually see him that night? Are you sure it was him who came back?"

Her brow furrowed.

"You are the first person to ask me that. Now that you mention it, no. No I didn't… I just assumed."

'Assumed'. Finch could imagine Brookman's reprimand.

"May I see his room?"

Du Plessis set down her teacup and paused. She fixed him again. She had a thespian's sense of timing.

"*Heer Dokter*, let me ask *you* a question."

It seemed good grace to allow her. He flung open his palms and settled back on the divan.

"How long have you been in South Africa?"

"Two-and-a-half, nearly three months."

"My Louis, God rest his soul, could trace his lineage in the Cape back over 200 years. French Huguenots. There have been Dutch here since 1652, Portuguese since the 1480s. There have been Europeans in South Africa longer than they have been in the Americas. For some reason, history has never accorded us the same legitimacy."

"I'm sorry, I don't quite understand—"

"Doctor, you come to my house unannounced. You drink my tea. You are polite. But you poke around. You seem to think that you can just walk in and put everything to right. The British seem very convinced that they can just walk into a stranger's house and put everything to right."

Finch felt a flush of anger.

"Madam, that is dangerous talk."

"Before there were British in my house, there *was* no danger."

He bit his lip. She softened a little.

"Doctor, I love this country. If you've been here even three months, then I believe that you will have begun to love it too. You, me, we are guests in this ancient land. Please to God, let us not rip it apart."

Finch wondered if this wasn't the most sensible thing he'd heard throughout the entire South African crisis.

Now it was his turn. Humility.

"Mevrouw Du Plessis. I thank you for your hospitality and your time. You have been candid with me, I shall be candid with you."

He took her lead and let the pause hang pregnant.

"The truth is, I did not know Cox that well and warmed to him no more than you did. He was a character, make no mistake, and a decent CO on the whole. I had no idea about his life outside active service other than he'd been in South Africa for a year or so, before the war, a regular rather than a volunteer. He was British, yes, but colonial British, a man who had spent much of his career in India. That is where his family reside."

She nodded her understanding.

"Admittedly, it is curiosity that has led me to your door because I still find it strange that a man of his position should have met his end in such a sordid manner. Knowing how the authorities work, I imagine they will have been quite officious and not accorded you or your business any great sympathy. And, yes, too, Inspector Brookman thought I might be of assistance when it came to Cox's personal effects."

He sat forward again.

"But I am also asking these things to spare myself. Most likely, questions will be asked of me by Cox's family, his friends, his loved ones. I feel it is only proper that I am apprised of the facts, if only that I might be judicious with them when it comes to administering soothing words."

Du Plessis stood up and gestured towards the door.

"Please."

Finch followed. She ushered him into the hall, then up the creaking, rickety staircase with its warped steps and unstable, ornate banister. Onto the landing, much brighter thanks to a skylight, faced four doors. She produced a bunch of keys from her skirt pocket and turned it in the lock of the one with a brass number three screwed to it.

There were two rooms within: a small sitting room with a settee, a low table and a chair; beyond that a bedroom, from which the window opened out, with a large bed, a chest of drawers, a washstand and wardrobe. The suite was airy and cool. Quiet. Pleasant.

That said, it had the standard artefacts familiar to the traveller – cheap framed floral prints, a bookshelf with a few dog-eared volumes, the faint smell of mothballs.

She opened the wardrobe for him. There was not much inside. Two khaki shirts hung from wire hangers, a pair of braces. A drawer yielded underwear and socks. By the washstand were toiletries and shaving tackle. Anything of use to the enquiry, Finch guessed, Brookman's men would have removed.

Under the wardrobe was an empty kit bag, a bespoke one, more like a carpet bag.

Finch pulled it out and examined it. He turned it this way and that, pawing at every seam, tugging at the linings.

"Something wrong, Heer Dokter?"

"Cox was a man of surprises," he said.

She shrugged and rolled her eyes.

"Did the police take anything, do you happen to know?"

"Some papers, I think. They were on the desk. There…"

There was nothing on it now bar a blotter and an ink well. In a drawer there were some pencils, a worn guide to Cape Town and a street map. Finch leafed through them. There was nothing of Cox's.

Mathilda was calling up the stairs. He was clearly detaining her mistress.

"Thank you. I have kept you long enough."

"If you wish, I can pack what's left of his things. You can return to collect them. When are you leaving Kaapstad… Cape Town?"

"Tomorrow."

"You are going back to the Front already?"

"Not directly. First I head to Paarl."

"Paarl?"

"Conference. Royal Army Medical Corps. I go up to the Front from there. Due back with my unit on the 29th… But I'm not leaving till the afternoon. I could call on my way if that's convenient. Say two-ish?"

Finch took a last look out of the window. He could see the drainpipe and could imagine portly old Cox huffing his way down it.

"Very good," she said. "Two, you say?"

He didn't answer. Something had caught his eye. Brookman's men weren't as thorough as the inspector would like to think.

The mantelpiece was not quite flush with the wall. In the crack, something had slipped down. It looked like card, or paper.

Finch took out his penknife and inserted it into the gap.

"Do you mind?" he asked.

She shook her head.

Carefully he eased it out.

It was a slightly creased photographic print – not framed, but within a rough white border – a moodily lit portrait of a brassy-looking woman in a tight bustier and fish-net stockings, sitting astride a dining chair that had been turned round the wrong way. She held a cigarette holder in hands that were gloved to the elbow.

He flipped it over. It was signed, '*My darling Lenny, Love Vesta x*'.

"Vesta...?"

'*V*'?

"Some kind of singer or dancer. Some kind of harlot."

He propped it against a candlestick.

She got her door key out, the signal for Finch to leave. He hastened on his way.

"My apologies."

Down in the hallway he fumbled for a shilling and offered it to her.

"Please. For your trouble."

Her hands remained by her side. She nodded at a small glazed earthenware pot on the dresser. It stood next to a large carved wooden statuette of a panting and slightly cross-eyed King Charles spaniel which watched lopsidedly over an assortment of knick-knacks.

"For Mathilda."

Finch deposited the coin. He turned to shake Du Plessis's hand.

"Until tomorrow."

"Tomorrow."

Back outside, the sun was blinding. Once through the gate onto the dusty street, Finch examined Cox's wristwatch again, hoping that he had understood the instructions from his bellboy about which trams went where and at what hour.

By the tram stop, to ease his stiff knee, Finch leaned a hand on a telegraph pole and gave it some cautionary exercise, gently easing his leg back and forth.

He was not a great believer in fate but in this case made an exception. There, posted right in front of him, was a bill for a burlesque review at the Gaiety Theatre. At the top, in bold case, above an assortment of comedians, singers, jugglers and novelty acts were the words 'Vesta Lane'.

Chapter Twenty-Four

The Nama dead were buried within the rocky corral. Again the ground was unyielding, but this time the men were undaunted in their digging. It was an act of catharsis as much as tribute.

Mbutu hacked at the ground with a flat stone. His fingers bled but he did not care.

Though the Nama do not say it, Mbutu you are a curse.

This time the fallen were given separate graves. They were aligned east–west, laid next to each other so that the dead would face the rising sun. The plight of the Nama dictated that things should be done speedily. Already the bodies had been bound in white cloth – excess material ripped from the petticoats of the women's voluminous skirts.

When the bodies had been laid in the shallow cuts, the Nama gathered round. One of the women came forward and recited what sounded, to Mbutu, like a poem. Three or four others took turns in giving a brief eulogy. Hendrik faced his people and uttered a short speech about his friend Stefaan.

"Good man," he intoned to Mbutu afterwards. "Good man."

Then, one of the blind men was led through to the front. He was middle-aged, bearded, dishevelled. He reminded Mbutu, to a degree, of Samuel, the man who had befriended him on the train.

Mbutu, you are a curse.

His appearance was deceptive. The man had the voice of an angel. The song he sang carried no obvious melody or tonal structure but was light, child-like, lyrical. For a moment, Mbutu was lost in memories of the songs sung by the elders in Basutoland.

When the testimonials had been concluded and whatever loose soil there was had been shovelled on top, the graves were again mounded with small rocks, forming cairns. It was to prevent the bodies being eaten by wild animals, he was informed.

While the womenfolk tended to the fire and stirred the broth, the men gathered. There had been much discussion prior to the burial, only a fraction of which Mbutu was privy to.

The gist of it was that while they could survive hiding in the rocks, it was but a temporary arrangement. Certainly they had been right to conceal the horses and dispose of the soldiers' bodies, but it was only a matter of time before others came searching. They could only explain away so much.

Clearly the Nama had to move on. What they needed to know was whether it was now safe to return to their villages and rebuild them or to seek sanctuary elsewhere. Resolution would only come from someone scouting the land round about. There were only seven able-bodied men in total now. It was decided that two would go out into the bush and reconnoitre on horseback.

It did not take long for fingers to be pointed at Mbutu as one of the chosen. He could ride, as they all could. But he had also lived among the white men and knew their ways. He spoke their language. Mbutu objected at first, though saw the logic. In which case, the selection of his riding companion was also obvious – Hendrik. He was the only one with whom Mbutu could converse.

They would take two horses each – two in reserve – plus water, the biltong, the map, a carbine apiece and ammunition. The other rifles and two pistols would remain with the defending Nama.

The men spoke in furious clicks. Hendrik was urged to address Mbutu.

"Soldiers stop… find horses… return… money," he said.

Mbutu asked him to repeat and then understood.

If they ran into a patrol they would claim that they had found the horses. They would say they had set out to return them to their rightful owners, hoping for a reward. It would be a more plausible scenario now that they would be riding with all four animals and with the saddle kit intact – save, of course, for the guns.

"But if they… If take… cap—?"

"Capture? If they capture us?"

Hendrik drew a line across his throat.

"Not from here."

He waved his arms around to indicate their camp.

"We not know."

Mbutu got it: if they were seized, they were to betray nothing of the others.

"But how would the pair of us explain how we came to be here in the desert?" asked Mbutu.

"Like you. Train," said Hendrik. "Train. Jump."

Mbutu asked Hendrik to tell the others that they would be back by sundown. Should they have failed to return, it was fair to assume the worst.

The sun was well up now. They would have to leave immediately. Mbutu took the officer's map from its leather cylindrical holder and unfurled it on the ground. He weighted it with stones at the four corners. The Nama were curious. To them it was a picture, squiggles and lines, not a geographical representation.

It was a one-inch Ordnance Survey map. Mbutu tried his best to explain how it worked, but even he could see that much of the land in these parts had not been surveyed. Great chunks of the Karoo remained blank. Nonetheless, from the position of the railway, he worked out, as best he could, where they were presently situated. They were four or five miles from the tracks, somewhere north-northwest of the Beaufort West junction.

He called the white woman forward. Based on the information that she had given, drawing in the dirt with a stick again, he pointed to the various settlements that lay approximately where she had indicated.

There was one, according to the map, that matched the name the girl had tried to pronounce. This must be it. He pointed.

Mrs Sutton gave no reaction.

He said it. Not Vankalik… *Vankilya*.

This time she nodded.

It lay further to the northwest, about 20 miles away. There were other villages beyond – unnamed, the Nama had no need for them; tiny dots of civilisation that were mere afterthought for the cartographers.

As he sketched them out, there were murmurs of acknowledgement. Mbutu now doubted that he and Hendrik could make it there and back in a day, not in this heat. They would extend their return till sundown tomorrow and camp a night in the bush. They added bedrolls to their kit.

Mbutu and Hendrik were given a bowl of the broth and some water. The horses had been led round, out from the depression.

As they made to leave, the others gathered. Hands reached to touch the arms of the two men, to wish them well.

They turned to climb up the boulders. Mbutu heard Emily call his name. He crouched to her level. She ran and flung her arms round him.

"Please, will you find my father?"

"I cannot promise, but I will try to find out what has happened to him, yes."

She squeezed his neck tight. He thought of his own boy and tears formed in his eyes. He wiped them away before she could see.

—

Within an hour the rocky hump had retreated to a dot. With no cover, the heat was searing. The horses were allowed to amble at their own pace, eating the scant vegetation as they wished. Again they took shelter under quiver trees to sit out the midday sun.

Though Mbutu was an experienced outdoorsman himself, Hendrik had the advantage of local knowledge. He was from a race of people who were at one with this land. The most precious commodity was water. The need for it was accentuated by the dry, salty biltong.

When Mbutu went to take a small drop from his canteen, Hendrik stopped him, grabbing his wrist forcefully. He pointed. There were some bushes nearby with leathery leaves and thick thorns. They bore a green bulbous fruit that looked like a spiky gourd. He picked one, split it in two with his knife then pulped the fibrous membranes within, yielding a few sips of not unpleasant liquid. They picked the rest for use later.

After taking turns for an hour's sleep each, the other on watch with his rifle ready, Mbutu unfurled the map. They should soon emerge – if his estimations were correct – in a dry riverbed leading them approximately west. Nothing would have flowed through the gully, maybe for years, but such things could yield a borehole.

The sun had begun its descent. This time they swapped to the reserve horses. Hendrik had lavished great care on their mounts, leading them to scrub he knew they could eat and feeding them some of the gourds himself. He also ensured they got the best of the shade. The going had been hard for their trusty steeds. They were lean and muscular and clearly well-groomed, well-exercised, but the environment was gruelling enough for even the indigenous wildlife.

Mbutu was not wrong. Soon they were in a gently winding gully with sculpted walls and a stony bottom. It was surer footing for the horses, which seemed to snort with pleasure at the change of terrain. With the sun going down, the blessed relief of shade began to spread in the lee of the banks. And then, in a bend, Hendrik saw it, a small dark impression that looked little more than a rabbit hole.

Hendrik dismounted and walked over brandishing an enamel mug. He lay prone and thrust his arm deep in, reaching around. He came up with a mugful of thin, sandy mud. After dipping a finger in and a cautious taste he offered a handful to the horse he had been riding. It sniffed at it, then turned its head away.

He emptied his mug on the ground and smacked his hands together to wipe off the dirt.

"No good."

Mbutu tried to explain that if they could sieve the mud through cloth, through a shirt, they could easily draw some liquid. Hendrik shook his head. He pointed to the ground around the hole.

"No animals."

There were no footprints. The wildlife had spurned it too.

"Good water… many."

Within half an hour they were back in the bush again. The ground rose slightly and the patchy grass grew thicker. Springbok bounded away in the distance. Every now and then some small unseen creature would scuttle out of their path.

It was an hour from sundown when Mbutu first saw it – what looked like a thin black vertical line, as if a child had taken a pencil to the paling sky. The closer they got they could see that the streak of darkness was smoke.

Chapter Twenty-Five

The Gaiety Theatre downtown bore its name with an ironic grin. Finch felt as though he had walked into a bear pit – a triple-decked heaving mass of khaki where the air reeked of alcohol, sweat and cigarettes. The fug that hung over the stalls, rising up to the gods, was barely penetrable to the houselights.

Finch had procured himself a tuppenny seat though it, too, was something of a misnomer, for all inside the auditorium were standing, even on the balconies, some literally hanging from them, others having scaled the walls to perch on ledges or swing from drapes and light fittings.

The men seemed to form a single organic entity, a heaving mass, whose movement was dictated less by what was happening on the stage but through its communal swerves to avoid the flail of fists or another drunk Tommy nonchalantly relieving himself.

Out front, the raked stage was awash with broken glass, the remnants of the reception reserved for acts that did not meet with the audience's approval. On Finch's entry, a hail of beer bottles was already greeting an unfortunate duo named Max & Pal – a man and his performing poodle, the poor pooch yelping in terror as it abandoned its hoop-jumping to bolt for cover.

The following performers, a juggling/acrobatic troupe, the Flying Niembaums, fared little better. Though, from where Finch stood, their act was of such questionable quality, performing feats you could witness in an average school playground, that he himself was almost inclined to launch a missile of his own.

In the pit beneath the harsh phosphorescent glare of the footlights, the tinny house band struck up an off-key oom-pah introduction for the next Christian to be thrown to the lions. While the conductor looked nervously over his shoulder, the Master of Ceremonies strode out into the spotlight. He was a small man wearing a black dinner jacket. His thick black hair and lustrous moustache seemed to have been borrowed from someone several sizes larger.

"My Lords, ladies and gentlemen," he began, barely audible, "all the way from beautiful Birmingham. One of the finest voices in the Empire. Singing a song made famous by the great Harry Lauder, would you please give a warm Gaiety welcome to Mr Arthur Krebbs."

To a volley of abuse, the safety curtain was winched back and there, standing against a crude painted backdrop of an English country garden with rose bushes, a swing and white trellis, was a portly man dressed in a child's sailor suit, grotesque rouged cheeks, blacked out front teeth and carrying a giant red-and-white swirled wooden lollipop. It was a spectacle so absurd, so incongruous, that for a moment the baying mob was stunned into a hush.

The orchestra picked up the tune and Arthur Krebbs began in a wavering falsetto.

"Two little boys had two little toys," he trilled. "Each had a wooden horse…"

Within an instant, the audience had regained its senses. A barrage of projectiles flew towards the stage and the man tried to shield himself with his oversized confectionery. Professional to the last, he edged off slowly, his face locked in a resolute showbiz rictus.

A bottle of pale ale soon evaded his swatting and glanced off his forehead, sending a jet of blood across the boards. As he staggered off stage right, a black houseboy was dispatched with a mop, his readiness implying such spillages were not an irregular occurrence.

A chant went up, starting slowly from the back, building momentum, then accompanied by handclaps and foot stamps in 2/4 time. The theatre was shaken to its core. Dust rained down from the rafters.

"Ves-*ta*," it went. "Ves-*ta*… Vest-*ta*… Ves-*ta*."

The flustered MC scampered back on, straightening his askew wig. This time he carried a large speaking trumpet. He cast an eye to the wings, was given some kind of assent then nodded to the band leader.

"My Lords, ladies and gentlemen," he boomed. "Back by popular demand… the Queen of the Cape, the sweetheart of South Africa… Please give a warm Gaiety welcome to the one and only…"

He was sounding more like a boxing announcer.

"The delightful…"

Huge cheers.

"The delectable…"

Animal-like baying.

"MISS VESTA LANE!"

The cacophony of wolf-whistles was so loud it distorted the eardrums. And then suddenly there she was, prone, head casually propped on one hand, borne on the outstretched arms of three muscular black men who were stripped to the waist wearing baggy pantaloons and turbans.

They set their mistress down and then stood still, arms folded, like court eunuchs, while she sauntered out before the footlights – curvaceous, dressed in the kind of black basque and high boots that the showgirls wore at Maxim de Paris. Clearly older than her stage persona suggested, Vesta Lane was overly made-up, with unnaturally dyed copper hair pinned in a bun beneath an undersized top hat, fastened at a jaunty angle.

The soldiers didn't care. For those who'd been cooped up in barracks or at sea, or witnessed the carnage at the Front, the sight of female flesh, especially the white expanse extending from the top of Vesta's stockings, against which she was now twitching a riding crop, was enough to bring the house down.

The escorts retreated, Vesta entered into some crude badinage with one soldier she picked on then started up a husky, slightly off-key ditty, full of indiscreet double entendres about her passion for 'riding', slapping her own backside for good measure. She tossed her hat into the crowd, releasing a cascade of her artificially hewed hair, causing yet another scrap to break out.

It was a spectacle, all right, Finch had to concede. He was not sure if Vesta believed in what she was doing or if she were wryly sending up the whole burlesque genre, which, if so, afforded him a sneaking admiration.

No sooner had the show finished than a number of soldiers rushed the stage, locked in combat with the bouncers while Vesta was hustled away. It was the key for the whole auditorium to erupt in one huge communal mêlée. Whistles blew, there were MFPs now forcing their way through to inflict order. Truncheons flailed.

Finch seized his moment. He eased his way down to the front. In the corner was a fire exit. Pushing the metal bar, he found his way into the backstage area that was both unlocked and – in view of the manpower now required front of house – unguarded.

Behind the scenes, it was cramped, poky, dimly lit. He was in a narrow corridor. Up ahead, around the corner, he could hear shouting. Approaching gingerly he put his head round, saw a knot of people pushing and shoving and darted unnoticed into an alcove behind some water pipes.

Through the jostling bodies he could glimpse Vesta Lane's name on the door, emblazoned in lipstick red upon a bright yellow star. Some soldiers, drawn like moths to a flame, were being rebuffed by two men.

Staying military personnel, men trained to fight, was no mean feat. But you wouldn't want to mess with this pair. The first, the younger, was sinewy, muscular, bow-legged, scrawny like a lightweight boxer, and with a long, bent, broken nose to go with it. His suit and bowler gave a veneer of respectability, but there was no mistaking a man of violence.

The other, middle-aged and greying slightly, was an even more impressive sight. Another who looked like he'd stepped out of a ring, but this time from a bout of all-in wrestling. He was huge, a man mountain, maybe 6ft 5ins and weighing what, 20 stone? The thick beard lent him a bruinesque quality.

The duo made light work of the drunken Tommies, who were soon sent packing towards the stage door out to the street. But they were persistent, these admirers. From the opposite direction approached another man.

Finch held his breath, squeezed in tighter. The man passed close enough for Finch to get a whiff of the French cologne and observe that this caller was a civilian, a gentleman. He wore a powder-blue suit of silk cloth, a felt fedora with a maroon velvet band and carried a large bunch of gladioli done up in patterned paper bound with a big pink bow. On his shoes were strapped white spats.

And then Finch saw it, glinting in the muted gas light – on the man's left little finger, a diamond.

The man gave a diplomatic cough and the two heavies turned, then stepped aside. The gent rapped a *rat-tat-a-tat-tat* tattoo with his cane's silver head – in the shape of an eagle – and Finch heard a female voice utter 'Come in', followed by a squeal and a chuckle before the door was closed behind them.

The corridor now seemed painfully quiet. He was sure he would be noticed any second but, mercifully, for a full 15 minutes or so, Finch remained undiscovered while the two bodyguards smoked, discussed their respective fortunes with betting on the nags, the talents of a new and reasonably-priced Chinese prostitute at a bordello known to them both, and the finer points of how to immobilise a man with a single finger applied firmly behind the ear.

When the gent re-emerged, Finch was unable to follow for fear of exposure. Before the man put his hat back on, Finch got a clear look at him – medium height, slim, blue eyes, wavy, sandy hair, clean-shaven. As if some kind of privileged guest, the man was escorted away.

Finch seized his chance. He slipped over to the dressing room, knocked in the same pattern as the man had done previously and smoothed himself down.

The female voice from within called out, 'Ashley?'

He avoided confirming this as fact and waited for the door to be opened. Vesta Lane didn't even look at him, swinging it open, having already turned to pour two generous glasses of Gordon's gin, rattling at the bottles and glasses on her dressing table, splashing into them a token measure of bitter lemon.

The dressing room was cramped. It had a rack of gowns and outfits, a hand-painted chinoiserie floral screen, a cluttered dressing table and mirror with illuminated bulbs around the outside. A striped couch ran along one wall. On a small round table, from a chipped ceramic vase, sprouted the bright spray of gladioli.

Vesta had on a red Japanese kimono, the riding boots had now been replaced by a pair of fluffy pink slippers, her copper-coloured hair, albeit with greying roots, cascading in waves over her shoulders, a black feather boa around her neck. The kimono had a fiery dragon shooting flames across her shoulders. He – probably more likely a *she* – seemed the perfect emblem for her.

Vesta Lane lit herself a cigarette which she held in a long dark-wood holder and turned, brandishing the two glasses. All pleasantry slipped.

"Who the hell are you?"

"Miss Lane. My name is Captain Ingo Finch of the Royal Army Medical Corps…"

"I need a doctor I'll get one myself."

In close-up the pancake make-up seemed vulgar – an orange mask with bright red lipstick extending beyond the natural line of the mouth and thick black Cleopatra mascara.

"I just wanted to let you know how much I enjoyed your show…"

"Get in the queue."

"…and felt it my duty to visit you out of respect for Major Leonard Cox."

The name turned her face to thunder.

"Lenny?"

She sucked hard on the cigarette.

"That bastard."

"Forgive me, I don't think I expressed myself clearly. Respect for Major Leonard Cox… the *late* Major Leonard Cox."

Silence.

Vesta downed her own gin and retreated to the dressing table to start on the second. She sat on her stool, wringing her hands, the upper of her crossed legs jiggling nervously, the fluffy pink slipper wafting in a state of high animation.

"Stupid bloody war."

He spelt it out as tenderly as he could, but it still sounded coarse.

"I'm afraid he was killed right here in Cape Town," he said. "Christmas Eve… Murdered."

She stared off into middle distance and drew again on her cigarette.

"He had it coming!" she snapped.

She stood up, the signal for Finch to leave. Her kimono flapped open revealing the tantalising inches of pale thigh flesh that had driven a thousand Tommies wild. Finch had not enjoyed female company in a while himself. He tried not to look and turned instead to the flowers and saw the handwritten card wedged between the stems and the signed initials "A.K."… Ashley K.

"If I might be so bold, Miss Lane, what exactly do you mean by that remark?"

"What's it to you?"

"I was a colleague of the major's. I wanted—"

She yelled towards the door.

"Bonzo… Steve…!"

"He had a watch… an engraved watch that you—"

"I don't know what the bloody hell you're talking about… Bonzo…! Stevie!"

Finch bade a swift farewell and exited, saw that the coast was still clear and made for the stage door.

Suddenly, from out of nowhere, a man appeared. Finch ran slap bang into him. The man was skinny, wore a silk shirt, had bouffant hair, carried some kind of make-up kit and spoke in a manner that seemed oddly feminine.

"Can I help you?" he lisped.

Behind him, Finch heard an, 'Oi you!' and the two bouncers were after him. Finch pushed silk-shirt aside and hobbled away as fast as he could.

For a big man, the bearlike bodyguard was nimble and soon upon him. He swung a meaty right hook but Finch ducked and the fist collided with the wall, producing a yelp of pain. Such was his size and the narrowness of the corridor, Bonzo the bear-man − Finch assumed he was Bonzo − had inadvertently blocked the way for his more sprightly colleague.

"Don't you ever fucking come back here again!" the young one was shouting from behind the man-dam as Finch slipped out into the crowded street.

"Bitch," added silk-shirt.

The bear, nursing his hand, stumbled after Finch, adding for good measure up the alleyway: "You show your face again and you're fucking well dead."

−

Finch's growing confidence with the city's public transportation enabled him to hop two trams back to Adderley Street and limp his way to the police station on Wale.

Unsurprisingly given the hour, Brookman was not present, but Finch left a lengthy note with the desk sergeant.

It was gone midnight, but the streets were still busy. Finch made his way back to the Belvedere feeling smugly satisfied with his amateur sleuthing.

In the lobby he nodded goodnight to the late-shift desk boy and climbed the stairs. He had reached the landing when he heard a bump from within his own room. There could be no mistake about its provenance.

Conscious that it was way too late for the maid to be turning down his bed, Finch proceeded with caution, flipping the safety strap off his holster. Unfortunately, the creaking floorboards betrayed his advent. There were a couple of thuds and the clang of what sounded like someone scuttling down the fire escape.

Slowly, with his Webley service revolver raised, Finch pushed at the door. It swung open. As he struck a match to light the lamp, he saw that the room had been ransacked, the sash window wide open, its wooden shutters swinging in the night breeze. He hurried to it, leaned out and thought he could see the shape of a man running down the street.

He yelled: "Stop!" but it was pointless.

Turning back he saw the intruder's handiwork. His clothes had been strewn over the floor. The drawers from the dresser were hanging out, the wardrobe doors flapped open. On the bed was Cox's cardboard box, upturned and with the Major's belongings similarly scattered.

He checked through them. Whoever it was had helped themselves to the ten shillings from Cox's wallet, which lay unfastened on the bed blanket, and Finch's own useless pocket watch, which he had left on the bedside table. But that was it.

Finch had nothing more of value in the room. His own wallet was on his person. Any papers he didn't need to hand, he had deposited in the hotel safe. Everything else, at first glance, appeared to be present.

Almost. Finch sat on his bed, sighed and reached for his beloved Talisker.

They had taken his bloody whisky.

There was a knock on the door – the bellboy, wanting to know if everything was all right.

Chapter Twenty-Six

It was the horses that reacted first. As the humps of the huts within the kraal became defined, the animals whinnied and scuffed. It was the smell – not the obvious aroma of burning, but of the sickly, fetid one masked by it. Of rotting. Rotting flesh.

Mbutu and Hendrik dismounted and tethered the horses to a lone baobab. Mbutu fanned his bush hat in front of his face then wrestled his red spotted kerchief up from around his neck. Hendrik rummaged in the saddle bags and found the yellow rag that had been used to wrap the officer's pistol. He pressed it over his nostrils. Each man grabbed his carbine.

They advanced, creeping forward slow and low. Smoke was wafting on the gentle breeze, the thin pall that they had seen at a distance was rising from the embers of a large wooden structure to one end of the village of Vankilya. In the dry heat and with a light wind, a fire could keep burning for days.

Their ears became attuned to an ambient hum – flies. There were black clouds massed over several mounds strewn.

They were soon upon the first heap. The insects buzzing over it were worked up into such a frenzy that the arrival of the two interlopers resulted in them swarming around them too. Mbutu and Hendrik flapped at them.

Beneath the cloud were the remnants of a cow, the thin emaciated cattle of the veld that were the lifeblood of the natives. It was now just a deflated hide draped over bones. The eyes, lips and tongue had been devoured. Rancid blue/grey entrails spewed from its belly. As they moved on, black masses were feasting on beasts in similar states of ruination.

In the desert, it was a wonder that no carnivore had binged upon the flesh. But the reason was the same as the one that had prevented any animal from drinking fetid water.

"*Vleis*. Meat," said Hendrik. "No good."

Satisfied that there was no one about they moved on. They counted 19 dwellings within the kraal – *haru oms*, the basic round huts fashioned from a rush-like matting.

Unlike the larger buildings, the native dwellings had not been burnt or ransacked, but left abandoned. All that remained were the meagre possessions of the Nama people – wooden cooking and household utensils, spears, rudimentary bedding and the odd trinket, beads, hand-carved figurines for the children. Although again, flies had made swift work of any uncovered foodstuffs, largely dried meat and seed cakes. Whoever was here had left in a hurry.

The huts were gathered in a rough circle about 20 yards in diameter. In the communal space the dirt had been scuffed and kicked up furiously.

Hendrik knelt down. He called Mbutu over and pointed. It was the impression of a boot, one with hobnails. There were plenty more. There had been soldiers here without question.

Mbutu saw something glint in the dust and picked it up. He handled in his palm the spent casing of a bullet. He removed his carbine and detached the magazine. The bullet was of the same calibre, from the same type of weapon.

A cattle pen fashioned from branches had had its entrance left open, explaining why the cows had wandered. Nearby was a well, a much deeper, wider borehole. Next to it was an iron hand pump and, behind, a covered wooden water tank raised up on a latticed support structure. The water source must have been bountiful or it would not have sustained a permanent settlement.

Mbutu activated the pump. After several rusty cranks some muddy brown liquid choked out into the trough then became more fluid, running clear, smelling fresh.

Hendrik tasted it and decreed it to be drinkable. They each took a turn slaking their thirst then gleefully pumped the water over each other's heads.

Near the well was a meagre vegetable patch. It had had a basic irrigation system rigged up, channelling water from the tank, following the rows of root vegetables.

To the eastern end of the village were three wooden structures that were still smouldering, the timbers reduced to blackened, charred embers.

The first, it appeared, had been a low, simple hall, its roof beams collapsed. There had been homemade benches. There was a blackened book flapping in the dirt – *Cobham's Flora of Southern Africa*. Given the barren wilderness that surrounded them, it was a largely redundant text. But the zeal of a missionary was a force of nature, Mbutu recognised. The building, its walls a whitewashed wattle and daub, had been a schoolhouse.

The second one was most likely a home, a bungalow. There were some metal kitchen utensils and a bathtub that had survived the flames. There was a low wooden fence and a rudimentary garden.

The English and their gardens.

Though there was not much left of it, it was obvious what the third and largest building was. It was raised up on a higher platform and faced east–west.

Like the graves of the Nama.

It had had steps leading up to its double doors.

Poor Emily. Is this where you hid?

If her father, Missionary Sutton, had remained under the church floorboards, there is no way he could have survived the inferno. Mbutu picked up a stick and began poking about in the embers. The heat was still strong. There was still the glow of orange and silver/white flecks amid the charred wood. It was impossible to tell if there was a body in there.

Mbutu scuffed at something in the dirt – a large brass crucifix.

A light gust blew in and made the embers glow angrily, fanning them like a bellows. Ash swirled in the air. It stung Mbutu's eyes. He turned his back.

It was then that he saw it. The wind had stroked some of the soot away. It was a picture… an engraving… an ornate carved elephant, tusks proud, trunk raised, trumpeting against a backdrop of palm trees. It had been etched into a silver panel, now lying forlornly in the cinders. He went to brush the ashes away, burnt his fingers and cursed. The alert Hendrik raised his carbine.

Mbutu signalled that it was okay. He removed his shirt, bound it round his right hand and brushed at the panel again. A few wipes revealed a beaded border, a surround. The metalwork was exquisite. It was a rendering of Africa, but not the Africa of these parts.

He jabbed around it with the stick, removing dirt and ash. He thought at first it was a tray. But no, it was the lid of a box.

Further digging revealed a hinged handle. With his wrapped hand he pulled hard. It was wedged under a timber. He tried again, freed the box and fell on his backside.

Its metal had been dulled but there was no mistaking it was made from silver. And the art wasn't African at all. The elephant looked different. It had small ears, a domed head. Conclusively, riding on its back was a plump, mustachioed man in a high-collared jacket. On his head was a turban with a feather and a jewel in it.

The British had soldiers who dressed as such. There were similar men who had worked for the mining administration in Kimberley, their wives and daughters dressed in brightly coloured silk. From across the sea… From India.

The box was about 18 inches long, 12 across and six deep. It had a lock but no key and a lid attached by two elaborate hinges.

Hendrik returned with a jug half filled with well water and made the box hiss. He fiddled at the keyhole with his knife but to no avail. Mbutu took a turn. He tried to unscrew the hinges but the blade of the knife was too broad.

Shooting the lock off was out of the question. Though they were sure there was no one around for miles, the sound would carry. Plus they could not afford to waste the ammunition.

They resorted to a more primitive method. Hendrik stood over it and hammered at it with the butt of his rifle. On the third blow the lid sheared off and papers fluttered in the breeze. Mbutu ran after them, stamping at them with his feet.

The two men then hunched over the box. The interior was lined with worn green velvet. Inside were more papers, letters largely, and a handwritten book, a journal of some sorts. The book was of cheap material, bound in card and frayed blue linen, the jottings hand-written in a spidery scrawl on feinted paper.

To Hendrik, who had never written a word, they were simply objects of bemusement, the white man's affectation. To Mbutu they were otherwise. He leafed through them. It was official correspondence mainly – a permit from the Cape Government allowing the missionary to ply his trade; a receipt for the bathtub; some correspondence with a vicar in Port Elizabeth, an ongoing debate over liturgical interpretation.

The English. Not to worship God, but how to worship God.

Mbutu stuffed everything back in the box. He would read it thoroughly at their next rest. He put his shirt back on and crammed the box into a saddlebag. The lid no longer fit securely. A square piece of card fluttered down.

It had been inserted between the pages of the journal. It was a photograph of a man with huge mutton chop sideburns in a cleric's dog collar. He was standing stiff and uncomfortable with his hand resting upon the shoulder of his seated wife. She seemed much younger than him, not unattractive. A baby girl bedecked in flowing lace was cradled in her arms. She was slightly blurred, out of focus, amusingly unable to sit still during the film's long exposure.

It was the mute woman and Emily. On the reverse was handwritten, 'Lichfield, March 20th, 1893'. Not yet seven years ago.

They wandered further around the village. There were more bullet casings and, here and there, splashes of blood. More flies.

They tracked the footprints as best they could. A group of men had come from approximately the direction they had, some by foot. Either side of the marks were hoof-prints which continued out of the village to the western side with further activity around a low mound of freshly dug earth.

Both men had witnessed enough death to know what this was. At about 20ft long and 6ft wide, it amounted to a roughly-hewn trench with the desert soil shovelled back on top. Around the mound the ground was spattered with white powder.

Mbutu recognised it from the disposal of corpses after an outbreak of lung sickness in the mine camps of Kimberley – quicklime. They were staring at a mass grave.

"Devil soldiers," growled Hendrik. "Devil soldiers."

Suddenly, with a panicked whinny, one of the horses reared up.

Hendrik ran. It happened too fast for Mbutu to register, but in a flash, as soon as he reached the baobab, Hendrik had gone to ground his arm rising up and slashing down, the sun glinting on the blade of a knife. A moment later he stood. Hanging from the hand of his outstretched arm, almost down to the ground, was the limp carcass of a snake. Mbutu approached gingerly. It was a light copper colour, almost yellow. In the dirt, Hendrik scuffed his foot toward the severed, hooded head of a Cape Cobra.

He tossed the body aside and made a claw like gesture with the first and second fingers of his right hand, imitating fangs.

"Bite… Kill."

It was a signal to leave. The light was thinning. They should make as much headway as they could then find a place to camp. The snake made Mbutu nervous about sleeping out in the open.

As they rounded the horses, Hendrik kicked something and it skittered along the ground. He grumbled and rubbed his toe.

Mbutu bent over the object. It was cylindrical, like a can, the kind the British kept their condensed milk in. Its circumference about the same size as the circle made by touching together the thumbs and forefingers of two hands, no more than about ten inches in height and painted an olive green. The lid had been sheared off, the edge jagged. It was empty but still had a noxious smell from within, sulphurous, like eggs.

Stencilled on its side were symbols and combinations of numbers and letters that Mbutu did not understand. Above them was a black skull and crossbones.

–

Heading northwest they carried on riding towards the cluster of tiny settlements from whence Hendrik and his people had come. They would check them at first light.

Half an hour out of the village they stopped to rest the horses.

They sheltered in the late evening shade of some smooth reddish rocks. Mbutu took the opportunity to leaf through the journal.

As he pored over the insufferably neat, insufferably elaborate longhand, he was able to determine certain information.

Missionary Sutton had been posted to Vankilya by a Dean Ephraim Newbold of the Christian Friendship Society, which ran the Cape regional missions from a provincial headquarters near Paarl, way over towards Cape Town.

Moving onward, Mbutu found further references to Dean Newbold, a man whom Sutton clearly held in high regard – the official communiques being, mercifully, typed.

As the war had proceeded, Newbold had been encouraging his missionaries to usher displaced natives to a settlement – a 'refugee encampment' – that Newbold was himself administering. The Christian Friendship Society had an arrangement with both the Cape Railways and the British Army to use spare rolling stock to move people south to Paarl, provided they could get first to Beaufort West.

Beaufort West. That place again.

Sutton being Sutton – the man, it was evident, had a stubborn survivalist streak – he had declined the invitation. The war had not touched that part of the Karoo he had explained in his final epistle. And even if it did, he had unswerving faith in the word of Jesus Christ to dull the blade of the sharpest sword.

Mbutu tried to explain all this to Hendrik. He indicated that he comprehended – but Mbutu was not wholly convinced.

When the temperature had dropped, the men remounted and rode on. The other Nama villages were only a few miles distant but, as Hendrik explained, lay across a valley of some sort.

Despite his time in the Karoo, Mbutu was simply not prepared for what lay ahead. As they sauntered along, Hendrik, seemingly noting some local landmark – a rock, a bush, Mbutu wasn't sure – raised a hand and bade Mbutu stop.

Hendrik tethered his two horses to some hardy acacia, and walked forward. He stopped, turned and beckoned for Mbutu to follow. Mbutu did so, rather too casually for Hendrik, who shot out an arm across his chest to make him halt.

Though, at ground level, the same terrain seemed to continue rolling on towards the horizon, what now lay before them, only inches from their feet was a chasm maybe a hundred yards across and some several hundred feet deep – remnants of an ancient river that had carved its way through the rock, hewing stratified walls of red and brown.

They shielded their eyes against the setting sun glaring directly at them. The dying rays kissed the land to a pinkish gold. To Mbutu it was beautiful. Below them an eagle swooped, circling something way down in the shadows.

He asked Hendrik how long it would take to cross the gorge. To reach the villages.

"Not here," he replied. "Cross… up…"

He pointed north.

"Many hours. Half day."

There was a sudden whip, a *zing* and puff of dirt that exploded from the rock to Hendrik's right. It was followed by a crack that reverberated around the ravine like a thunderclap.

Mbutu grabbed Hendrik by the arm and pulled him down behind a rock. He shielded his eyes and tried to see. On the other side, across the gap, someone was standing with the setting sun strategically behind them.

Moving round the rock and squinting through the gaps in his fingers, Mbutu could see two soldiers with rifles and another, probably an officer, with binoculars pointed right at them.

Though he and Hendrik were in cover now, the horses, some yards behind them, were out in the open. If the soldiers felled the horses...

They do not want to kill the horses. They want to recover the horses.

Crack-*zing*. Another shot. Close. Another puff of dirt.

"Quick," cried Mbutu.

He manhandled Hendrik into a depression and they scuffed along on their bellies to the bigger outcrop of smooth pink rocks further back.

They could hold out till nightfall, but that would gain the soldiers a precious hour or two. By Hendrik's reckoning it would take some hours to head up-valley and cross, but that was a vague estimate. Military men were resourceful. Could they climb straight down into the ravine and up? They may already have men over on this side. They had to get out of there. NOW.

Their pre-conceived cover-story about returning the horses was clearly naive. The men of the raiding party would have been missing for long enough. That black men were now riding their horses would simply have confirmed their deaths as fact.

They had the soldiers' horses but they also had their guns.

Mbutu signalled to Hendrik. They must get to the horses, reach for the saddles and the sheathed carbines.

Crack-*zing*. Crack-*zing*.

As long as they were behind the precious horses they were safe, shielded.

They scurried low along the ground as shots whistled over their heads. They pulled the rifles free and on a nod of understanding, Hendrik fired a shot across the gorge, which made the horses buck. It was nowhere near its mark but showed that they meant business.

Mbutu need to untether the reins of all four steeds from the acacia bush. They exchanged another glance. They knew they must preserve their ammunition. But – *bang!* – a covering shot was vital.

Once the horses had been freed, they kept within their equine shield, walking them into the lee of the big round rocks.

It could not be determined with absolute certainty but, with the light almost gone, they were convinced enough that there were no soldiers on their side of the ravine. They mounted their horses, then rode for their lives.

Chapter Twenty-Seven

Finch rose early. Feeling that his stiff knee might benefit from stretching, he took a tram to the Company's Garden in view of a gentle stroll – having first, as had been requested by the police, lodged a note with hotel reception informing of his whereabouts.

It was set to be a glorious day, already warming. The birds were in full song. Finch wandered the straight geometric paths between the rows of shrubs set before the great white edifice of the Parliament building. Save for a pair of middle-aged women walking arm in arm, to whom he doffed his hat, Finch had the place to himself.

The garden had been founded by the Dutch East India Company in the days when Cape Town – *Kaapstad* – was a way station on the long haul to Batavia. Back then, this patch of fertile ground, watered by canals of fresh water running from the slopes of Table Mountain, was the Company's lifeblood, the reason Jan Van Riebeeck had been sent to fortify this distant southern outpost.

Finch stared in wonder at a small pear tree. It had been planted in 1652, the year Van Riebeeck landed, its plump green fruit still ripening nicely. The Portuguese explorer Bartolomeu Dias had rounded the Cape in 1488, a plaque reminded. By comparison, Columbus was a New World arriviste.

A cough interrupted Finch's drift.

"Good morning, Captain."

It was Brookman, extremely chipper.

Finch didn't know whether his advent was a good or a bad thing.

"Good morning, Inspector."

Brookman stood beside him, gazing at the tree. Finch remembered something he had learned from a psychologist – women faced each other when talking, men conversed while contemplating some mutual object of fascination. Probably the reason that sporting events were so popular.

"I see you have found the forbidden fruit, centrepiece of our little Eden."

"Makes you think," said Finch.

"Certainly does, sir. Certainly does," Brookman ventured. "Just wanted to say thank you for the information you passed to us last night."

Finch nodded.

"Of course, ordinarily, I'd have slapped your wrist for mounting your own little freelance operation," he said, his face now twisting into something of a mock frown. "But, given the circumstances, I can only add, 'Well done.'"

Finch breathed a sigh of relief.

"You'll be able to find him, Fancy Dan… Ashley K?"

Brookman was subtly leading Finch back towards the street.

"In custody as we speak."

Finch discreetly checked Cox's watch. It was not yet nine o'clock.

"Fast work."

"All down to you, my friend."

Finch grinned. Smug satisfaction. And *friend*?

–

Half an hour later, Finch found himself at the police station again, his presence required to confirm another identity, not of Cox this time, but of the man responsible for his passing. In the cab, Brookman ran through the particulars – the subject's name was Ashley Kilfoyle; he had arrived in the Cape two years ago from Portadown, Ireland; he was a gentleman of means, newly acquired, but a loner – no family, no wife, no sweetheart. His wealth had come from speculation on the precious metals markets.

Kilfoyle owned a villa in Hout Bay but found that it made him even lonelier and thus spent most of his time at his city apartment not far from the waterfront, walking distance from the Officers' Club and the other gentlemen's attractions. He had been arrested there at dawn. A search of his apartment revealed Cox's missing glove, which had been left lying casually on a coffee table, and a crocodile skin notebook which matched the stationery given to the cabbie. It had had a page ripped from it with a corresponding tear along its length.

Mrs Ans Du Plessis had already been summoned to provide witness, given her previous testimony as to a man matching Kilfoyle's description turning up to argue with Cox at her guest house. So now, explained Brookman, if Finch could just confirm Kilfoyle as the man he had seen at the theatre last night, the law would take its course.

On the way, Finch told Brookman about the intruder in his own room. Brookman listened attentively but suspected nothing sinister. Given the items that had been taken – the pocket watch, the money, the whisky – it could be dismissed as a burglary. The city had gone crime-crazy, he reminded. Never had this much Old World money poured into this particular bit of the New. Policing was stretched and the thieves knew it.

Unfortunately, the Belvedere was a budget hostelry. Such things could be expected in an establishment populated by transients. He hadn't wanted to alarm Finch, but it was the Belvedere's third break-in in as many weeks.

"There's one thing I don't get," said Finch. "Why take the money from the wallet and not the wallet itself? Seems rather… I don't know, fussy?"

"Petty cash has no trace, unlike a piece of someone's personal and identifiable leather."

As they approached the police station, a man exited and stopped to hold the door open. He wore a smart, beige double-breasted suit and a Panama hat and had a clipped brown moustache set in a kindly pink, slightly puppy-fat face. Green eyes twinkled. Finch would have put his age somewhere around the same as his own.

"Why thank you, good sir," trilled Brookman, happiness personified now that he had got his killer – *and* beaten the Military Foot Police to the punch.

"Good morning, Inspector."

"Allow me to introduce Captain Ingo Finch of the Royal Army Medical Corps," Brookman offered.

"Ah, Captain," the man sighed. "Delighted to make your acquaintance."

He noted Finch's bemusement.

"Rideau," he added. "Albert Rideau."

In his head, from the card, Finch had assumed 'Albert' to be pronounced the French way – *Al*-behr. But he was wrong.

Gloves were clearly the garment of the hour, for when Rideau extended his hand to shake, he kept his fine, black velvet ones on.

"Forgive me, an accident," he apologised.

"And please forgive me, Mr Rideau, for not getting back to you. The last 48 hours have been something of a whirl."

"Quite, quite," concurred Rideau, staring at the ground, shaking his head, his tone turned mournful. "Terrible business. Truly terrible. Beggars belief."

"Mr Rideau was an old associate of Major Cox's," explained Brookman.

"India," Rideau added. "Fellow spearman. Eleven years. Bought up my commission and came to the Cape. Business opportunity. Tinned fruit. Lo and behold our Lenny gets a posting, we rekindle our friendship. And then… *this*…"

Though Finch hated to admit it – how subtle his institutionalisation – civilians were becoming objects of mistrust. That Rideau had once worn khaki put him at ease.

Rideau perked up again.

"But listen, I hear you've been very good to old Coxie, tidying up his affairs and whatnot. The least I can do is buy you lunch."

"That's very kind of you. But really, I couldn't. Plus, I'm rather—"

"Nonsense. Any friend of Cox's…"

The 'friend' thing again.

"I'm afraid, I'm being shipped north again this afternoon."

"Already? What time's your train?"

Rideau was persistent, he'd give him that. Finch unfolded a scrap of paper from his pocket on which was scrawled, in pencil, various travel details.

"4.07… But I have to check out of my hotel and also have an errand to run. To be perfectly honest—"

Rideau was already on his way up the pavement to commandeer the cab they'd just vacated.

"Then we'll dine early. Wherever you need to be, whatever time, have you there in a jiffy…"

Resistance was futile.

"…What say half past eleven, La Rochelle? Unless the inspector…?"

The detective waved a hand, indicating that he would not need to keep Finch for long.

"La Rochelle's not to be sniffed at," Brookman whispered to him.

"Very good, Mr Rideau. Thank you."

Rideau climbed up over the running board, the cabbie twitched his whip and the horse began clopping off. Rideau leaned out over the side.

"Please," he shouted. "*Albert.*"

Brookman's office was its usual cramped, dingy self. The paperwork which had seemed more than enough a couple of days ago, now towered in piles on his desk, the table and the windowsill.

The inspector rummaged for an ashtray, they took seats and the ritual of smoking began. No sooner had they lit up than there was a knock on the door – Krajicek. He bid them good morning and bustled over to hand Brookman a typed document, positively beaming.

"Just as we thought," he trilled while the detective scanned the details. "Major Cox had consumed enough alcohol to have felled an elephant, but he was killed, as we suggested, by a combination of factors. There was the oral administration of a massive overdose of a liquid opiate, almost certainly laudanum. But trauma inside the throat, vomit and the flooding of the lungs, confirm that the poisoning was compounded by suffocation due to a large foreign body blocking the airway – the handkerchief. In short, if Cox wasn't already unconscious, the drug would have rendered him so, allowing the killer to stifle him with ease."

Finch nodded a 'thank you'.

"Most intriguing," Krajicek chirruped, rubbing his hands with what almost seemed glee.

Krajicek scurried off. Brookman got up and indicated for Finch to follow him across the corridor. This time they did not enter the interview room, the one where Pinkie Coetzee had been held, but went through a door next to it into a narrow cramped, darkened space. Along one wall was a window.

The other side of the glass, seated the same side of a worn table, with two empty chairs opposite, were two men. They did not look up. It was a two-way mirror. Brookman put his finger to his lips.

The first man, Finch knew, was Ashley Kilfoyle, dressed in another smart suit, this time a cream linen number. His wrists were cuffed. He still wore the ostentatious white spats. Without his hat, with his wavy, sandy hair on display, he looked younger than Finch remembered, but it was, without question, the same man.

The other was a bald, stern-looking fellow in pinstripes, leafing through some documents.

"Legal counsel," whispered Brookman.

He let Finch observe for a moment.

"So?" the inspector asked.

Finch nodded.

"That's him."

"Absolutely certain? You'd swear to it?"

"Absolutely."

Brookman made for the door. Finch followed. Brookman put his hand up to stop him.

He kept his voice low.

"I shouldn't really do this, but I think you deserve to see what's about to happen. But please, not a sound."

Finch nodded again.

"And not a single word to anyone."

Finch indicated that he understood.

Seconds later, Brookman was the other side of the glass with his trusty corporal, Pienaar, in tow.

Above the glass was a grille. The sound was reasonably clear. The solicitor's name was De Villiers, Finch learned, clearly an expensive brief and one who preferred that his client said absolutely nothing. He was fussing over the technicalities of Kilfoyle's apprehension and whether the arrest was legitimate.

Brookman paid little regard to the overture.

"You know I've just come from a meeting with a colleague of Cox's," he said, directly to the suspect. "Another brave man putting his life on the line, while others swan around, drinking, whoring… murdering."

"I would ask you to refrain from making unsubstantiated allegations, Detective," interrupted De Villiers. "Opinion has nothing to do with this. We are to keep to the points of law."

Brookman came round the table and began walking up and down behind the suspect.

"For a soldier in a war to meet such an ignoble end is a cruel thing. It will be even harder for Cox's wife and children to stomach."

"Please, Detective!" blurted De Villiers. "My client is here to assist with your enquiry."

To Brookman, the lawyer was a ghost. Finch knew it all to be part of the theatre of interrogation. Kilfoyle, meanwhile, stared straight ahead. He fiddled with the diamond ring on his little finger and appeared to be whistling silently to himself. Given his circumstances, it seemed a questionable tactic.

The lawyer was not done.

"I also request that, as my client's agent in this interview—"

"'*Interview*'?" scoffed Brookman.

"...that you address all questions to me."

Kilfoyle, seated to the right of his representative, reached out a hand and touched De Villiers' forearm.

"Really, it's fine," he said, his voice tired, bored.

"Mr Kilfoyle," urged the lawyer. "It would be prudent—"

"The man is just doing his job."

He looked up at Brookman, a haughtiness to his tone, as if this were just some irritable inconvenience.

"Detective... Inspector? Please, ask me your questions and I will do my best to answer them."

He had wrong-footed Brookman; his lawyer, too, who exhaled a sigh of exasperation. Brookman scraped out a chair, sat down opposite his suspect and stared him in the eye.

"Very well," he said. "Let's get it out of the way. In the early hours of December 25th, the body of Major Leonard Cox was discovered on the stoep of the Esperanza Guest House on Atlantic View Drive. His death had been brought about under suspicious circumstances. So, I am asking you—"

The lawyer cut in. Kilfoyle sneered defiantly.

"Mr Kilfoyle, you have not been charged. You are not obliged to answer."

This time it was Brookman who did the wrong-footing.

"Kilfoyle," he continued. "Did you *like* Major Cox?"

"*Like?* Good God, no. I despised the man—"

The lawyer tried to stop his client but it was in vain.

"I'm sure even the most amateur policing will reveal that we had argued in public on more than one occasion."

Brookman checked his notes.

"You visited him at his guest house on the morning of the 24th. The landlady heard you threaten to kill him."

"I was probably not the first that day."

"This is no time for flippancy, Kilfoyle."

"*Mr* Kilfoyle," corrected De Villiers.

"We have a cabbie who can place you at the hansom cab rank and is witness to you helping Cox on board. Your handwriting matches that of the address that had been written. It was inscribed on a piece of paper ripped from your very own notebook."

Brookman slapped both items down on the table, right in front of him.

"Circumstantial evidence," blurted De Villiers.

"I hear both you and Cox had become pretty cosy with a certain music hall performer."

Kilfoyle affected a theatrical voice.

"'The face that launched a thousand ships and burnt the topless towers of Ilium?'"

"Beg your pardon."

"Helen of Troy... Doctor Faustus."

Brookman stared blankly.

"Kit Marlowe...?" Kilfoyle offered, faux helpful.

"Don't play smart with me," Brookman snapped. "You and Cox were seen gambling in recent weeks, playing cards. Did he owe you money?"

"He now owes me a cab fare plus generous gratuity."

"Don't push me, Kilfoyle—"

"*Mr* Kilfoyle..." chipped in De Villiers again.

"The glove. How do you explain the presence of Cox's glove in your own flat."

"I've already told your estimable officers. I picked it up. He'd dropped it. I'd intended to return it. It's certainly no basis for an accusation of taking a man's life. Or are you going to arrest me for theft? I'd be pretty bad at it. No self-respecting thief takes a single glove."

Brookman was not running this show. Not at all.

"I'm tired," yawned Kilfoyle, "I should like to lie down."

In a flash, Brookman had kicked the chair from under him. Kilfoyle landed on his back.

"Ashley Reginald Kilfoyle, I hereby charge you with the murder of Major Leonard Armstrong St John Cox."

He turned to Pienaar.

"Corporal..."

Pienaar let in two waiting constables. They made swift work of scooping Kilfoyle from the floor and escorting him from the room.

"I'll see you lose your job over this," yelped De Villiers.

Brookman ignored him.

Chapter Twenty-Eight

At the insistence of Mbutu, they turned their horses north. It would mean wasting precious energy travelling in the wrong direction but there was hope that, should the soldiers pursue them, they would be leading them astray.

After about a mile-and-a-half they came to another depression, a dry riverbed similar to the one they had traversed previously. In the orange glow of twilight, they selected the two fittest horses and took them to one side.

Hendrik watched as Mbutu removed his shirt and bound it round the front right hoof of the first horse. Mbutu used his undershirt round the next hoof, his trousers and a ripped piece of bedroll round each at the rear two.

He mimed out to Hendrik his plan, that these horses must not be leave hoof prints. Hendrik understood and began binding the legs of the second horse.

Once done, Mbutu pointed the two weaker horses northward and whacked them each sharply on the rump. They galloped off into the gloom, continuing the false trail.

Mbutu and Hendrik led the remaining two softly across the riverbed. They headed for a cluster of sweet thorn.

A fire was out of the question, though the lack of one would bring the danger of wild animals. They would have to remain alert.

They took turns on watch, carbines at the ready. With only two horses now it would be hard going.

The sleep was fitful. In the almost oppressive silence, predators could easily be heard, shuffling around, the odd growl in the distance. The horses were uneasy and in need of constant soothing.

Creatures, we depend on you. Please do not let us down.

Come the first rays of the sun they were on their way. It was hotter than the previous day and, throughout the morning, the horses suffered greatly.

They were forced to ride while looking back over their shoulders continually, but, mercifully, no pursuers emerged from the shimmering haze.

By mid-morning they were forced to rest – a baobab tree, more rocks. In what shade they could find there was better chance of sleep than at night-time. As before, they took turns on watch, Hendrik first.

For Mbutu, the sleep was light, a mélange of dreams and recollections and anguished thoughts. He had not had any meaningful rest since he left Kimberley.

I will get back there.

He thought of Beaufort West and of pushing his way through the gangs of eager black volunteers to take his place on the train north, and of the Boer besiegers being swept away.

A scream.

Hendrik!

Instinctively he reached for his carbine and crept low to his companion who was sitting with his back against a rock, clawing frantically at his shirt collar.

Mbutu scanned the land, assuming, at first, that he had been shot. But there had been no crack of a rifle. There was not a soul, not a creature to be glimpsed.

No. Please let it not be so.

There, on the ground, scuttling away towards the shelter of a rock, was a tiny scorpion. Its size was not relevant, but its colour was. The darker a scorpion, the less potent its sting. This one was a pale amber, almost translucent. Its venom could be lethal, depending on where it had stung.

Hendrik was clutching at his neck. On the left-hand side Mbutu saw a welt, swollen an angry red even against Hendrik's brown skin, right on the jugular vein. The scorpion must have crawled down onto him or tumbled under his collar. Either way he must have brushed at it, causing the tiny creature to react in the only way it knew.

"Hendrik. You must keep still. Your heart—"

But it was no use. It was over in a second – no words, no struggle. One moment Hendrik was alive, the next he was quite dead. Mbutu felt for a pulse, for breath. There was none. Hendrik was slumped in a sitting position, legs out before him, head lolled forward onto his chest.

Mbutu, you are a curse.

Though his own heart told him to rest a while, to accord poor Hendrik some kind of burial or goodbye, his head told him that he must go. And go now.

Did it really matter that Hendrik's earthly remains were not to be buried beneath a pile of stones? He laid him out on the ground, said farewell and thank you. Animals would see to the rest. It was all dust to dust.

Switching horses, Mbutu rode the remaining hours across the desert, stopping only when absolutely necessary and praying he could trust his navigation. Late that afternoon, the rocky corral appeared on the horizon.

As he approached, heads appeared, a handful of men came out to greet him. The empty saddle told its own story.

Sheer force of will had overcome his exhaustion but, once dismounted, he could barely stand. He was given water and broth.

One of the Nama, a thin young man, probably no more than 18, was pointing… pointing east.

"*Soldate.*"

Soldiers.

"*Vanoggend.*"

This morning.

He held up his hands and counted off on his fingers. Eight.

East. Soldiers now lay in the way of Beaufort West and the railway. Go on his own and he could sneak through, Mbutu was sure of that. But to attempt it with a party including women, children and blind men… and the Suttons?

"Hello."

A tiny voice. Mbutu sat up. Standing before him was Emily. She hugged him. Her mother lingered behind her. The Nama were going through the saddlebags. Waving away the advice that he should rest, Mbutu got up and rescued the ornate silver box.

The lock and hinges were now bent and broken from its enforced opening.

"The elephant box!" Emily exclaimed.

She looked up at him.

"Daddy?"

He crouched down. Children respected honesty.

"My child, the village, the church, the homes, have been destroyed. It is very unlikely, almost certain that your father did not survive. I am very sorry."

He glanced up at her mother. She stared impassively. Emily did not betray emotion at what seemed mere confirmation of something they had already accepted.

"Thank you," she said.

Mbutu opened the lid and pulled out the photograph. Emily smiled bittersweetly. Her mother remained expressionless.

Then, with greater purpose, Mbutu got out the ledger with its letters of correspondence stuffed within. He pointed.

"Mrs Sutton. Here… I understand that your mission was in contact with headquarters in Paarl… a Reverend… a Dean Newbold there?"

She nodded. He extracted a typed sheet.

"See… this place, sanctuary… this encampment for refugees. Your husband had deliberately chosen not to comply with Newbold's request to send the villagers down to there."

He detected the faintest of shrugs.

"This is very important. Was there any reason for him to suspect that it might not be a safe place to go?"

Slowly the woman shook her head.

Others were gathering round now.

Mbutu stood in the centre of the corral and beckoned the remaining Nama around him. He tried his best to explain that they were no longer safe where they were. There were soldiers off to the north and west. They had shot at him and Hendrik. They were the ones who had attacked the corral.

He summoned the youth he had spoken with. He asked to him to repeat to his people that eight soldiers had since been seen this morning, off to the east.

In which case they had no choice but to leave. It was what Hendrik had been building towards, waiting for the right moment. Well, that moment was now. The route to the railway was cut off. Their villages had been destroyed. Stay put and they would lose any fight against armed troops.

Someone asked about heading north to De Aar, the next significant railway junction on the way back up to Kimberley. Would the whites there be hostile to them?

They would, said Mbutu. There were military camps all around the place. Word would be out.

He forewent the map and did as Hendrik had done, sketching it out in the dirt, drawing a gentle arc that began at Kimberley in the north and rolled south-southwest through De Aar to Beaufort West before curving into a more defined westerly course for the last leg of the journey to Cape Town.

They were currently in the bush in the region of the bend, he marked, which meant they were already two thirds of the way along this grand route.

In which case, they should continue in that general direction, towards the Cape – but not by following the curve of the railway. Instead they should shortcut across it in a straight line.

By his estimation it would take three days across the harshest of terrains. They would be reliant solely on their own wits, but his faith in the Nama was absolute. There were no people more hardy or resourceful.

They must head towards here…

He drew an 'X'.

Paarl.

Chapter Twenty-Nine

When Finch arrived at La Rochelle, the sign hanging in the door greeted him with a single word – '*Fermé*'. The awning was still unfurled, the pavement chairs stacked.

Assuming Rideau to have miscalculated, Finch prepared to wait. No sooner had he turned, surveying the trickle of oncoming pedestrians, than there was a rattle of bolts. A small man with an elaborate curled moustache popped his head out.

"Monsieur?" he asked. "Captain... Captain Finch?"

Finch nodded. The man wore a white shirt, black bow tie and long white apron.

"*Vite...* Come," he beckoned.

Inside, the man re-secured the door behind them. The tables were unoccupied save for one slap bang in the centre. On seeing Finch, Rideau stood, all smiles.

"Sorry, old chap, should have explained, Henri does me the odd favour on occasion. Out of hours."

The man who'd led Finch in bowed.

"Monsieur Rideau is a special customer."

"And Henri owns the best damned restaurant in Cape Town," added Rideau, patting the man on the back, at which Henri the owner blushed, then snapped his fingers.

A waiter appeared with a tray bearing a jug of water and two glasses of Pernod. Finch always found the taste of aniseed a little overpowering, but he toasted the two men and sipped politely.

Half an hour off opening time there was already a heady garlic-laden aroma wafting from the kitchen. There was a clatter of utensils and a hubbub of activity behind the scenes, wisps of steam glimpsed through the slatted saloon doors.

Despite the summer sun, the shuttered restaurant was dark – dim enough for there to be a candle on the table. It had crisp white tablecloths, sun-drenched impressionist-style paintings on the walls, vignettes of country and small-town life in the Midi. From the ceiling hung baskets and old-fashioned wooden cooking implements.

Rideau gently removed his velvet gloves. His fingers were cut and grazed with a couple of fingernails taped up, the middle two fingers of his right hand. He showed them off like war wounds.

"Found this early edition Steinway," he said. "1855. Idea was to do it up an sell it on but I just fell in love with the thing. Tone like you wouldn't believe. Rich, deep... You play at all?"

"Was pretty handy at the clarinet once. Wish I'd kept it up."

"Never say never. Music is a great tonic... Anyway, been up late the last few nights sanding the thing down. Whoever owned it previously had coated it with this thick brown lacquer... varnish. God knows why. Really mutes the sound. Almost impossible to get off. Can't take a flame to it so have to scrape it off shred by shred, then rub it down by hand. Frustrating, I can tell you. Takes its toll."

Finch noticed something over Rideau's shoulder. On the zinc counter stood a huge clear-glass vase. Swimming in it were a dozen or so small, pink-skinned, black-eyed frogs. They looked like little naked people.

Rideau saw what was amusing him.

"Good old Henri. A sense of humour," he said.

"Rideau – is *that* French?"

"Back in the mists of time. Paternal line hails from Guernsey. But me? I've spent more time in India than anywhere. Part of that curious imperial breed. Prick me and I bleed for England, though I've spent not more than a handful of years in the Mother Country. Boarding school. Father was a civil servant. Moved around. I was actually born in Halifax, Nova Scotia. Shall probably pop my clogs elsewhere on the map painted pink. India was what I knew for much of my adult life. But have to say, love it here. *Love* it. Home now. Of course this war's a damn beastly mess."

"Wars are, Mr Rideau... Albert. I'm afraid I know that all too well."

"Indeed... Saw active service myself, just minor insurrections really, usual Sub-Continental stuff. Bouts of pitchfork-waving that interrupted our polo. That said, there were some unpleasant things to witness. But, Captain, nothing, nothing like this—"

"Please... Ingo."

"I can't begin to imagine, Ingo... Old Coxie had written to me about the sterling work you RAMC chaps were performing. Heroic, he called it."

"He did?"

Rideau lowered his voice.

"Confessed that he felt a little useless. You fellows doing the spade-work, saving lives, and him, a cavalryman, filling out chits."

"He needn't have felt that way," said Finch, glad at least that Cox had imparted this confession. "We can't all be firing bullets. We couldn't function at all without expert administration and there was no doubting the Major's knack for it. Really licked us into shape. Pen mightier than the sword and all that."

He sipped his Pernod.

"There are times when I, too, have felt somewhat misplaced," he continued. "I was a general practitioner. One minute I'm lancing boils, next thing I'm performing battlefield surgery alongside men far more capable than myself."

Rideau tutted a sound that said 'nonsense'.

"If you've saved so much as one life..." he boomed. "Your very good health, sir."

Finch smiled. They clinked glasses again.

A waiter appeared with some bread and two plates of quail's eggs. The war had clearly not affected supplies.

"Listen," said Rideau. "Seeing as we're doing this against the clock, took the liberty of asking Henri to rustle up a selection of starters. Guinea fowl for the main. Anything not to your liking, do say."

"No objection whatsoever," said Finch, cutting into the tiny yolk.

"Not bad," said Rideau, savouring it.

"You know, Albert, I have to confess. Although I served with the major, I knew him for three months only. It wasn't a personal friendship but a professional one. He was my CO. I don't want you forming the opinion we were bosom pals."

"Understand, old boy. Don't think anyone is misinterpreting."

Finch didn't know whether to say it, but the Pernod, at noon, on an empty stomach, had removed a layer of inhibition.

"Truthfully, on occasion, I found him a little... *frustrating*."

Rideau smiled.

"Who didn't? Could be a horse's arse. Ample evidence of that."

"But, by and large, he was always fair with me. That night… Magersfontein…"

"Was just reading about it. Terrible. Terrible."

"…he was forced to put me in a dangerous situation. I know, in retrospect, it was not a decision of his making. Just following orders. Was not in a position to apologise – rank and all that – but I know, through his action he was saying sorry."

"Poured you a good old drink, no doubt."

"He did that."

They clinked glasses again.

"Poor fellow."

"To Major Leonard Cox," said Finch.

"To Coxie," added Rideau.

They ate in silence for a moment. A waiter arrived with an armful of small dishes – garlic mushrooms, pâté, more bread, olives, pickled artichoke – which he fitted artfully onto the crowded table.

"And to Detective Inspector Harry Brookman," Rideau said. "Good man, Brookman. Rather him than the Military Foot Police, I tell you."

Finch nodded.

"You know he was something of a war hero himself?" Rideau offered.

"Really? I had no idea."

"Discretion being the better part of valour and all that. Never mentions it. But I looked him up a few months back. Zulu War. NCO, Natal Native Contingent. Distinguished Conduct Medal… Isandlwana."

"Good God."

"One of the few to get away. Now *that* was a bloodbath all right." Finch nodded.

"You know him from previously?"

"A year or so ago…"

He waited to swallow a morsel.

"…organised gangs were pilfering fruit from the cannery… Own a factory in the Eastern Cape… Not just sundry items, whole crates of fresh produce. Sophisticated operation, selling it to city restaurants on the black market. That's how I got to know Henri here. Had been on the wrong end of it himself. Every cloud, as they say.

Brookman, cunning fellow – a Hebrew you understand; you know, Dreyfus and all that – cracked the case with a clever sting operation."

There was a pause. Rideau's head hung sorrowfully for a moment.

"I don't know whether you know, but I was with Cox the night he was…"

He hesitated. He couldn't bring himself to say it.

"I didn't," said Finch.

Brookman had been under no obligation to divulge such details, he knew. The detective was well-versed in keeping his cards close to his chest. Maybe he had engineered this very meeting so that Rideau might unburden himself.

Rideau sensed his candour might be unsettling Finch.

"All on record," he hastened. "Went over it with the inspector in great detail. We were at the Officers' Club. Cox had been playing poker. Never been one for cards myself. Or gambling for that matter. But when I arrived, Coxie was already half-cut. Absolute cert the others would take him to the cleaners…"

He turned wistful.

"You know he never used to be like this, Ingo. Back in India. He was always a character, make no mistake – funny, liked a drink, prone to pomposity. But, underneath it all, was an absolute brick. God's truth, *that* Cox you'd have loved. The devil got to him over here."

"The devil has got to a great many men."

"Felt it my duty to spirit him away, get him sobered up. My place up at Wynberg. Kip the night. Sleep it off. Didn't want him embarrassing himself either at the club or back at his guest house. Spot of bother with the landlady, he said. Bit of a dragon."

"You were looking out for him. Friends do that."

Rideau blushed. He carried on.

"Anyway, while there, word was that this Kilfoyle character had showed up. Must have been an ex-military man in some capacity or they wouldn't have let him into the club. Didn't see him myself but knew that Cox owed him a wedge. There were accusations of Cox having welched on it. Not good form. A gentleman doesn't do that. And Kilfoyle was a volatile sort, so I gather."

Rideau explained how he had helped Cox find his coat and walked him – supported him – outside into the street. He then sat him on a bench while returning inside to settle his bill. Once that was done he had gone back to procure them both a cab, but Cox was no longer there.

"Just assumed he'd either managed to climb into one all by himself... there's a rank nearby. Or some kindly soul had stepped in to help him. Asked a couple of people thereabouts. They confirmed the latter. Someone had popped up to lend a hand. This 'Good Samaritan'."

He turned mournful again. His eyes cast down.

"Next thing I hear is that Coxie's dead. Our Samaritan wasn't quite so good after all..."

He growled it out.

"...Bastard Kilfoyle."

Henri appeared with an earthenware jug of the house white, a Burgundy. Rideau resumed his composure, tasted it and nodded his approval.

"Local wine, you know, but the vines were transplanted from Chablis. Soil perfect, climate most equable. I tell you now, South African wine can compete with the very best. My next business move. You know, if you should choose to stick around after this show's over, we'll need good men, whatever their field of expertise."

Finch smiled. It was a compliment, meant sincerely or otherwise. But he was right. For a house white it was of exceptional quality. Crisp, dry. Rideau looked Finch in the eye.

"Ingo, may I be candid."

"By all means."

"I wanted to meet you for the very reasons I said, helping Cox and all that. Saying thank you. In some ways you're my final link, being the last person to spend substantial time with him, official capacity or otherwise. At some point I'll be back in India. His family will want to know what happened... and about you. But I also..."

He stared down into his drink. Finch was glad that someone else had been thinking along the same compassionate lines.

"Please... Go on."

"You see there's something still bothering me. Something doesn't add up. If Kilfoyle offed our friend, why on earth kill him by such an elaborate method?"

He paused, suddenly realising he might be revealing information to which Finch was not privy. Finch understood. He offered a quid pro quo.

"It's all right, I'm familiar with the details," he explained. "Was there at the mortuary."

"Of course you were. I'm sorry. It's just that until they get a noose round Kilfoyle's neck, one must exercise caution."

"You think he'll swing?"

"I'm not a betting man, as I've said, but for this I would place a substantial wager."

Finch reflected for a moment. He was as anxious as anyone for justice to be done but his gut told him that an eye for an eye wouldn't solve anything. There had been enough death this past three months.

"But anyway, Ingo. What I'm saying is, regardless, I think there's more to this than meets the eye. I tell you, I'm convinced of it. If you've heard the stories, you'll know Cox was a mixed-up chap. But he was a good sort underneath, as I've said. Leaves a lovely wife, Isadora, and three children. The oldest, Peter, is about to become a Lancer himself... No one, none of them, deserves this."

Finch wriggled awkwardly.

"I have to ask you, Albert. But Cox's wife, Isadora, did her middle name begin with a 'V'?"

"A 'V'...? No, it's Susan."

"Might 'V' be from a pet-name?"

"Not that I'm aware of. Why on earth do you ask?"

"Major Cox wore a wristwatch, a good one. It bore an inscription dedicated to him. A loving inscription. From someone identified only as 'V'..."

He wasn't sure whether Rideau knew about Vesta Lane. He kept it neutral.

"You know, I hate to raise it with such a good friend of his, but there's good reason to believe that Cox wasn't... putting it delicately... entirely in honour of his wedding vows."

Rideau stared for a moment. He raised a stick of asparagus, bit the end off, savoured it, swallowed.

"You have to understand... A colonial marriage. How shall I say, it's built on a different kind of foundation. Months, years away from home..."

"An inscribed watch. There seems to be more to it than mere physical release," ventured Finch.

"Look, I do know this... He and Kilfoyle had got into some silly schoolboy spat about an actress, if that's not overstating her talents. Music hall performer. Bit of a tart in my opinion..."

Rideau did know.

"...but I hadn't thought that to be anything more than a bit of infatuation, maybe a bit of bravado in terms of whom his rival was. Peacocks strutting their stuff."

"You do know Cox and Kilfoyle had been arguing about something... *someone*, in the immediate run-up to his death. Kilfoyle had threatened to kill him over it."

Rideau blew out a hiss of disapproval.

"I do, and I understand where you're coming from. But honestly, selling everything down the swanee for *that* woman...?"

Finch decided to say it.

"Vesta Lane?"

Rideau nodded.

"I mean, have you *seen* her, for God's sake? Come on."

"You did concede that Cox had been a horse's arse of late."

Rideau gave a wry grin. It gave way to a sudden look of panic. "This watch. If it were to be shipped back home it would cause..."

Finch hitched up his left sleeve to reveal the offending item. He undid the leather strap – awkwardly given it was newish and stiff – and handed the timepiece over.

"Gosh, I remember him wearing this," he sighed, examining it front and back. "Fairly recent acquisition. Had no idea it was a gift. A gift from a lady friend..."

There was incredulity in his voice.

"...from Vesta?"

"Though it prudent to keep it on me," Finch said, stretching the truth a little. "There's was a break-in at my room... The Belvedere."

Rideau exhaled a whistle. He turned the watch over again.

"Must admit I was a little surprised they'd put you up there. You know they've had a spot of bother of late."

Rideau handed the watch back.

"Glad I held on to it," said Finch, strapping it back on. "Zeiss. German. Keep it out of harm's way."

Rideau shook his head.

"You know, the more I hear about this business, Ingo, the more I don't like it."

Rideau took a moment, as if wanting to lay it out correctly.

"It's not the question of Kilfoyle's culpability," he said. "He had the motive, all right – the debts, the love rivalry. I heard, too, about

194

the unwelcome visits to the guest house and the death-threat he made. But something about this just doesn't sit right. I mean, this sudden resolution. It's too neat. Too tidy. Too convenient. Too quick. And, heavens, this poisoning business. Unless the coroner—"

"I'm afraid, I believe Krajicek... the deputy coroner... to be correct on this."

"You're the medical man. I wouldn't take issue."

Rideau dabbed his mouth with his napkin.

"I'm pretty sure Brookman feels the same way about it all, too, but for his own good reasons is keeping his counsel. Not giving us the whole picture. Playing the long game."

"Funny you should say that…"

Finch tried to check himself but it was too late.

"…Brookman didn't once mention the question of poisoning during his interrogation of Kilfloyle this morning."

Damned Pernod. Damned wine.

Not two hours gone and he had already betrayed Brookman's confidence. Rideau either missed the admission or chose to spare Finch's embarrassment by saying nothing.

"But you're right," Finch added swiftly. "I'm not entirely comfortable with the outcome either."

"Tell me," said Rideau. "You said Cox and Kilfoyle might have been arguing about someone. Did Cox ever mention any other names. Not a woman… I mean associates, enemies?"

Finch shrugged a no.

"Anyone, perhaps, by the name of…"

He looked around then whispered it.

"…Moriarty?"

"Moriarty? You mean like Sherlock Holmes?"

"Exactly."

"No… Not that I recall. Although…"

He *had* heard it somewhere. Where?

"Although?" asked Rideau.

"I don't know. Rings a bell. Can't think… But why—?"

"It's a name that's cropped up, that's all. For obvious reasons I'm guessing a pseudonym. Moreover it's a name that seemed to surface anytime some misfortune was about to befall Cox, muttered in conversations, overheard from behind closed doors. Cox was always furtive about it. But that name kept coming back."

Finch racked his brains. Moriarty. Where, oh where?

"Don't worry, Brookman's fully aware of all this," Rideau assured. "Not trying to go behind his back. It's just that I think what happened to Coxie, it's part of something… *bigger*."

"Bigger?"

"Much bigger."

Henri arrived with the guinea fowl – two plump browned birds on what looked like a cranberry sauce base. A couple of waiters appeared to fuss over the cutlery and napkins and refresh the drinks.

"Be a good chap," whispered Rideau. "You hear anything, let me know. Within the bounds of what's right and proper vis-à-vis the investigation…"

Was that a little acknowledgement of Finch's indiscretion?

"…You have my card. And, likewise, if I—"

"You can contact me via regimental HQ," offered Finch. "Might take a while but a letter will get to me eventually."

A waiter flipped the door sign to '*Ouvert*' and proceeded outside with a large metal winding handle to crank open the awning.

Chapter Thirty

Once again, Finch found himself walking up the path to the Esperanza guest house. It was now quite hot, far more humid than the previous day. He was damp with sweat under his tunic.

Already he regretted drinking at lunchtime. He had a headache coming on. All he wanted now was water.

Finch rapped at the door and Mathilda answered. She issued only the faintest of smiles, looking a tad embarrassed, and ushered him into the cool front sitting room with its loud clock and stern old Heer Du Plessis gazing down.

He could hear footsteps on the stairs and stood in anticipation of his wife's entry. It was, instead, an army officer. The uniform was Royal Artillery, a second lieutenant. He carried his left arm in a sling. Though his most striking feature was the black patch over his left eye. There were healing burn marks down the left side of his face.

He saluted. Finch returned the gesture.

"Captain Finch?"

"Yes."

"Mrs Du Plessis asks that you join her upstairs. Major Cox's room."

"You are part of the enquiry?"

"No, no, sir. A guest here."

The man saluted again.

"Need to be off, sir."

"Thank you. Very good."

He exited, bidding a jolly 'Good afternoon, Mathilda' as he left.

Finch climbed the creaky stairs to where he found the door to room three ajar. He pressed his palm against the door but it would only go so far, blocked by something.

He squeezed in, catching his brass buttons on the jamb. It was the bedstead that had caused the obstruction, twisted out of position. It had been stripped bare, the mattress strewn at an angle, tufts of feathers exploding from deep knife slashes hacked into it.

Faded rectangular patches on the pale green wall paint correlated to the smashed framed floral prints lying on the floor, the pictures cut from their frames. A pillow lay next to them. The glass-breaking had been done artfully.

Finch looked around. The wardrobe doors hung open revealing nothing within except hangers. Empty drawers protruded from the chest. From the mantelpiece and a small bookshelf, a few ornaments and cheap volumes had been piled to one side. The curtains had been ripped off the pole and lay in a heap.

Mrs Du Plessis had slipped into the room silently behind him.

"An insurance investigator."

"Insurance investigator?"

"Exactly," she hissed.

"Who were they?"

"They…? Just one man. Strong looking. Knocked at the door this morning. Said very little. Presented me with a letter from the Cape Town Authority, something about my hotelier's licence and a routine check of the deceased's room. I showed him upstairs and left him to it."

She rolled back the rug. A section of floorboard had been prised up then replaced.

"Didn't hear a thing apart from some scraping of furniture. Assumed it was standard practice. Sent Mathilda up to ask if he wanted tea. She tried the door but he'd locked it. Sent for me. Knocked. No answer. Knocked again, harder. The door opened, he squeezed out. Brushed right past me and out of the house. Not a word."

"You've told the police… Inspector Brookman?"

"Mathilda ran a message over to the police station earlier."

"Did anyone else witness this? The artillery officer maybe?"

She sighed.

"He picked his moment. Waited till Mathilda and I were alone."

"Did he threaten you in any way?"

"No. He seemed cold. How do you say, *detached*? But I had no reason to suspect. No reason not to let him in. There's been a lot of paperwork. You have a murder, people take interest.

"There appears to be nothing taken from the room," she added. "The shirts, the few personal items that you saw, I had already packed them for you. Downstairs… the carpet bag."

Finch saw the Vesta Lane print on the mantelpiece. She had fallen over face first.

"What else can you tell me about him?"

"A suit. Smart. Looked the part. Like I say, broad, strong. Oh, and the hair... *Rooi*... Red."

In her no nonsense fashion, she moved the conversation on. What had happened had happened.

"Tell me," she asked, "when you return to England, will you be calling upon the major's widow in person?"

Finch explained that Cox's family lived in India.

He went to the window and stared out. Beyond the backyards, the ground rose sharply up to Signal Hill, the coarse grass of the slopes dotted with tumbling natural rubble. When he turned round a moment later, Du Plessis had squeezed back out of the room. He heard another door crack and a drawer slide open. She returned with a small bundle of papers.

"Then it is safe to give you these."

It was a tattered stack of personal correspondence tied up with a red silk ribbon.

"I thought it prudent to remove them."

Finch undid the bow and began thumbing through the missives, which had been folded and reinserted in their envelopes. There were maybe 20 or so, all bearing Cape postage, all uniformly addressed in a decorous, looping feminine scroll – some directed to Cox's regimental HQ, the rest to a local post office box. The most recent, a telegram, had been sent only on December 24th, Cox's last full day on earth.

"They were in the back of wardrobe. See here..."

She opened the door. It creaked. She indicated below a lower shelf and what appeared to be a false panel at the rear, about one foot square. It was now split and wrenched open.

"I saw wood shavings. I thought mice. And then I noticed. The screws."

The heads of the four that had been holding it in place were shiny with use, not varnished over. The police had missed it but not the eagle-eyed ransacker.

She was fortunate indeed that this man had not figured her as the letters' remover.

Finch pulled out a few sheets at random. It was largely expensive pale blue bond. Each letter, some several pages long, commenced: '*My*

Dearest Leonard' and concluded '*With all my heart, V*', or a variation thereof. To Finch, even from a cursory inspection, it was patently clear that 'V' was not Cox's wife... neither was she, barring a gross misjudgment of character, Vesta Lane.

"Does the inspector know about these?" Finch asked.

She shook her head.

"Can I keep them?"

"Do with them what you feel necessary. Please be discreet. I know what it is like to be widowed. Why make that poor woman suffer any more? But act with caution. If you choose to give them to the police, then I only discovered them this morning. You understand?"

Finch nodded. He was not sure how much Du Plessis knew of the details of Cox's death but felt that she was owed some kind of explanation. He told her as much as he could without betraying police trust.

He concluded with the detail that there was a man now in custody for the murder but that Cox had been killed for a reason – A woman? A debt? – a motive that was not yet clear.

"You must promise me, Mevrouw Du Plessis. If anyone suspicious calls upon you, if you are concerned about anything at all with relation to Cox, you must contact Brookman immediately."

He was satisfied by her look that she had understood.

He followed her out. Down in the hallway he stuffed the bundle inside his tunic. On the dresser by the front door, the one with Mathilda's tip jar, the carved cross-eyed spaniel panted at him. On the floor beneath it was Cox's carpet bag, done up with string – the remainder of his things.

He hoisted it by the leather handles. They shook hands.

"I'm so sorry you have been caught up in all this, Mevrouw Du Plessis. I truly am."

She shrugged, as if to blame it all on fate.

He patted the bundle in his tunic, assuring discretion.

"Thank you," he said. "And Happy New Year..."

"Goodbye, Heer Dokter," she replied, flat, expressionless.

–

Out on the dusty street, Finch checked Cox's watch. He had less than an hour before his train left the main station. His hansom cab, generously laid on by Rideau, was at the bottom of the slope, waiting patiently. He waved to the driver and it began a languorous *trit-trot* out from the shade of a jacaranda.

Half an hour later he was amid the khaki chaos of Cape Town railway station again, a military man once more. Under the vaulted roof, the noise – of men, of barking sergeants and of the chuffs and hisses of shunting locomotives – conspired for an almighty din.

Across the forecourt was the army postal desk where harassed clerks, army NCOs, sought to make order of the great scrum of men trying to avail themselves of its services.

Finch hated doing it, but handed his kit bag to a porter and summoned a second one to carry his two items for postage – the box and the carpet bag – then limped his way over and pulled rank to carve himself a route through to the front of the queue, not without some cursing from the men of the lower orders.

Du Plessis had tied a brown paper label to the carpet bag. The box, the one with Cox's clothing, but minus the Zeiss watch, was now layered in thick brown paper.

Finch also retained Cox's wallet. The burglar had deemed the small slab of tattered leather to be of no intrinsic worth. To Finch there was something about it – the scrap of paper with the name '*Shawcroft*' upon it, even the crumpled chemist's shop receipt. He had lodged it in the waist pocket of his tunic, under which bulged the bundle of Cox's letters.

Ten minutes later he had relinquished the last of Cox's worldly goods, to be headed in the direction of the harbour and a steamer across the Indian Ocean. Lord knows when they might arrive in the Punjab, though he always marvelled at the magnificent ease of transit – of both goods and people – to and from the most far-flung reaches of the Empire.

Though he had already sent a letter to Mrs Cox, expressing his condolences, he had inserted another note to explain that these were personal items and how he thought she might like to have them. He was, again, very sorry.

By a quarter to four, Finch had pushed past the pale, fresh-faced tyros bound for the Front. Those who returned would be weathered, grim-faced men.

He found his way into a second-class compartment, his kit bag slung on the luggage rack above his head by the Indian porter whose heroics earned a greater tip than might have been expected.

Across the way, as he had seen on arrival, ambulances waited to take away the wounded from the incoming trains. The invalids were being siphoned off so as not to shock those champing at the bit to see some 'action'.

For a moment he ventured that he was just arriving, that all that had passed in the previous three days was just some dream.

Christ. Was it just three days?

The platform guard blew his whistle. The locomotive yielded a great hiss and an iron shudder.

Chapter Thirty-One

The train trundled out of the station, out of the hubbub, past the blithely wandering rail gangs. It chugged past the rickety black shanty towns, the immense slopes of Table Mountain receding behind. It was not that far to Paarl, 40 miles or so, an hour's ride. Paarl would mark the end of Finch's communion with urbanity. Further up the line lay nothing but heat and death.

The six-man compartment was full of officers this time. The sheer volume of men heading north, now that the troopships had started docking, made it difficult to believe that the Boer Republics could hold out for long.

Finch had managed at least to procure a seat by the window. He nodded a mutual greeting to a fellow RAMC captain he assumed to be there to attend the same conference.

Once underway, once everyone had settled down to their editions of the *Cape Argus* or their penny novellas, he removed the red-ribboned bundle of letters from his tunic. It earned him a knowing look from the lieutenant-colonel of the Royal Canadian Dragoons seated next to him.

He felt like a voyeur – he *was* being a voyeur – but he knew he would have to sift through the missives if he were to find out what on earth had been going on with Cox. If anything came to light, he would of course pass the letters on to Brookman.

The reality was there was not one grieving widow here but two. The first a wife, a mother; the other a lover – a lover right here in the Cape, unable to express her sorrow or to learn the details of the fate that had befallen her clandestine paramour. Maybe she didn't yet know he was dead?

Should there be nothing criminally incriminating in the letters' contents, he swore that, when next in Cape Town – whenever *that* might be – he would track down 'V' and return the letters personally.

There were 23 items in all. The earliest letters pre-dated the war, going back to April, when Cox had first been posted to the Cape. Some were addressed to his regimental HQ, others to a post office box. The last, the telegram, had been delivered directly to Cox at the Esperanza guest house, shattering the scrupulous secrecy maintained up till then.

The first letter, penned on April 20th, 1899, was short and relatively curt. It began 'Dear Major' and thanked Cox for lunch the previous day with a polite wish that they 'might avail themselves of the opportunity to luncheon together again under similar circumstances.'

Within two weeks, the Major had become 'Dear Leonard'. By the end of May he had evolved into 'My Dearest Leonard'. Come June he was 'My Darling', 'My Sweet', or, in particularly effusive communications, 'My Dear Sweetest Darling'.

'V' was a constant, though from pretty early on, the initial was preceded by 'With Love' or 'Love', 'All my love' or variants thereof.

'V' clearly found Cox to be a charmer, someone who had brought some much-needed fun and laughter. It was apparent from the outset that she, too, was married. In the first few letters the prose were studded with references to both her shame and her understanding that 'in the eyes of the church' she had 'broken sacred vows'.

The eyes of the church, he noted. Not the eyes of God.

The epiphany seemed to have been reached in late June, resulting in a particularly lengthy epistle of the 29th, a nine-sided epic of deep soul-searching which concluded that, instead of an acceptance of her own, apparently miserable domestic lot, the damsel should now seize the outstretched hand of her shining knight. And so it continued blissfully and apparently thrillingly through the onset of the South African winter.

On August 11th, following what appears to be their first lovers' tiff – something to do with a day trip to Simon's Town and a recklessness that caused them to be almost spotted by someone she knew – there came a reference to Cox's drinking. There were certain things about him she had been prepared to overlook thus far, she professed, but that issue needed to be addressed 'should they have a future together'.

In the sweet make-up afterwards, 'V', it seems, and Cox too, had pledged to leave their old lives behind and start anew... in London. Cox had a friend, an importer/exporter of canned goods. He was going into the wine trade. Cox was sure said friend would need an agent in England.

Rideau? Given the willingness with which he had extended an offer of employment to Finch – no matter how hypothetical – the fact that no such thing had been dangled before Cox spoke more about the major's trustworthiness than anything else.

'V' appeared to live in Stellenbosch somewhere, clearly a woman of means, for there were references to household staff and her '*gilded cage*'. She had married young, some 23 years ago, she had referenced, which must put her in her early 40s now.

To her great regret she had been unable to bear children, one of the reasons, she cited, why her husband had begun to treat her with contempt.

They were British but had come to South Africa because of '*his blasted job*', something that entailed long hours, much time spent away from home and, she suggested, plenty of womanising. They had lived in the Cape for three years. Her social life was one of society functions in the company of dull Imperial wives.

She mentioned something about her husband's dealings with Milner – one supposed the Cape Governor himself – which probably meant that 'V''s husband was a Government official or a high-ranking civil servant.

The more Finch read, the more he understood that Cox was on the verge of upsetting some very powerful people. 'V' admitted as much. There were several instances where she urged caution; that revelation of their union would cause a scandal.

Other than that, 'V' appeared to be highly intelligent, passionate and – if Finch had deciphered their secret code correctly – sexually adventurous. Once she had accepted her own infidelity, she was driven only by doing what was '*in her heart*' so that her conscience '*could be free*'.

In September, Cox was moved up to Beaufort West as the war drums began sounding. The letters from that point went via his regiment. The new, cool, more formal tone, marked not only a change in emotion but the reality of military censorship.

She '*understood all too well*' the new circumstances, something he had been apologetic about. She understood, too, of his frustration with his new posting, seconded to the RAMC. She assured that '*saving lives*' was as important as '*taking them*'.

On October 11th, when war was declared, she urged Cox never to hold back from doing his duty, but prayed that he would keep himself safe. As he moved up to the Front, she told him how proud she was of his part in attempting to relieve the dreadful siege of Kimberley, sparing its poor women and children from the '*beastliness*' of the Boers.

Cox didn't mention any names, but his vaunted admiration for the doctors under his charge concurred with Rideau's expression of Cox's appreciation – something that warmed Finch to his old CO.

She longed to see Cox again, wrote 'V'. He hinted that he might have leave come Christmas.

Unfortunately, the lovers were never to reunite. On his return to Cape Town they were unable to undertake an immediate reunion due to her Imperial wifely duties, but had planned to rekindle their flame on the 27th – *today*. Her husband would be away again. She had hoped to sneak into Cox's hotel room tonight, this very night, in Paarl.

But then… on December 24th, dispatched at two minutes past eleven in the morning, came that final panicked telegram:

ONTO US ++ PAARL IMPOSSIBLE ++ WILL EXPLAIN ++ BE CAREFUL ++ SO SORRY ++ VERITY

Verity. Not 'V'… '*Verity!*' In a moment of alarm she had let her guard slip – and even, noted Finch, paid extra for the lettering.

Finch had barely had time to finish reading the letters when the train began to slow. As the line curved in to the Paarl station he could see the great smooth, domed Paarl Rock.

When the train came to a bumpy halt, the usual scramble began as soldiers disembarked and porters, hawkers and everyone else mobbed the carriages, resulting in a collision of two opposing human waves.

The officers and civilians in second class waited patiently in the corridor, carrying their briefcases or dragging kitbags.

As Finch stretched forward, turning and stooping to the right to drag his, he was unaware of the blade that swung with well-rehearsed efficiency, thrust upwards, piercing his tunic under his left armpit.

Chapter Thirty-Two

Finch hailed a cab. As he stood kerbside, he had a cold-shock moment of realisation.

The letters!

He swung his kit bag into the buggy, asked the cabbie to wait and turned back against the human tide, trying to retrace his steps. It was a futile mission. As he limped on, head down, scanning the ground, he bumped into people randomly, eliciting muttered expletives.

He navigated his way back to the platform, hoping that the bundle could have fallen out on the train. But then came the shrill blast of the guard's whistle. The carriages were already pulling away.

He cursed loudly at the train and then at himself.

"Sir… Sahib."

A turbaned Indian porter was gesturing. His tunic.

Awkwardly Finch felt at his side. The porter pointed more specifically.

Finch removed it.

Down the right hand side there was a long straight slash that revealed the silk lining within. He had seen such handiwork before, on Cox's jacket. Whatever implement had been used to cut through the cloth had been very sharp indeed. Whoever had done it had been skilled.

What the hell—?

In a state of sweat and fury, he limped towards the exit.

When he re-emerged, the Coloured cabbie saw the jacket draped over Finch's arm and the slash. Such things happened here in crowds all the time, he said. Someone looking for money. The captain *did* have money?

The disgruntled Finch assured him that he did.

Pick-pocketing or not, Finch had at least had the good fortune to have read everything and committed the important details to memory. As soon as he reached his lodgings, he would put them down on paper.

The Peerlberg Hotel was set amid some fine high-gabled Dutch architecture. Finch found it hard to fathom for a moment that we was in Africa. Inside, the hotel was modern – airy, cool and rambling with a large entrance hallway. There was a trestle table set up beneath an RAMC flag – three horizontal bands of cherry, blue and gold – at which he had to register with some cheery underlings.

A bellboy hovered to take his kit bag to his room, Finch asked reception if he could make use of a sewing kit.

"Finch. I say… Ingo."

It was the welcome voice of his old pal Hawley Jenkins.

"You hear about Cox?"

"Had to identify the body—"

"Jesus. Can't bloody believe it."

"Not exactly a dose of seasonal cheer."

"Every day out here is Christmas," Jenkins deadpanned.

He was being called away.

"This evening. Grab dinner? Must tell all. Jesus—"

"Love to," said Finch. "But I've got to break bread with the new CO."

"Exactly," said Jenkins, issuing a mischievous grin.

He grabbed Jenkins' hand again and shook.

"Congratulations, Hawley. You deserve it. Glad, at last, that they've trusted us not be babysat."

"Have to borrow that sewing kit… Crown I need to add to my epaulettes… Though not the circumstances I'd anticipated."

As soon as he had registered for the conference, picking up his agenda, Finch went upstairs to his shared room. It, too, was light and airy with wooden floors, a balcony and a mosquito net draped over each bed. The other occupant, a lieutenant, was sprawled on his, leafing through a penny dreadful. He scrambled to attention. Finch stood him at ease.

The lieutenant was full of questions. He hadn't yet been to the Front.

Finch had to stop him. His first order of duty was to dig out his leather-bound notebook. He sat at the room's desk and spent a full three-quarters of an hour writing down everything he could remember, interrupted only by the occasional chortle from the lieutenant, evidently enjoying his novella, and a knock on the door and the bellboy brandishing a needle and thread.

After he fixed his tunic, Finch spruced himself up, spent 20 minutes leafing through an incongruous tourist handbook entitled *Warner's Guide to the Cape* and, at seven o'clock, descended to the main hall for a lecture by the RAMC's surgeon-general.

The troop surge was an open secret. Soldiers were docking at Cape Town, Port Elizabeth and Durban from all over the Empire – a quarter of a million men in the field.

It was now official that old Redvers Buller had been relieved of his command. Painful lessons had been learned, it was admitted, a rare concession on the part of Her Majesty's Armed Forces. Buller, formerly one if its stars, was the sacrificial lamb.

The officer gave a near eulogy on behalf of the Boer soldier, a brave and resourceful character from whom Tommy needed to steal a trick or two.

Kimberley and Mafeking were still under siege. So too, in Natal, was Ladysmith. It was these that had captured the public's attention back home. It was all the Boers could cling on to. Break the sieges and the war could be wrapped up in four to six months. The two Boer Republics didn't have the manpower to withstand a protracted assault.

Afterwards they were poured a glass of sherry and had a chance to mingle. Jenkins came over and introduced Finch to a fellow medic named Doyle, a big-framed Scotsman with a handlebar moustache, who now lived on the south coast of England and whose interest seemed focused on sport, primarily Association Football, styling himself as a goalkeeper.

"Can you bat?" he added.

"Doyle also plays for the MCC," Jenkins interjected.

"You're a man of many talents," quipped Finch.

Doyle smiled, exchanged some more pleasantries and then moved on.

"Pretty versatile, now you mention it, old A.C." said Jenkins.

"A.C.?"

"Arthur Conan."

The Welshman was smirking.

"My God, that was *him*…? I have *The Sign Of The Four* in my kitbag… If I'd have known I'd have—"

"…behaved liked a besotted schoolgirl," laughed Jenkins.

Over dinner, Finch told Jenkins all that had happened with regard to Cox though, for the sake of propriety, held back the information about the mysterious Verity.

Finch was going to elaborate on the various other incidents and characters that had drifted in and out over the last few days but, realising Jenkins was in demand, and through a number of interruptions at their table, kept it to the facts, an act that brought Brookman's voice echoing in his head.

Jenkins, in his new guise, had evidently been busy.

"Been assembling information for a delegation to High Command. From what we're hearing it actually had some impact. Penny's finally dropped. This isn't the bloody Crimea. Been a rude awakening."

Sure enough, Jenkins had to move on. Left alone, Finch finished his sea bass, drained the bottle of Chenin Blanc – two gourmet meals in one day, he sighed – and returned to exchange small-talk with his colleagues.

There seemed a new air of professionalism about the RAMC. Tomorrow, he was informed, he would be assigned an assistant. There would be greater emphasis on the aftercare of the wounded. Field hospitals were no longer to resemble ad hoc abattoirs. They knew, by now, what to expect in terms of the volume and the type of casualty. Hospital ships would soon be stationed offshore to relieve the over-burdened city military infirmaries.

There was a basic problem with the British Tommy. He was not fit, a legacy of industrialisation and squalid urban living. The general standard of health in Great Britain was appalling – men were frail, malnourished and diseased before they even got into the field – although, it was noted, the colonials seemed in finer fettle. Ensuring fitness and quality of a soldier's diet would make for a more efficient fighting man and improve his chances should he be wounded.

As for the military campaign, there was a new sense of purpose there, too. The Boers were to be re-engaged at the Modder River, it was whispered, for the big push on Kimberley. Relieving the city would provide a huge political victory.

Finch could see it now, the headlines in the *Daily Mail* and *Morning Post*, crowing about the salvation of innocent women and children from the clutches of the barbarous, baby-eating Dutchmen.

Finch was not alone in thinking that, admirable though the new sense of professionalism was, they were still not addressing a crucial issue – disease.

From his personal experience already of an outbreak of typhus among the troops, it was shaping up to be a bigger threat to the Empire's armies than anything the Boers could throw at them. Not just armies but civilians too. Clean water, sanitation and hygiene were fundamental. Had Florence Nightingale taught them nothing?

Jenkins appeared again. He proffered a crystal tumbler. Finch swirled the pale amber liquid and inhaled its aroma with deep satisfaction.

"Talisker. Hawley, you bloody beauty."

Jenkins clinked a glass of his own.

"Chin-chin."

They chatted briefly about the disaster of a typhus epidemic breaking out and the prevalence of dysentery among large encampments.

"Not just the men, Hawley, but the women, the children and, God knows, the poor blighters who've been ridden over roughshod in all this... the natives."

Jenkins felt the same way. They had discussed it enough in the past.

"Politics, Ingo," he confided. "On paper it's all abstract. It's a case of demonstrating it to the brass, letting them bear witness."

He took another sip.

"And, tomorrow morning, mark my words, they *will* bear witness. They will."

Chapter Thirty-Three

There were only two of them selected to undertake the task – Nurse Sullivan and herself. Though they had all been sisters-in-arms, Annie was glad to be away from the hospital, away from Hanwell in particular.

The shape of the war was about to change, they were told. Units were being reformed. They would be assigned new duties.

Paarl had seemed the very model of genteel civility, with its neat vineyards, its fine Dutch architecture and its stunning mountain backdrop. The great Paarl dome reminded her of the pictures she had seen of Ayers Rock.

The town, however, was certainly not for their delight. No sooner had they stepped off the train than an RAMC corporal appeared to usher them into a clapped-out, covered mule wagon.

For an uncomfortable two hours it clopped north, winding through a mountain pass into flatter, more arid lands. The heat rose.

The corporal was annoyingly evasive about their destination, his summations amounting to a deliberate 'You'll see' or 'Just you wait'.

But eventually, in the distance, there it was. You could smell it before you could see it – a swelling mass of humanity, an amorphous human lake set in a great dusty crucible. A dirty streak of air hovered over it. It was the biggest number of people Annie had ever seen assembled in one place, thousands upon thousands of them – and all, apparently, as they neared, Africans, black Africans.

They stopped 100 yards short of the encampment – if you could even call it that, for there was only a smattering of tents.

"Here we are, Shangri-La," quipped the irritating corporal, hopping out over the tailboard. He delved into his pocket and pulled out a linen surgical mask which he began tying on.

"What, they didn't tell you?" he shrugged.

He held out a hand as if to help them down, then withdrew it.

Their long, thick skirts and buttoned up tunics were utterly impractical for their duties, let alone clambering over tailboards, but they were used to it. Both women were dripping with sweat. It was an everyday occurrence.

Annie looked ahead to the throng. For such a large body of people it seemed calm. As they followed the corporal, the smell became overpowering and they reached for their pocket kerchiefs.

It was the stench of human excrement, of a vast crushed makeshift city devoid of sanitation. Then Annie realised – the ambient hum; it was not voices, it was flies. The black cloud hovering over it was flies.

"Wait here."

The corporal stomped off ahead and down an arbitrary walkway through the human mass towards one of the few tents visible. He returned accompanied by a puffing, red-faced, middle-aged man who wore a battered Panama, a faded pink shirt, braces, canvas trousers, scuffed boots and the black bib of a clerical dog collar.

"Good day, ladies," said the man, seemingly untroubled by his surroundings. "Dean Ephraim Newbold at your service."

He proffered his hand in salutation, then nodded at the corporal.

"Right you are, Cedric. Shake a leg."

The corporal returned to the wagon, unceremoniously dumped the nurses' kitbags on the ground, then instructed the driver to wheel the cart around. He clambered up on board.

"Enjoy your stay," he shouted.

"Oh, don't mind him," dismissed Newbold, swinging his arm out full stretch to herald all before them.

"Welcome to Cape Government Native Emergency Resettlement Station No. 624-16. Or as I like to call it, Camp Eureka. Population 30,000… give or take. Depends on the time of day."

"Eureka?" asked Annie.

Newbold turned, the signal for them to follow. He pointed to their kitbags.

"Sorry, not the Ritz."

They dragged them behind them.

"Theory of displacement. You know, Archimedes… sat in a bathtub, water sloshed over the sides. What we have here is human displacement. War plonks itself down in the tribal lands, these poor folk are the overspill. We've got Xhosa, Basuto, Matabele, Tswana, Tsonga…"

There were no boundaries, no fences or gates. It had determined its own limits. One moment the women were walking across dirty ground, the next they were picking their way past bodies... emaciated bodies... poor forlorn wretches stretched on the ground or huddled together. Some alive, some dead. Those that were living were barely more than skeletons. No one spoke. They just sat exhausted, listless, eyes dull, unfocused.

"Oh yes, Swazi too," said Newbold.

The younger children were a shocking sight, their round distended bellies an aberration – all ribs and angular joints and eyes sunk deep within sockets. They looked suddenly elderly, as if accelerated artificially along their life cycles. Large angry flies crawled around mouths and nostrils at will.

Malnutrition and starvation were just the start. A place like this, given what the nurses knew about what was already happening among large concentrations of soldiers, would be a breeding ground for dysentery and typhoid.

"Local missions gather them in as best they can. They, too, then find themselves on the front line or can't cope with the influx. Send them down here to us... And then, of course, we can't cope with them either."

"Missions... you're not an army chaplain?" asked Sullivan.

"Christian Friendship Society, my dear. Doing the Good Lord's donkey work here in the Darkened Continent. Despite the government's lofty title for it, camps like this are run purely as civilian operations, by volunteers. The army, the government, no one wants to know... I say we have 30,000 here, that's by mid-afternoon when the new arrivals have swelled the numbers. Come morning up to 500 could have perished. State of equilibrium. We were burying them at first, but, what with the typhus, we find it more expedient to cremate. Keeps these beggars away..."

He flapped at a squadron of particularly attentive horseflies. In the distance, black smoke rose.

"Jesus," snorted Annie.

"...would be proud of you. The reason you're here, the reason the Good Lord brought you ladies here, is to help us. The instructions are for you to have a good look around. Please, go where you will. Take stock, impart some basic medical knowledge to my helpers... and then, the crucial part, further your observations to the party of army VIPs who will be arriving for inspection tomorrow morning."

He noticed looks of disdain.

"Actually, in this case, I'm glad for some joined-up thinking. A few wise heads in the Medical Corps realising that the Empire can't wash its hands of all this, must take responsibility. Doesn't sell the war well. And if the army pushes on into The Free State and the Transvaal, like they're all saying... well, it won't just be natives cast adrift, but Europeans, too."

"You don't have enough medical staff to care for these people?"

"My dear girl, other than some St John's Ambulance, I don't have *any* medical staff. Me? I scare up sacks of mealies and buttermilk; furnish old clothing and blankets; recite the Scriptures."

"Dear God," said Sullivan.

"...moves in mysterious ways," added Newbold. "...moves in mysterious ways."

They stepped into a large tent. There were some 15–20 casualties laid out on the floor. Young white women and Coloured female orderlies were attending to the sick. They were mostly elderly or children, some mere babes in arms, their coughs hacked painfully, the weaker ones rasping forlorn little life-or-death struggles.

"Other than a few medicines we can poach from the Red Cross, we're relying on what little fresh water we can find. That plus tenderness and prayer."

The nurses dumped their kit bags and stepped forward to help. He put his hand up to stop them.

"First, I need you to do something."

He led them to the other end of the tent and opened the flap. Apparently they had come in by the rear entrance. Out front, a queue stretched on forever. Newbold registered the shock on their faces. He had meant it that way.

"Here we must also *play* God."

He pointed at the queue.

"Go down the line. Anyone you think over 60, anyone who, in your estimation, has a less than an eight-in-ten chance of survival, turn them away."

–

That night, neither Annie nor Nurse Sullivan slept. They rose at dawn and took a mere mouthful of the mealies offered at the food station.

Annie was not religious but found Newbold an endearing man and complied, head bowed, when he read a brief prayer.

In the orange glow of daybreak, they aided his staff in their near impossible task, another logistical one – a question of sorting through the human debris, organising disposal of corpses, deciding on the odds of survival of the sick, and making sure not to waste precious food or time on those who were lost causes.

Annie and Nurse Sullivan gave practical advice to Newbold's loyal Christian soldiers, whose medical knowledge extended to little more than emergency first aid.

But with so many cases, where on earth to begin?

When the sun rose fully, Dean Newbold called them. He pointed back up the trail. There was a puff of dust. Another wagon was approaching. They watched at distance as it came to a halt where theirs had done and a party of officers disembarked, loosening stiff limbs after the long road haul up form Paarl. They seemed to be going through the same ritual of shock, though she noted that the corporal *was* handing out surgical masks this time.

"You'll have to pardon me," said Newbold. "Got to show these fellows around. Want to make it absolutely clear what we're up against. Only way we're going to help these people is with proper resources. And you, ladies…"

Annie and Sullivan looked at each other.

"*Us?*"

"They'll be asking your opinion. You're part of our diplomatic offensive… our charm offensive… There's one officer in particular. Welsh chap. Hopes to bring us under the RAMC umbrella and start coordinating aid with the Red Cross."

The corporal led the men to the edge of the camp. Newbold came to greet them, bellowing his somewhat insincere wish that they'd enjoyed a pleasant journey. He steered them towards the main tent on what looked like a similar sort of tour he had conducted yesterday.

Fifteen minutes later, Newbold re-appeared with the officer party, about six or seven of them, heading in their direction. No, not all military… there was a civilian… he was scrawling in a notebook.

"Ladies," boomed Newbold, "please welcome our distinguished guests."

Two were RAMC, the others included a braided army high-up and two other officers plus an adjutant sergeant.

One of the RAMC men, a major, a man of medium height with thick black hair and dark twinkling eyes, stepped forward. His accent was distantly familiar to Annie. From when she was very young. Her great grandfather. The Welshman?

"No need to stand on ceremony," he said, addressing them directly. "First of all, I'd like to thank you for the help you're giving here. Though the most important thing you can assist us with is a bit of practical input. Thought it good to see all this through the eyes of those on the sharp end – you nurses."

There was a snort from behind him. A colonel, a rotund man with a white walrus moustache was now looking rather ill behind his surgical mask.

"Damn good work," he seemed to mutter. "Damn good work."

The sergeant, a thin man with a clipboard who looked like he'd rather be anywhere else, announced that they would be taking statements shortly.

The civilian, meanwhile, continued scribbling furiously. In a brief instant he looked up.

"John Simmons, *Cape Argus*," he said, doffing his bowler.

A journalist, thought Annie. Clever.

"The reason you two were selected for this rather unpleasant assignment," the major went on, "is that, with the reorganisation you were on your way up the line anyway. And what more effective witnesses than the very nurses put forward as mine and the captain's assistants."

Annie and Nurse Sullivan looked at each other. It sounded like recognition of sorts. They should be happy. But with what lay round about them…

The major took a peek at the sergeant's clipboard. The colonel next to him was turning a shade of green.

"Nurse Sullivan?"

She nodded.

"You'll be with myself. And Nurse…"

He was prompted.

"…Jones?"

Annie did the same.

"You're assigned to Captain Finch."

An RAMC officer had been staring off into middle distance. At the sound of his name, he turned. He was tall, reasonably trim. He had pale blue eyes, dark brown hair. When he pulled down his surgical mask she saw that he had a clipped moustache.

She recognised him, but wasn't sure from where.

Then the penny dropped. She uttered a word under her breath. "Bastard."

—

After the questioning of the nurses, Jenkins informed Finch that he was escorting the inspection party back to Paarl. It was a two-hour-plus slog. They should get going. Nurse Sullivan would go with them.

Jones expressed a desire to stay and help at the camp until the last possible moment, which Finch respected. He felt a moral obligation to do likewise. There would be another wagon along in a while.

Finch kept a discreet distance as the two women bade a hasty and fond farewell. Finch thought he detected the brief glint of a tear on Jones' cheek but she wiped it quickly and flashed him a steely glare.

Finch did not know what to make of her. Amplified by his three-month remove from the social company of women, he judged her to be attractive. She was clearly dedicated to her work but also had a contemptuous air about her.

He had been warned about colonials and their natural obstreperousness, the Antipodeans in particular, though from his personal experience, professionally he had never found them wanting either as soldiers or as medical personnel.

Indeed, compared to the average Tommy, the Australians especially seemed a wholesome, superior breed. Their bush troops, adept at firing from horseback and in terrain not dissimilar to that which they were encountering in South Africa, marked them out as most worthy adversaries of the Boer commando.

Jones' attention was suddenly turned. From the main tent, a Coloured female orderly was beckoning. She wore a starched head-dress exposing only her face, suggesting she might actually be a nun.

"Excuse me," said Jones and headed off.

He noted the lack of a 'sir'.

A moment later, after conferring, she turned back.

"You might want to see this," she called.

He deliberately displayed no acknowledgement.

"Sir...!" she was forced to add.

Jones moved with purpose. He had difficulty keeping up. She and the nun/orderly led him along another arbitrary walkway towards an awning under which stood the trestle tables and barrels of mealies being stirred by more of Newbold's flock.

Another female orderly, a short, flustered white woman with a pinched face and a large crucifix around her neck, was trying to form a queue from what appeared to be new arrivals.

The short, pinched woman pointed.

"Down there... Down *there*."

"How long?" asked Annie.

"About an hour?"

They proceeded towards a spreading shepherd's tree under which were gathered some of the new arrivals, squeezed into the retreating shade.

They were different to the others, Finch noted, the smaller, slighter, lighter-skinned aboriginals, or Khoisan people, once the only human inhabitants of this land. They had long been marginalised, pushed to the badlands.

The Coloured orderly whispered something.

"She says they are Nama," repeated Jones. "From across the Karoo."

"They have crossed it on foot," said the orderly.

"Jesus."

"But that's not all," added Jones.

She led him around the tree. The forlorn rag-tag gaggle was already in the process of assimilation – speechless, lifeless. Sitting amongst the Nama was a black African man. He had a rough beard and wore a ragged blue-checked shirt and a battered bush hat. Sweat stained his clothes and neckerchief.

And, cradled in his arms, fast asleep, clad in a filthy pinafore dress, was a young blonde, white girl.

Behind him, Finch saw a white woman – a skinny, crazed-looking individual kneading her hands.

The black man raised his head and fixed Finch with tired, blood-shot, but kindly eyes.

"Please, can you help us? We have come a long way."

Chapter Thirty-Four

The man was looking down at him. Standing with his back to the sun, it was difficult to make out his features. Mbutu had been told that he was a doctor. When he raised his hand to shield his eyes, he could see the man was also in army uniform, an officer.

"You speak English?" he was asking.

"Yes."

Mbutu was so tired, so hungry, it took every ounce of willpower to fight the raging desire to lie down and close his eyes. He feared that he might never wake up.

"The nurse tells me that you crossed the Karoo."

Did the doctor not believe him? Or did the doctor not believe her?

The nurse was kneeling down, attending to the white mother.

"Three days. On foot," Mbutu sighed.

"Is that possible? You have women, children, elderly—"

"The Nama people are hardy, resourceful, can live off the bush."

They are also very trusting. They put their life in his hands. He led them to where? To here? This hell? Mbutu you are a curse.

The doctor turned to the white woman and addressed her. She flinched and averted her gaze.

"Madam. Is it true what this man says?"

The word of a black man counts for nothing.

She began to quake. She drew up her knees and buried her face in her hands.

He bellowed his question again.

"She cannot talk."

"Cannot talk?"

"She has lost her voice. Shock."

"Shock?"

"She… her daughter… these people have suffered a terrible ordeal."

The doctor studied him.

"You are not one of them… not Nama."

What did it matter?

"Basuto."

"From Basutoland?"

"From Kimberley."

"How the hell did you get out of Kimberley?"

Mbutu said nothing.

The doctor officer did his best to crouch down to his level. It was an awkward manoeuvre, stiff, unbending. He had injured his left leg.

Emily was still asleep, cradled in Mbutu's arms. The doctor stroked her blonde hair.

"This girl…"

He nodded at the white woman.

"…Her mother… They are from Kimberley too?"

Mbutu exhaled. He was exhausted enough.

"Please, sir," the nurse interrupted.

Her accent was unusual. Not from the Cape, not British.

"He's right," she said. "She's mute."

The word of a black man counts for nothing.

"They have endured a lot," said Mbutu.

Awkwardly the army doctor got to his feet and walked around the tree, observing.

"Some of your party, the men… are blind?"

"Please," said Mbutu. "Help us. Weakest first. I will explain all."

"I will be the judge of such things!" the doctor snapped.

It was for show, thought Mbutu. The officer pretended to mull over the situation. But he would concur.

"Right," he continued, addressing both the nurse and the nearby Coloured orderly. "Run someone over to the food station, fetch them buttermilk, some mealies."

He turned back and spoke to them all, not knowing whether they understood.

"Then you can all get some well-earned rest."

"Newbold," said Mbutu. "I cannot rest until I speak to a Mister Newbold… a church man."

"Dean Newbold is busy. He's gone back to Paarl. Will be there until this afternoon."

He seemed uncomfortable in authority, thought Mbutu, insecure, playing out a charade of giving orders.

"Then, for the sake of these people, I need to speak to someone I can trust."

The doctor crouched down and looked him in the eye. No one else could hear.

"What is your name?"

"Mbutu. Mbutu Kefalaze."

"Mbutu, my name is Captain Ingo Finch of the Royal Army Medical Corps. I am a doctor. You can trust me."

—

Only when he was satisfied that his people had been fed and watered did Mbutu speak. He was deathly tired but told the doctor that which seemed prudent.

Emily awoke but preferred to cling to Mbutu rather than seek succour from her mother or any female attendant.

In her own childish way, as she sat cuddled up to Mbutu, sipping on some buttermilk, Emily corroborated elements of the tale he told, with Mbutu judiciously silencing her when it came to the parts he would rather remain withheld.

They had walked over three days, stopping during the midday heat and at night, lighting a fire and keeping watch to maintain safety from predators, he said.

They had brought the goat with them, which had been milked and slaughtered en route – he did not mention the ample meat the two horses had provided. They had obtained water from surface wells, boreholes and from plant leaves. Miraculously no one had died.

He told Finch how he, personally, had been tricked out of Kimberley on the pretence of running a message for the army and that he had been forced to ride the train south. He had been turfed out into the wilderness and had been saved by the Nama who were themselves seeking refuge after their villages had been destroyed.

He explained to Captain Finch that the child's father… the woman's husband… was a British missionary named Sutton. He had been one of the casualties. After the attack, the two white females had fled into the Karoo.

Soldiers, British soldiers, had come after them. Mbutu and a colleague had gone northwest to the villages to validate the Suttons' story but were chased away by more troops.

"British soldiers?" asked Finch incredulously.

"It is the truth."

Finch exhaled.

"My dear fellow, I'm afraid you're mixing up your combatants. These were clearly Boers."

"They wore British uniforms."

"They were Boers masquerading."

"Doctor, Captain. I heard their voices. Please, I ask you to believe me."

"How did you get to these villages? If they're where you say they are, that's some distance."

Mbutu. You fool. You cannot say by horse.

Emily looked up at the officer.

"Please, sir. What Mbutu says is true."

Thank you, child.

Mbutu pulled her in close.

"This poor creature has seen things no child ought to."

He reached behind him for his canvas bag. He pulled out the smashed elephant box.

"Here…"

The captain set it before him, opened it and leafed through the contents. He stopped at the photograph.

"Emily, this is you? Your mother?"

She nodded.

He opened the logbook. Mbutu pointed a finger.

"See… the letter. Dean Ephraim Newbold."

The captain rubbed his chin as he picked through the assorted correspondence and telegrams.

The British. It is only true if it has been written.

The doctor captain handed the photo to the girl, put the correspondence back, then closed the lid.

"Mbutu," he said. "I don't doubt that you are an honourable man. I don't doubt, either, that you and your people have endured great hardship. I assure you that we will repatriate little Emily and her mother. But the reality is there are 30,000 people here, very sick people. This is a war, terrible things happen… to everyone."

Mbutu had forgotten something.

223

"Doctor Captain. What if I told you that before Emily's village was destroyed, they marched in a column of men, white men... in shackles?"

"Shackles?"

"Prisoners. They marched in prisoners. They too were killed by the soldiers."

"Now steady on—"

"They were not killed by bullets."

The captain stood awkwardly and turned to go. He beckoned to his nurse. The officer personality resumed.

"Jones. Once you have completed your duties here, give the Red Cross instructions to pack the two whites on to Cape Town."

Mbutu saw her roll her eyes. She did not care for her *baas*.

"And whatever did so," yelled Mbutu, "also blinded these men!"

He pulled from his bag the hessian headwear, the rough sackcloth material into which had been fastened two round, glass eyeholes with the strange orange rubber beak.

"Captain. Doctor!"

He turned back. Mbutu threw it to him. The officer doctor instinctively put out his hands to catch it.

Chapter Thirty-Five

They faced south and watched the wagon creak down the dusty trail. The ever-chipper Newbold bounded out over the tailboard.

"Captain… Nurse Jones…" he beamed, striding towards them with great purpose, seemingly unbothered by his lengthy round-trip.

"…I think it is safe for us to be optimistic. By the sounds of it, we are to receive some long overdue material and financial assistance here at our little assembly. We are now officially an army-sanctioned centralisation point – a Concentration Camp. Or as I would rather, Congregation Camp."

"He's a good man, Captain… *Major* Jenkins," echoed Finch.

"Has his head screwed on…" said Newbold. "And thank you, Nurse Jones. Sterling work, my girl."

In truth, Annie did not feel as though she had contributed much at all.

"You're welcome," she said anyway.

The sarcastic corporal hopped down from the driver's seat. His boots crunched in the dirt. Reflexively, he went to help Finch, the officer, with his kitbag.

"Cedric, please… we have ladies…" blurted Newbold.

The corporal huffed and hoisted Annie's bag first.

Finch informed Newbold that his prediction had already proven correct. The camp had, this very morning, taken in its first white refugees.

The news caused the smile to drop. On hearing that they were survivors from a church mission to boot, he bade a terse farewell and hastened off down the walkway, stomping round bodies, waving over his shoulder.

Annie took her last sad look at the amorphous human mass and its apocalyptic black cloud.

She and the captain then climbed on board the wagon and, with an orchestrated jolt on the part of the tiresome corporal, it set off for

Paarl. They were the only two passengers but, for the tiresome journey back through the mountain pass, neither spoke, subject solely to the aural backdrop of the corporal's whistling and the languid *clip-clop* of the two mules. The presence of an officer had put paid to the NCO's rudeness at least.

She watched as Finch made notes in his leather-bound journal, something she had remembered him doing that day in the coffee shop. Now, as then, he seemed lost in thought.

He had certainly not remembered her. Or if he did, he had done a magnificent job of hiding it.

After well over two hours the Paarl rock came into view, followed by the order and neatness of the Dutch colonial town.

Passing the whitewashed, high gables of the town's centre, they alighted at the train station. The corporal passed the captain's bag down and, with a parting shot of petulance, heaved Annie's over the tailboard.

When the captain's back was turned, he could not resist a parting, lascivious gesture – some insinuation that Annie and her new officer ward were going to engage in intimate relations.

Oblivious, the captain pulled a scrap of paper from his pocket, checked the scribble and announced that they still had more than an hour until the next train bound northward. They had a long, uncomfortable, overnight journey ahead of them, he reminded, although Annie suppressed a minor thrill at the revelation that she would, this time, be travelling in second class.

He pointed to a tea shop across the road with tables on the pavement set beneath bright yellow umbrellas.

It was late afternoon, the place was empty. They ensconced themselves and ordered their drinks from a waiter evidently unprepared and not exactly grateful for the advent of custom. Finch opted for rooibos tea, she herself preferring Ceylon.

A sudden and welcoming cool breeze blew, ruffling the dangling cotton fringe of their umbrella. Annie supposed she carried the smell of the camp with her. She could not tell. If she did, she hoped that the wind would do something to purge it.

Captain Finch insisted that he would be paying the bill and that the least he could do was to treat her to a slice of cake. She politely declined. It didn't seem right.

The few words spoken were confined to polite chit-chat but the captain seemed to have something he wished to get off his chest. It came awkwardly.

"Nurse Jones, I realise that this is probably not the assignment you had been anticipating," he began, entering into something that sounded like a rehearsed speech.

Is that what he had been writing in his notebook?

"…and, as a consequence, have now become separated from your colleagues, but you come with the highest recommendation and we have much work to do. For both our sakes…"

He hesitated, not quite at ease with the text.

"…I think we can at least attempt some civil discourse."

The patronising bastard.

"For example, where are you from?" he said, horribly forced.

"Sydney."

"You were a nurse there?"

"Yes."

"Where did you work?"

"The Sydney Hospital."

She did not elaborate. He sighed in exasperation.

"Did you like it there?"

Did one 'like' a hospital?

"It was well-run, clean, unlike—"

"Caring for the wounded in wartime can be a shock. I've been here three months. It's still not easy."

She stirred her tea, staring into the cup. Tea had become a ritual. Very British.

"Not just the war wounded," she said.

"What we witnessed today is a tragedy," he conceded.

She reversed her decision and selected a slice of sponge gateau from the cake stand. It oozed strawberry jam and a thick white cream filling.

"May I ask *you* something?" she said.

"Nurse Jones, I do not wish to press the point. But the correct way to address me would be to employ the occasional 'Sir'… 'Captain'… either's fine. 'Doctor' if you really must—"

"That native, this morning," she carried on, "the one accompanying the two white females…"

He nodded.

"What was that all about?"

"Lord knows."

"What was that he threw to you?"

"From the mines, I think. Some kind of breathing apparatus… But the mother and child *will* be taken care of. Poor blighters."

"They're all poor blighters."

He removed a silver cigarette case from his inside breast pocket. She noted some improvised needlework down one side of his tunic, under the armpit. The thread was green but did not match.

"Smoke?" he offered.

"Not really."

"You mind if I do?"

She shook her head. He tapped out a cigarette, lit it and exhaled skyward.

"And which is why we need to keep on top of things, Jones…"

The breeze wafted the smoke away behind him.

"…Reverend Newbold… *Dean* Newbold is correct. This is just the start. As the war pushes northwards, there'll be plenty more lost souls like that mother and daughter we saw today. The army can't allow that to happen."

She didn't like the implication. Camps full of dying blacks seemed inevitable. The army's real objective was to stop such a fate befalling displaced whites.

"The papers, they'd have a field day, you understand."

He went on to tell her a little bit about himself but she demonstrated little interest. When he probed her for further background information, she kept it curt, sleepwalking through the main points of her recent experiences, avoiding any mention of her civilian life.

She had spent four weeks in the Cape Town Military Hospital, she said. What they had witnessed there had upset her – all of them – but the nurses had done their duty.

"Cape Town is a beautiful city."

What a pointless thing to say.

"Did you get to see any of it?"

"We had little time off. When we did, we were heavily chaperoned."

Had it jogged his memory?

"Not surprised," he replied. "By day, Cape Town's a treasure. I long to return and explore it at my leisure, some day, when this nonsense is over…"

He paused. The war? Nonsense? An unwitting but probably truthful summation.

"But you've got to be careful. And by night… men, drink…"

She reflected for a moment of her cloistered existence these past few weeks. She yearned for a time where life would not be straight-jacketed.

"Most of our excursions were confined to all-female tea parties up at the mansion," she explained.

"The mansion?"

"The benefactor of the nurses' home."

He seemed lost in thought again. Was he forming a mental picture?

"Sir Frederick Hancock," she added.

He smiled in recognition. He exhaled a silent chuckle.

"Rather you than me."

Rare candour, humour. Was he human after all?

She suppressed an impulse to laugh in return.

"On the odd Sunday afternoon that enough of us were available, he and Lady Verity would invite us over. They have this beautiful house—"

"Wait, wait… Lady Verity…?"

"Yes."

"Lady Verity Hancock?"

"Yes."

Lady Verity Hancock!

He seemed excited. She couldn't understand why.

Chapter Thirty-Six

Lady Verity Hancock. But of course!

As a benefactor of the nursing home, knew Finch, there would have been ample opportunity for Cox to have run into her... back before the war, when the RAMC was still a work in progress – lots of Cape Town functions, receptions and hobnobbing with the politicos.

Cox, you sly fox.

But oh, Cox, what had you got yourself into? Finch could picture the scene – the lonely-heart wife, the stuffed-shirt husband. But the cuckold in question was no poor civil servant. He was Sir Frederick Hancock, personal envoy to the Marquess of Lansdowne, Secretary of State for War, architect of British foreign policy in South Africa.

No wonder Lady Verity was paranoid. No wonder Cox was being warned off.

Public knowledge of their affair would have been scandalous – a humiliation for Sir Frederick and social suicide for Lady Verity. But, politically, it would have been crippling, coming at a critical juncture of Britain's involvement in the Cape.

And it would also...

Finch had a sudden sharp realisation.

...make those letters a valuable political weapon, a means of blackmail.

Was that why Ans Du Plessis's guest house had been ransacked? Was that why his own hotel room had been burgled, his tunic sliced open?

Inspector Brookman was suddenly very present in Finch's mind. He would have to pass this information on to him right away.

Nurse Jones was staring at him.

"I'm sorry," he said. "It's just that I know the woman, of sorts... Lady Verity Hancock."

"You do?"

"I was just surprised and delighted to hear that she had taken such a personal interest in the doings of the nurses," he improvised. "All most benefactors want is their name on a plaque."

"She was nice," she added.

But telling Brookman. How to do so? His possession of the letters would amount to withholding evidence, especially now the 'other woman', as it were, was proven to be someone other than Vesta Lane. Even if Du Plessis took the blame with regard to holding them back, there was no denying that Finch had also sat on them, read them…

What if he bent the truth a little?

The cogs whirred… Yes… Ans Du Plessis had only found them belatedly, that was they had agreed. She had given them to him yesterday to post to Cox's widow alongside his other possessions. He had, after all, been charged with that responsibility.

Yes, yes… He was about to include the letters in the parcel to India but – gentleman to gentleman, Brookman – had grown suspicious of their nature and decided to have a peek to avoid further upset for the wife. He was in a hurry, boarding a train, and had no chance to return them. He was doing so at the first opportunity. And now it was an emergency. They had been stolen.

He pulled out his notebook, uncapped his pen and made notes. He must rehearse his lie.

He looked up. Nurse Jones was growing bored and was quite happy to show it. She had drunk her tea, demolished her cake, and had since leaned over to retrieve a discarded *Cape Argus* from the next table.

Communicating the information to Brookman would not be easy. It was sensitive material. He could not risk writing it openly in a telegram. In any case, it required too long an explanation. He could get it tapped out in a private Morse message, but again it wasn't secure.

He would have to write a letter. Tonight, on the train, he would put it down on paper. When they stopped at Beaufort West or De Aar he could get it to Brookman via the army mailbag. If not possible there, then at the terminus at Hopetown. Chances are the letter would reach Brookman tomorrow or the day after.

Nurse Jones was examining the front page with its headline:

ROBERTS AND KITCHENER TAKE CHARGE

The paper, like just about everyone, was cheerleading the army's new leadership.

Sending a letter still seemed slow. If he'd been in Cape Town, he'd have hobbled round to the station right there and then. He could seek out the local police station here in Paarl but it would take a while to run through the backstory to some local bobby and, even then, much of the information was still privileged.

If only to…

As he glanced down at Jones' newspaper, his blood ran cold. For the first time since that moment when the coroner's sheet had been pulled back to reveal the dead white face of Cox, he felt truly shocked. He could taste a sudden rise of vomit.

"You all right?"

No, he was far from all right. His head spun. For there, over Jones' shoulder, at the bottom right hand side of the front page, in a neat box, ran a minor headline:

Suspect in RAMC murder enquiry found dead

He snatched the paper right out of her hands.

"Hey!"

But there it was, in black and white… Mr. Ashley Kilfoyle of Hout Bay, formerly of Portadown, Ireland, recently charged with the murder of Major Leonard Cox, had been found dead in his Cape Town jail cell. The means of his death were not disclosed.

"Don't move," he told her.

Armed with the newspaper, Finch hastened towards the post office building across the road, over on the same side as the station. He hobbled in through the door. It had a tiled floor and a high ceiling, overly grand. It was cool, quiet, virtually empty.

There was a middle-aged woman in a straw hat being served at one of the positions along the long counter, but the rest were free. She had two Pekinese dogs flitting around her skirts. They yapped at him.

The smell. He must smell.

A plain-looking female assistant, early 20s, looked up. She had a strange cast to her eye – an outward squint, giving the impression that she was looking at someone over his shoulder. He turned. There was no one there.

"Can I help you, sir?" she said.

He decided to pick one eye and stick with it.

"Please, I need to use your telephone."

"Our telephone?"

"You have one for public use?"

"I'm afraid it's by appointment. Do you have—?"

"It's rather urgent."

The look on his face, he was sure, had done the trick. She pointed to a side room.

"Shilling deposit, thruppence per minute once you have been connected."

"I'm afraid I've never used one before."

"A telephone?"

"No."

"If you could just wait there, sir."

She placed a wooden 'Closed' marker at her position and ducked under a hinged flap.

"Please, follow me."

Inside, the candlestick telephone stood on a desk with a worn wooden chair before it.

"You have the number... the exchange?"

He didn't. There was a notepad on the desk and a pen on a chain. He dipped it in the inkwell and scrawled, "Detective Inspector Brookman, Cape Town Police."

He reached into his pocket for a shilling but she was suddenly in a hurry, fumbling for a handkerchief. She then cranked a handle on the stand, unhooked the receiver and tapped the lever beneath it.

"Cape Town... Police Station if you please."

He could hear the crackle of a voice on the other end. The woman looked up at him.

"Wale Street?" she asked.

Finch nodded.

"Would you kindly connect me. Thank you."

He could hear electronic squeaks and pips. It took another half-a-minute during which the poor woman pretended to stem a running nose.

There was a response. The woman adopted a more formal tone.

"Good afternoon. I'm placing a call from the General Post Office in Paarl. I have a gentlemen here who would like to speak to..."

She read from the note.

"Detective Inspector—"

"Brookman," prompted Finch.

"Brookman."

She passed the receiver.

"Listen here… Speak here… Allow a second or two to avoid overlap. Bit of a delay."

She hustled to the iron-framed window, took a wooden pole with a hook and reached up to pull open the hopper.

"And when you've finished, please hang up the receiver."

She scurried out.

Finch pressed the receiver to his ear. There was the crackle of static, then a voice.

"*Hello…? Hello?*"

Amazing. A voice from 40 miles away.

"Inspector Brookman?"

It took a moment for a reply.

"*This is Desk Sergeant Norris.*"

Disappointment. Finch found himself talking slowly and unnecessarily loudly.

"Sergeant Norris. This is Captain Finch of the RAMC. We met the other day. I had been assisting Inspector Brookman with the Cox murder enquiry. It is with the greatest urgency that I need to speak to him."

There was no reply. He began to reiterate when the sergeant's voice came back. He missed the answer.

"I'm sorry, could you repeat—"

"*The inspector's not here, sir. Won't be back for some time.*"

Finch cast a glance at the newspaper.

"Kilfoyle… What on earth happened?"

There was a pause.

"*I'm not at liberty to say, sir.*"

Damn.

"The inspector. Can I leave him a message?"

"*Of course, sir.*"

"Tell him I have information which may be of vital importance to the enquiry."

"*Very good, sir, but I think you'll find it's an open-and-shut case now.*"

"Sergeant. You must pass this message on."

"*How do we reach you, sir?*"

"I'm in transit. You can leave a message for my unit at the Hopetown telegraph. But, I stress, it is most urgent."

"*Right you are, sir.*"

"Thank you. Goodbye."

"*Goodbye, sir.*"

Finch sat for a moment. He wondered whether he should try and contact Rideau, for he too had had suspicions. He would surely pass the information to Brookman on his behalf.

But then the shock became something else – a chill supposition that his own delay in passing on the letters could somehow have expedited Kilfoyle's death, whether it be at the man's own hand or that of others.

A female voice interrupted him.

"*Hello?*"

It was the telephone.

"*This is the operator.*"

"Hello."

"*Would you kindly replace the receiver.*"

He hung up.

He paid the woman at the counter, who had for the olfactory comfort of her customers opened several other windows and already totted up the bill, then limped outside. As he crossed the road, he saw that Jones had procured herself a second pot of tea. She did not look in the best of humour; less so when he performed an about-face in the middle of the street.

Finch made his way into the train station and checked the departure board, then Cox's watch. Their train, the 6.15, was due in about 20 minutes' time. There were already troops assembling. But there was also a later one leaving at ten minutes past eleven. Their orders were to report at Hopetown by noon tomorrow. Catch it and they'd still arrive on time.

There *was* one other thing he could do...

Finch hurried as best he could back to the tea shop.

"Nurse Jones?"

"What?"

"I'm afraid this may sound a little unorthodox..."

She did not appear enthused.

"Lady Verity Hancock."

"What about her?"

"The mansion. It's in Stellenbosch, right?"

"Yes."

"Do you remember where? Would you recognise it?"

235

"Recognise it?"

"The building."

"I think so."

Finch laid down some coins to cover the tea and cake. The waiter rummaged in his apron for change but Finch told him to keep it.

"Tell me, how far is Stellenbosch from here?"

The waiter shrugged.

"I don't know... 15, 20 miles?"

Finch stepped into the street. There were taxis idling in the sun. He put thumb and forefinger to stretch his lips and gave a shrill whistle. One of the buggies sprang into life. It trotted over. The Coloured cabbie looked down.

"*Baas?*"

"Could you take us to Stellenbosch?"

"But the train—" Jones protested.

The cabbie did not look sure.

"Long way for my mule. And for no return fare."

"How much to take us to Stellenbosch, wait half an hour, then bring us straight back here?"

"Man, that's a three- to four-hour round trip. I don't know, 15 shillings maybe, but—"

"A guinea. I will give you a guinea."

The cabbie's face lit up.

"These your bags?"

He jumped down to load their gear.

"You know what, let's leave them at the baggage counter," said Finch.

The cabbie helped Finch cart the two kit bags to the desk where they were checked in. The man at the desk seemed to labour forever at filling out the receipt.

When finally offered, Finch grabbed it and, with the cabbie in tow, re-emerged into the sunshine. Jones was not amused. Finch explained about the later train. It did not alter her demeanour.

Finch helped the reluctant Jones up then clambered on board after her. The cabbie wheeled the buggy around and headed for the road south.

As the sun started to lower in the sky, the vineyards which seemed to stretch on forever were bathed in a pink-orange glow. With the whitewashed gabled buildings and pretty churches, they were a world away from Camp Eureka. It reminded Finch of a trip he'd once taken to Tuscany.

There were few people about. On the outskirts of town, as ever, black folk ambled around the paltry shacks that constituted their neighbourhoods, exiled to the margins.

As the buggy carried on its way, roughly parallel to the train line, they heard the toot of a whistle and saw the smoke as their intended locomotive approached.

Christ, Finch. I hope you know what you're doing.

Save for the odd wagon, the road was empty, though behind them a lone horse, kicking up dust, slowly gained on them. Nurse Jones just stared ahead. He would have some explaining to do. Again, Finch got out his trusty notebook and jotted down the points that needed addressing.

After about an hour, the great Paarl rock had long retreated from view and the low sun in the west was stinging their eyes when there came a sudden snap, like that of large dry twig being broken in two.

The mule lurched to the side and the cabbie struggled to control the animal as if something mechanical had fractured.

Snap!

It came again. The mule snorted, the cabbie cursed.

Only then did Finch realise. That sound and its accompanying echo...

Magersfontein.

It was a gun... a rifle.

Crack-*zing!*

Someone was shooting at them.

Chapter Thirty-Seven

The cab listed over to port, its steering gone. The broken axle was now scraping along the gravel, the mule thrown into a state of skittish panic.

CRACK! Another shot.

Finch heard the bullet thud into the earth bank to their right.

The driver was struggling, pulling hard on the reins as the mule began to rear up.

"Get down!" yelled Finch and reached up to grab him by the back of his collar. Finch wrestled him onto the boards. He landed hard, uncomfortably, shocked.

"The vines. Go... GO!"

He stared at Finch in a daze.

"My mule."

"No time—"

Finch pushed the man out.

"Go! KEEP LOW!"

His mule was on its side, eyes wide and white, struggling against the weight of the harness to upright itself, kicking out at nothing. The cabbie loitered for a moment, then staggered off. Finch grabbed Annie's hand and dragged her in the same direction.

CRACK!

They dived between the vines and ran as best they could along a straight earth furrow. The soil was loose and powdery. Running in the 'V' of the furrow was awkward, but the gradient, which sloped away gently, carried them along. Up ahead, the cabbie stopped and turned, out of breath, his look one of utter confusion.

"They're not after you," barked Finch, motioning with his arm. "Go! Hide till the coast is clear."

They could hear the rattle of hooves.

Finch took Annie's hand again and pulled her with him.

Magersfontein. He had a sudden thought of young Miles.

"No straight lines. We zig-zag."

She nodded. They ran on. The adrenaline masked the pain in Finch's knee.

The cabbie branched off to the left, lolling through vines, crashing right through the thin wooden sticks of the trellising and creepers.

Finch threw a glance over his shoulder. He saw a flash of white – the horse. He heard it pant and splutter and its hooves scrape to a halt. There was the squeak and clink of tack.

"Now!" he urged Annie, and they ducked right between the head-high creepers, smashing right through.

Ten yards along, the next furrow, they burst right again, repeating the manoeuvre several times.

After a minute or two they stopped. Finch pressed his finger to his lips. She nodded.

The pursuer made no sound. Had he stopped also?

CRACK!

Another bullet. It fizzed through the leaves. A red splash appeared on Annie's chest.

NO!

Finch was splattered too, right across the face. But he could taste it... Grape!

Too close. Much too close.

They ran on instinctively, ducking low. He didn't need to lead Annie this time, crashing on across the lines, vine after vine, trellis after trellis.

Instinctively they doubled-back and both hit the floor, prone.

Gradually Finch lifted his head up.

There!

A glimpse. Brown riding boots, slowly and noiselessly stalking in their direction, four or five furrows along, each step placed carefully and skilfully.

Annie pointed upwards. Where they had crashed through, there remained a ragged gaping hole. Their route was obvious. There came the ominous click of a rifle bolt.

You idiot, Finch. You have a gun yourself.

He crawled his fingers down to the holster. But...

His Webley was gone. The security strap flapped open.

The brown boots stopped. Finch saw a hand reach down and, by its stock, pick his service revolver out of the dirt.

Finch stretched his hand. A large stone. It was the oldest trick in the book but he grabbed it, twisted round and hurled it as far as he could in the vague direction they might have continued running.

It landed with just the correct degree of rustle.

For what seemed forever, the boots remained still. Then, mercifully, slowly, they turned, down the slope, as if he and Annie were still fleeing away from the road.

Finch could hear Annie's breath being brought under control. He felt his own heart pounding inside what seemed his head as, there, right before them, into their own furrow, not five yards away, the man stepped between the vines through the gap they had made.

But he was facing away from them. Not once did he turn in their direction. Had he done so they were sitting ducks. Instead he was creeping away, his rifle raised, the webbing strap wound tightly round his left hand like a marksman.

The light was fading but Finch could see the man wore a dark suit, blue or grey, and had close-cropped sandy, reddish hair. He had a thick neck. His shoulders were broad, muscular.

Ten yards further on, the man picked his way through into the next furrow and continued to proceed away from them.

The sun was fully down, its vestigial glow diminishing. Nightfall would be their salvation. If they could just hold on a little longer.

Sure now that the man had moved some distance away, they crawled back in the direction they had come. Some 30 or 40 yards on Finch signalled it safe to rise and continue on foot, hunched low.

They lay again and almost willed the last light away, saying nothing.

They had begun to relax when they heard footsteps once more tramping through the dirt. This time they were not those of a stalker but of an impatient man, a man stamping in anger back to his steed.

Again came the scrape of hooves, but then…

Another shot. A whinny. He had finished off the poor mule.

There was an equine snort and a creak of leather. The man made a clicking sound and the horse wheeled round. Slowly it receded from hearing.

Annie turned to him.

"I don't care who you are. What the bloody hell is going on?"

Finch got to his feet and rubbed his cursed knee.

"Here…"

He extended his hand. She refused it.

In the thinnest of light he saw her stand and brush the dirt off her skirts. She had lost her hat. Her hair had been pinned up but there were tresses that hung down. She made a rudimentary attempt at re-fastening them.

"This way," said Finch.

He turned and hobbled off up through the vineyard in the direction of Stellenbosch. To affect an air of cocky calm – though he felt anything but – he plucked a grape and popped it in his mouth. He spluttered and spat it out. Not yet ripe by some distance. He heard her contemptuous snort behind him.

"There's no way we're going to get up to the Front tonight," she said. "I'll be listed absent. I have written orders."

He turned and faced her. Her eyes were dark, scowling.

"No, you're in my charge now, your orders come from me."

"Fat lot of good that's done me——"

"NURSE JONES!" he yelled. "Like it or not, you are a nurse, I am a captain. You will do as I bloody well say. You hear?"

She nodded silently, resentfully.

"Now in case you hadn't noticed, someone just tried to kill us. They may well try to do so again. I don't know what the hell's going on any more than you do, but until such time as we can get to safety, all we've got is each other."

He checked Cox's watch. He could barely read it. She was right. There was no way they'd make it back to Paarl. He wondered whether they might pick up another train at Stellenbosch. He was clutching at straws.

Their bags!

At least they were secure. But he'd packed his journal in his. Now he wished he'd kept it on his person. There was incriminating inform-ation within.

At his command, they carried on walking for another 20 minutes till they could see the lights of houses. When they came to the end of the row of vines there stood a water pump.

"Here…"

Finch worked it and Annie cupped her hands under the spout. Then she did the same for him. They sipped at the cold, rocky liquid which emanated from deep in an aquifer. Annie took a kerchief, wet it and wiped the grime from her face.

Finch eased himself down to sit on the ground against the low wall which surrounded the pump.

Annie seized her moment. She ran as fast as she could.

"Shit."

Finch hoisted himself to his feet and made after her. It was agony but he gained on her. Had she not been encumbered by her thick skirts she would have been clean away.

He grabbed her arm, she smacked it away.

"Please!" he implored.

"Get off me."

She struggled on. It was no use. He lunged, thrust both arms around her waist and as gently as he could under the circumstances, pulled her to the floor. He landed on top of her and rolled off.

"I'm sorry… really sorry."

Suddenly she was on top of him, swinging wildly, with hard fists. He raised his arms to protect his face then grabbed her wrists. He pushed her onto her back and held her firm.

"Please, Nurse Jones…"

Her knee rose up and caught him in the groin. Pain seared up through him. He doubled over.

"I'm going into Stellenbosch to find the nearest bloody police station."

"No!"

She was off again, running. Finch dug deep and sprung after her. This time he brought her down in the nearest approximation he could muster to a rugby tackle. He stayed on top of her and held her arms fast.

"Get off me, you bastard!"

Finch felt her body beneath him. His right thigh nestled between her legs. The sexual suggestion of their entanglement was obvious. It embarrassed him.

"Please, Nurse Jones. It is vital that you at least hear me out. Give me a chance to explain myself. Let me do that and you are free to make your own decision as to your next course of action."

"You bloody pervert."

"Please, I implore you."

Slowly he released her wrists. She did not resist. He flopped back on the ground. She sat up, panting.

"I'm afraid I've been caught up in something... something of magnitude."

"Well whatever it is, why not just march down into Stellenbosch, find the local police station and tell them what just happened?"

"No."

"Why not?"

He hesitated.

"Because I need to speak with someone first."

"Who?"

Finch sat up. He chose his words carefully.

"Nurse Jones. I know that as a medical professional you will be familiar with the concept of confidentiality."

She nodded.

"Can I trust you?"

He thought of Mbutu and his need for assurance.

"What do you mean?"

He turned to face her directly again, looking her in the eye, holding the stare. He softened his tone.

"I'm speaking now as a person, not as an officer. Whatever you may think of me, I need to know that I can trust you. Completely and utterly."

She shrugged an 'if you must'.

"Listen. I'm deadly serious. I'm appealing to you. Do I have your word? Your solemn word?"

"I still don't understand—"

"Please. I need to know. This is absolutely crucial. Not a word to anyone about what I'm about to tell you."

She hesitated, then said it.

"You have my word."

"You promise?"

"I promise."

He had nearly got her killed. She had a right to know. Plus if anything happened to him...

And so he began.

Over half an hour he told Annie everything. For her part, she was a good listener. He imagined the number of deathbed confessions and desperate ramblings she must have been subjected to over the past few weeks. She asked no questions, just nodded her head, asking him only to repeat the odd piece of information and clarify details.

Afterwards she sat in silence. Finch felt a pang of guilt that this young woman now, too, carried knowledge upon which there was, evidently, a very heavy price.

"Of course, if anything happens to me—"

"Then I know nothing," she said.

"Thank you."

"So that's it then? You want to speak to Lady Verity?"

"Yes. And after that we should do as you suggested, turn ourselves in."

She stood.

"How's your knee?"

"My knee?"

"You've been hobbling on it all day."

"There are men in this war who've suffered far worse."

"Then come on."

It appeared for a moment as if she were extending her hand to help him up. He raised his in return. But she was merely reaching over his head to crank the water pump again.

She sipped straight from the spout then turned. Finch made heavy weather of getting to his feet. His body's natural anaesthetic was wearing off.

"Lady Verity's house," she said. "I think I remember where to find it."

Chapter Thirty-Eight

Finch hobbled after Annie. She had breezed on down the dirt pathway to a gate. Beyond it, the path reached wooden steps cut into the embankment which descended to the road proper.

At the bottom of the steps, Annie stopped and looked westward. In the street lamps' yellow glow, Finch could see the row of fine mansions and villas that curved around the avenue of Stellenbosch's northern limit.

There was no traffic. Apart from the gas lamps it was quite quiet, though in the distance they could hear the muted hum of activity in the town. Outside one house, about 100 yards ahead, they saw a man shuffling up and down the pavement.

Finch pulled Annie out of sight, into the shadows.

"Is it him?" spluttered Annie.

"Security guard. But best not to be seen by anybody."

Despite her display of confidence, he could feel Annie shaking.

He tried to calm her.

He explained to her that his impulsive rush to Stellenbosch had probably saved them. The man who shot at them was surely loitering in Paarl. Leaving suddenly like that had made the man panic.

She thought for a moment.

"So he wasn't intending to kill you... kill us?"

"Believe me, firing with a rifle like that, he meant harm all right."

"I don't understand."

"What I mean is, if he'd been in Paarl, he'd have had ample opportunity to bump me off then... and with a greater chance of success than firing at distance from horseback."

"So he was trying to ward you off, keep you away from something?"

"It's a possibility."

"Maybe, given what you know about Cox... could he have been trying to *capture* you?"

Finch mulled it over. Was this the man who had stolen the letters from him on the train? He tried hard to visualise. He had seen him before, he was sure of it?

"If I... we were suddenly deemed expendable, I'm not convinced that would be so—"

"Following you, then. You're leading him somewhere."

If Finch had seen the man before, it made a sort of sense. But he could hear Brookman's voice echoing in his head, reminding him to stick to the facts.

"But again, why fire at us?" he said. "If you're following someone, expecting them to lead you somewhere, you don't suddenly charge after them down a country lane. And why alert them to your presence even?"

"What if you have a clue to something? You're on a path to finding out information he wants... but stray off that pathway, speak to the wrong people, and his mission suddenly becomes void?"

"You have a fanciful mind, Nurse Jones."

"Lady Verity. You're not meant to speak to her. Our ginger friend had you covered, but your dash to Stellenbosch turned him skittish."

Finch suddenly felt vulnerable again. If she were right...

"We can't hang about here. We've got to move."

"Again?"

He grabbed her hand and ushered her back towards the gate.

"If you're correct – and I'm not necessarily conceding that point – but if you *are* right, wouldn't he be here? Wouldn't he be lying in wait?"

"I thought he headed back to Paarl."

"I'm no expert, but farm country? I'm betting the vineyards are riddled with paths and backroads."

They climbed the steps and hurried back into the sanctuary of the vines. By the water pump they sat and assessed the options. Making contact with Lady Verity was a long shot. She might not be at home. Even if she were, what guarantee was there that he could gain access to her – and alone?

If they could find the street, Annie explained, she was pretty sure she could identify the residence. It was nearby, she thought, near a church, a small one, white, wooden...

Cautiously they skirted along the edge of the vineyard. Up high they had a good vantage point. The houses before them reeked of money. They were elegant and beautifully kept with the gardens out front usually behind a wall or high hedge. Generally they were in the Cape style, built low with shuttered windows and a veranda.

One, its owner presumably in sympathy with the wine region, had fashioned his house after a miniature French chateau. Even the stone looked authentic.

The air was fresher now. There was the smell of flowers, jasmine… night blooming. Crickets chirped. The peace reminded Finch of his visit to the Mount Nelson. It was only a few days ago but seemed like a lifetime.

Reaching the end of the street, finding no landmark that caught Annie's attention, they turned in the other direction, retracing their steps.

"There!"

The millionaires' row was intersected by a street that ran through to what seemed the centre of town. On the corner of the first block, a small steeple poked up.

"You sure?"

"Got to be."

Finch rooted around in the vines. At the end of each row, the trellises were supported by a stake, cut from a tree branch. He pulled one up and snapped it across his knee, the good one.

"Here…"

He gave her the half with the whittled point. The broken end was sharp, splintered.

"We hug the wall all the way, in the dark. No talking. Any sign of our friend, we withdraw."

She nodded.

"I should go first," she said. "I know what I'm looking for. Someone needs to keep an eye out behind us."

"Very good."

They climbed over the fence, Annie wrestling with her skirts, and scrambled down the bank as quietly as they could. They crossed the road to the intersecting street. The road had a pavement and they stuck to it, keeping close to the walls and hedges.

There were lights on but no pedestrians about. From within open windows they could hear the sounds of gentility – the clinking of cutlery, the tinkle of a piano. Somewhere, someone on a violin was making a hash of a minor scale.

The church on the corner was not much more than a chapel. There were no lights on. While Finch kept watch, Annie peeked round the corner.

There was a sudden rustle which startled them. A tabby cat shot across their path.

"This is it, I'm sure," she whispered, pointing ahead. "One of these up on the left."

To Finch there was no doubt which one. Out the front stood two uniformed members of the Cape Police.

They crossed the road as discreetly as possible and huddled into a side gateway to a building two doors along.

There was a metallic clang. From seemingly nowhere a rotund black maid appeared emptying rubbish into a dustbin.

"Good evening," whispered Finch.

"Good evening, mister," she replied.

She shrugged, turned and waddled back through a side door.

"We need to get a move on," he said.

But Annie had already gone, striding purposefully.

"What the hell—?"

He grabbed her arm to restrain her just as she was turning the corner.

"I'm sorry," she said, "but this is ridiculous. There are two policemen right there. Let's just…"

"*Shhhhhhh!*"

She pulled herself away but he grabbed her from behind and put his hand over her mouth.

"Look!"

There, standing with the two policemen, making small-talk, sharing cigarettes, was the red-headed man. He had his rifle slung over his shoulder. Beyond, his white horse was tethered to railings. There was a peal of laughter at some joke.

Finch released his grip.

"Now do you understand?"

She said nothing. She didn't have to.

"Even if we got past them – past him – there's no way I can just march up and demand an audience with Lady Verity Hancock. It was a stupid idea."

"We could pose as a medical deputation."

"Look at us."

They were both ragged and dirt-covered.

"How about if we—"

"Jones, what are you doing?"

Unseen by the police guards, she crept along, then darted across the front of the adjacent building to where an alleyway ran down the side of the Hancock place. Finch cursed and hurried after her.

The house was bounded by a wall atop which sat a neatly boxed screen of thick leylandii making for a height in total of about 7–8ft. Spaced along the wall at regular intervals were square, ornamental brick towers; they were flat-topped, crowned with a square slab.

"I think I'd better do this," said Finch and did his best to climb up. His knee had other plans.

"Link for hands," said Annie.

"What?"

"Give me a leg up."

He intertwined his fingers. She planted her high-laced boot in his palms and was hoisted up. Crouching, with her head just peeking over, she could see in.

"There's grass," she whispered. "Looks soft."

"No, it's too risky."

It was too late. Annie had swung herself up onto the top of the hedge and was suddenly gone.

Finch could do nothing else but follow. He made a meal of it but he clambered onto the hedge, rolled over and jumped down, tumbling right into her.

The building was made of a pink-reddish soft stone. They watched from its shadows. The gardens were lush. Even in the gaslight you could see they were an explosion of colour. Across the lawn, in the cobbled courtyard, a shiny black landau waited with two horses champing at their bits being held fast by a valet.

Then, two black servants emerged from the front doorway and walked to two large, glossy, wooden gates. Slowly they went through the business of bolting them back in position. As they did so, the two Cape policeman were in full view, though the red-haired man was now gone.

The policemen took their positions either side of the gate in what seemed a set routine. As they did so, deep conversation came from within the house. A white driver appeared. He swung himself up into the box seat. The landau was well sprung, it tilted over.

Behind emerged two men, one a man in his 60s in top hat and dark suit. He had full grey side whiskers and a rather sour expression. A generous belly strained at his trouser waistband.

"Sir Frederick Hancock," whispered Finch.

A servant opened the door to the landau and lowered a step. A second man, younger, slimmer, similarly dressed, helped him up. He nodded to the driver who twitched a whip and the two blinkered geldings, their tails tied up, began to walk.

"Quick," said Finch.

At ground level there was a window open, the sash halfway up. Chancing that the lack of light within indicated it was empty, Finch manhandled Annie through. He followed. They could hear the landau squeak and scrape out through the gate. Then the horses picked up speed to a trot.

"Now," said Finch, "we just have to hope that his wife is at home."

They were in a side room of sorts, one filled with stacked chairs and trestle tables.

They sneaked to the door. It led straight into the hallway. It was brightly lit with an electric chandelier. The walls were oak-panelled. The floor was made of black and white tiles. There was a Queen Anne divan with light blue upholstery and a round, dark wood table upon which sat a tastefully arranged bowl of fruit.

The front door closed and the two black servants traipsed back in followed by the valet. Finch and Annie ducked back from view as he came towards their room and pushed open the door.

"Under here," urged Finch and they slid beneath the main table which had been draped with a protective sheet.

The room was also electrically lit. The valet flipped a switch and it was illuminated instantly. He was young and square-jawed and stood looking round the room in the manner of someone who'd forgotten what he had come in for.

He shrugged, went over to the window, pulled it down closed, then, on his way out, reached for a large ring of keys that he kept on his belt.

He found the one he was looking for, turned the light off, then began to pull the door closed.

No.

Suddenly a voice called out, one of the servants: "Mister Paul. Mister Paul."

"What now, Noah?" he groaned.

He stamped off to supervise his charge.

Finch and Annie emerged and went to the door. From upstairs they could hear the voice of an Englishwoman instructing a maid – something to do with the bed linen – and the woman insisting that the maid leave whatever it was till the morning.

There was no one in the hallway.

"Come on," said Finch and Annie followed him to dart across the black and white tiles to the swirling patterns of the maroon stair carpet. The impressive staircase doubled back on itself on the way up to the landing. The landing itself had an overabundance of busts, vases, potted plants and feathery leaves.

Up ahead, at the end of the corridor, a door was ajar.

"Very good, Christine," the woman was saying. "Good night."

"Good night, ma'am."

They squeezed into an alcove and the maid, a young black woman of 17 or 18, hurried past bearing a stack of crisp, folded sheets. She went down the stairs.

"Is that her?" asked Finch, nodding towards the door.

Annie signalled a 'yes'.

"Right, here we go."

They smoothed down their clothes and Finch went and knocked.

"Come."

Finch entered first. The room was some kind of parlour, lit by an overhead electric arrangement of tulip-shaped glass casings. It had a chaise longue and two armchairs, pale blue and Queen Anne, matching the ones downstairs. A gramophone player with its large trumpet stood on a low table. Finch was minded of Jenkins.

By the window, writing at a desk next to a potted palm, was a middle-aged woman in a white linen blouse and long dark blue skirt. Her chestnut brown hair, with a fleck of grey, was tied up in a bun.

"Excuse me, Lady Verity?" ventured Finch.

The woman turned, a look of surprise on her face. Her half-moon spectacles fell and hung on the gold chain around her neck. At her throat was a blue cameo brooch. She had unusual blue, almost violet eyes and clear, lightly tanned skin.

"Who are you?" she asked and stood up right away.

Finch guessed her age to be about 45 but she had the athletic physique of someone ten years younger, a horsewoman maybe.

"And how did you get here?"

Finch cleared his throat.

"Please ma'am, it is with urgency that we need to speak with you. I am Captain Ingo Finch of the Royal Army Medical Corps and this—"

"Nurse Annie Jones of the New South Wales Army Nursing Service Reserve," added Annie, stepping forward.

"Christine!"

Finch made the flapping, palms-down gesture of a man urging another to keep their voice down.

"Please ma'am, just a moment of your time—"

"CHRISTINE!" Lady Verity barked again, louder.

They could hear the patter of feet below.

"I don't care who you are… or what state you're in…"

She looked them up and down disapprovingly.

"…but you can't just come barging in here like this. If you are on official business then kindly make an appointment."

Christine the maid appeared at the door. Lady Verity breezed right past them, trailing a light musk of sandalwood.

The maid looked concerned.

"Christine. Tell Paul to inform the police detail that we have intruders."

The maid nodded and scuttled off.

"Now, I kindly ask you to leave, Captain."

She motioned to the exit.

"Please ma'am. Sorry for the interruption," urged Finch, "but it's the only way we could speak with you—"

"I'm warning you."

She held the door open for them to leave.

"It's about Cox… Major Cox."

At mention of the name, Lady Verity's face slid from its steely resolve. Her violet eyes glistened.

"Cox?" she asked.

Finch nodded.

She turned to the corridor.

"Christine!"

They heard a 'Yes, miss' from the stairs.

"My mistake entirely. I'd completely forgotten. The captain and the nurse *do* have an appointment with me after all."

"Very good, miss."

"Not a word of this to anyone, you understand? And see that we are not disturbed."

"Yes, miss."

She shut the door and looked Finch in the eye. Her voice cracked. "Go on."

Chapter Thirty-Nine

It was quiet, eerily so for such a large mass of people. All Mbutu could hear around about him was the rasping and wheezing of sleep or the pained gurgling of those for whom slumber was to become permanent. There was the occasional, distant wail. The place stank of death. It *was* death. Mbutu had noted the pall of smoke from the pyre as they had arrived.

Mbutu you are a curse.

He clutched the strange hessian head-sack. The officer-doctor had briefly examined it then tossed it back to him. He wasn't sure whether the man had given serious thought as to what it might be. Neither had the other man, the blessed Dean Newbold.

The officer-doctor had not long departed when this other white man came striding towards them. Around his neck was the dog collar of a holy man.

A Man of God. God left this place a long time ago.

The man seemed kind, concerned. He was informed of their plight and nodded silently, with furrowed brow. Despite his attempts to be even-handed, to treat the Lord's children all the same, his immediate concern was for the well-being of the two white females.

"My poor dears," he began and took a hand each in his. When the woman did not speak, he grew confused. Little Emily tried to explain but could not get her tongue round the name of village from whence they had come, her description of events thereafter delivered as one would expect of a child her age – not presented in a logical order, glossing over important aspects and with emphasis placed on insignificant details.

"Four days ago, hunting for food, we came across Mrs Sutton and her daughter Emily," explained Mbutu. "They have been on the run from great danger."

"*Sutton?*"

"Yes, Sutton… They are the family of the missionary at Vankilya."

"Is this true?"

The little girl nodded.

"Then where… how…?"

Mbutu spared the child. He discreetly shook his head indicating that Missionary Sutton no longer walked God's earth.

On his knees Newbold embraced them both.

"Please," said Mbutu. "I need to show you this."

From his bag he withdrew the silver elephant box and handed it over, as he had done previously to the army doctor. Newbold opened it with great curiosity and began leafing through the papers like the captain.

Mbutu indicated the huddled, sightless men nearby.

"Something terrible happened in the villages."

It was then that he had produced the strange hessian sack again, which Newbold pawed at but with as little regard as the doctor-captain.

Newbold informed the Suttons that they would be evacuated on the first available wagon. They could have use of his tent for this evening.

"But Mbutu—" protested Emily.

"I'm sorry," said Newbold, lying as nicely as he knew how. "There isn't much room."

Emily had hugged Mbutu, hugged hard. The embrace felt final. He sensed the wetness of her tears on his neck.

"Do not be afraid my child, you are safe now. Mister Newbold, he knew your father. He is a missionary also. He will take care of you."

The woman gave a faint trace of a nod.

"Thank you for what you have done… what *all* of you have done," said Newbold.

"May I keep this?" he added of the elephant box now under his arm.

"It is not mine. It is theirs."

And with that, Newbold put his arm round the Suttons and led them away.

—

That was some hours ago. It was dark now, getting cold, the heat of the day evaporating fast into the cloudless night with its breathtaking splash of stars and the great Southern Cross constellation shining down on them.

Though every fibre in his being screamed exhaustion, Mbutu's mind was too active for easy sleep.

He did not feel safe with the hessian head-sack in his possession. It was evidence of some act of evil.

Devil soldiers.

He took it out of his bag again, wandered past and over bodies to where the camp reached its natural limit. On his knees, and with his bare hands, he scooped out soil.

It had blindsided him, but as he patted the last handful down, searching for a mental marker should he wish to retrieve the object, a hurricane lamp came swinging towards him.

There was a flurry of voices.

"That him?"

"Think that's him."

"They all look the bloody same."

Three men, one in plainclothes, a light-coloured suit, and two soldiers, all with kerchiefs tied round their faces.

"What's he doing?"

"Covering over his shit."

"Whole place is a shithole."

The first soldier held the light close to Mbutu's face as he sat.

"You the one who found the white woman and her daughter?" asked the plainclothes one.

"Who wants to know?"

"You can cut that out, shit-boy," snarled a soldier.

The other laughed.

They had a hand under each armpit and were hoisting him to his feet.

"You're to come with us," said the plainclothes one.

"Right, you heard the man."

They marched him back through the human mass, walking so swiftly his tired legs kept giving out under him.

"And they said you were fast," scoffed one soldier.

More laughter.

"For a coon."

"Where are you taking me?"

"You'll shut your bloody mouth 'til asked."

The plainclothes man was carrying the lamp.

"Up here," he said.

There were only a few tents in the camp. This one, a large sturdy structure behind the fire pits, contained sacks of grain. There were no staff around. The walking turned into a drag, the toes of Mbutu's boots scuffing along in the dirt.

The plainclothes man nodded. The two soldiers manhandled Mbutu up against the central supporting post, as solid as a ship's mast. One worked quickly with some rope to tie his hands behind it.

Ominously, the plainclothes one removed his bowler, his jacket and started rolling up his sleeves.

Please, if this is a place of God, show mercy.

"Right, we want to know what *you* know," he said.

"Know?"

"The Sutton woman has told us everything."

It is a lie, the Sutton woman cannot talk.

"Where did you go? What did you see?"

"I don't—"

In a sudden whirl, the man's fist landed square in Mbutu's face, splitting his nose open, sending excruciating, electrifying pain shooting up into his brain.

Mbutu collapsed, sliding down the post to the floor, slumping in an awkward pile.

The man casually went to a trestle table, upon which had been set a bowl of water and a towel. He carefully and theatrically washed his hands.

"Right," he told the soldiers. "Pick him up."

I can hardly see, hardly stand.

He took his time.

"Again. What do you know?"

The blood dripped from Mbutu's nostrils and choked in the back of his throat. He had barely had a chance to open his mouth when the knuckles connected with him again.

Chapter Forty

"Please, sit," said Lady Verity and indicated for them to take the settee. She placed herself on a high-backed chair, the coffee table a buffer between them.

"You knew Leonard?" she ventured, her voice tremulous.

Her use of the past tense suggested that she had already learned of his fate.

"He was my CO," said Finch.

"Captain Finch… yes, yes, Captain *Finch*. He spoke very highly of you."

"I was with him up until the retreat… the redeployment. Then, in Cape Town. On leave. The police called me in to identify the—"

He checked himself.

"It's all right, Captain…"

She pulled an embroidered lace handkerchief from her sleeve and dabbed an eye. She seemed to stiffen, correcting herself, not wishing to betray anything.

"Major Cox," she added, "was a liaison for the Nurses' Initiative. A very helpful man."

"He was a good man, yes," echoed Finch, trying not to sound too insincere.

Lady Verity eyed Annie.

"New South Wales, you say?"

"Yes."

"You know we lived in Victoria for two years. Melbourne. Wonderful city."

Finch noted her use of 'we'. Matrimonial solidarity.

She regarded Annie further.

"You look familiar."

"I came here to the house, about a month ago. Tea."

She scrunched her face in willed recollection.

"Cape Town Military Hospital. The Australians. How could I forget?"

Annie was not sure how this was meant.

"You're all doing a splendid job," Lady Verity added, affecting the tone of officialdom.

"Thank you."

She returned to Finch.

"But Captain, might I ask why—?"

"Why we are here?"

She eyed them further. No matter the last-minute sprucing up, their clothing and boots were dirty. There was a rip at the hem of Annie's skirt. Finch had lost some buttons from his tunic front. He was still conscious that they smelled.

"Lady Verity, we have some explaining to do and I suspect not much time in which to do it."

"I see."

"But if it's not too much of an imposition at this difficult moment, might I turn this around and ask what you know of Major Cox's death?"

The word upset her. She tried to stop her voice from cracking. She picked at an imaginary thread on her skirt.

"I don't understand."

"What exactly do you know? What were you told of the circumstances?"

"If any information is required of me, I shall be communicating it to the police myself," she scolded.

Finch thought for a moment of Ans Du Plessis.

"Lady Verity, I'll not beat about the bush. Lives are at stake here."

It seemed to strike a chord. Lady Verity rose, hastened to the door, opened it, checked there was no one on the landing, then closed it again.

She returned to her seat but this time kept her voice low.

"Please, you cannot come here like this making wild and fantastical accusations."

"I'm accusing no one."

She regained her detached air.

"This is a time for grief, for reflection on a life cruelly lost," she declared, falsely sanctimonious. "Major Cox has a wife, you know, a family…"

It seemed to Finch a rather tardy, rather hollow consideration.

"But if you are really that insistent on knowing, I was informed of Major Cox's passing by one of our committee members. He said that Leonard... Major Cox... had been killed... murdered... while taking a hansom cab to his lodgings."

"That is correct."

"An opportunist, some thug trying to steal money, they thought. But I then read in the newspaper it was one of his peers, this Kilfoyle, who had been arrested."

"That is correct."

"I had heard the name Kilfoyle before... Leonard... Major Cox... said that..."

She returned to her handkerchief. A fissure in the facade.

"I'm sorry, you must forgive me."

"Not at all," soothed Annie.

"It's just, for such a kind man, a soldier. To meet his end like this..."

She fought it valiantly but began to crumple. Finch afforded her the dignity of composing herself.

"Lady Verity, I assure you, we are absolutely not intent on causing you further distress."

"Then why—?"

He gave a theatrical cough.

"May I speak frankly?"

He could see that she feared a revelation. Her eyes darted here and there then settled on Annie.

"Nurse Jones knows all that I do," said Finch.

"Oh."

"In Cape Town... the police... I was placed in charge of repatriating Major Cox's effects. Included within were some personal items that—"

"Personal items?"

"Correspondence... letters."

"Do you have them?" she cut across.

"No."

There was a glimmer of fear.

"Then who does?"

"I'm not sure," he confessed. "They were stolen from my person."

"*Stolen?* Are you sure?"

"Absolutely. And rather artfully."

Her voice cracked again.

"By... by *whom*?"

Finch shrugged.

Lady Verity got up and walked to the window. She stood and gazed down to the street, moist-eyed. She remained that way while Finch sketched out the details of what he knew and what was permissible to share – but he mostly spoke about the letters, not the intimate details of them but enough to suggest that he was familiar with their contents.

"You had no business reading them," she snapped. "Whoever this woman may be, such things are a private matter."

Finch explained that he had had no idea of the identity of 'V' until the final telegram. He had not meant to pry. He had, he said, and stretching the truth a little, peeked at the letters because they had been passed to him in confidence with the express wish that he evaluate whether they should be forwarded to Cox's family.

"I am a doctor," he added. "The sanctity of privileged information is my stock in trade."

Her tone softened.

"I see," she said.

She came back over and sat down. Her hands were shaking.

"There is also this..."

He undid the engraved Zeiss watch and handed it to her. She turned it over and stroked the inscription.

"No matter the scrupulous secrecy, I'm afraid you were always going to give yourself away," said Finch. "The last item of correspondence. A telegram. You signed with your Christian name..."

"It's all right, Captain," she sighed. "You no longer need to press your point."

She lowered her head and gazed at the watch's words, caressing them. Eventually her voice came, painfully, sadly. She even affected a little ironic laugh.

"I'm afraid I've been a bit of a fool, haven't I?"

She handed the watch back, but Finch gestured that she keep it. She smiled her thanks and nodded at a porcelain water jug on the drinks cabinet.

"Please, would you mind?"

Annie went over, poured some into a nearby whisky tumbler – fine, ornate crystal – and handed it to her. She looked up.

"You say that what is said here is confidential?"

They nodded. She sipped her water then dabbed her handkerchief in it, patting at her throat and neck.

Said Finch: "We need to know if there's anything that has happened recently that may have led to Major Cox's death—"

"Why on earth should I tell you?"

"...and that if you have any suspicions at all, can shed any light, then please make this information known to the police... to the detective leading the investigation, Inspector Brookman."

"And compromise myself?"

"Brookman is a fair man. I'm sure there are ways of guaranteeing anonymity."

She exhaled a sarcastic hiss.

"I doubt it."

Then paused for a moment, mulling it over.

"No one is judging you, Lady Verity," stressed Finch.

"Come, come, Captain. *Everybody* will be judging me."

"I know this can't be easy," he said.

She blushed and dabbed at her neck with her wet handkerchief again.

"Very well. I met Major Cox... Leonard... about six months ago," she said, rather terse. "As you have deduced, and there's no point in hiding it, yes, we became friends – more than friends. You see, my husband and I are married but have lived separate lives for some years. I married young – 18. He was already established in his career. In his 30s... To be a ministerial wife, foreign postings, beautiful homes, it can turn a girl's head."

Annie thought for a moment of her own ex-fiancé Edward.

"As a ministerial wife I have certain responsibilities... duties. What I didn't appreciate was that, as part of those duties, I was expected to accept when my husband sought..."

She hesitated over the word.

"...'relations' elsewhere. He has a mistress in Cape Town, you know. Will be staying with her tonight. The Cabinet is in late session. Of course, if any of this got out... Leonard... this whole beastly business... it would be I who was cast as the scarlet woman."

Annie reached over to lay her hand on Lady Verity's.

She drew breath and continued.

"I can't deny that when I first met Leonard he presented something of a thrill. War Office function. The first man to approach me, to pursue me in 30 years. Can you imagine? Before I got trapped in *this…*"

"It's okay," soothed Annie.

"…suffocated by this blasted Imperial charade."

She released Annie's grip to wipe her eyes.

"It was meant to be a bit of fun, but feelings changed, developed—"

"Lady Verity," Finch interrupted. "I know from the tenor of your letters, your final telegram, that there was a panic, an urgency… that you felt that someone was on to you…"

"We wished to avoid discovery, naturally."

"Pardon me, but it seems to me to be about something more."

Her eyes had been locked on his but flickered away for a moment.

"You see," he said, "I do not believe that Cox was killed randomly at all."

She bit a knuckle.

"Might I ask if you've read the newspaper today?" Finch added.

She threw a quizzical look.

"I looked at the *Argus* and the *Gazette* at breakfast, yes."

"Not the late editions?"

She shook her head.

He produced the page he had ripped from the *Argus*, laid it on the coffee table between them and spun it round to face her. She picked it up with the care of an archivist handling a literary relic, and took a minute to ponder the news of Kilfoyle's death.

"Are we supposed to feel sympathy for this man?"

"Lady Verity, I'm not sure that Kilfoyle murdered Major Cox at all. I think he was set up. I think someone got to Kilfoyle before he could demonstrate his innocence. It certainly deflects from Major Cox's death being about something… *more*."

"More…?"

All of a sudden she looked scared.

"That is what I have been trying to determine."

"You think blackmail?"

It was a likely assumption, but again Brookman's voice echoed in his head.

"Possibly. Has anyone approached you in the last day or two?"

She ignored him, she was talking to herself now.

"It would ruin him, ruin us. No, they couldn't possibly—"

"They? Who's '*they*'?"

Her eyes pleaded with him.

"Captain Finch. Please, be a friend to Leonard in death as you were in life. Leave him be."

"Lady Verity, it is not my wish to play the amateur sleuth. Far from it. With some vigour I have been trying to contact Inspector Brookman. Unfortunately I have been in transit to the Front. We were in Paarl this afternoon when I read the news of Kilfolye's death. What with the theft of the letters, I decided to head straight to you."

"Thank you."

"But on our way here someone followed us, started shooting at us."

"Shooting? Are you sure?"

"Someone tried to kill us all right," said Annie. "We gave him the slip in the vineyard. Square, stocky fellow... red hair—"

At this description, Lady Verity stood up.

"You must go! Go now! It's not safe."

She hurried to her bureau, reached underneath, felt around and pulled free a small brown letter envelope. She came back and pressed it into Finch's hand.

"What is it?"

"Please... Go...!"

She ushered them to the door. Satisfied that the coast was clear, she then hustled them along the landing. Though carpeted, the wood creaked heavily. They went through glass French doors and onto a balcony overlooking the rear garden, with an iron spiral staircase that led down to the patio. The lawns stretched off into the darkness.

"This time of night, with my husband gone, there are just two men, posted out the front—"

A male voice came from behind them.

"Ma'am...? Ma'am...? Is everything all right."

"Fine, Paul!" she bellowed.

She turned to Finch and Annie.

"Go now! FAST! Your lives are in danger."

Finch held the envelope.

She put her hands to his, cupped them and curled his fingers round it.

"I'm afraid you are right, Captain. This is about something of great consequence. Something I feel in my conscience I ought to make known."

Her eyes darted back and forth. Now he understood. She was being watched.

"By your own staff?" Finch whispered.

She nodded. There were footsteps on the landing. She turned.

"It's all right, Paul. Just getting some air."

She spun back to face Finch again.

"God speed."

Annie was already halfway down the steps.

"Captain. Come on!"

Lady Verity hesitated over something, then said it.

"Moriarty… You must find Moriarty."

The man called Paul was almost upon them.

"Lady Verity… ma'am?" he called again.

"Really, I have to go," she said.

And with that she went back inside.

Chapter Forty-One

The pain was like nothing Mbutu had ever experienced. His nose was broken, no question about that. Though he could not raise his hands to check, he sensed the bridge had been shattered. Mashed cartilage had pulped up underneath.

He tried to open his mouth. His jaw clicked awkwardly on the left side. With his tongue, through the metallic-tasting pool, he probed around and felt several upper teeth loose. Two or three had been broken, their edges ragged and sharp. He tried to spit out the fragments, but his effort was pathetic, just a long viscous drool.

However, the greater agony came in his neck where it had been jarred back and forth by the blows, an electric jolt shooting up behind his left ear.

Mbutu strained to look upward but couldn't twist his head, couldn't open his left eye. The skin had been pulled tight by the swelling.

The main man, in blurred silhouette against the hurricane lamp, was standing casually, nonchalantly. He was cleaning his hands again, fussily.

From the side, a bucket of cold water was sloshed over Mbutu's head. It made him choke and splutter.

The two soldiers grabbed his arms and hoisted him back up to a standing position. His legs could not take his own weight. The men had to hold him there. They pulled his arms tightly, roughly, behind his back, behind the pole.

The plainclothes one scooped up a piece of paper from the table. To Mbutu he did so with the ease of someone browsing the society circulars he used to run between the big Kimberley houses.

"Mbutu... Mbutu Kef... Kef-a-leze?"

Do not speak my name. Do not dishonour it.

His tone was flat, methodical, unemotional.

"We didn't know who you were exactly. But we knew you'd show up somewhere."

He had the grey facelessness of the bureaucrat sycophants Mbutu saw cosying up round Cecil Rhodes – a thin, drawn face, dark beady eyes.

The man said the next bit sarcastically.

"We must thank our friend the Dean for being so thorough in documenting the comings and goings in this human toilet."

The soldiers laughed.

"Wh… what do want?" Mbutu groaned.

He wished he'd said nothing.

"To come straight to the point, and to begin with – two Lee-Enfield carbines."

The guns. We should have discarded them. They were taken from us when we arrived.

"We're not fools. The serial numbers…"

Serial numbers?

"…match those from a cavalry patrol that went missing southwest of De Aar three days ago."

He casually returned the paper to the table.

"So, anything to say for yourself?"

The silence lingered for some 30 seconds, then… BAM! …came the hardest blow yet to his face, the right side this time. He was down on the floor again, his face in the dirt. Then, more water, another hoisting.

He doubted whether he could survive many more.

"I would advise you, for your own comfort, to speak."

Comfort?

Think. Think fast. What had you worked out with poor Hendrik?

"We found the weapons… My party, we crossed the Karoo… Three days," he pleaded.

"Why on earth cross the Karoo on foot? Or are you people really as stupid as they say?"

Why, Mbutu?

"Because we wanted to come here, to Paarl."

The man gave a snort of derision.

"My dear fellow. Even the most simple of natives would have found his way to the railway."

Think, Mbutu.

"I had fled from Kimberley. Did not trust—"

The man put his hand up to stay the words.

"Is it because you had just murdered British soldiers?"

"No!"

The man nodded. The blow this time came from behind, a rabbit punch to his right kidney. His legs buckled and he went down. The pain was not a stab, nothing that reached a crescendo and then subsided. It was a sustained deep sting through his innermost organs. It sent Mbutu into an added spasm of panic.

"The women. Mrs Sutton... her daughter. Where did you find them?"

Mbutu squinted upwards. This pain. Could they help him? Could they make it stop?

"We – the Nama, myself – we were hunting for food," he panted. "We found them in the wild. Hiding."

"Mrs Sutton claims that you – your little band of savages – raped her."

The long sting continued. He closed his eyes. He willed it to go.

"What? NO!"

It is a shameful lie. Besides, she cannot talk.

"The rifles. You found rifles in the middle of the desert? You just happened to stumble upon them?"

Think, Mbutu.

"No, we found bodies. Four of them."

Good, the number. It lends weight to the story.

"We buried the men. Prayed for them—"

His words were cut off by a kick to the stomach. He was winded and gulped for air.

"We thought Boers..." he groaned. "We were afraid... we moved on."

"No horses?"

Think Mbutu. Were there horses in your story? If you found bodies, would horses still be there?

"No, no horses."

More water. He was hauled to his feet again.

The man took his time.

"Three days ago, two natives armed with Lee-Enfield carbines engaged in gunfire with a British reconnaissance party at the gorge near the village of Vankilya – one Hottentot, one Bantu. The Bantu was wearing a blue-checked shirt. The same kind of filthy rag you are wearing now."

Think Mbutu.

"They were riding British cavalry horses. One of them was identified as the grey mare belonging to a Lieutenant Masterson of the Special Expeditionary Force. So, let me ask you again. Were there horses?"

Mbutu. THINK!

The man's fist connected with his left cheek. He slumped but, this time, was not allowed to fall.

"I... I..."

Another fist cracked his right eye socket.

Mbutu screamed: "Yes. Yes. There were horses, there were horses!"

Think of Hendrik.

"We were returning them."

"I can't quite hear you."

"We were returning them. I said there were no horses because I feared you might accuse us of stealing them."

The man cracked a faint smile.

"I can assure you that an accusation of theft is the least of your worries."

The soldiers chuckled.

"So you rode off into the back of beyond, to the northwest, just on the off-chance you might run into some British soldiers, and all rather nicely and conveniently hand their horses back?"

"Yes."

"Why not take them to Beaufort West... De Aar?"

"Because—"

The man hit him hard, but seemingly effortlessly, in the solar plexus. Mbutu's diaphragm went into spasm. He gulped wildly, like a fish that had been landed on the riverbank.

"And where are the horses now?"

"Don't... know," he panted.

The man curled his knuckles into a fist again. The act alone was sufficient now to elicit information.

"Two ran off. The others—"

"What about the others?"

"Across the Karoo. We used them for transport. And then—"

"And then what?"

"And then... for—"

"For what?"

"For meat."

The man was mock apoplectic.

"Meat?! FOOD?!"

Mbutu said nothing. Slowly, he slid down the pole. The man was over him.

"Well let me tell you, you bloody cannibal…"

The soldiers tittered.

"Those horses belonged not to me, not to the army, but to Queen bloody Victoria. You mean to tell me you ate Her Majesty's horses?"

Mbutu looked up.

"Yes."

Hands washed again, the man started to roll his sleeves down then re-insert his cufflinks. His next words came casually.

"Well that just about does it, Mr Kefaleze. I regret to inform you, you are to be executed at dawn. Given that you've already feasted generously upon the British Crown, don't expect a last meal."

No! It cannot happen like this.

"I have a wife. A son," he protested.

The man said nothing. One of the soldiers helped him on with his jacket and lifted the tent flap for him to exit.

Mbutu, think! THINK!

"A black man," yelled Mbutu, "accused of all that you say. Why not just shoot me right here?"

The man stopped.

Slowly he returned and squatted down. He pulled a kerchief from his pocket so that he wouldn't have to touch him directly and cupped Mbutu's chin. It brought a wince of pain. His neck.

The man's dark eyes were expressionless, ruthless.

"I know for a fact," hissed Mbutu, "that Mrs Sutton uttered not a word about anything."

The man stared on, unblinking.

Mbutu, keep your counsel. Give them nothing and your life still has value.

The man clicked his fingers. He was handed something wrapped in cloth, something angular and heavy. He unrolled it directly into Mbutu's lap.

A crucifix. A brass crucifix tarnished by fire.

The man took out his pocket watch.

"Sun-up's in about three hours. I suggest you have a good hard think about what you saw, what you know. More importantly, what the Suttons saw."

And if I do, I will have sealed their fate.

"Tell me nothing, tell me lies, I'll put the bullet in you myself."

Chapter Forty-Two

Once over the wall, Finch and Annie moved as fast as they could, hugging the hedges and fences, keeping to the shadows as before. Clear of the vicinity, they huddled in a chained gateway.

"Right, let's think about what's next," panted Finch.

"What we need to do is turn ourselves in to the nearest police station and explain everything as soon as possible," Annie spluttered.

"No."

"What?"

"The man, our red-haired friend. You saw how cosy he was with the police."

"That means nothing. He could have been asking for the time of day, a light, anything."

"Why take the chance? You saw how Lady Verity reacted when we described him. If there are political ramifications to this I'd rather steer clear of the bumbling local bobbies and take this directly to Brookman."

"The army then... The town will be crawling with soldiers. We find a friendly officer—"

Finch blew out his cheeks.

"Again, I'm sorry. Any officer worth his salt has got far bigger things on his mind right now. They'd just refer us to the Military Foot Police."

"Is that such a bad thing?"

"Believe me, I've seen how they operate..."

He shook his head and exhaled a whistle.

"...The quicker we get to Brookman the better."

He looked south towards the lights.

"More than that, we have to anticipate what our trigger-happy friend will be expecting us to do. There are only so many times we can slip through his grasp."

"So?"

"I don't know for sure," said Finch, "but shouldn't we head for the least obvious place? Hide out?"

"You mean double back the way we came?"

"Or just head in the wrong direction altogether."

She didn't sound enthusiastic.

"So we're not going to Cape Town tonight, either?"

Finch pulled up his sleeve and looked reflexively at his left wrist. He had no timepiece.

Annie had her nurse's fob watch pinned upside down to a ribbon on her uniform.

"Just gone eleven," she said.

"Too late. Besides, wouldn't he have the station and cab ranks covered?"

She sighed.

"Then where to this time?"

She followed Finch to the corner and, once again, carefully, they looked round. A few blocks down they could see people.

"That's the main drag, right?" asked Finch.

"I think so."

"Follow the road west or south and you're on your way to Cape Town."

He turned and pointed north.

"We already know what the Paarl road's like. Plus we'd have to go back past the Hancock place. In which case why not go east—"

"East?"

"Just for a while."

She rolled her eyes and huffed, then started out ahead of him.

–

After some more zig-zagging through the backstreets they hit an unlit path, a rutted wagon trail. They had already passed a road sign indicating they were proceeding broadly in the direction of Franschhoek. Ahead, in the moonlight, were the silhouettes of more mountains – jagged this time, ominous.

They knew better than to talk more than necessary and ploughed on down the trail for another hour.

Finch felt the pain in his knee keenly. Annie, though physically strong, was encumbered both by her skirts and her boots, which had a low heel. In the dark, they were both stumbling over stones and ruts. More than that, the boots had given her blisters.

Several times they stopped so that she might sit and soothe her feet, the skin shredded at her heels.

"We can stop for the night if you like," said Finch. "Yes, we should stop."

"Don't feign chivalry on my account," she winced. "I'm fine."

"There's only so far we can run. We're safe for the moment. If we can get a few hours' sleep. Take it in turns."

To their left was a field; to the right, woods.

"The field's too exposed," said Finch.

She pointed to the trees.

"No. This is still Africa. Some pretty unpleasant creatures about."

"Then what?"

"First sign of civilisation, we'll find somewhere."

A further ten minutes on they came to a narrow river and a flat, slatted bridge crossing it. Annie climbed down and bathed her feet. Turning inland they could see lights.

"We stay close," he said. "We hug the riverbank, we watch."

A short while later they were huddling behind bushes on the scrubland that led towards a cluster of buildings on the road out of Stellenbosch.

The main one, a walled, grand 17th century building in the Dutch gabled fashion, with smallish, shuttered windows, looked like part of a winery. There were men, and some women, coming and going. Buggies loitered outside. The women were finely dressed, the men too, but mainly in khaki.

Whispered Finch: "It's a hotel."

Finch checked his wallet. He still had money, nearly three pounds.

"Right, wait here," he said.

"What?"

"Don't move…"

Annie panicked.

"You're going to just waltz in and grab a room? I thought you meant a barn, some old farm shed."

"We stumble out of the wilds and the first place we hit is a hotel? I say kismet."

"But—"

"Indoors, amongst fellow officers. Might be the safest place yet. Hiding in plain sight."

"And how about me?"

"Don't worry."

Annie watched in exasperation as Finch brushed himself down then, in the dim light emanating from the hotel, limped across the road.

The building had high stucco walls, a red-tiled roof and an ornate iron double gate into its courtyard. Finch made his way in, as carefree as he could convey. He turned and gave a nod, then disappeared into the lobby.

It seemed to take forever but, 20 minutes later, he was back out, limping across the road towards her.

"Right. All set. Third floor on this side. I've been up to take a look."

He pointed to the western wall. It was a more recent extension to the property.

"I'm afraid budget won't stretch to a second room. And we'd be sure to arouse suspicion…"

He turned awkward.

"…if we went in together."

Annie wasn't sure she felt comfortable with the thoughts and considerations that had obviously gone through his head.

"Go around to that side," he said. "Wait back in the trees there. You see them?"

"Yes."

"I'll go to the room, turn the light on and lean out. I'll signal to you when it's safe."

"How do I—?"

"See, the fire escape…"

She nodded.

"Give me another five minutes."

—

Annie went to the line of jacaranda trees across a lawn. The air hung heavy, the crickets in full chorus.

There were several gas lamps already glowing on the four storeys on that side.

275

Eventually, on the third floor, two windows from the right, a new lamp was lit. The sash window was pulled up and what looked like Finch leaned out and beckoned. She doubted whether he could see her. He had faith in her.

She looked back and forth then crossed the grass and reached the iron fire escape. She unhooked the ladder to access it – it creaked and grated way too loudly. The rungs clanged as she progressed.

Passing the second floor she saw a large man in his undergarments sitting in an easy chair, reading a book. On reaching the third floor, Finch helped her in. He locked the window and pulled the curtains closed behind her. She saw he had bolted the door and slid the security chain across.

"Added bonus. They have a telegraph office here," he enthused. "Just sent a cable to Major Jenkins. He knows about the Cox murder and some of the shenanigans. He's my CO now, *and* a friend. He'll cover for us."

"You sure?"

"We speak to Brookman first thing, get the next train up. We'll still be in Hopetown by evening."

There was a small sigh of relief.

"Bad news is it's too late for dinner. But took the liberty of ordering room service… sandwiches, ham, cheese and a pot of coffee. I hope that's—"

"Thank you."

There was, pointedly, only one bed. A big double one on a framed brass bedstead. Finch bade her sit on it… to 'make herself comfortable' while he took the armchair in the corner.

The room was reasonably clean. It had a washstand and a jug. Across the way, he said, was a bathroom and water closet, though they'd have to be careful leaving the room.

Annie removed her boots and rubbed her feet.

"Would you like me take a look?" offered Finch.

She declined.

There was a knock on the door. Finch pressed his finger to his lips. On the dresser was a large vase. At his signal, she grabbed it as a makeshift weapon and positioned herself on the blindside of the jamb.

Finch looked out through the spy hole. He sighed in relief.

"Room service," came the call.

Finch slid off the chain and undid the bolt. Annie pressed herself into the corner as the bellboy, in tunic and artfully skewed pillbox hat, placed the tray on the coffee table. He made an over-elaborate fuss of indicating every item on the plates, enquiring as to whether the coffee should be poured right away. It seemed of deep concern to him.

Finch pressed a coin into his hand, screening Annie the whole time.

"Thank you, sir," he bowed and scuttled out.

They ate in silence, working diligently at a generous slab of bread, cured ham and something that resembled cheddar. The coffee was hot.

They had almost forgotten it, but when they had finished, Finch pulled the brown manilla envelope from his pocket. He tipped the contents onto the counterpane. There sat a lightweight darkened brass key, about the length of a thumb joint, barrel-ended, with a triple-looped grip that gave the impression of a miniature carpet beater.

Annie examined it.

"Looks like the kind you lock an upright piano with."

"Small. A locker, a latch, who knows?" shrugged Finch.

"And what did she say? That name? 'Moriarty'?"

"Heard it before... From Rideau, for one. He's the villain in the Sherlock Holmes stories."

"Rideau?"

"No, Moriarty."

"Sorry, never read any."

"My goodness, you should."

He was going to mention that he had a novel in his kit bag, but thought better of it.

"So what does it mean... the name?"

She handed the key back.

"Might be real, probably a pseudonym, a codename. All I know is we have to find him."

"Or *her*."

"Yes, I suppose... or her."

"She couldn't be more precise as to Moriarty's whereabouts, Lady Verity?"

"No."

"Fat lot of use... Sounds like she doesn't know who Moriarty is herself. She's asking you to find out. Using you."

"She wouldn't do a thing like—"

"Oh *please*."

"Really, I must insist—"

"Then why keep the key? If she were that committed to her noble cause, why not get off her fat backside and use it herself?"

"She's a public figure. It's not that easy. I'm guessing Cox gave it to her for safekeeping and probably didn't reveal its use, perhaps to protect her," Finch mused. "It was a leap of faith on her part to entrust it to us."

Annie rolled her eyes.

"What is it with men? One handsome woman, even one as old as dear old Verity—"

"She's not that old."

"…and you lose all sense of reason."

He got out his cigarette case and lit himself a Navy Cut. As an afterthought he offered the case to Annie. This time, she took one.

"You think that's why that man's after us? To lead him to Moriarty?" she ventured, her tone more conciliatory.

He exhaled.

"Or is his job to *stop* us getting to Moriarty…" said Finch. "I'm not sure of anything."

"Were you ever?"

"Nurse Jones—"

"You can cut out the pompous captain act. You don't wear it well."

Jesus, was he that transparent? Finch was truly speechless.

He held the key up, pretending to examine it. Then, suddenly inspired, went over to the dresser. There was a key in the lock of one of the smaller top drawers. He removed it and held the two together. They were of a similar design, though theirs was smaller.

"I just don't know," he said, shaking his head.

He motioned for her help. Together they dragged the dresser over to barricade the door.

"Better safe than sorry," he said.

He returned to his chair and perched on the edge. He was hesitant but eventually got to his point.

"Nurse Jones. I… I… Once again I apologise for the situation I have put you in. I promise you I will do everything in my power to resolve this matter. Tomorrow, first thing, we will go to Cape Town and put it right. You have my solemn promise that you will not be held responsible for failing to report for duty. The blame is entirely mine."

She nodded her thanks. For the apology, if not for the rest of it.

"Now, please, I suggest we get some sleep. The bed. I insist you take it. I shall sleep here in this chair."

He pulled a cushioned footstool close to him to enable him to stretch out and Annie gave him one of the blankets and a pillow. It was awkward, yes, she thought, but not as bizarre as some of the other activity that had gone on today.

"Goodnight, Nurse Jones."

He extinguished the gas lamp.

"Goodnight… Sir."

Annie, stared up into the dark. Her mind was still active, racing with thoughts, but she heard the soft, unconscious breathing of Finch across the room and felt relief, at least, that he was able to get some rest.

There was no telegraph office, she guessed. Or not one open at that hour. He had made that up for her sake.

It took her a while to slide into oblivion.

—

Finch had left the curtains open a little so that they might wake with the sun. Day was breaking. He had a brief moment of amnesiac calm before the bubble was pricked and the weight of their predicament descended on him.

He got up and began his daily business of stretching. He tried to stop himself, but watched Annie lying serene and peaceful. Her dark hair was down around her shoulders. He was minded of the day that he had first seen her, in the coffee shop. She was beautiful.

Of course he remembered her. How could he not?

He touched her shoulder and roused her. She awoke with a start.

"Come on," he said.

He would go downstairs, check out of the hotel, and grab as much as he could from the breakfast buffet. She was to exit via the fire escape again and meet him at the same spot in the trees. She was to leave it ten minutes. She was not to answer the door to anyone – *anyone!*

As quietly as they could, they manoeuvred the dresser out of the way. Satisfied that the coast was clear, Finch left and Annie locked the door. She waited the designated ten minutes, then hitched up the sash window to begin her clanking descent down the fire escape.

The guests had yet to stir, the curtains remained drawn, but at the bottom, as she swung down off the ladder, she bumped slap bang into a handyman walking along the path, armed with a sink plunger and a spanner. But he saw that she was making a getaway from what he assumed to be a gentleman's room, smiled and threw her a wink.

She made her way across the lawn to the trees. She was desperate to relieve herself and, in Finch's absence, squatted amid the undergrowth further in.

The birds were lively this morning, the dawn chorus resounding, though her thoughts flashed back immediately to the red-haired man and the fear returned. The sun's rays were growing stronger, she could feel their warmth. Death seemed an interloper on a day like this.

She stood again at the tree line. Eventually Finch appeared. His limp was not quite as pronounced as yesterday and his tunic bulged with what appeared to be pastries. One had already fallen out onto the gravel of the drive and he was smiling for once, like a mischievous schoolboy.

Finch did not see her returning his impish smirk. For, as he came towards her, she shot straight back behind a trunk. From behind, running straight at him, were two burly men in uniform. Their caps bore red crowns. They wore red and blue armbands and white webbing. Military Foot Police.

One wrestled Finch to the floor and held him in an arm-lock, face in the dirt, while clamping on handcuffs behind his back.

The second man, a sergeant, was bellowing at him.

"Captain Ingo Finch. You are under arrest."

"Arrest? For what?"

"The assault and battery of Lady Verity Hancock."

Chapter Forty-Three

Mbutu sat with his back against the post. His hands were numbing from the thin rough rope that cut into his wrists, his shoulders strained and ached from the way they had been forcibly contorted behind him.

Pain does not matter anymore. Mbutu you must think.

By rights he was a dead man... and a black man. Did a slender chance of survival now seriously hang on his ability to incriminate the Suttons?

He had brought them all – the Nama, the Suttons – on a three-day trek to this place. It was supposed to have been a refuge, a sanctuary.

Mbutu, you are a curse.

It was dark but light would soon come. It would come fast.

There seemed only one thing he could do – say nothing. His life would be in their hands now, these men of the British Crown. These men with the guns and the authority. White men. They would walk through the entrance before him and casually determine his fate. They would expend more energy ruminating on their choice of breakfast.

To his left he was aware of someone moving along the side of the tent. It had already come.

Please God. Let my son know that I only ever meant good.

The shape came close, the moon not bright enough for a silhouette, but enough to give the impression of a man... but a man, it seemed, who was struggling for breath.

The huffing and puffing did not befit an assassin. Whoever it was, whatever it was, did not carry the menace that had accompanied the others. There was some clawing at the tent flap and the large black shape crouched in a most ungainly fashion. It was trying to squeeze itself under. It entered, rolled over, pawed at the air above as if looking for an invisible hand-hold, then managed to right itself and pop on its hat.

The figure came behind Mbutu. The flash of blade made him suddenly doubt his instincts. He strained away from it. Then it fumbled at his wrists, severed the rope and accidentally nicked his forearm.

"Sorry."

Dean Newbold was helping Mbutu to his feet.

"Listen, we haven't much time," said the cleric.

"The Suttons... are they safe?" Mbutu asked.

"They will be."

Newbold beckoned Mbutu to the flap. It was hugely painful for him but Mbutu got down on all fours, eased himself into position and rolled under.

"I'm afraid the smell got too much for the guards, so they've taken themselves off site. Back at sun-up. But we've got to hurry."

Newbold pulled Mbutu to his feet. He bade him put an arm round his shoulders and carried on without pause. Newbold did not have the bearing of an athlete, but he was a big man, strong, felt Mbutu. Secure.

"I'm afraid little Emily told them all they need to know. Thought she was being helpful. Whatever ungodly business these men are involved in... Quick, across here..."

They were heading towards the northern perimeter.

"I don't know what you saw out there in the wilds, but whatever you did, none of you were supposed to. Missionary Sutton was not due at that village until next month. But he had zeal. Asked my permission to arrive early, to begin God's work at once. If only I'd..."

They were stepping over bodies towards a rough, informal pathway that led down to the shepherd's tree where they and the Nama had first sat. To Mbutu the vast, silent, unseen human carpet was eerie.

"The Nama?"

"I took the precaution of dispersing them amongst the general population. But we know where they all are. We will relocate them to another mission as soon as possible. I will oversee it myself."

"All of them? You can do that?"

"As it still stands, for a short while at least, this is a civilian camp run by the Christian Friendship Society. The Lord's authority still holds good here."

Not Godless after all.

"The man who questioned you, interrogated you," said Newbold. "He is not regular army. Some kind of intelligence officer. He wants to remove the blind men to Cape Town so that they can have their medical data recorded. Something about experiments."

Mbutu started to turn back.

"Then we have to help them."

"Not 'we'... 'I'. I will get them all to a safe mission. I can tweak records. Then we can sneak them back to the Nama lands. You, meanwhile..."

Behind the tree sat Mrs Sutton and Emily. The little girl ran up and hugged Mbutu.

"You've got to get out of here, all three of you."

He led them further. Emily held Mbutu's hand as he staggered along.

Suddenly there was a light up ahead.

"Down!" urged Newbold.

The four of them hit the ground, Mbutu doing as best as he could to support his own wrenched neck.

The light came closer. It was one of the soldiers from earlier. He was swinging his hurricane lamp back and forth.

"He hasn't noticed you gone yet, or we'd have heard him raise the alarm," whispered Newbold. "Must be looking for the Suttons."

They were lying among the human carpet – the amorphous, wheezing black mass of sick and dying. The light swung closer towards them.

"I would say needle in haystack," hissed Newbold, "but given our skin colour. And my size..."

Mbutu did his best to shrug off his jacket. His shoulders screamed with pain.

"Mrs Sutton, Emily... huddle in close," he urged. "Cover your heads."

The light moved close, less than eight yards away and then began to retreat. They could hear the man complaining of the 'bleeding stink'. He was pressing his kerchief to his face.

The people immediately around them seemed either asleep or so weak, the best they could do was turn their heads and watch silently.

It caught them by surprise but, from somewhere, an emaciated black arm reached out and touched Mrs Sutton on the cheek. She screamed but no noise came. Startled, she went to get up, making a commotion. Newbold dragged her back down and held her fast.

The light, which had been moving off, stopped.

"Oi?"

They said nothing.

"Someone there?"

They froze.

"Come out and show yourselves!"

Newbold, even prone, was too conspicuous.

"Oi… I said come out. Now!"

Newbold eased himself up to his knees, a look of sheer innocence across his face.

"Oh, hello my good fellow," he said.

"Mr Newbold?"

The light was coming towards them again.

"Don't you ever get no sleep, sir?"

Newbold pretended to be tending to a sick female, the one who had reached out and touched Mrs Sutton. Mbutu held Emily and her mother firmly, keeping his jacket across their heads.

"Alas, not when there's God's work to be done," he said.

He stood up and walked towards the soldier, preventing him from coming closer.

"And might I ask what you're doing out here, my boy? This is not a place for a lost soul."

"That woman… the British one. 'Er and 'er daughter. You seen 'em?"

"They are in my tent."

You are a fine actor, Mister Newbold.

"No they're not."

"Sleeping like babies," said Newbold. "Come on, I'll show you…"

He strode up to the soldier and threw his great arm round his shoulder. The man didn't appreciate it.

"You sure you looked in the right one," the Dean added.

"S'all right," the soldier said, uncomfortable.

He turned and ambled away, lantern swinging again.

Newbold hastened back over.

"Come on."

Two hundred yards on, clear of the unofficial camp border was a clump of acacia. There were two horses tethered, standing patiently.

"The grey. She's my own," said Newbold wistfully. "And the bay…? Ask me no questions, I shall tell you no lies."

Each horse bore stuffed saddlebags and plump deerskins.

"Enough here to last a few days."

"Where do we—?" asked Mbutu.

"Here."

Newbold pressed into his hand a small, round, flat tin. A compass.

"There's your map in the saddlebag."

The British and their maps.

"If you worked in the surveying gangs, then you'll know how to use both in tandem."

Mbutu nodded.

"Head north," instructed Newbold. "Round the escarpment. You know this country better than any now. You've lived off it before. You can live off it again. Stay clear of the railway line and the army camps along it. The Coloureds are raising their own people at Calvinia. Their own push against the Boers. Travel with *them*. Use sound judgement."

"But where...?"

Newbold cut him short, fiddled with the grey's stirrups and motioned for Mbutu to take the bridle to hold her steady. He bundled Emily in both arms and swept her up into the saddle.

Newbold turned to her mother.

"Mrs Sutton. Do you ride?"

The woman gave no indication.

"Not well, but she can," offered Emily.

"Good," said Newbold. "Not side-saddle I'm afraid. Astride. But you'll find it easier."

He lowered the stirrup and bade the woman put her left foot into it. She refused.

"Mrs Sutton!"

Her eyes flicked to Mbutu. He nodded that she should do as Newbold asked. Newbold extended his arms. He grabbed her lower leg, helping spring her upwards. He told her to swing her right leg over and squash up behind Emily. She gathered her skirts and did so.

"Be good to Bessie," he said. "You'll not find a more tolerant creature."

He went to the front and rested his cheek on Bessie's nose. He stroked her face tenderly.

"Goodbye, old girl. Look after them."

Bessie seemed to snort a farewell of her own. He gave her a tap on the rump and she ambled off.

Mbutu did not dally. He shook hands and tried launching himself up onto the other horse. But, physically, it was beyond him. Newbold did his best to heave him up. Mbutu grabbed the pommel and clung to the reins.

"Thank you," said Mbutu.

Newbold panted.

"Kimberley," he said.

The word made Mbutu's heart leap.

My wife. My son.

"They say the siege will soon be broken. Go home, Mbutu. Go *home*."

There were two lights swinging now, moving faster in their direction.

"The head covering. That sack. The one I showed you," said Mbutu.

Newbold nodded.

"The tree. One hundred paces west. There's a flat round stone."

"Go!" Newbold exerted. "God bless."

He gave Mbutu's horse a shove and it, too, disappeared into the darkness.

They rode through the remainder on the night. By dawn the ground had opened out onto the plains, the vast grasslands that would extend ultimately to the desert of the Karoo and way beyond into the vast interior.

By mid-morning, civilisation had long retreated. They were on their own. This time Mbutu carried the knowledge of the Nama with him. As the wilderness was the white man's enemy, so, too, it could be their friend.

They found quiver trees and rocks to give them shade and Mbutu lit a fire and cooked a small ration of mealies. They would rest, he announced, through the heat of the day and proceed in the afternoon. He would set a snare for a rabbit.

"And if soldiers come?" asked Emily.

"That is a chance we will always have to take."

Mbutu stood watch, scanning the horizon to the south while the Suttons slept. For once they looked at peace.

Newbold was a man of God, a man who abhorred violence, but he had also had the foresight to include a carbine.

As the heat began to recede, Emily sat up and rubbed her eyes.

"Did they come, Mbutu?"

"No, child, they did not come."

"Are we safe?"

He looked deep into her young blue eyes.

"I can never guarantee it," he whispered. "But I will do everything in my power to protect you... to protect your mother."

The woman was stirring. Slowly she eased herself up, reclining against a rock scoured smooth by a millennia of wind and stone. Mbutu handed her a deerskin, instructing her to take only two small sips.

"Where are we going?" asked Emily.

He smiled.

"Home," he said.

The woman looked at him, her eyes framed by her usual worried countenance. But, for the first time, weak, awkward words passed her lips.

"Thank you."

Part Three

Chapter Forty-Four

There was a blur of white somewhere up above Finch. It was too bright for stars, the wrong shape for the moon. There were two lights spinning. Then the twin glows merged to become just one.

As Finch willed his eyes to focus, it became apparent that he was no longer outdoors, it was no longer night-time. He was in a darkened room, the daylight issuing through a small barred window situated up high.

Aside from the fuzziness, there was a foul chemical taste in his mouth, accentuated by the parch dryness. He didn't need to be a medic to know that he'd been drugged.

He was lying on his side. The stone floor appeared to have a thin scattering of straw upon it. The walls were bare, a grubby whitewashed brick.

Finch was becoming aware of another sensation – cold. He was shivering. Slowly, awkwardly, he managed to sit. He hugged himself and turned his tunic collar up, pulling it tight round his neck. Now, not just his knee hurt but his left bicep too. It was sore, tender, bruised. Someone had injected something into him, crudely, right into his arm, right through his tunic.

The room was about 10ft square. There was a heavy wooden door with iron hinges, a store of some sorts.

Slowly Finch got to his feet. He felt wobbly, like someone fresh off a fairground ride. He reached to steady himself on the wall. When he pulled his hand away it was wet. He saw now, there was a red streak with a white print where his palm had been.

Blood. Not his own.

He took a handful of straw and wiped at his hand, disgusted. He staggered to the door and tried it. That it was locked was an inevitability.

He made an effort of pounding on it with his fist, but his hands were difficult to coordinate. He tried to scream, but it was a weak protest. He was aware that his speech was slurring, his tongue swollen and dormant.

In the corner was a bucket, presumably for ablutions. But there was also an enamel mug. He shuffled over to it. It contained water that was stale, a touch fetid. It made no difference. He drank it right down.

As his senses began to return, Finch tried to recall what had happened. It started to come back – Annie, the hotel, the MFPs…

Nurse Jones! Had she been interned too? He hoped, for her sake, that she had remained hidden.

His feeble attempt at shouting had had an effect nonetheless. Within moments there was the rattle of hobnails and the clanking of a chain and keys. There was an MFP opening the door and a sergeant clomping in.

"Captain Finch."

The man's cap peak was pulled down hard over his eyes in the affected manner of a drill sergeant.

Finch measured his reply.

"I demand to know what's going on."

"You were read the charge on your arrest."

The arrest?

"I was also drugged on my arrest."

The sergeant was as officious as Harmison had been.

"Orders."

Finch's mind was becoming clearer.

"You have no right to detain me."

The private exited and returned with a crude wooden stool.

"Sit down, Captain."

Finch did so. He extended his left leg and rubbed his knee.

"Where am I?"

"In the charge of the Military Foot Police."

"No, *where*…?"

"In the charge of the Military Foot Police."

"What time is it?"

"Afternoon."

"No, the time?"

The sergeant raised his voice.

"And I told you, afternoon."

"If it's afternoon, you've detained me from rejoining my unit, assuming this is the 29th of December?"

The sergeant said nothing.

"Surely you can't arrest someone in anticipation of their going absent?"

But it was coming back to him now, the charge... something to do with Lady Verity. An assault?

"Can you account for your movements over the past few hours?"

Christ, what had happened?

"I was in Paarl, the RAMC, then I visited a refugee camp. This is all a matter of record."

"Why did you go to Stellenbosch?"

'Go' to Stellenbosch? If he were still in Stellenbosch, they'd have said 'come'.

"*Warner's Guide to the Cape.*"

"What?"

"It recommends it highly."

If there were any doubt about his returning consciousness, the stinging slap across the face brought him right into the present.

"HOW DARE YOU!" screamed Finch.

He tried to rise but the other MFP had come behind him and held him down by the shoulders.

"MIGHT I REMIND YOU THAT YOU HAVE JUST STRUCK A SUPERIOR OFFICER!"

There was no reaction.

"There are two witnesses who can place you at the Hancock residence at around ten o'clock last night, the Lady's maid saw you announce yourself."

"I do not deny it. I have nothing to hide."

"Why were you there?"

"Lady Verity and I have a mutual colleague. Or, should I say, *had* a mutual colleague, my former CO. He was killed – murdered – in Cape Town, a few days ago. Again, a matter of record."

No response.

"I was charged with responsibility for tidying up Cox's affairs. As Stellenbosch was not far from Paarl—"

"There was a nurse with you," the sergeant cut across. "Where is she?"

God bless you, Nurse Jones, you got away.

"I don't know."

"You then proceeded to the Egremont Hotel."

"Seeing as you arrested me in its grounds, may I congratulate you on your excellent detective work, Sergeant."

Another slap. This time it was worth it.

"You checked in alone. The girl, where did she go?"

Christ, they were stupid.

Finch shrugged.

"The witnesses – the maid, a valet – claim that Lady Verity was in an agitated state. That she had tried to evict you—"

"At first, yes. She had just lost a close friend. She was upset."

"…and that soon after your departure, she was found in her chambers. She'd been roughed up quite badly."

"Something you'd know about."

The irony was lost as another slap was delivered. It left Finch's left ear ringing.

That was it, Finch lost it.

"I'M TELLING YOU AND YOU'D BLOODY WELL BETTER LISTEN!!! I HAVE BEEN ON THE RUN THESE PAST HOURS BECAUSE A MAN HAS BEEN FOLLOWING ME – WITH CONSIDERABLE MENACE. I HAVE REASON TO BELIEVE HE ALSO TRIED TO HARM LADY VERITY AND WAS IN THE VICINITY AROUND THE SAME TIME AS I WAS. YOU CAN CHECK WITH THE POLICE DETAIL GUARDING THE HOUSE. THEY'LL—"

There was another slap. Harder.

With it, hobnails rattled as the MFPs left and the door was bolted and locked from the outside.

–

Finch had no idea of the passage of time. There was no doubt in his mind, as he lay curled in a ball on the floor, that the red-haired man was the one who had assaulted Lady Verity – if indeed she had been assaulted at all and this wasn't just some ruse to bring him into custody.

Or maybe she had panicked and pinned it on him?

In his cold semi-sleep he heard the door lock, clank and the bolt rattle open. The light that brought him to came not from the window this time but a hurricane lamp close to his face. It hurt his eyes. The hiss from it was ominous, like a cobra ready to strike. It was otherwise dark, the light from the window long gone.

There were three men upon him now, different MFPs to the ones who'd entered before. Without word, he was hauled to his feet by two of them and marched forcefully out of the cell, pushed from behind by the third.

They said nothing, Finch said nothing. At the end of the corridor was a door. Through it and Finch was into an office where a Military Foot Police officer, a captain like himself, sat behind a lamp-lit desk, scrawling at paperwork. He looked up momentarily to gesture that Finch should be deposited in the chair opposite him, then he returned to his labours.

The MFPs exited. Only when he was finished did the man look up. He was middle-aged, a little on the chubby side and bald, a few strands of hair oiled across his pate. His narrow, squinting eyes were housed behind round wire spectacles.

He scanned the document before him.

"Captain… Finch?" he read off, as if Finch were the next patient at a busy doctor's surgery.

"Yes."

"I trust my men have been looking after you?"

Was this sarcasm, wondered Finch, or was the man oblivious to what went on a few doors down?

"Quite attentive. You know, I'm going to write to Mr Warner and ask him to include this place in his next edition."

The man raised his gaze again. The joke was either lost on him or he chose to ignore it.

"Does your definition of care involve drugging?" added Finch.

The man screwed the cap on his fountain pen and blotted his writing.

"Ah yes, sodium thiopental," he said. "Prescribed by our medical officer. We thought it would give you some rest, allow you to gather your thoughts."

"You really have been most kind."

He ran through the next bit as if brushing off an irritant.

"Captain Finch, my name is Captain Anthony Franklin of the Military Foot Police. I am an attorney of law. I have been appointed your legal counsel."

"Legal counsel. For what purpose?"

"A court-martial."

"On a trumped up charge of battery…? Enforced desertion?"

The man did not answer. He got up from his chair. His Sam Brown belt was fastened a little too tightly and rode up above his generous belly. It reminded Finch of Cox.

Damned bloody Cox.

"You know, what happened to Lady Verity – what you *did* to Lady Verity – is a terrible thing," he said.

"You mean what I am *alleged* to have done."

"It would cause great embarrassment to Sir Frederick."

The man moved behind Finch, slowly pacing up and down, making it difficult for Finch to look him in the eye.

"Have you heard nothing? I did no such thing. I told your men earlier what happened and what I think is the most likely scenario."

"It would prove both scandalous and most likely detrimental to the war effort at a most critical juncture," the man continued. "Treachery, no less."

"I'm no expert, but shouldn't defence counsel be asking me what happened and how we can best mitigate any charges levelled?"

The man paid no attention. He went back to the desk, hovered over it, and scrawled a note.

"However, I believe it is within my purview to have any such charges deferred if you can assist us in the search for a certain individual."

Finch said nothing. Was the man asking him to sell out Nurse Jones?

"Moriarty," he said. "What do you know of Moriarty?"

Finch sighed. He slumped back in his seat.

"Will everyone stop talking to me in damned riddles. I really don't know anything. But I have heard the name, yes, and, I must admit, I'm getting a little curious myself as to who the hell he is."

The man appeared to issue the slightest of frowns, as if Finch had unconsciously told him something of import. He leaned forward on his palms.

"I will ask you again, Captain, what do you know of Moriarty?"

"I know that he's the hottest ticket in town."

"What do you know of Moriarty?"

"Nothing."

"What do you know of Moriarty?"

"I believe you just asked me that."

The man made a humming noise, one of pondering.

"Captain Finch, according to a cable from the office of the Provost Marshal, on around noon on…"

He scanned another document before him.

"…the 12th of December, you entered into a private parley with a detachment of Boer commandos at Van Doorp Farm, Magersfontein."

Finch spluttered his incredulity.

"What? Are you seriously—?"

"It, too, is a matter of record."

"For Christ's sake, man, I was ensuring the transfer of wounded. Under the terms of the Geneva Convention—"

"The previous day," the man cut across, "you collaborated with the enemy in the field…"

Finch folded his arms.

"This is beneath contempt."

"…and then did not return to your post for a full five hours after that."

He shot a look of daggers at his inquisitor.

"You have nothing to say, Captain?"

"Absolutely fucking nothing…"

Finch spat the last word out.

"…Captain."

Franklin scrawled another note.

He then went to the door and opened it. He gave a nod and the three MFPs marched back in.

"Captain Finch," said Franklin. "We can do this the easy way or the hard way. The choice is yours. But, mark my words, we *will* find out this information… who this Moriarty is."

Any pretence of civility swiftly evaporated. Two MFPs grabbed Finch under either armpit and yanked him forcefully to his feet. The other shoved him in the direction of the door.

Cell door open, they launched him into the darkness. Finch careered across the floor and crashed into the slop bucket, then the wall. He writhed on the floor, holding his knee. But it was not over.

"Strip," barked one of them.

"What?"

"I said strip. Your clothes. Hand them over. Everything."

"I'll do not such thing."

A hobnail boot came down hard on his damaged knee.

Reluctantly and desperately, Finch complied.

Finch did not sleep this time. He lay in the dark and, for the first time in a long while, offered up a prayer.

As the thin light of dawn began to leak through the small window he heard the crunch of boots again, the shuttle of the bolt as an MFP opened the door. Finch had steeled himself for the worst. All he could do, he knew, was to roll into a ball and protect his vital organs when the blows came.

The man, Franklin, was standing over him now. But he had Finch's clothes in a bundle under his arm, his boots in his hand. He threw them at him.

"Captain Finch, you are free to go," he said.

He pointed to the door.

"A procedural matter."

"That's *it*?!" screamed Finch as two MFPs moved between him and their officer. "You drug me, beat me, humiliate me and then just tell me I'm able to go. Casually. Just like that?"

Finch pulled his clothes on as fast as he could.

"Like I say, a procedural matter," said Franklin. There was a faint smile. "I'm sure the army would regret any inconvenience—"

"INCONVENIENCE!"

Finch, half-dressed, flew at Franklin. The MFPs held him back then swept him out into the street, threw his boots after him, and slammed the metal door behind him. In the dawn light, on the pavement, Finch could see that the door was unmarked. It bore no evidence as to its use within and sat squeezed between the entrances to warehouses and stores, most of which had their metal shutters pulled down.

After the stale interior, the cool fresh sea air hit him instantly. There were gulls cawing. They were at the Cape Town docks.

"Captain Finch?"

He turned. There, a few feet away, stood the genuinely comforting sight of Inspector Brookman.

"Come on," the detective urged. "I could get fired for pulling a stunt like this. Had to tell some lies to get you out."

He motioned to him to hurry.

"Carriage around the corner."

Finch could barely walk, Brookman saw and lent assistance while Finch carried his boots.

"Thank you, Inspector. Thank you."

"Thank your little friend."

As they rounded the corner, Finch saw Annie sitting in the back of the buggy.

"Nurse Jones!" he exclaimed.

The inspector helped Finch up beside her. She made him comfortable, took a handkerchief and gently wiped his face.

"Did you save me a pastry?" she asked.

For the first time in a while Finch smiled.

Brookman climbed up to the driver's seat, twitched his whip and the dapple grey horse took off.

The docks were coming to life. A crane was winching up a netted pallet. Along the cobbled dock byways, they wound past piles of crates and boxes.

Brookman yelled back over his shoulder.

"Lady Verity... You were set up..."

"That's what I was trying to tell them."

"Though she *was* roughed up."

"Is she okay?"

"She will be. Is keeping tight-lipped about it. Scared to talk."

"It was him, the red-haired man?"

"Don't know. But from what Miss Jones has told me, he'd be the number one suspect... he was after something. Information. But was disturbed. The household staff put two and two together—"

"And I made four."

"Afraid so."

He urged the horse on.

"There's a high-stakes game being played here," said Brookman. "Something you... the pair of you... have got yourself caught up in. Me too for that matter."

"Inspector, who the hell is Moriarty?" asked Finch.

"That would seem to be the question of the hour."

They came off the dock road up towards Strand Street.

"Right, heads down," said Brookman. "You can't afford to be seen. And I certainly can't afford to be seen with you."

They ducked as he wheeled the buggy off to the right, crossing the oncoming lane. Up ahead were Military Foot Police, an unusual sight so early in the day, their presence generally aligned with drinking hours.

"I have reason to suspect this lot are in on it," he added, nodding in the their direction.

Brookman slowed to a trot as they edged up an alley behind some coachworks and came to a halt. He sprang down and opened the door.

"What the hell's going on Inspector?" asked Finch.

"I don't rightly know, Captain. But I do know you need to make yourselves scarce."

"Why?"

"I'm sorry, but I can't explain. I really wish I could."

He helped Annie out then both extended their hands to Finch.

"Trust no one," Brookman added. "The MFPs let you go – for now – but they'll be watching out, ready to reel you in at any moment. There are others out there too who would mean you harm. You already know that."

Finch reached for his left boot. He prised up the inner and was relieved to find what he'd been looking for.

"Inspector, what's this?"

It was no longer in its envelope.

"You mean other than it being a key?"

"It was given to us by Lady Verity. Something to do with Cox. Maybe what her assailant was looking for."

Brookman examined it.

"One thing I do know is locks."

He pressed it back into Finch's hand.

"It's a barrel key. A modern one. No more than about five years old."

"A latch key? A locker?" asked Annie.

"Desk or bureau. Small compartment or drawer."

The tension returned to his face.

"But there's no time. Please go, hide, lie low. Keep out of sight. If you must move, do it in a crowd or after dark."

"Why?"

Brookman ignored him. He reached inside his jacket and pulled something from under his jacket.

"Here…"

It was a Webley, like the one Finch had lost, though a more recent model, shiny and oiled.

"…you'll need this."

Finch clutched it.

"You took it from me, threatened me," said Brookman. "Are we clear?"

"No. Not clear at all."

"Disappear for a day, maybe two. If you can find out anything in the process, anything to do with this Moriarty, any of this business, then please do. But by all means, be careful."

"Cox and Lady Verity. You knew they were—"

"I did… High society is small society, Captain. People talk."

Finch felt relief, at least, that his failure to disclose the letters had not prevented Brookman's knowledge of their affair.

"Now go. Please. Keep out of the way. I will find you. I promise."

Chapter Forty-Five

Finch and Annie watched Brookman depart as silently yet dramatically as he had arrived.

The coachworks smelt of wood and resin. There were cartwheels stacked behind a chained metal gate at the alley's dead end; the rest of it comprised shuttered lock-ups. Opposite the entrances ran a grubby brick wall. By a puddle, a stray black and white cat picked over the carcass of some small bird or rodent.

It was still early. They would be conspicuous until the rush-hour crowds and the cover that they would afford.

"So what now?" asked Annie.

"I wish I knew."

He leaned against the wall and pulled on his boots. She offered to help but he insisted he was okay.

"Don't know about you, but I don't much fancy hiding out for two days," she said. "Brookman said something about finding out as much as we can, if we were careful. His hands must be tied."

"Thank you," said Finch.

"For what?"

"Saving my bacon."

She was evidently not an easy recipient of praise.

"Only thing I could think of. Had enough money to get a taxi cab from the hotel to the tram terminus. Hung around for the dawn service to start up."

"How did you know where to find me?"

"Brookman said that the Military Foot Police used a number of hidey-holes around town for their more high profile 'guests', as he put it. We've been calling at them one by one. Taken hours. You know he hasn't slept in God knows how long… He mentioned another name… Hartson, Harrison?"

"Harmison."

"That's it. Raised him on the telephone. Used him to buy you some time. Brookman was supposed to deliver us, both of us, straight to Harmison, that was the deal, all part of the ongoing investigation, which is now in MFP hands… I got the impression this Harmison was not exactly the sharpest knife in the drawer."

Finch laughed.

"So?"

"So what?"

"So what do we do?"

Finch went to the end of the alley and looked round the corner. There were still two Military Foot Police on the seaward end of the main drag.

He wasn't sure how efficient the lines of communication were. They still might be on the lookout for him as the supposed assaulter of Lady Verity. The problem had been compounded by the fact that, in the past few minutes, courtesy of Brookman, he'd also been reinvented as a hostile, armed fugitive, one also absent without leave.

Though the alley was a cul-de-sac, its line extended across the other side of the road running through to the street that ran parallel to the thoroughfare of Buitengracht.

"How's your knowledge of the city?" he asked Annie.

"Better than yours probably."

"The next road over, what is it?"

"Bree… Yes, Bree Street."

He rubbed his face. His cheek still smarted.

"Do you know Bloem Street? It's around here somewhere, I think."

"Few blocks inland."

"You sure?"

"Pretty."

"In that case, I do have one idea."

He sensed scepticism.

"What?"

"The RAMC's official headquarters are at the Cape Town Castle, but the bulk of the work, the day-to-day admin stuff, is conducted from an office on Bloem Street. Cox was based there before hostilities broke out. I know he would have reported there again on return to Cape Town on the 24th. He still kept a desk there."

"What are you suggesting?"

"That we go in and take a look around."

Her expression conveyed that she didn't concur with it being a good plan.

"Why not?" he urged. "RAMC personnel in an RAMC building? It's not illogical. 'Hiding in plain sight.' Remember?"

"Look where that got us last time." she said.

"If there are MFPs outside the building, or anything looks out of the ordinary, then we'll steer clear. I promise."

"Surely they'll have posted someone there?"

"Not the sharpest knives in the drawer. Remember?"

It was her turn to smile.

"What time is it?" he asked.

"Quarter past seven."

"Right, follow me."

He led her to the end of the alley.

The odd cart and wagon had begun to clop past. They heard the clang of a tram and the fizz of electricity in the overhead cables. It was trundling downhill towards them.

"Right," said Finch.

He grabbed her hand.

"Let's go."

As the tram drew close, they saw it was packed with workers headed for the docks. As it passed them, obscuring their view from the MFPs on the corner, Finch dragged Annie across the street.

He was more incapacitated than he thought. He caught his foot in the track and stumbled. The tram had continued on, leaving them completely exposed, but the MFPs hadn't looked their way. Annie helped him up. They ducked into the alleyway opposite.

"Thank you again," he panted.

They followed the alley, past a line of refuse bins, to Bree Street. It, too, was exhibiting the first signs of life. Sure that there were no Military Foot Police, Cape Police or anyone else of obvious threat, they hastened north, keeping close to the storefronts.

Onto Bloem Street and the block was dominated by a gleaming modern office block, all cement and glass that could only, estimated Finch, have been built in the 1890s. It had about ten storeys and the ground level, the reception area, was nothing but plate glass with a revolving door situated in the centre. Above it were the words 'Warwick House'. Again, there seemed no evidence of danger.

"The RAMC haven't got the whole building," said Finch. "It's shared with other businesses, some tied to the services, some commercial. I came here once, but that was it."

A woman of about 30 years of age was walking in their direction on the other side of the street. She had a long skirt, white blouse, a dark bolero jacket and a straw boater. She stopped outside the building, wrestled some keys from a leather satchel and began unlocking a glass door, starting with the lock at the top.

"This is our chance," said Finch.

He led Annie over to the woman.

"Good morning," he said.

"Good morning," she replied, still reaching up.

"I wonder if you could help us?"

She crouched to undo the bottom lock set in a metal bar at the foot of the door, then stood and eyed them up and down. Lord knows how they presented, wondered Finch. He alone hadn't shaved for three days.

"I'm afraid we're not open till eight, sir. There won't be any medical corps here till then."

"Which is why we need your help. You see, the nurse and I, we're due to leave for the Front this morning."

The woman shook her head.

"Just terrible, this business. Just terrible…"

She fumbled with the keys and put them back in her satchel.

"…My brother, Terrence. He was at Colenso. What he wrote to me… It's just shocking."

"It must be difficult for you," soothed Annie, touching her elbow.

"Not knowing's the worst," said the woman, her voice a little shaky. "You spend every day hanging on the footsteps of the postman."

Annie extended her hand and introduced herself. The woman reciprocated.

"Daisy," she said. She jabbed a thumb towards the inside. "The receptionist."

"Daisy," ventured Finch. "I'm afraid we lost a dear colleague of ours recently, a Major Cox."

She shook her head again and exhaled loudly.

"I heard," she said. "Saw him only the other day. He was home on leave, the day… the day he was…"

She gazed off into the middle distance.

"…Such a nice man… Oh, it's just so awful."

She pushed the door open and let them in. She proceeded behind the front desk.

"If you want to leave a note for someone here, I'll be sure—"

Finch pulled his most sombre face.

"It's more personal than that," he intoned. "You see Cox was my commanding officer. We served together at the Front… Magersfontein."

He hoped that the word would add resonance.

"In these unfortunate circumstances I've been charged with taking care of his personal effects… to forward them on to his dear wife and children. I'm afraid I'm only in Cape Town very briefly."

"Oh, I see."

Finch delved in a pocket. Yes, he still had it – the requisition order Brookman had filled out, intended for Ans Du Plessis, but worded to the same ends. Daisy glanced at it but didn't read it, accepting it at face value.

"We were wondering if we could take a quick look," added Annie. "See if there's anything that ought to be included. Photographs, mementoes…"

It was obvious they had placed Daisy in an awkward position.

"But honestly, if it's an imposition, we understand," Annie continued. "The police will be able to do the same. It's just that his things will probably end up in storage somewhere."

She turned back towards the street, nodding discreetly for Finch to follow.

It worked.

"Look, I shouldn't really be doing this," whispered Daisy. "If the caretaker were here."

She went to the glass door and locked it from the inside, then returned to the desk. She rifled through more keys, unlocked a case on the wall and removed yet another bunch. She went towards a door in an internal wall and unlocked a latticed cage screen, which she slid back on concertina hinges. She beckoned for them to follow her into a confined space.

"What's this?" asked Annie.

"An elevator… a passenger lift," said Finch. "See…"

On the wall next to it, Finch pointed to the brass signs for the assorted outfits that occupied each floor of the building – several shipping companies, an accountancy firm, a telegraphy company and, on the eighth floor, Royal Army Medical Corps.

The lift was an Otis, Finch read off the floor plate. The Otis Elevator Company had done very nicely out of the new mania for building upwards, such devices commonplace in cities like New York, and proliferating elsewhere. He had ridden in them a few times in London.

Daisy slid the caged door back across, threw a large lever and punched a button. With a jolt, they took off. Annie grabbed Finch's hand reflexively, then let go when she realised what she was doing.

"My stomach!"

Daisy laughed.

"It does that the first time."

They followed Daisy down a corridor past closed doors to the Excelsior Shipping Company and Masthead Telegraphic Incorporated. The third door along door was adorned with the letters RAMC. She found the key, then opened it.

Within were several desks each piled with papers. There were a couple of telephones. On the wall was a large map, buried under a forest of coloured pins.

"Through there," said Daisy, pointing to a side room. "The Major used to park himself in there."

"Thank you," said Finch.

"Ten minutes. Please don't dally. The caretaker clocks on at quarter to."

"We'll be as quick as we can," assured Annie.

Daisy prised the key off the ring.

"Lock up after yourselves and bring this back to me. Have to use the stairs, I'm afraid."

Said Finch, hamming up the sincerity: "Major Cox's family would appreciate what you've done for them."

When her footsteps had retreated down the corridor, Finch closed the main door and locked it from the inside. They then went into the small office. They felt the receding hum of the elevator.

Inside there was one desk with a telephone. Unlike the ones in the main room it was remarkably uncluttered – just a blotter, some pens and a large, lined desk notepad. The pad was devoid of any writing whatsoever, with the exception of the bottom right-hand corner which, given the impression on the page beneath, had had something scrawled on it before being torn off.

Finch went behind the desk and sat in the wood and leather swivel chair. Turning round, he saw there was another building of similar height on the opposite side of the street off to the left. But straight ahead, unobstructed, lay an impressive view over the docks and the sweep of Table Bay. The sky was a clear blue, the morning sun already shimmering on the water, a haze blurring the horizon.

Down one side of the desk were three drawers.

"Brookman said a desk, right?"

Annie watched as he pulled out the key Lady Verity had given them. He tried it in each lock.

"Nope. None of them. Too small."

He tried to wrench the top drawer open but it remained fast, as did the second. When he pulled on the bottom drawer, the largest, it jolted open to reveal nothing but a half-drunk bottle of Mount Gay rum.

He eased out the cork, sniffed it and took a swig.

"Medicinal purposes," he said. "Here…"

He handed it to Annie and she did the same. She stood for a moment gazing out of the window.

"Great view," she said.

Her momentary drift was shattered by the sudden shrill ring of the telephone. Finch looked at her.

"You think it might be Daisy? We haven't long."

"Why don't you answer it?" she said.

"You think I should?"

"Jesus, it's not going to bite."

Finch unhooked the receiver and put it to his ear.

"*Captain Finch?*" came the tinny female voice.

"Daisy?"

"*No, sir… this is the Cape Town exchange.*"

His blood ran suddenly cold. How could they know?

"*Connecting you now, sir…*"

There was a man on the line.

"*Captain Finch?*"

"Who is this?"

"*Shawcroft.*"

"Shawcroft?"

"*I'm watching you from the building across the way. You have about 30 seconds before the MFPs bust in. Get out!*"

Finch could feel the hum from the elevator shaft. The lift was rising.

"*The fire escape,*" the man urged.

Even though the main door was closed, they could hear the clang of the elevator gate. It was followed by a tattoo of hobnails on the corridor's shiny linoleum.

"Nurse Jones, the window," Finch motioned.

There was a rattling of the doorknob, followed by loud banging.

"We know you're in there!" boomed a voice.

There was a crunch as someone rammed a shoulder into the door.

"*Cape Town Races. Noon.*"

The man hung up.

Annie swung open the casement window. Finch ushered her onto the metal fire escape.

"Who was that?"

"I'll explain."

They clambered down the eight floors into another alleyway.

As they reached the bottom, a head poked out from Cox's office, an MFP.

"Oi you! Stop!"

Finch was scuttling away as fast he could.

"Wait," said Annie.

Two MFPs were now out of the window and thundering down.

"Here…"

She was lifting up the bottom section of ladder, a drop-down segment, trying to unhook it.

"I'm becoming an expert."

Finch saw what she was doing and helped her. Removing the section would mean a two-storey drop. The ladder clanged to the ground.

They disappeared up the alley and merged into the burgeoning morning crowd on Bree Street. When they had cut across a succession of roads and alleyways, they wound their way through the stalls of Greenmarket Square. The stall-holders were setting up trestle tables that were flowering into colourful displays of fruit, vegetables, African tribal jewellery, cheap clothing and assorted knick-knacks.

Satisfied that no MFPs were evident they diverted behind a garment store and skulked, once again, in an alley alongside bins, crates, boxes and pallets. There were workmen delivering racks of clothing off the back of a flatbed cart straight into the tradesmen's entrance.

Pausing to catch breath, Finch explained to Annie about the warning phone call.

"Shawcroft? Where have we heard it before?" she asked.

Finch unbuttoned his breast pocket. Of all Cox's personal effects, the only thing he had managed to retain was the wallet. The intruder at the hotel had taken the ten shillings from within. But in the rear section, behind a silk divider, the other items remained – some 1d and 2d stamps, a receipt from a chemist's shop and a scrap of paper. He showed it to her. It was lined and ripped from the bottom right-hand corner of a notepad. On it, written in pencil, was one word – '*Shawcroft*'.

"Here," said Annie and produced a large orange which she had purloined from a stall. "I don't usually hold with such behaviour but, given the situation."

The fruit was huge, plump and took two hands to hold. She bit into it to break the surface, then dug her nails in to start peeling. As a coil of orange skin fell to the floor, she broke the flesh into two halves. They both gorged silently. To Finch, the tangy fruit was like a shot of pure energy.

"Extenuating circumstances," he said. "Though I did have some change on me."

"So, Cape Town Races?"

He wiped his mouth on the back of his hand.

"Over at Kenilworth."

"How do we know we can trust him, this Shawcroft? Just because he tipped us off about the MFPs doesn't necessarily make him on our side."

"We don't know. We'll have to take a chance. Tread carefully. See what he wants."

"Did he say what he looks like?"

"No."

She mused for a moment.

"What size are you?"

"What?"

"Your size. Chest, collar, waist—"

"Why?"

"We can't go dressed like this."

The delivery men had gone in, the clothes racks were temporarily unattended.

"As you say," she added. "Extenuating circumstances."

Chapter Forty-Six

The thunder of hooves sent a shock through his body. Finch was suddenly minded of the Boers at the farmstead at Magersfontein. Even the smell – of turf, earth, sand and beast – was evocative.

He thought for a moment of Swanepoel, a man ostensibly civilised but who would then have seemed to have been responsible for a monstrous act. The execution of the wounded had been pushed to the back of his mind amid all that had happened of late. But when Finch recalled it, he grew angry.

He would not forget. And when this episode was over, he would not the let the army forget it either.

The pack came into the home straight and a shiny, sinewy black beast – its jockey in green and gold silks – was a full length ahead, nearly two by the time it tore past the winning post, the pursuing riders smacking their crops, the wide-eyed equines snorting and frothing.

The visceral thrill of a group of horses running flat out drew on its association with a cavalry charge, Finch supposed – or rather the romance of a cavalry charge. Not too far north from here young men on horseback, swords drawn, were being mown down casually by men with machine guns. Cavalry were a dying breed, in every sense.

There was an added perversity for Finch. The race meeting – with its culinary fineries and champagne and high fashion – was taking place not only in the face of a war but amid it. All around the southern suburbs were army camps. They had colonised every square inch of open ground. Indeed, much of the day's clientele was made up of officers. The remainder, it seemed, was comprised of those whom the war was treating well.

After the first race, the band of the Scots Greys was wheeled out to march up and down before the grandstand. In its ceremonial red – where combat troops were now filth-covered men in khaki – it too peddled the legend.

The regiment had just arrived in the Cape, the crowd was informed. It would be at the vanguard of the relief of Kimberley, an announcement that brought a rousing cheer and the waving of hats.

In joyous celebration, the tic-tac men took to their soap-boxes and fistfuls of bills changed hands.

While the band played on, Finch kept in the centre of the throng and fingered Brookman's revolver in the right-hand pocket of his jacket – part of a rather tight, light brown suit, his army shirt and tie and brown boots fitting the ensemble. He could raise and fire it without removing it, he had rehearsed. He prayed it wouldn't come to that.

Finch kept moving and turning, scanning the crowd. He could not see Annie directly but knew exactly where to signal should they choose to abort their mission or, in the worst case scenario they had discussed, Finch be beyond salvation.

The sudden whiff of perfume in the air combined with the whirling wisps of cigar smoke took him to other glimpses into high society – Ascot, Henley, punting on the Cam…

Did you go punting on the Cam, Swanepoel?

…promenading alongside the Albert Memorial – events he had only experienced briefly and uncomfortably.

He conjured images of his own dear mother, since deceased, and how as a child she had attended the Great Exhibition at the huge Crystal Palace in Hyde Park. She used to regale his wide-eyed self with stories of the wondrous new inventions demonstrated – the camera, the telephone, even the elevator, which were now everyday reality. The pace at which technology proceeded flummoxed him. The age of sail was nearly over. The dear old horse itself, it was said, would be soon be replaced by the new automotive carriage. In this very war, army scouts were using Marconi wireless sets – communication without cables.

A man with a megaphone gave the final run-though of the runners and riders. Despite such advancements, Finch doubted if anyone more than 3ft away could understand any of the announcement.

He watched as the hands on the clock on the grandstand nudged round to noon. Right on time, the tape went up, the horses bolted. There was a huge roar. As the crowd surged forward, he jostled to keep himself visible to Annie.

"Captain Finch?"

They had run through the drill so many times that Finch's first instinct was not to turn and face whoever it was who had come up behind him, but to grab his right earlobe, the signal that contact had been made.

The man laid a timid hand on his elbow. He was having to shout.

"Captain...? Captain Finch?"

The man was of short to medium height, balding, overweight, his forehead glistening with sweat. He reminded Finch of a garden gnome, a beardless garden gnome in a grubby worsted suit.

"Shawcroft?"

The man nodded.

"...Of the *Evening Post*."

There was a gasp as a horse on the far side, wobbled, then a burst of relief as the jockey steadied his mount.

"You're a journalist?" Finch blurted. "How did you—?"

"No time."

There was an urgency about the man. His eyes were bloodshot, glassy.

–

Annie waited beneath the main grandstand. For her part, she had stolen a maroon skirt and jacket with a large crocheted beret into which he had tucked up her hair. Not that in the dark, presently, it made any difference.

Before she and Finch had taken up their positions, they had reconnoitred the racecourse and found it to be the best place to afford both a vantage point and somewhere to remain hidden. In the wall at the back of the stand, alongside a trench that had been roped off for building work, they had found a door that led to an enclosed storage area under the angled boards of the seating.

In the light of a solitary window she could see the rubbish that has accumulated on the dirt floor – things that had fallen through the gaps from above – coins, combs, handkerchiefs, a lady's fan, tickets, ripped-up betting slips.

As the horses came into the home straight, the shouts of the spectators reverberated down through the walls. When people rose as the horses came into the final furlong, there was a resounding *rat-a-tat-tat* as the sprung wooden seats slapped up.

The window afforded not a view of the course but away to the side, to the paddock and winning enclosure, the place where they had agreed Finch should position himself.

She could see him – just – deliberately and conspicuously bare-headed amid a sea of hats, looking this way and that, then gazing periodically in her direction, trusting that she would be watching out for him.

There was an almighty explosion of applause as the winner crossed the line. They had been in place for 15 minutes now. She could just make out her fob watch and hands that showed it was almost noon. If Shawcroft was about to make himself known, it would be now.

Despite the care they had taken, Annie was suddenly discombobulated by the fact that she was not alone. She did not see anyone but could register a presence. Whoever it was, she supposed, could sense that they'd startled her.

A voice came eventually.

"Good day."

It was English, flat, unemotional. The noise outside and above could well have masked the sound of the man's entry, but the door, when she had opened it, had cast a pool of midday sunlight. Whoever it was must have entered ahead of her. He had been waiting.

"Good day," she replied, affecting to portray no fear.

She looked out at Finch. He was oblivious.

The man came closer. In a sudden lull, she could hear his shoes crunch. He remained several feet away but was now positioned behind Annie, between her and the door. She could see his shape, sense his being.

He said nothing more. The silence lingered.

"Shawcroft?" asked Annie. "Are you Shawcroft?"

With her eyes re-adjusting to the gloom after looking out of the window, he pulled something from his pocket. A kerchief? No, gloves. Leather ones. He began easing them on. He took his time.

"What do you know of Shawcroft?" he asked.

"Nothing."

The crowd was becoming active outside the window. The winning horse was being led into the enclosure. They were on their feet. The seats above repeated their *rat-a-tat-tat* volley. The man could do with her as he willed. No one would know.

There was an icy calm to him.

"Is Shawcroft meeting you here?"

She said nothing. He repeated the question, the tone more incisive.

"No... I..."

"No need to be alarmed, Nurse Jones."

He *knew* her?

He stepped closer still.

The sash window. It didn't appear locked. She would have to slide the bottom half up... if it didn't jam, they usually did. The dust suggested the frame was not well maintained. Even in her long skirt she was adept enough to hoist herself over the sill, but she could not outmuscle this man.

"Who is Moriarty?" he asked.

"What...? I don't know."

Then, from the corner of her eye she saw Finch, amid the throng, as people jostled to congratulate the rider or pat the horse. He was raising his right hand to touch his ear. In which case who was...?

The man with Annie watched her turn and followed her line of vision. The space was suddenly filled with light, momentarily blinding her, as the door swung open.

"*Here...*"

Shawcroft pressed a rustling bundle into Finch's hands. It was soft, wrapped in brown paper, tied up with string.

Around them the crowd swirled. Patrons were shouting the name of the winning jockey, offering up hands to shake his as the horse was led right through, parting the crowd.

Shawcroft's voice quavered. Sweat beaded on his brow.

"It was found in the Somerset Road Cemetery."

"I don't understand."

He looked back and forth, then hissed it out, as if the words themselves were poison.

"Moriarty. Have you found Moriarty?"

"Who is Moriarty?"

He lowered his voice and spoke rapidly.

"Moriarty holds material, information of great worth, Captain Finch. You must know that. Your man... a big price."

They were being jostled. The man clung to Finch now, grabbing his lapels, almost begging. His breath was stale, dehydrated.

"Seeking Moriarty puts you in great danger," Shawcroft urged. "Mere knowledge of Moriarty can—"

People were looking at them, pretending not to when Finch returned their gaze. He wedged the parcel under his arm and prised the man's fingers from his jacket.

"You're making a spectacle of yourself, Shawcroft... Believe me, I'm as desperate as you to find out what's going on here."

This time it was Finch who did the lapel-grabbing.

"So, answer me... Who the hell is this Moriarty and just what has he got?"

He shook Shawcroft hard. The man gave a shriek, a pathetic one, like a child. Heads turned again.

Finch suddenly felt the weight of Shawcroft as he collapsed into his arms and softly toppled forward. There were gasps. A woman screamed. He had space around him, people were pulling back.

The band struck up again: *The Bonnie Banks o' Loch Lomond*.

Finch eased Shawcroft to the ground. In the middle of his back, between the shoulder blades, was a single blood red blot soaking outward. Whatever implement had been used, it had been sharp, thin and long.

Finch rolled Shawcroft over. The eyes were open. He felt for a pulse in his neck. There was none.

"HIM! It was HIM!"

A woman in a white gown with an elegantly feathered hat was pointing right at Finch.

"Someone!" she continued. "*Someone!*"

Others joined in.

"I say, you!" growled an elderly gentleman with a monocle.

"Stop him! Stop that man!" yelled another.

Not far away Finch heard a police whistle. He picked up the bundle and barged his way out as fast as he could.

–

Annie saw Finch shoot his right arm straight up in the air, the sign to get out – and get out now. He was hurrying her way. Something had happened. Fingers were pointing.

For a moment she saw another man turn back in her direction. Though she had not seen him fully, she knew instinctively it was the same one who had been with her not a minute before. And now, in the daylight, she saw it, the red hair. Though he couldn't see her, he knew she could see him. He looked coldly in her direction. And then he was gone.

Chapter Forty-Seven

Finch ran towards the main gate, then threw a sharp left past a vending stall selling tea and sandwiches till he reached the back of the grandstand.

"Through there!" Annie yelled.

The building work – where ground had been broken to lay new foundations – continued all the way to the perimeter fence. A section of the iron railings had been removed, to be replaced with a makeshift screen of rough wooden slats held together with wire.

They crossed a duckboard over a trench and parted a section of it, climbing through into the trees that lined that area of the course.

They could hear the whistles and shouts but kept their nerve to weave through into what seemed the boundary of a public park, where mothers and nannies wheeled perambulators and young children of the well-to-do chased each other round and round. Inevitably, there was an encroachment upon it by army tents.

Finch and Annie determined to head in what they believed to be the least obvious direction, not a route out of Kenilworth but back into it, around the side of the racecourse.

Following the line of it for a few more minutes, the whistles and shouts receded. They were now at the far side, opposite the grandstand. With an accompanying rumble, the next race thundered past, the hooves sending up great clods of turf, the faces of the jockeys locked in grimaces of concentration. The roar from the crowd suggested business as usual.

A few yards further on and there was a line of sandy-coloured boulders which bounded a concrete drainage channel. About 6–7ft across, it was almost bone dry, just a thin trickle of water ebbing gently down the centre.

They eased themselves down and followed the channel till it entered a tunnel, no more than 5ft high but tucked under some thick undergrowth. They ducked in and stopped. Catching their breath, they slipped down into seated positions, their backs against the wall, Finch stretching his bad leg straight out.

Feeling safe for a moment they each blurted out their version of events and quizzed each other over the details.

"So our man Cox paid a 'big price'?" said Finch. "So did poor old Shawcroft. Not exactly news, is it?"

Annie's eyes narrowed.

"Maybe that's not what Shawcroft meant by 'big price'."

Finch could hear Brookman's voice. "The trick is to listen."

"This information, the documents, papers, whatever…" she said. "Seems Cox and Lady Verity had been intent on taking it to a newspaper. It's the logical place for an exposé, after all. But—"

He beat her to the punch.

"You mean rather than give it to the journalist… to Shawcroft… they were going to *sell* it to him?"

Annie nodded. She uttered a disapproving sigh.

"Not really the great noble purpose sainted Verity was espousing."

Finch rubbed his chin.

"Unless Cox was going solo, trying to extract some personal advantage out of the situation. He owed money all over the place. We know that. Maybe she trusted him with the information, but he cashed it in. Or was about to."

"You mean before he went and stashed it with this Moriarty person?"

Finch shrugged a non-committal 'yes', but it was their best estimation so far.

"Well we know we can discount our red-haired friend as Moriarty now," said Annie. "I mean, sure, he seems to crop up every time that name is mentioned, but he asked *me* what I knew of him."

"It's like I said, I think he's on the hunt for Moriarty as much as we are. When Shawcroft referred to danger, he didn't suggest it was Moriarty himself who was dangerous, it was *association* with Moriarty."

Poor Shawcroft. The parcel was now sitting right there in Finch's lap. He removed his penknife, slit the string and folded back the wrapping. There, on a bed of brown paper, sat a folded coat – a lightweight army coat.

He shook it out and held it up by the shoulders. It was three-quarter length, khaki and made of a gabardine-type material rather than serge.

It had regimental brass buttons down the front and as fasteners on the epaulettes. It bore the scuffing of wear and tear, especially at the elbow and around the collar. It was caked in mud down the left-hand side but was otherwise unremarkable. However, there was no mistaking to whom it belonged, or rather had formerly belonged. On each epaulette were the crossed spears of the Queen's Royal Lancers.

"Major Cox?" asked Annie.

Finch nodded.

"Remember, there was some confusion as to whether he had his coat on him in the hansom cab? Rideau mentioned he had helped Cox find his coat, suggesting he had it with him. The cabbie, Pinkie Coetzee, also remembered the Good Samaritan – Fancy Dan – throwing the coat onto the seat after Cox. But when I collected his belongings there was no coat inventoried. The jacket, yes, but no coat."

"So what's going on?"

He stared hard at the garment.

"What's going on, as you put it, is that I have no bloody idea other than the fact that the coat must be of considerable significance for Shawcroft to have risked his life over it."

"You're sure he's dead?"

"Absolutely. Our red-haired friend... assuming it was him... was pretty damned clinical. Stiletto knife or some other kind of thin, puncturing weapon. Knew exactly what he was doing."

As the adrenaline subsided, the enormity of what had happened was at last beginning to sink in. They sat in silence. Finch thought of Annie alone with that man, at his mercy.

"You were bloody lucky," Finch said.

She shrugged off the sympathy.

"But how does it explain the coat being found in a cemetery?" she asked.

"Maybe it was thrown out of the cab in frustration. I mean there can't have been a struggle... Cox was comatose. Maybe the killer ran off with it and then decided to hide the evidence? Bury it, perhaps? That would account for the mud."

"So how did it come into Shawcroft's possession?"

Finch hissed out his frustration.

"Lord knows."

"The second cabbie," mused Annie. "You said there was a second cabbie, right?"

"Corroborated Pinkie's story. Yes."

"He said he had seen someone matching the description of the killer, the 'well-dressed gent' in the same location an hour later... the Somerset Road Cemetery... only looking somewhat dishevelled, and this time heading back into town?"

"He did."

"Well what if this gent had been looking for Cox's coat... rooting around for it in the gardens? If he'd hopped out there like Pinkie said and was still in the same place an hour later as the second cabbie reported, only this time muddy – it adds up."

Finch rummaged through Cox's pockets. They were deep and had the usual accumulation of fluff, debris and now dirt.

In the left-hand pocket, however, he touched upon something hard and smooth. He pulled it out.

There, held between his thumb and forefinger was a small, brown, glass bottle. There was no stopper and, save for some liquid residue, it was empty. An adhesive label from a chemist's store was attached to it on which had been typed the words: '*Major L. Cox. Prescription. Laudanum. 4 fl.oz.*'

—

He handed the bottle to Annie.

"We tend to use chloroform at the hospital," she said.

"Us too, but this stuff is preferred. As opiates go it's more powerful, though it's in pretty short supply at the moment."

He put his left forefinger over the neck of the bottle and upturned it. The remainder of the liquid trickled out. It was brown, almost the same hue as the bottle. He sniffed at it.

"Laudanum all right."

"And that's what Cox was killed with?"

He wiped his hand on his trousers.

"Ultimately he was suffocated, but if the killer used an entire four fluid ounces on him—"

"He was a goner anyway?"

He nodded.

She took the bottle from him and had a sniff for herself.

"You think this is it? The actual murder weapon?"

"I don't know, Annie…"

'Annie', she noted. He called her Annie.

"…but I'm guessing that whoever did it either poured it straight into his mouth or onto the handkerchief – he was dead drunk, helpless, remember? What we do know, according to the cabbie, is that the kerchief, Cox's own kerchief, was stuffed in hard as the coup de grâce."

"And then the bottle was put back into the coat pocket and the coat was tossed out," she recounted. "Which would explain why someone was hunting for it."

Finch hesitated.

"I don't know. It just doesn't seem very well thought-out. I mean, you kill someone, throw out the murder weapon and then spend an hour rooting around trying to *retrieve* it again… and unsuccessfully."

He remembered what Brookman had also said: 'The history of crime is littered with some pretty stupid villains.'

"Then the murder, it was spontaneous," she enthused. "Not pre-planned… a fit of pique… or something opportunistic."

Her brow then wrinkled.

"I still don't get the laudanum thing."

"How do you mean?"

"Well, why would Cox be carrying laudanum in his pocket. And why get it from a chemist? He could have helped himself to it at any of the field hospitals or at RAMC headquarters. He was surrounded by medical supplies and could sign a chit for pretty much anything he wanted. And look. The label. The date…"

It was displayed boldly – '*December 24th, 1899.*'

"…he'd only purchased it on the day of his death."

"It *is* odd," Finch conceded.

"You think he was an addict? You do hear of it."

Finch blew out a sigh.

"Why do you think that?"

"He had no business procuring laudanum for legitimate reasons. He wasn't a doctor."

"Cox was many things, but not an addict."

"How would you know if he were an addict or not? Addicts are secretive."

"I think I'd have been able to tell. I spent an awful lot of time with him. He fulfilled his duties under extreme pressure."

"All the more reason for seeking a release."

"No. There was never any suggestion that his judgement wavered. I mean army life, the midst of battle? It simply wouldn't have been feasible."

"Then what about if he were *coerced* into buying the drug for someone, maybe someone who *was* an addict? We know in Cape Town he kept some pretty louche company."

Finch thought about a statistic that the police were always fond of quoting, about killers being known to their victims. Certainly if someone had murdered Cox with a bottle of laudanum – *that* bottle of laudanum – they would have had to have known that Cox had the bottle on his person.

"And if Cox had only been in town a few hours," Annie concurred, "then it must have been someone familiar to him."

"Do you have your handbook," Finch asked briskly. "Your Medical Corps handbook?"

She snorted with derision.

"Great thing like that…? It's in my kitbag. Christ knows if I'll ever see that again."

"Of course. Sorry."

"Why?"

"I seem to remember something from when we first landed in the Cape. Something aimed at thwarting the black marketeers. A rule."

"What rule?"

"Laudanum. It's on the restricted list, I'm sure of it. Not widely available for civilian use. Certain drugs can only be purchased over the counter in the presence of a medical professional who acts as a co-signee. Cox wasn't strictly medical personnel, but he ran his own little RAMC fiefdom and had all the accreditation… Nurse Jones, I think we're on to something."

She was Nurse Jones again.

Finch took the bottle back. Though the name of the prescription had been typed, the label itself was pre-printed, bearing the name of the chemist. Below the date, in small, faint green type at the bottom, it read: '*Kaapstad Druggery.*'

Finch still had Cox's wallet on his person. He pulled it out, opened it and teased out the receipt that had been nestling in the back. It was a bill for six shillings and tuppence made out on the same stock, green on white stationery. It also had an address: '*127 Burg Street, Cape Town.*'

"Look!" he exclaimed, pointing to a scratchy pharmacist's scrawl. "The prescription was issued in Cox's name. But it says '*Cox OBO*'."

"On Behalf Of?"

"Right."

"On behalf of whom?"

"Doesn't say."

"So you mean the killer was actually alongside Cox when he bought it?"

"It's a probability."

Finch's boyish enthusiasm was suddenly replaced by a look of stone.

"Kilfoyle," he said.

"What about him?"

"There's absolutely no way he could have done it. Think about it. For one, his movements could be accounted for much of that day. He certainly wasn't hanging around with Cox on a visit to a chemist's store. On the contrary, Cox had been avoiding Kilfoyle."

He reasoned it out with her. That night, outside the officer's club. Yes, Kilfoyle could have helped the drunk Cox in the street, albeit reluctantly… Cox's glove probably came off in the process, Kilfoyle merely picked it up, took it home for safekeeping, exactly as he had said.

"The stumbling block," he continued, "is that the cabbie, Pinkie, had described the 'well-dressed gent' putting Cox in his cab, paying him, writing down the address, walking off and then having a change of heart and returning. But what if this returning gent was, in fact—"

Her eyes flashed in agreement.

"A *second* man?"

"Exactly! A different person entirely… a case of mistaken identity… Maybe this Moriarty character…? Maybe the red-haired man?"

He began parcelling the coat back up.

"Remember I told you about the stitches and the slash in the lining of Cox's jacket… where something had been sewn in crudely and later sliced out? Same thing happened to me, remember, with the letters, on the train…?"

"Yes."

"Well what if that person killed Cox to get at it? Whatever it was. Documents… papers…"

He began patting his own pockets. He undid the button on the left breast pocket and pulled out a crumpled business card.

"There's someone else who's suspicious of the official line. Someone who knew the secret life of Cox better than any."

He handed it to her.

"Albert Rideau?" she read.

"We can't do this on our own," he said. "And until Brookman reappears—"

"Would he help us?"

"He would. He's as sceptical as we are. He may well have found another piece of the puzzle in our absence."

In the distance they could hear shouting again. This time, it was accompanied by the sound of excitable, barking dogs.

Finch got to his feet. He offered his hands and pulled Annie up.

Chapter Forty-Eight

Rideau's apartment was in Wynberg, just southwest of Kenilworth, only a mile or so distant, the route taking them away from the city, something they hoped would be in their favour.

Having been spotted at the racecourse, it was Finch who was the more conspicuous now. He buttoned up his jacket, turned up his collar and, thanks to some quick-thinking on Annie's part, 'acquired' himself a Homburg hat from a park bench.

As insurance, they walked apart, dog-legging through the backroads till they arrived on the main street within minutes of each other.

Wynberg – 'wine mountain' – was founded on its vineyards, though unlike rural Stellenbosch, out to the east, it had become absorbed into the suburbs. Nonetheless, it maintained its sedate country feel with its verandas and stoeps and dirt roads.

Rideau's home, according to his card, was on a street named Hangklip. They found it easily enough, set back from the main thoroughfare, one of a row of townhouses in what looked like converted offices, from perhaps what was once the local bank. The door, with its shiny black paint and brass knocker shaped like a lion with a ring in its mouth, looked to Finch like a vague homage to 10 Downing Street.

It was early afternoon and the residential streets were quiet. While Annie hung back, loitering behind a lamppost, Finch walked up the three steps to the door marked number four and rapped.

There was no answer for a while, though Finch thought he sensed some movement behind the ground-floor window. It unnerved him and he began to beat a retreat, walking backwards down the steps and almost tripping over.

Suddenly the door cracked open.

"Finch?"

It was Rideau.

"What the hell?" he continued.

He peered out, his eyes darting back and forth.

"Sorry to drop in on you like this."

"Are you alone?"

"No."

Finch gestured and Annie stepped forward into view.

"Nurse Jones of the New South Wales Army Nursing Service Reserve," he introduced. "I'm afraid we're in a spot of bother."

"You can say that again," said Rideau. "There have been military police up and down here all day."

He opened the door and beckoned them in.

"Quick!"

The cordiality did not last long. Once inside, door closed, Finch and Annie found themselves staring down the barrel of a gleaming revolver – a Colt, Finch recognised. Its handler was not smiling.

"Look, I'm sorry to do this to you, old boy," said Rideau, motioning for them to raise their hands, "but I've heard some pretty unsavoury things – some rough stuff with Lady Verity; that you escaped police custody; are on the run. Was at the police station this morning."

Finch eyed Rideau. He was in shirtsleeves with a lilac silk paisley patterned waistcoat over the top, which matched his cravat. There was a breadcrumb on his moustache.

"You can add a charge of murder if you wish."

"Murder?"

"You'll read about it soon enough. Kenilworth Races. Someone set us up."

"It's true," chimed in Annie. "They've got it in for us."

Despite the gun, Rideau didn't look threatening to Finch. He was ex-military but didn't carry its bearing. Finch was more concerned about an accidental discharge of the weapon.

"Look, maybe you should put that thing down."

"You seemed a decent chap at lunch. But now *this*…?"

Keeping his hands raised, Finch turned sideways, slowly.

"Albert. In my right-hand pocket you'll find my gun, a Webley. I assure you it's my only weapon. Please… take it."

Gingerly, Rideau edged over. He put his hand in and pulled out Finch's pistol. He held the stock by thumb and forefinger and laid it, slowly and deliberately, on a nearby occasional table.

The place was tastefully decorated, observed Finch – polished floorboards, some oil landscapes of India on the wall. Above the dado rail the paper hung in cream and pink stripes. Through the doorway into the living room he could see a fine Persian rug, a divan and, in the corner, still in some state of disrepair, the grand piano he had evidently been working on.

"You know I could turn you over to the authorities," said Rideau. His hands appeared to be trembling.

"But you won't," said Finch.

"And why not?" huffed Rideau.

"Because you and I know there's something completely bent about Cox's death. Brookman admitted as much."

"It was he who saved us and put us on the run," said Annie.

Rideau's brow furrowed.

"Brookman? *Really?*"

"At the police station, did you see him?" asked Finch.

"Actually no. Said he was away. Some urgent business or other."

"It's tosh. He's gone to ground, too, minding his own back till he can pull us back in."

The parcel had fallen to the floor. Finch prodded it with his boot. It rustled.

"Plus, there's this."

"What is it?"

"Have a look."

Without removing the gun or his gaze, Rideau crouched down. He undid the string and ripped open the paper. He pulled at it and saw the epaulettes.

His brow wrinkled with curiosity again.

"*Cox's?*"

Finch nodded.

"How on earth did you come by it?"

"I see you've just had lunch," said Finch, nodding to Rideau's moustache. "Rustle us up some food, put the kettle on, and I'll reveal all."

Rideau stood. His voice was firm.

"I need to know I can trust you. I'm not joking."

"You have my word."

"Mine, too," added Annie.

He didn't seem convinced, but Finch could sense intrigue getting the better of him.

"Finch, you profess to be a gentleman. This business with Lady Verity. I admit, I just can't square that with you. You don't strike me as the type. But I want you to look me in the eye and say it again. Promise me that I can trust you or, by God – and it brings me no pleasure to say so – I'll use this thing."

He waved the gun for emphasis.

Finch was under no illusion that, ultimately, Rideau would shoot if he had to. He did as commanded.

"Then all right," said Rideau. "Come in."

He pocketed Finch's gun and, at the point of his own, motioned them towards the sitting room.

"Stop right there!" Rideau yelled.

Finch froze.

"Your shoes... boots."

"What?"

He pointed the gun at their feet.

"House rule."

Only then did Finch see that Rideau wore a pair of pointed, soft-leather Moroccan slippers.

"Yours too, Miss Jones."

She shrugged, caught Finch's eye, and they both attended to their laces. Rideau lowered the weapon but did not relinquish it.

"Lapsang Souchong, Darjeeling, Earl Grey...?" he asked.

"Beg your pardon?" said Annie.

"Tea. What kind of tea?"

"Rooibos?" enquired Finch.

Rideau nodded.

"And for you, Miss?"

"Just tea. *Tea* tea."

–

Rideau went through to the kitchen, leaving the stocking-footed pair perched on the divan. There were further paintings – one over the fireplace of something French and impressionistic, of genteel folk lazing on a riverbank. It would have been at home at La Rochelle, thought Finch.

There was a bookcase crammed with leather-bound volumes, a large wooden globe from a bygone age with misshapen continents and Terra Australis not yet charted. There were potted ferns and an antique barometer.

The mantelpiece contained some ornaments – small nudes, mischievous plump boy cherubs. Finch did not recall Rideau making any reference to a wife.

In the corner, he could see that the piano was standing on a folded tarpaulin. The lacquer had been almost completely removed to reveal rough, raw wood. Sandpaper, a wooden sanding block and a plane lay on the floor.

"Nice place," said Annie.

"Thank you," came the voice from the kitchen. "A useful pied-à-terre. Just an apartment. My main home is at Bathurst, in the Eastern Cape, near the cannery."

"Cannery?"

"Fruit, Miss Jones. Pineapples mainly."

Rideau returned with a tray bearing two teapots, the necessary crockery and some French-style baguettes sliced up and lined with some thin, holey cheese. Annie did not wait to be asked and began devouring with gusto. Finch followed.

Rideau exited and returned again, rather proudly, with a plate of fresh sliced pineapple and two small forks. The smell was potent.

Annie put down the remnants of her sandwich and tried a slice. The juice ran down her chin.

"God, this is delicious."

"My sentiments entirely," Rideau smiled. "It is my personal mission to share the produce of Eden with the world."

Finch poured the tea and explained, as succinctly as he could, all that had happened to them since they had last met. Rideau stood and listened intently. When Finch came to the part about the red-headed man, Rideau interjected.

"Wait… I've seen him. Burly fellow, had on a blue suit. He was there, loitering around the police station… that day you and I met."

"Are you sure?"

"Yes, yes… he was right there on the corner. You know, when I got into the cab… And I've seen him since. Damn, where was it…?"

"He's very dangerous, Mr Rideau," urged Annie. "If you see him again…"

331

Rideau was lost in thought.

"Cox's guest house, that's right. The old dragon. What's her name…?"

"Du Plessis."

"I don't know if I'm imagining it but, now you mention it, I think I saw him around there too. That road that slopes up to the house. Yes, he was at the bottom. Not doing anything, just standing there, by a lamp post. I'd gone, like you, to pay my respects. Get a look at where poor old Coxie met his maker."

He turned mournful.

"He looked pretty athletic, I must say, a military type. I thought he was something to do with the police investigation. A bit of muscle. Keeping tabs."

"Definitely muscle. It was he who turned over Cox's room."

Rideau mulled it over. Though it had happened two days previously, this particular piece of information had been kept from him, he said, though probably because there was no Brookman around to keep him up to speed.

"So *he's* this Moriarty fellow, then? If he's instrumental in all this business, what does he know? What does he hold?"

Finch shook his head.

"He's not Moriarty."

"No?"

"Unless he's playing an elaborate game of bluff. He's on the trail of Moriarty as much as we now are. *If* we are."

"And you're no closer to finding out who?"

"Afraid not."

Finch finished off the remainder of their story, bringing them right up to the moment they had knocked on Rideau's door. Their host silently processed the information, nodding his understanding.

When he was done, Rideau came and sat in the armchair opposite them. He perched on the edge, then gave a theatrical cough.

"Captain Finch… Ingo?" he said. "I'm afraid it is me who now has to be honest with you… with both of you."

"How so?"

He paused for a moment, assembling his words.

"That day we met. Lunch. We were being frank, open, sharing information. I suspected that you were telling me almost everything, but not *completely* everything."

Finch and Annie threw each other a look.

"You let something slip, then checked yourself. You said that you'd been present at Kilfoyle's interrogation. I purposely didn't pick you up on it."

Finch knew there was no point in denying it.

"I'm sorry."

Rideau waved a hand, as if flicking away a fly.

"Really, it's fine. Totally understood. We'd only just met. It was a big ask but, as a consequence of your doing that, I thought I ought to keep something back for myself, too."

He turned to Annie, then Finch.

"I would like to offer a most sincere apology. What you went through to get to Lady Verity... being chased, shot at and all... and now all this business. I feel a great burden of responsibility. You see, I *did* know about Cox's affair... with Lady Verity. I deliberately chose not to reveal it... to confirm that she was 'V'. I mean, Cox had told me in confidence, for one. I simply hadn't fathomed on you figuring it out and tracking her down like that. Had I known—"

Finch exhaled.

"Albert, it's fine. There are certain things about which one should be circumspect. We only made the dash to Stellenbosch on learning of Kilfoyle's death. But now you mention it, who else knew? Brookman suggests it wasn't quite the *amour secret* they believed. Small circles and all that."

Rideau shrugged.

"Very few, I would imagine. I think I was the only one he actually confessed it to. Well, that was my understanding. I suppose, try as they might, there must have been suspicions, tongues wagging. Her staff, etcetera, as you've already intimated. But the pair of them, they'd have done their darnedest to keep the lid on it. There was too much at stake. Although, might I add, I believe they genuinely loved each other. Whatever you've heard about Vesta Lane or any other strumpet..."

He turned to Annie again.

"Forgive my language, Miss Jones."

"It's okay."

"...they were just silly schoolboy fascinations."

"I hear you," said Finch.

"Lady Verity was not the half of it, though. This trouble that Cox had got himself into. Remember I said he was in way over his head. It was something big, I tell you. Something explosive. I believe something to do with state secrets. Of that magnitude. Something that came as a consequence of dipping his toes in these new forbidden waters. I'm guessing this is where our friend, this mysterious Moriarty, comes into play."

"It would be the assumption—" said Finch, checking himself too late.

"You know, Brookman loathes that word."

Rideau smiled, Finch did the same. Rideau then turned serious again.

"Remember the two Coxes I spoke of – one the honourable family chap, the other the womaniser, gambler, drinker?"

"Yes."

"Well this is a case of the bad Cox for you. From what I deduced, Cox knew the value of the information he had come across. He knew it would be devastating. But rather than place that information in the correct hands – those of the authorities – he tried to profit from the situation…"

Finch and Annie caught each other's eye again.

"…Had debts, you see. From what he'd hinted, he was about to sell the information to a newspaper. To a journalist—"

"Shawcroft."

He nodded.

"Maitland Shawcroft of the *Evening Post*. I never heard Cox's direct mention of that name, but once you start making deals like that, word gets out… If I knew, then others certainly did… I must add here again that I've told all this to Brookman. He knows way more than he's letting on, as we've already determined. Detective's prerogative. It's probably why Cox was silenced… why Shawcroft himself has now been silenced."

"What about the coat?" asked Annie.

"Yes," Finch added. "The coat. It was handed over as if Shawcroft were trying to tell us something."

"And it was found at the Somerset Road Cemetery, you say?"

Annie nodded.

Rideau rubbed his chin.

"I don't know. What do *you* think?"

"That it was tossed out en route," said Finch.

"By your second Good Samaritan, the one you described? The one who knew about the laudanum bottle in the pocket?"

"Exactly."

"And so you now think it is he who killed Cox?"

"There's a strong chance."

"Not Kilfoyle?"

Finch shook his head. Rideau exhaled sharply.

"My word, if you're right... and I say *if* you're right... that would be a colossal embarrassment for the police. I mean Kilfoyle dying in custody and everything. I told you, the whole thing, it was too neat, too tidy, too quick. But even if he wasn't directly involved in Cox's murder, I can't believe Kilfoyle didn't have *something* to do with it."

"I'm not so sure, Albert. I'm not defending him. Don't get me wrong. But the more one looks at it..."

Finch stood. He eyed the carriage clock on the mantelpiece. It was almost a quarter past three.

"Albert, I have a plan. But I must hurry."

Finch had already thought through a course of action but had wondered how to go about it. Now they had a safe haven from which to operate, he could proceed. He would head to the chemist, he explained, to the Kaapstad Druggery, in the city. He would find out just who it was with whom Cox had co-signed for the purchase – if not a name to hand, then an identity, work it backwards from there.

"I say, steady on old chap," blurted Rideau. "You're a marked man. Can't go waltzing about like that. Lie low here. Wait for Brookman to seek you out. He said he'd come and find you, didn't he? Don't play the sleuth. Let *him* deal with it."

"It's Brookman I'm worried about, too. The Military Foot Police and the Cape Police seem to be pursuing separate agendas. Something's not right. He's caught in the middle. It's pretty extreme what he did. If people are being eliminated in the hunt for Moriarty, or this so-called privileged information, and he knows more than we do, then he's a prime target."

"Sir, are you sure?" blurted Annie.

'*Sir*' he noted.

Now Rideau stood, too.

"No. Listen. This is preposterous. You two stay here. Rest. Freshen up. Help yourself to some more tea, more food. Let *me* go. I can be there within the hour. No one will think twice."

"Won't work," said Finch. "You don't have the credentials. Won't know what questions to ask."

"You can brief me. I'm a fast learner… Seriously, you need to keep your head down."

He gestured across the room.

"The minute you step outside that door—"

"He's right," urged Annie.

"I'm sorry," said Finch. "But Albert, you're a marked man too. Anyone who's had a brush with this thing is. I'm going. And going alone. That's the end of it. Nurse Jones. You stay here. That's an order."

Rideau grabbed Finch's arm.

"Think for a minute. What difference does it make if we get this information now or tomorrow? I repeat, let Brookman handle it. The more I hear, the more I believe we should stick together. Safety in numbers. This is reckless."

Finch was already at the front door.

"But, blast you, if you *are* intent on playing the hero," he admonished, "don't use the front door… And don't, for God's sake, go dressed as you are!"

Rideau disappeared off down the hall and into what Finch supposed was the bedroom. He returned with a beige suit on a hangar.

"Might come up a bit short in the leg, but it'll do."

He held it up against Finch. It was double-breasted with a fine, chocolate pinstripe.

"Don't worry, not one of my best."

Finch got changed into it right then and there. As much as he liked Rideau, he felt no urge to experience his boudoir.

"And don't forget this," said Rideau.

He reached in his pocket for Finch's Webley, handed it over, then stood back to admire the new attire.

"Not bad, Ingo. Not bad at all."

He tucked a chocolate brown silk handkerchief with cream polka dots into Finch's top pocket.

"There…"

Finch transferred his personal effects, then pulled on his boots. He took the empty laudanum bottle from Cox's coat and slipped it into his new jacket pocket.

Annie appeared.

"Good luck," she said.

Rideau steered Finch down the hall passage. At the end he unlocked a door that led across a small garden to a wall with a wooden gate. Rideau went ahead and unbolted it.

"Left," he said. "Go to the end. Once you hit the street, turn right. It looks like the road is taking you away from the main drag, but it curves back 100 yards down. Cape Town tram stop's opposite."

Finch looked him in the eye.

"Thank you, Albert."

"And for God's sake be careful. Get back here as quickly as you can. Take no risks."

Rideau extend a hand. Finch shook it. Then he was gone.

Chapter Forty-Nine

The Kaapstad Druggery was a ramshackle affair – an explosion of bottles, jars, boxes and packages that blocked out a good portion of light from the window to the street. Finch was thankful for that. There were MFPs out and about. He had seen two on a street corner not 100 yards away. A civilian suit – even one as finely tailored as Rideau's – could only provide so much cover.

The owner of the chemist shop, a small Indian man, stood behind a desk, barking instructions to somebody out the back in a subcontinental tongue. He wore a white coat, had pomaded hair and bore the scowl of someone habitually disaffected.

The bell over the door jangled but the man did not look up as Finch approached, continuing his instructions to the person behind while checking off items on a list. When, finally, he did acknowledge Finch, it was not with the countenance of someone keen to offer assistance.

"Excuse me," Finch began. "I wonder if you can help me?"

"Very busy," he said, stripping the English language down to its basic components.

The man's unswerving discourtesy made Finch smile.

"There is something funny?" asked the man.

"No, not at all."

"Being chemist, serious business. Serious business."

He went back to his list.

Finch cleared his throat.

"I have a request for a purchase."

The man said nothing.

"Four fluid ounces of Sydenham's Laudanum."

The man looked up.

"You have prescription?"

Finch shook his head.

The man waved his hand as if to shoo Finch away.

"Must have prescription from doctor."

"I *am* a doctor."

"Doctor not need come. Doctor send errand boy."

A nameplate on the counter bore the name Mr Dev Mokani. The man broke off again to address his unseen colleague behind him, in Gujarati, Finch guessed.

"Mr Mokani…?"

The man turned, momentarily perplexed by the familiarity.

"I repeat, I need to purchase four fluid ounces of laudanum."

"Laudanum very scarce. Not cheap. Especially now, with war."

"I understand."

"Priority is Royal Army Medical Corps."

Finch produced his identity card.

"Captain Ingo Finch of the RAMC," he announced. "I am currently out of uniform, on leave."

Mr Mokani examined it, then disappeared into the back of the store with it where the instruction of his unseen assistant continued in earnest. It seemed to take an extraordinarily long time and with a great deal of yelling, the clanking of a typewriter and the repetition of Finch's name and rank to boot. But, eventually, the chemist returned with a bottle which he flashed briefly before Finch and popped into a small brown paper bag.

"Six shillings and sixpence."

He'd already put the price up, noted Finch.

Finch opened the bag and pulled the bottle out – same kind, same label as the empty one in his pocket, only this time with his own name upon it.

"Is this how you sell the drug?"

"What do you mean?"

"No instructions?"

"You are doctor," said Mr Mokani. "You know dosage. Six shillings and eight pence."

"Sixpence."

"That is what I said."

He lowered his head and continued ticking off items. He patted the counter, indicating that Finch should deposit his coins.

"Mr Mokani, I have a confession…"

The chemist looked up, brow wrinkled.

"...I am not actually here about laudanum. Well not *this* laudanum anyway."

He placed the bottle on the counter. The man huffed.

Finch reached into his pocket and produced Cox's bottle. He showed the label to the chemist.

"This was purchased from your store on the 24th of December. Christmas Eve. I am afraid that the army officer overseeing the purchase is... no longer with us. But, as a physician, I am concerned that the drug you sold him has been misused."

The man grew even more irritable.

"Misused?"

He snatched the bottle and examined the label.

"If this... Major Cox... has a problem with my service then I will wait till he *is* with us."

Finch let the silence linger.

"I'm afraid, when I say that he is no longer with us – I mean that he is deceased."

Mr Mokani shrugged.

"How did he die?"

"Laudanum poisoning."

"Oh."

"Now. Do you think you can help me?"

The man suddenly looked worried. He barked some more Gujarati over his shoulder.

"Are you sure was laudanum poisoning? Maybe something else."

"That's what the Cape Town district coroner has ruled."

The invoking of the authorities made the chemist uncharacteristically compliant.

"I remember the man," he offered. "RAMC identification, like you. But in different officer uniform. Cavalry."

"Are you sure, Mr Mokani?"

"Yes. Yes. Portly fellow. Belly."

Finch was experienced enough at all this by now to know that a slight twisting of the truth could be employed to great effect.

"As the cataloguer of Major Cox's personal effects, there appeared to be no instructions evident with his bottle of laudanum either."

"He was doctor, like you. Not need."

"He wasn't. An RAMC officer yes, but a lay person, not a medical professional. Such a thing – a leaflet or sheet containing recommended dosages, side effects and so forth – should have been supplied, tied to the bottle. I'm afraid you have breached pharmacist's rules, Mr Mokani. Something I would be compelled to report. Unless—"

"Unless what?".

"If you remember Major Cox, you'll recall he was co-signing on behalf of somebody else. Do you remember who? If you could give some clue as to his identity—"

"Why?"

"Because I believe he may have been the one who wilfully administered an overdose of the drug to Cox."

"I do not understand."

"Whether you understand or not is by the by, Mr Mokani. I just need to identify the other person."

Mokani rubbed the back of his head. He screwed his face up.

"Was a man."

A man? Finch had always assumed the other person was male but now admonished himself for automatically eliminating 50 percent of his suspect pool.

"A gentleman," Mr Mokani added.

Finch was beginning to tire of this particular designation. Most of those so-called over the past few days had proved to be anything but.

"Well-dressed… Yes, yes, I remember," Mokani continued, warming to his new purpose. "Afterwards, two men argue. Outside. On pavement. Waving arms. Raised voices."

The man suddenly disappeared, ducking down below the counter.

"Mr Mokani?"

No response.

"Mr Mokani, I must insist—!"

But Finch could hear him rummaging before reappearing with a narrow wooden drawer pulled from a filing cabinet into which various receipts, invoices and slips had been filed, separated by index cards.

"It's recorded, the man's name's recorded?!" yelped Finch.

Mr Mokani yelled at his assistant again then started flicking through.

"…22nd, 23rd, 24th," he went, stopping at the correct date. He pulled out a clump of chits and rifled through, placing them into a pile as he went, like a croupier counting winnings at a casino.

"Here."

He stopped at the one he had been searching for, handwritten on his store's stock, pale green stationery.

Finch did no wait to be offered it. He snatched it up.

"Hey!"

What Finch read not only confused him, but suddenly infused him with a paralysing fear.

—

Rideau returned to the sitting room.

"He's a good fellow but quite headstrong," he said of Finch.

"Stubborn is a better word," said Annie.

Rideau smiled.

"But he'll find the information he needs," she added.

"You mean like on your little excursion to Stellenbosch?"

"Exactly. No stopping him once he's got the scent."

"I just hope he's careful. If the police, regular or military, pick him up, he'll be up before a court-martial. Men have been shot for less."

Any sense of mischief suddenly evaporated. Rideau looked embarrassed for his lack of tact.

"You really think they'd do that?"

"I don't make light of it, Miss Jones. There's a war on. Little sympathy for miscreants when brave men are dying by the thousand."

He checked his words.

"…not that Finch isn't being brave. Far from it. I think to have pursued this thing… whatever this thing might be… has demonstrated remarkable fortitude."

"Stubbornness," said Annie.

Rideau couldn't help but raise a smile again.

"But listen, have to stay positive. Get to the bottom of it and the police… Brookman… will explain the whole situation to the army personally. I'm sure of it. And if your captain has the ear of his new CO like he says, I'm sure this will be straightened out. Not only that but we can find out finally what the hell this thing is we've all been caught up in."

He came over to take her plate. There was barely a crumb remaining.

"Look, no point moping about… Miss Jones, please don't be coy, but I'm guessing, from the looks of things, that you're still a bit peckish."

She nodded mischievously.

"Being a fugitive from justice burns a lot of energy."

"In which case let me rustle you up something else."

She went through a charade of polite protest.

"Come, come, it will be my pleasure."

He beckoned for her to follow him through to the kitchen. Inside it was scrupulously neat, the pots and pans hanging from an overhead rack, scrubbed as shiny as mirrors, the shelves packed with bottled oils and spices. A string of fresh garlic dangled. There was a train of dried, purple chillies.

In the centre was a wooden work surface, again immaculately clean. On the far side was a range with a wood burner underneath. The flames were flickering.

"An omelette, Spanish omelette... tortilla?" he said. "I have fresh eggs, onions, garlic, peppers, ham. Cream from the dairy this morning. No chorizo unfortunately, but then you can't have everything."

"A what?"

"Cho-*ree*-tho. Kind of spicy sausage."

She was leaning in the doorway. She hoped she didn't sound ignorant.

"Sounds good," she said.

He twirled a heavy frying pan, put it on the range and, with a theatrical flourish, drizzled some olive oil from an unnecessary height.

"Forgive my excesses. I was in Valencia a couple of years ago. Couldn't resist taking a cookery course. The chefs were all big show-offs."

"You've been to Spain?"

"All over Europe," he explained, passing her a chopping knife and a large white onion. "If you don't mind... Will speed things up."

"Not at all."

"Part of the fun of researching the fruit-canning business. The Mediterranean mainly. Valencia for the oranges, south of France, Italy... Greece for the olives. Then sailed from Marseilles to the United States. Spent most of my time in Florida. Oranges again, bigger ones. Then down to Uruguay... town called Fray Bentos. A British company has started canning corned beef there. Meat not fruit, but same principle."

He joined her at the work area, thumping open a bulb of garlic.

"You're a well-travelled man," she said.

"Bloody itinerant more like, if you'll pardon my French. Was born on the hoof. Canada. Grew up in India. Now here. I sort of crave inertia, actually."

He tossed the onions and garlic into the pan. After months of hospital and army stodge, Annie found the smell intoxicating.

"But look at *you*," he said. "Australia... South Africa... You're a volunteer, so must have a sense of wanderlust, a taste for adventure... Either that or you're running away from something."

She fixed her eyes downward.

"I'm sorry," he said. "I didn't mean—"

She looked up.

"It's quite all right. I guess you could say it's a case of both."

He kept her busy, showing her the best way to gut and slice a green pepper, with the ham lined up next for dicing. He cracked six eggs into a bowl, added cream and began to whisk.

"You know I've been to Australia, too. Wonderful place. Like the Cape in many ways – the climate, the lifestyle. Sydney, Melbourne, Brisbane. Of course, they teased me something rotten and quite mercilessly. I mean me, this exotic fruit..."

Annie wondered whether this was a turn of phrase or a private confession.

"...but I tell you, Miss Jones, once you've weathered the storm, you're in the club. There's nothing they won't do for you."

The pan fizzed into life.

"They... *we* can be a bit brutal."

With the ingredients cooking up nicely, Rideau poured on the egg mixture.

"I can add a few crumbs of crushed chilli. Will blow your socks off."

She shook her head.

"Probably a wise decision."

The contents of the pan were coagulating nicely.

"Only question is do we save some for old Finchy, or scoff the lot?"

Her conspiratorial chuckle suggested the latter.

"Right you are. Mum's the word."

There were two wooden stools alongside the work counter. He gestured that they should eat there. While she made herself comfortable, he arranged the plates and cutlery.

She hadn't seen him do it but, evidently, he had uncorked some wine. Two cold glasses of a pinkish hue had been placed before them.

"A Grenache rosé," he said. "I tell you, the Cape's got a lot going for it."

She raised her glass. Rideau clinked his against it.

"To Finch," he said.

"To Finch," she replied.

To complete the epicurean overload, Rideau slid a hot and colourful half-moon of fluffed omelette onto her plate.

"Bon appétit."

So perfect did it seem to her she was compelled to eat in silence, savouring every morsel.

Rideau took it as a compliment. Only when he was fully satisfied that she had finished and, with great insistence, couldn't possibly manage another mouthful of anything else, did he clear the plates and take them to the big, deep enamel sink.

She rose to help him and stood at his side.

"No, no, I insist," he said.

He turned on the tap and fetched a scrubbing brush and a small box of soap flakes from the shelf above. While the water ran, he removed his silver cufflinks, placed them on the sideboard and began rolling up his sleeves.

It was then that Annie saw it, down the inside of his left forearm – a contusion, a line in blue and black.

Chapter Fifty

Finch clutched the chit, absorbing the word, then dropped it in disgust. He did not really know what he had expected to discover inscribed there next to Cox's name – maybe that cursed moniker Moriarty, maybe someone else's entirely – but there it was, in stark, typed, black and white: '*Mr A. N. Rideau.*'

There could be little doubt that Rideau – perceived ally Rideau, a man in whom they had just confided their secrets – was most likely complicit in Cox's murder; his professed act of caring for his old colleague just bogus – a front, a means, probably, to extract further information from them.

Not just today, but in the restaurant. Yes, he too had enquired after Moriarty, hadn't he?

And Annie… Annie had been left alone with him.

Instinctively, Finch turned and rushed to the door. He then stopped and raced back to scoop the piece of paper from the counter.

"My invoice," yelped Mr Mokani.

The doorbell jangled and Finch disappeared, at which the chemist came out from behind his counter and skittered onto the pavement after him. Finch, hobbling as fast as he could, was already round the corner.

"You are thief!" bellowed the chemist. "Stop thief!"

The commotion caused heads to turn. A woman in a bottle-green dress asked if everything was all right. An older, grey man in a top hat, his much younger wife on his arm, stopped to gawp.

A passing Cape policeman came over.

"What seems to be the trouble?"

Mr Mokani huffed and puffed back.

"This man here," explained the first woman. "He claims to be the victim of a robbery."

"Not claims. I am victim," Mr Mokani corrected.

The policeman eyed him up and down as if his accusations were to be regarded with more cynicism than that of a white man.

"Please. You must chase!"

"This is your shop?" asked the policeman, evidently uninterested in pursuit.

"Not shop. Pharmacy. But please. Man he get away!"

"A chemist's," chipped in the woman helpfully.

"And who stole what exactly?"

"Man. Stole invoice. Run away. Limping. You catch him."

"An invoice?"

"A bill," offered the man in the top hat.

"Isn't that a good thing?" quipped the copper. "He can come and steal my bills if he wishes."

A few onlookers chuckled.

The man in the top hat felt compelled now to tender an opinion in Mokani's defence.

"Keeping one's books in order is paramount to good business practice," he trumpeted.

"If you say so, sir," said the policeman.

"I *do* say so."

"And so do I," said Mr Mokani.

"Don't get smart with me."

"I *am* smart. I am also out of breath." He waved towards the corner. "You must apprehend thief. Quickly."

"Who was this man?" asked the policeman.

Mr Mokani pointed up towards the corner.

"Hurry or you lose him."

"Who?"

"*This* man…"

Mr Mokani pressed a brown folded card into the policeman's hand – Finch's military identity card. The policeman opened it and, in an instant, put his whistle to his lips. A sharp blast and a colleague was running up the pavement towards him, pushing people out of the way, eliciting grunts of disapproval.

"Him," said the first policeman, flashing the card, pointing at the name. "It's *him*!"

Rideau began rolling his left sleeve back down, though he knew there really was no point. He had registered the flicker of shock on Annie's face, even though she had sought to mask it.

"I'm afraid you weren't supposed to see that."

He reached behind him to untie the apron and, in the same move, produced his revolver. She had assumed he had put it aside, but it had been there all along, tucked into his waistband behind him.

"I'm terribly sorry, Miss Jones. I had been enjoying your company so. You are a most convivial guest."

He shook down his sleeve. She could not help but look at the bruising. He was an enthusiastic auto-injector.

"I'm afraid you must forgive my little affectation," he said, throwing down a glance. "Three years ago now. Appendicitis. Took the damn thing out but… complications. Laid up in hospital for five months. Left me with a taste for something I've been unable to shake off since."

Annie looked at the table. The two glasses of wine sat there. While they remained unchanged, everything else, their circumstances, now had.

"What do you want?" she asked.

He shook his head as if not knowing where to begin.

"The captain has just put himself in great danger to help us," she added.

"He has, hasn't he?" mused Rideau. "And if you consider the effort he's expended on behalf of old fool Cox, a man he disliked almost as much as I did, then you absolutely have to give him full marks for decency."

With his free hand he reached for his wine glass and drained the last mouthful. He motioned for her to do the same.

"Please, no point in wasting it."

"I wouldn't drink with you now if you were the last man on earth."

Rideau smiled.

"Come, come. No need to be quite so melodramatic. You still know very little about me. Are jumping to all sorts of conclusions. I'm no more a monster now than I was five minutes ago."

"It doesn't alter the fact that you've now got a gun pointed at me."

He ignored her.

"Please…"

He said it firmly and steadily.

"...I just need to know – Moriarty. *Who* is Moriarty?"

Annie's first instinct, curiously, was one of offence. Had she and Finch really conveyed an air of deceit? They had been nothing but honest.

In which case, did her safety now rely on pretence that she knew more than they had been letting on, or an emphatic repeat of their denial?

"What do *you* know?" she asked.

He gave a supercilious chuckle.

"Very clever," he said. "But a response that is not going to win you any favours. Now, I repeat—"

"Why?"

"Why what?"

"Why are you doing this?"

"This?" he wagged the gun. "I thought that was more than obvious."

"No... Why...? Why do you need to know who Moriarty is?"

He seemed momentarily perplexed.

"My poor sweet dear," he patronised. "The same reason *you* are after him. Don't think I didn't have a good poke around in that office desk myself. Bottle of rum wasn't it? And we all know Cox had long given up sewing those blasted papers into his jacket. Abandoned that little trick before he went off to the Front. It's just about then that our Moriarty comes on the scene. Keeping the goodies safe for Cox's return, only now holding on to them indefinitely, it would seem. However, you obviously got one step further than me if you hooked up with our man Shawcroft. So, I need to know. Who—?"

"And what if I tell you nothing?"

He exhaled.

"Please, let us not let this become vulgar."

She saw that he seemed to relax slightly, as if threatening people with weaponry was a reluctant last resort; that he'd much rather continue to play the bon viveur.

No matter. The fact was – pretty as his gun looked – he was a man with an instrument of death. It was aimed at her.

The work surface was on her left. Rideau hadn't removed all the items. The chopping board and the large kitchen knife she'd used, its blade flecked with onion peel, were close. If she could just reach...

"Look, I don't know quite how to put this, but the identity of Moriarty is of immense value," Rideau went on. "As you've seen already, people have been killed over it. I'm sorry, but our friend Finch, that suicide mission… He'll be in police hands by now and with no Brookman around to defend him."

"Don't count on it."

He furrowed his brow in thought for a moment.

"Look… let's not make this anymore unpleasant or difficult. It's become complicated enough. I have a proposition for you. A third way. You lead me to Moriarty, I'll split the proceeds… say 70/30. The 70 to me, obviously."

"*Proceeds?*"

Annie moved towards him. Even though he had the gun, she was the one with the power, the one with the supposed knowledge. He took a step back.

"You *are* joking?" she snarled.

"A bull market as the stock exchange types like to say. We can make a killing."

She felt almost sorry for him. Rideau and his grubby little habit. She'd never met an addict but she had known drunks. It was the same thing. Men who could be charm itself and then lie and cheat to a selfish end. Whether one drank it, smoked it or injected it, it made no difference.

She shook her head at his shame.

"Then 60/40?"

She did not dignify it with a response.

"What you know, about Moriarty," he urged. "I assure you now your most prudent course of action is to share it with me. I have connections. If you're bound to me, you're secure."

"You're pathetic. You think I'd sell out Captain Finch for a few pieces of silver?"

"More than a few…"

In moving a step forward, she had now screened the knife. With her left hand she swept it off the table and held it point down, tucked into the fold of her skirt.

"…I warn you, Miss Jones. Please don't make this unpleasant. He'll be out of the picture by now, the captain. There's nothing you… *we* can do for—"

The air of confrontation was suddenly punctured by the sharp *rat-a-tat* of the door knocker.

"Finch!" squealed Annie and pushed right past Rideau.

"Miss Jones, I'm warning you, don't!" he protested, quite ineffectually.

She raced to the front door, slid the bolt and turned the handle.

"Captain Finch!"

But it was not Captain Finch standing on the doorstep. It was a solid, square, muscular man in a navy blue suit. His hair was...

"Miss Jones," said Rideau from behind. "I believe you have already met my associate, Mr Payne."

The man said nothing – simply stepped in and, without turning, closed the door behind him.

"Now, most heartily," Rideau added. "I would advise your full cooperation."

The man advanced towards her. His eyes were steely blue. Expressionless.

"A recurring pleasure," he uttered in his unfeeling monotone.

"Miss Jones and I were just having lunch," bantered Rideau, as if the whole thing had been mere fun and games. "Discussing the whereabouts of our mutual friend Moriarty."

The red-haired man... Payne... ignored Rideau. He came closer. He backed Annie against the wall in the hallway, raised his left arm, placing his hand on the door jamb just above and to the left of her head. His face was only a foot from hers. His right hand, ominously, remained in his pocket, brandishing something.

"Please, Miss Jones," said Rideau, the tone apologetic, embarrassed. "It would ease proceedings if you could enlighten Mr Payne as to both Moriarty's identity and his whereabouts. This whole business really is becoming most troublesome."

In a generally expressionless individual, even Annie could recognise disgust. Payne shot Rideau a look of contempt.

...And that was when Annie wriggled it to her right and, in one deft move, whipped the chopping knife up and over, plunging it straight through Payne's left hand, skewering it to the door frame.

He did not scream or yell, merely uttered a grunt of inconvenience as he tried to wrestle the knife free. But Annie was already hurtling down the hallway towards the back door.

"Please! Miss Jones!" begged Rideau.

She scooped up her boots, pulled the key from the lock, slammed the door shut behind her and locked it again from the outside, flinging the key into the bushes. She ran across the small backyard, exited through the gate and turned left into the alleyway, the direction she had heard described to Finch. There were already thumps against the back door.

Then she put her head down and, as best as her clothes would let her, charged... smack into the chest of a man in a smart beige suit hastening towards her.

"Nurse Jones. Thank God!" panted Finch.

"Get out of here!"

Chapter Fifty-One

This time it was Annie who grabbed Finch's hand. With boots in the other she was running in stockinged feet. She pulled Finch around, back towards the street.

"Rideau," she blurted. "He's—"

"I know."

The tram stop was up ahead. The cables crackled. One was near. As they hit the end of the alley, the number 36 was departing, heading into the city. It had started to rumble off down the tracks.

There was another sound, this time one of shattering wood. Fifty yards behind them, Payne had burst through the door. As they reached the high street, Finch glanced back over his shoulder. The man was sprinting towards them, arms pumping, knees raised high, striding like an Athens Olympian.

"What the *hell*?"

The tram was speeding up. They ran straight across the road, causing a horse cart to swerve. Annie caught the pole on the tailboard and shoved Finch up on board, throwing her boots after him. Though she had a handhold, she felt her feet become entangled in her skirt, stumbling now, trying to keep her balance.

Finch looked up. The red-haired man was closing fast. He kept one hand on the pole and reached out with his other to grab Annie's elbow. She locked her palm onto his forearm.

"Jump!"

She lifted her right leg high and pushed off hard with her left. Finch swung her mid-air and she landed one foot on the tailboard.

…But she was violently yanked back. The red-haired man, Payne, sprinting as hard and as fast as he could, had seized the hem of her skirt.

For the first time, she screamed. She wrapped her arms tight around the pole while Finch tried to wrestle her on board. Even at full tilt, the man seemed in control. He had immense strength in his arms, felt Finch. And he had been wounded. Blood gushed from an open slash in his hand.

Finch's gammy left leg still had its uses. He delivered a hard, sharp kick, landing his toecap on the bridge of the man's nose.

Payne lost his grip, staggered, fell and rolled over, before righting himself and resuming his chase. He too was limping now. But it was too late, the tram had cranked up enough speed.

Heads had turned from within. The conductor appeared – a small, older man with a wrinkled and bemused expression.

"What on earth's going on?"

"Someone behaving in an ungentlemanly fashion," said Finch.

"You all right, Miss?" asked the conductor.

"Fine, thank you."

She turned her face away so he couldn't register her upset. She kept her stockinged feet concealed beneath her skirt.

"Listen, there's one along every seven minutes. No point getting yourself killed over it."

Finch nodded.

"Where to?"

"Where are you headed?"

"All points to the docks."

"The docks it is, then… Two."

"Tuppence ha'penny."

Finch rummaged for change; the conductor wound the handle on the ticket machine hanging on the leather strap round his neck, then turned to go back inside.

"Any more fares?" he boomed.

"You want to sit?" asked Finch to Annie. "We're a bit exposed out here."

"Better not."

She tipped her head discreetly.

Nearest the doorway was a middle-aged man. He was reading the *Cape Argus*. The front page contained a bold headline:

KILLER AT LARGE

Underneath it, Finch saw, was a grainy halftone image… of himself, a cropped head-shot from the standard stiff portrait they had all had taken when they first joined up.

"Christ."

"I know. You'd think they have found something more flattering." He smiled.

Annie leaned against the hand rail and pulled on her boots.

"So he's our second man, you think…? Rideau," asked Finch. "*He* was the one who returned to climb on board the cab?"

She shrugged a 'yes'.

"Still doesn't make sense though, does it? I mean Rideau said he knew Cox no longer kept the documents on his person, that he'd passed them on to Moriarty, so he couldn't have been searching for them on board that night."

"Unless Moriarty had made contact by this point and the documents were *back* in Cox's possession."

"That runs counter to what Lady Verity and Shawcroft intimated. But it begs a question. If Cox were germane to the hunt for Moriarty, why eliminate him? Why not just follow him? Or coerce him?"

"More importantly," said Annie, "if you're an addict, why kill someone… your *supplier* of all people… and with the very drug that you so covet? There's no logic to it."

"Though it *would* explain why someone would be rooting around in the dark in the dirt for a coat… If he thought it had laudanum in the pocket?"

"Which would account for Rideau's damaged hands."

The sun was going down, the cover of darkness was on its way. Fortunately, the picture in the newspaper was a poor likeness, plus Finch was no longer in uniform. He was anxious to read the story but when the man got off at a later stop, he took the paper with him.

They alighted ahead of the docks, jumping off when it slowed down to sufficient speed. It was dark, there were plenty of people, including an exodus of dock workers. Despite the occasional glimpse of police, there was safety in numbers.

"Here," said Finch, pressing a penny into Annie's hand.

A few paces ahead was a newspaper vendor. Annie purchased the *Argus*. They stepped into an alleyway. It was hard to read in the gloom. Finch lit a match.

"Congratulations. Says you are responsible for the 'wilful extinguishing' of the life of a Mr Maitland Shawcroft, a reporter for the *Post*," she recounted.

Newspaper rivalry being what it was, Finch took grim, wry amusement at the fact that the *Argus* – despite the untimely death of a fellow professional – could not resist a dig at the competence of the competition.

Something did not sit right here either.

"But how did they know it was me?"

"You had a knife in your hand, remember?"

"No, I mean how did they *recognise* me?"

"I suppose they were on the lookout for you. Maybe there was someone in the crowd—"

He shook his head.

"Shawcroft. He addressed you by name?"

"Yes… but it was noisy, brief. I doubt very much that anyone overheard or was remotely paying attention."

"Shawcroft. Did he have anything on him? Had he written your name down?"

"Given his paranoia about our meeting, I doubt it."

"The RAMC offices then… Daisy. They could have traced your identity back to her. There were Military Foot Police after us there, not to mention you're a named fugitive."

He exhaled a hiss of suspicion.

"I'm not saying the paper knew in advance, but someone fed them the information pretty damn quickly. This whole thing, someone's been one step ahead of us."

"So what do we do?"

"Come on."

He took her hand and they ventured out into the street.

"Till guardian angel Brookman shows up, there's one more thing."

At the docks, even after nightfall, and despite the large discharge of workers, there were still soldiers everywhere. You could hear the shouts of the quartermasters as military cargo was stocked and logged, part of the unfathomable logistics of supplying over 200,000 regular and colonial soldiers, and with more than that number again still set to arrive.

They picked their way through the crates and boxes and a succession of backstreets and alleyways. The smell of seawater and oil was heady, the universal cocktail of the harbour.

It was cool now. Finch still hadn't got used to the transition from light to dark, heat to cool, that came at the flip of a switch at this latitude – so unlike the protracted summer evenings of home.

"There," he announced.

Ahead, across a slick cobbled square, intersected by redundant tram-lines, was a row of two-storey buildings that looked like they were once part of the shipbuilding business. Behind them was the water and a silhouette backdrop of masts, the cables and rigging tinkering on the breeze.

Opposite the central building was a row of hansom cabs, the horses idling. Even at this early hour there was the glow of lights and the sound of jollity from within. There were people going in and out, valets in red tunics opening doors.

"The Officers' Club?" asked Annie.

"The very same."

They watched for a moment. The acoustics were such you could pick out individual voices through the open windows – pompous English ones, noted Annie. You could also, even at this distance, smell the alcohol and cigars.

"The cream of the British Empire," sighed Finch.

Two days earlier, she would not have appreciated it as sarcasm.

A pair of army officers stepped out. They appeared to press money into the hands of a waiting steward who blew a whistle and beckoned. As he did so, the cab at the head of the queue jolted into life and the horse *clip-clopped* over.

"You have a plan?" Annie asked.

"We have the club before us; it's dark, there's a rank of cabs – the correct conditions. Why not take a look at the crime scene?"

Keeping to the concrete wall, which held back a crumbling earth bank, they skirted round the back of the cab rank. The buggies all shuffled forward a few feet as they advanced up the pecking order.

The first cab had wheeled round into the middle of the square; the two officers walked towards it and a valet opened the door for them.

"See, the cab doesn't pull up close, it turns a few yards out," he observed, "so that it can get a clear run at the ramp up to the road."

A bench was situated opposite the club, about ten yards from the door – wood planks on wrought iron supports and bolted to the floor; it abutted an ornamental obelisk with a bed of flowers.

"Accor7ding to the official version of events, Rideau parks the drunken Cox there," he said.

"…and his coat."

"Note that he does so himself. Unusual when this place is crawling with valets and sycophants."

"But not implausible. If he were trying to be discreet…"

"True. And then he goes back inside to settle the bill. Or so he claims."

"And Kilfoyle?"

Annie looked up and down.

"Kilfoyle comes from where?"

"His apartment is over that way," Finch pointed.

At the opposite end to the slip road, there were steps leading up out of the square.

"We know he was walking home when he stopped to help Finch. He then carried on his way, supposedly turning back after a change of heart."

"Look!" Annie whispered.

They hadn't seen them arrive, maybe they had been inside, but a pair of Military Foot Police were now standing guard outside the club.

Finch and Annie kept in the shadows and edged back round behind the taxi rank.

"We need to get out of here," she said.

"There's still a question I have to ask."

Keeping to the blind side, they went to the first cab and stood alongside the driver.

"Excuse me," asked Finch.

The Coloured cabbie looked down.

"*Baas?*"

"Do you know a man named Pinkie Coetzee?"

The man rolled his eyes.

"What's he done this time?"

"Nothing. Nothing like that. He's not in trouble at all. He helped us the other day. We want to thank him."

"Well he's not here. Not driving."

"His evening off?"

"No."

"Then what?"

"Dismissed. Doesn't work here anymore."

"He got the sack?"

"Two days ago."

"What on earth for?"

He shrugged his shoulders.

"Guessing the usual."

"Surely you mean the incident? The one with the British officer?"

"Don't know about that, *baas*. You have to ask him."

Finch and Annie exchanged a glance.

"You know where we can find him?" she asked.

"Don't know his address but my guess is he'll be at Sammy's."

"Who's Sammy?"

"A bar owner."

"Where's this bar?"

"Bo-Kaap."

She looked to Finch, he nodded.

"Can you take us there?" Annie asked.

The cabbie's face lit up like a beacon.

"Are you crazy, lady?"

"Crazy? Crazy why?"

"Come on, Missy. You... the gentleman..."

"Why on earth not?"

He phrased it delicately.

"It's not your neighbourhood."

"An unfamiliar neighbourhood is the least of our worries," snapped Finch.

The cabbie shrugged again.

"Whatever you say, *baas*."

They made to climb aboard.

"Oh, one other thing..." said Finch.

"*Baas?*"

"...can you describe me?"

"Describe you?"

"Yes. What do I look like? What am I wearing?"

The cabbie was growing tired of the nonsensical interrogation.

"I don't know... hat, suit..."

The driver twisted himself right round. Alongside the cab door, with the canvas roof up, they were almost obscured.

"The colour of my suit?"

In the glow of the gaslight, some ten yards away, it was obviously near impossible to tell. The cabbie shook his head.

"My face?"

The cabbie hunched his shoulders again.

"Look like a man with a lot of questions."

"Captain?!"

Annie was frantic. She pointed out through the other side of the cab. A man had entered the square, limping along, turning this way and that. He had a white handkerchief bound round his left hand. Payne.

"Sammy's Bar, Bo-Kaap," barked Finch to the driver. "Go, go, go!"

Chapter Fifty-Two

The bar was at the top of a cobbled street that ran upward towards Signal Hill. As they ascended, Annie sensed right away that she was in a different Cape Town. Even in the thin gaslight she could see that the tightly-packed terraced houses with their odd, sideways facing stoeps, were brightly coloured – painted orange, pink, yellow, lime green...

There was a heady waft of spices and smell of tobacco, the sounds of gentle conversation. Up and down the road were huddles of dark-skinned men in kufi skullcaps, some in long, baggy shirts. She saw the outline of a domed building... a mosque?

People were turning to look at them. On the walled stoeps, women in headscarves stared.

"What are we doing looking for a bar in *this* part of town?" she asked.

They had been walking up the centre of the road. Finch stepped to the kerb and approached a middle-aged man wielding a broom, sweeping around the front step of his house.

The man didn't seem offended. He pointed up the slope, the direction in which they were headed.

Brookman had filled him in on some of the local details and he imparted the salient facts to Annie – the Cape Malays formed one of the oldest communities in the city, descendants of the slave labour that the Dutch East India Company had shipped back from their colonies in Java and Malacca. They had brought their religion with them, part of the great spread from Asia.

Like other ethnic groupings in the Cape they were now of mixed race, the result of 200 years of intermingling between those of African, Asian and European stock that placed them under the definition 'Coloured' distinct from 'black' The Cape Malays were just one sub-set.

As Brookman had made clear, there was a real sense of grievance building amongst the Coloureds of whatever religious stripe. There were some powerful Cape Malay voices in local politics. While it had generally been accepted that the industrious Coloureds were pro-British, they had been denied the opportunity to do their bit for the Cape's defence, turned away at the recruiting posts.

What with the Cape Dutch, it was rumoured that groups were arming themselves as a precaution in case civil relations soured further.

As they neared the top of the slope, they began to hear music – a lively, rhythmic dance tune. Finch picked out a wild trumpet that was studding the air with frenzied staccato volleys. Around it there was laughter, gaiety. The bar was on a street corner. Outside, the crowd had spilled onto the pavement.

There were equal numbers of young men and women fraternising enthusiastically, flirty or coquettish, all seemingly enjoying themselves. Annie, victim of obsessive chaperoning, felt rather jealous.

There was no hostility as they approached, just a general bemusement that a white middle-aged man in a too-tight flamboyant suit and his rather bedraggled female companion should have ventured into these parts.

The bar, they saw, was not actually called Sammy's, rather The Hundred Yard Bar, though no one, thus far, had referred to it so.

Inside, more heads turned, then twisted back again and got down to business, which consisted, almost to a man... and woman... of enjoying the band.

There were bright paper garlands hanging from the low rafters between the lanterns. Beneath them, amid the packed clientele, couples danced in up-close free-form association.

Through the thick smoke, to Finch's eye, the ensemble was an unorthodox arrangement – steel-strung guitar, a plucked double bass and rudimentary drum kit. Over the top came that trumpet, played by a skinny man with closed eyes, his heaving ribcage outlined against his shirt, completely lost in the music – his wild and excited toots zipping up and down the scales, every outlandish flourish greeted with cheers.

They squeezed their way through the throng, towards the bar. It was really just planks mounted on bricks, behind it crates of pale ale that looked suspiciously like they had been intended for the army. The barman was a large man in a sweaty white singlet over which hung a brightly coloured floral shirt. He sucked on a toothpick.

"Good evening," Finch yelled. "Are you Sammy?"

"Who wants to know?" he said and went back to wiping glasses.

"My name is Captain Finch."

The man eyed him up and down.

"You police?"

"Army."

"There are no guns here."

"I'm a doctor, Medical Corps. I'm not interested in firearms."

He stacked some glasses behind him then returned to his wiping.

"I don't mean to be rude, Captain, but two white folks come here to my bar, it's not common. White folks come here, usually spells trouble."

The tune finished to an eruption of whoops and cheers. The bar was suddenly besieged.

"This is not a good time," he said.

"I'm afraid this is a matter of urgency."

There was already one young woman working overtime to keep up with demand as people shouted and jostled and rattled coins. They were begging Sammy to serve them, too.

He huffed, raised his hand to indicate that he would be one moment, and bellowed back over his shoulder.

"Gertie!"

A generously-proportioned woman hustled through the doorway and took over his spot. Sammy the barman then went round the side and beckoned them over.

"Can I ask you a question, Sammy?" said Annie.

"Go ahead, Miss."

"Your place. Why is it called the Hundred Yard Bar?"

He smiled and waved his hand towards the street.

"Down there... the Malays... the mosque..."

She nodded.

"Municipal law prevents me from selling alcoholic beverages within one hundred yards of it."

He pointed to the floor. Just in front of the bar, a white line had been painted across the stone.

"That there is the legal limit."

She laughed. He did too. But then his face turned serious.

"Now, what is it you really want?"

Finch spoke loudly and clearly.

"We're looking for a man named Pinkie Coetzee."

There was no reaction.

363

"Pinkie Coetzee. Cab driver. Do you know him? We were told he could be found here."

Sammy took a packet of cigarettes that had been tucked into the fold of his shirtsleeve, removed one, lit it, sucked in the smoke then exhaled, head pointing upwards, adding a lungful to the great smog that hung under the ceiling.

"Pinkie? I might do… Why?"

"He's not in any trouble," stressed Finch. "Far from it. In fact, he's been of great help, to us and to the police."

Sammy did not appreciate mention of the police.

"But I need to make sure he's okay… He'd been hurt, you see—"

The man dropped the cigarette on the floor, ground his foot on it and indicated that he needed to get back to pouring beer.

"Sure, I know Pinkie," he said.

He jabbed a thumb towards the rear. There was a pair of French doors, the woodwork battered and faded, a crack running diagonally across one pane.

They pushed the doors open and stepped through into a small yard. There was a lit candle on an empty bench table, intended as a romantic retreat. But in the light of it, a man was lying face-down on the ground in a stupor.

"Pinkie?"

Finch rushed to him, shook him and turned him over.

"This is your star witness?" asked Annie, incredulously.

Finch tapped Pinkie gently on the cheeks. He groaned. He was dishevelled, his shirt and trousers soaked in sweat, beer and vomit.

He half opened his eyes. They were bleary, bloodshot. It took a moment for him to register. Finch's presence here was evidently wildly out of context.

"Heer Dokter?"

Annie exited.

"Please, no more, Dokter," Pinkie added. "You already cost me my job."

"If there's anything I can do?" said Finch. "Speak to Inspector Brookman, speak to the taxi company…?"

Pinkie was not incapacitated enough to prevent him issuing a sardonic smile.

"Nothing you can do," he said, his voice weak, pained. "You know full well."

Annie returned with a jug of water. She handed it to Pinkie who, in one go, half drank it down, half sloshed it over himself.

"Pinkie, I'm afraid Nurse Jones here and I must ask you a few more questions."

Pinkie turned his head to eye Annie.

"I wish I never picked up that officer. Look where helping got me."

"Lives depend on it."

Finch pulled out his own cigarettes. He put two in his mouth, lit them and then passed one to Pinkie, who drew long and hard. Finch then produced his wallet. He opened it and brandished a ten shilling note.

"You think you can just buy me… the poor Coloured boy?"

Pinkie half-heartedly snatched at the money anyway.

Finch made an 'uh-*unh*' noise, the kind one makes when admonishing a child, and pulled it back.

He explained as clearly and succinctly as he could about their theory – that there could have been two Good Samaritans – one the Fancy Dan, the man who put Cox in the cab initially then walked away; two, a second man who returned to climb on board beside Cox.

Pinkie sucked on his cigarette.

"Yes," he said, "if that's what you say, I suppose there could have been two."

"The ring, the diamond ring," asked Annie.

"When did you see it on the man's hand…? When he gave you the address card, or when he returned to help on board Major Cox…?"

"Or both times?" added Finch.

Pinkie was fading, his eyelids closing. Finch slapped his cheek again. Harder this time.

"Come on Pinkie, ten shillings."

"First time. I saw… first time only," he whispered.

Finch turned to Annie.

"He conflated the two men, Kilfoyle and Rideau, just like we thought. He believed they were one and the same. Easy to do."

She nodded.

"But I'm not sure," Pinkie then added.

"Why?" said Finch.

"Because, Heer Dokter, look at me…"

He began a phlegm-rattle chuckle. It was hurting him but, the more it hurt, the more he laughed.

"I am drunk now. I was drunk that night, too."

"Shit," uttered Finch, with a tagged-on 'sorry' for Annie's benefit.

"Doesn't matter," she said. "Our theory. It still pans out."

Finch lay Pinkie back down… and tucked the ten shilling note into his filthy shirt's top pocket.

"What do we do now?" Annie sighed.

Finch stood and looked out across the Cape Town rooftops and dotted night lights.

"I don't know. Find out what the hell was so incendiary about some documents that would have driven a man to sewing them into his jacket."

"Or squirrel things away behind a false panel in a wardrobe."

Finch grew animated again. He was itching to do something.

"What?" she asked.

"Only place we haven't visited together…" he said, "…the only bit of crime scene we haven't re-examined is Cox's guest house. There must be something there. Maybe something Mrs Du Plessis neglected to tell us – she was pretty circumspect with her information. And if our red-haired friend has got our scent, then we'd better get out of here fast."

Chapter Fifty-Three

They took another short tram ride and hopped out at the stop on High Level Road. Ans Du Plessis was a tough customer, Finch explained, but neither immune to reason, nor – on account of the business with the letters – sentiment.

He wondered now whether those love letters had been sliced from his own jacket not as some means to blackmail but under the mistaken assumption that they might have been the documents that had been passed between Cox and Moriarty. Had they even thought, for a moment, that he – *Finch* – was Moriarty?

Other than the chirp of crickets, the silence of the neighbourhood was in stark contrast to that of Bo-Kaap. Up the slope of Atlantic View Drive there was the glow of lighting from within the houses but – as they stopped outside – not from the Esperanza guest house itself.

Finch undid the picket gate catch and let Annie pass through. As they mounted the wooden steps, the noise of the crickets stopped.

"What time is it?" he asked.

She twisted and turned to try and catch the gaslight on her watch, but to no avail.

"Can't tell… Must be after ten."

Finch pulled open the fly screen, rapped the knocker then pressed his face to the glass with its ornate ship and its billowing sails. There was no light from within.

"Probably in bed," he said.

"You'd have thought there'd be a guest up."

"Either out on the town or gone. Who knows? What with the Big Push, everyone might have moved on."

He rapped again. Hard. Nothing.

No windows were open. Annie went around the side passage. She tried the back door and the ground floor windows.

"All shut up back there, too."

"Only one thing for it," he said.

Finch got out his penknife and jabbed it into the lock, then rattled the brass, oval-shaped knob with its beaded surround.

"You'll never do it like that," tutted Annie.

From under her beret, she pulled out a hairpin about three inches long, then another the same. She crouched down, inserted both into the lock and worked them together.

The mechanism went '*click*'.

"How on earth…?" spluttered Finch.

"My brother," she said, pushing open the door. "Don't ask."

They stepped inside and closed it gently behind.

He called out a 'hello' and a second one for good measure.

Save for the heavy, resonant tick of the large carriage clock there was no sound.

Maybe, as Ans Du Plessis had said, the word had spread. Murder had been bad for business.

On the dresser in the hall – the one with Mathilda's tip jar and the silly cross-eyed spaniel – was a paraffin lamp with matches in an earthenware dish. Finch lit it. From the sitting room Heer Du Plessis scowled his disapproval.

On the wall, was a pegged board which bore the room keys. There were five guest rooms and five keys present. It seemed unlikely that everyone would be out at the same time, leaving their keys hanging there. The rooms must be vacant. Could Du Plessis's business have even been shut down as a consequence of the investigation? It seemed horribly unjust.

Finch took the key hanging on number three and directed Annie to the stairs. The boards creaked as they ascended.

Du Plessis's room was next to Cox's. It bore no number. He knocked but there was no answer. He hoped that she was okay; that she had merely been on a visit somewhere, perhaps a friend or relative. He tried again. Nothing.

They unlocked Cox's room. The bed had been put back in place. Finch set down the paraffin lamp and took a match to the bigger one on Cox's bureau. With a mirror reflector it threw good light.

"So what now?" asked Annie.

"We leave no stone unturned. Every nook, cranny. Every seam, every panel."

He pointed for her to start at the door. He would begin at the window.

"Must be something here… some clue to Moriarty."

While he worked his hands, feeling around the window frame and Annie did the same with the mattress and bedstead, Finch turned the various conversations over, pausing only to seek points of clarification from Annie.

Within the last few hours, a number of people – MFP lawyer Franklin, Payne and Rideau himself had enquired as to Moriarty's whereabouts. Rideau, Shawcroft and Lady Verity had also alluded to the fact that the elusive Moriarty had yet to be found. Cox had had documents of some importance that he had been stashing away but then, according to Rideau, before embarking for the Front, had passed them on to Moriarty.

Over the next half hour they combed scrupulously through the room and every crack in the walls, every gap in the window surround and skirting boards. They didn't have the tools to lift up the floorboards and had to take it as read that the 'insurance investigator', clearly now Payne, had found nothing when looking there.

"Come on," sighed Finch. "Let's go."

He extinguished the main light, grabbed the lamp and opened the door for Annie. He followed her and, at the bottom of the stairs, replaced the lamp on the dresser and began rooting around the various letters and bills that were stacked there, one of which was addressed to Lieutenant Ives of the Royal Artillery, presumably the officer he had met the other day.

In the two drawers immediately below were a battered wooden chess set, a ball of string, some stationery, envelopes and stamps. In the cupboard underneath sat a jumble of old crockery, knitting wool, table linen and, curiously, a small pile of Bibles – spares for the rooms, Finch pondered.

Was stealing them really a hazard? Maybe the war had driven the agnostic towards God.

"No use. Nothing here," he said, rising from a crouch and flexing his accursed knee.

But Annie was not listening. She was staring, wide-eyed.

"Look!"

"What is it?"

Amid the assorted chintzy knick-knacks, including what appeared to be a collection of porcelain thimbles set upon a lace doily, the wood-carved, cross-eyed spaniel leered back at them, tongue panting.

"What you call eclectic taste," sniggered Finch.

But Annie's arm was outstretched still, index finger jabbed forward. And then he saw it, carved across the plinth on which the dog sat, the single word:

MORIARTY

"It was never a person," yelped Annie.

Finch prodded at the ghastly ornament. It was about 18 inches high, heavy, made of a low-grade reddish wood and roughly hewn, the kind of thing one would pick up on a market or receive from a mischievous relative on the knowledge that the recipient would be compelled to put it out on display every time they visited.

But when he rapped his knuckles on it he could hear that the dog was hollow. He turned it round on the dresser, scattering thimbles which clinked and clacked. In the back was a flap set on two small hinges. And set in that was a keyhole.

He pulled out his key. This time it fitted. The little door opened. There, within the back of the dog, wedged in upright, curled in half upon itself, was a foolscap manilla envelope.

It was been jammed in good and hard, the top of it wedged up inside the pooch's head. Finch yanked it out. It contained what felt like a quarter-of-an-inch thickness of papers. The envelope bore stamped postage – *Cape Town, October 15th, 1899* – just before Cox would have moved north, Finch knew. The flap was still gummed. And, the address on the front, that of the Esperanza Guest House, had been written in Cox's own recognisable scrawl.

"Clever bastard," he exhaled. "That's how he kept it out of circulation. He posted it back to himself."

CRASH!

There was the smash of glass and a tinkling of shards. It came from the back of the house… the kitchen.

"Quick!"

Finch grabbed the envelope, took Annie's hand and in one frantic movement undid the front door, pushed the fly screen open and bundled her onto the stoep.

They ran down the path, opened the gate, then Finch tugged Annie, sharply, back down behind the orange blossom bush that ran along the side of the house.

He pressed his finger to her lips and reached into his suit pocket for the revolver.

In an instant the red-haired man – Payne – had burst out of the front door, careered down the front path and, seeing the front gate open, continued out into the street. They heard his feet flying across the dirt, the footfalls receding down the incline.

Finch looked up. They had missed it, but there, nailed to the veranda's upright post, was a notice. He could make out two bold words: '*POLICE – CLOSED.*'

They *had* shut her down. He felt for Ans Du Plessis.

"Least obvious route. Remember?" said Finch.

Behind the row of houses and the alleyway lay the rubbled slope of Signal Hill. In the dark it was a great, grey wall.

He pointed. "We go up, towards the battery."

"Are you sure?"

"Not really. But it's better than heading off down the street."

The small wall at the end was, by their recent experiences, an easily surmountable obstacle.

Not so the hill itself. In the dark it was heavy going. Finch estimated the summit to be 200–300ft feet up, its gradient about one in two. For every solid foothold, another would give way, sending stones and scree rubble thudding down behind them.

Finch took as much weight as he could on his right leg and extended his hand to Annie. Her skirts were again a hindrance. He pulled her, willed her after him.

"Follow the contours. Longer route but easier."

They wound back and forth and, eventually, up ahead, over to the right, they could see the silhouette of the Lion's Head, the great Sphynx-like rock that oversaw the harbour. Below, the other way, were the big naval guns of the battery. They had been in situ, in one form or another, since the British arrived during the Napoleonic War.

At the summit they sat and paused for breath. The air was cleansing and cool. Annie had a brief moment to catch the view. It was spectacular – the lights of buildings and ships all around, twinkling in every direction. On any other night…

"Christ!" blurted Finch.

"What?"

There, 100 yards, maybe 150 yards down behind was something moving, tacking left and right.

They threw themselves over the ridge and began scuttling down the other side. Perversely it proved more tricky than going up. Finch remembered some schoolboy fact about a hare and how it ran faster uphill than down.

"Don't brake against the momentum," he urged Annie, recalling his own training as a cross-country runner.

"Go with it. Use it."

"Bloody easier said than done," she groaned as they ran, stumbled, rolled and slid on their backsides.

Halfway down, Finch threw a glance back. He could see Payne up on the ridge, outlined against the night sky. He was closing. Then Annie squealed as she lost her footing, her control and tumbled forward, head over heels.

"ANNIE!"

For a moment she was a blur, a ridiculous rag doll whirl of limbs and skirts.

She came to a rest, still.

He scrambled down. She was flat on her back, winded.

"Right, we make our stand," Finch said and pulled out Brookman's revolver. He turned to face uphill. If he had to shoot the man, he would. There was no choice.

"No, no, I'm fine," Annie wheezed and eased herself up.

There were buildings below… homes. They were not far off Bo-Kaap again.

As they descended, the cobbled streets began to trickle down the hillside like watercourses.

"Does he know about the envelope?"

"The dog… Moriarty… the back was left open. He'll have put two and two together. Know that something was in there. This time we've got what he wants."

They lurched down through the steep suburban streets till the roads began to level. It was not far to the centre of town. They dashed across Buitengracht with its chaos of trams, Tommies, drunken Tommies and ones even drunker than that.

This time it was Annie who looked back. She yelled. Payne had narrowed the gap. Less than 100 yards. He exploded across the road with little regard for the traffic. There were shouts from the angry drivers of buggies and wagons.

They pushed into a narrow side-street. It had several pubs, the air thick with alcohol, smoke and profanity. The thoroughfare was jam-packed with soldiers. Amid a flurry of apologies, they forced their way between hot, damp, alcohol-reeking, khaki bodies. Payne, meanwhile, had been caught in human quicksand.

They heard a 'Steady on pal', and abuse aimed at him.

Annie turned. There was a flailing of fists and a surge that swept behind them and forced them onwards like a breaker rolling ashore. But they were Payne's fists. He had taken somebody on.

More shouts.

BANG! A gunshot.

Panic.

Men ducked and dived. A gaggle of female hangers-on, rough and overly made-up, screamed. Payne was charging on, unchallenged, his smoking pistol raised in the air.

Someone aimed a kick. It tripped him. He staggered. A boot swung towards his head but he dodged it and wheeled round, delivering an expert pistol-whip to his assailant.

Finch and Annie pressed on. They crossed another thoroughfare. Quieter this time.

BANG!

A bullet whistled past.

Finch pushed Annie round a corner. He raised his Webley and returned fire. The recoil jarred his wrist. He had had merely a token session at a range in Aldershot before departure.

My first shot of the war. In a city, at a civilian.

Payne ducked behind a pillar box.

They ran on. Finch saw the dark mass of the Parliament Building, before it the Company's Garden where he had strolled so peacefully the other morning.

The traffic was picking up again. They weaved between pedestrians and crossed between carts and buggies.

"Watch out!" screamed Annie.

There was a crackle of electricity and the clang of a bell.

Finch had not seen the tram. It was right upon them.

Annie threw herself at him, pushing him out of the way. As it passed it masked them momentarily. She grabbed the pole and helped him up onto the tailboard.

They cruised for only a few seconds, 200 yards or so...

"Oi!" yelled the conductor.

...before leaping off again.

Payne. Where was he? They'd lost sight.

"The Theatre District," remarked Finch. "We're in the Theatre District."

Above them were the bright lights of a marquee. They were completely exposed.

"Quick!"

Finch grabbed Annie's hand and they pushed straight past a queue of well-heeled attendees, barged aside the astonished commissionaire, charged past the box office, through the foyer and battered open the double doors straight into the auditorium.

The brushed red velvet and smell of flowers was in contrast to that of the Gaiety Theatre. On the stage was a full orchestra, the string section in the hum of tuning to the thin reedy tone of an oboe's 'A'. The conductor, rifling through sheet music, turned. But Finch and Annie were already down the raked aisle and, in what only induced stunned silence among the musicians, clambering onto the stage and an exit into the wings.

They plunged through a knot of stagehands tugging on a rope, whatever it was in the rafters counterbalanced by a bag of sand; then they forced their way on, down wooden steps, a corridor, past a dressing room where a male tenor was practising scales within, and out through the stage door into a dark, damp alley. The door was heavy and metal. Finch slammed it behind them. Leaning against the wall was a broom. He thrust the shaft through the pull-handle and the bar on the jamb, blocking it from the outside.

"Did you see him? Did he follow us in?"

"I don't think so," said Annie.

They were in a narrow alley between theatres. It smelt of sweat, showbiz, refuse and urine. Behind them was a dead end. Up ahead on the left, a few yards down, was the stage door to another theatre. Fifty yards ahead lay the glow and hustle-bustle of the street. And they could now hear police whistles.

"Right, let's get into the crowd."

But, as they moved forward once more, there he was, silhouetted against the gaslight, gun in hand, staring right at them. They were in a cul-de-sac, cornered.

Finch forced Annie behind him in order to shield her. He reached for his own gun but it was snagged in his jacket pocket. The more he pulled, the more entangled it became. Payne was walking towards them, slowly, his pistol raised and pointed.

There was a row of large dustbins to the right.

Payne aimed; Finch gambled and, as quick as he could, flung Annie behind them.

BANG!

In the dark, the shot missed, the crack reverberating deafeningly around them.

But Payne would not err a second time. He walked forward, walked closer.

It happened quickly and unexpectedly. The stage door to the other theatre was thrust open, whacking Payne on the arm, throwing him off balance. His pistol was sent skittering across the cobbles.

Standing before them, cast in the light flooding from within, was the bearded, bear-like bouncer Bonzo, the man-mountain minder in his battered bowler hat.

The Gaiety. They were at the back of the Gaiety.

"You!" he was yelling, though not at Payne, at Finch. "I thought I told you never to show your face here again!"

Payne was on his knees, feeling for his weapon. He found it.

"And *you*," Bonzo added, suddenly noticing him, "what the fuck do you think *you're* doing?"

Payne stood up. He looked at Finch.

"Give it to me. Give it to me… Or I'll take it."

He raised the revolver again, the other hand extended. Finch saw the blooded bandage round it.

"Oh no you fucking well don't," mocked Bonzo and whipped from his person a handgun befitting his size, with a 12-inch barrel and a calibre the likes of which Finch had never seen.

CRACK!

Before he knew it, Bonzo had loosed off a shot. It struck on the ground between Payne's legs, leaving a small crater.

"The next one's in your fucking head."

The police whistles were getting louder, closer, easing inevitably towards them. There was banging from within against the door Finch had jammed.

Payne turned and fled.

The bouncer's scrawny sidekick, Stevie, was poking his head out into the alleyway. He was eating a sandwich.

"What's up, Bonz'?"

Bonzo pointed at Finch.

"Him."

The sidekick spluttered.

"Is he fucking stupid or what?"

Annie hauled herself out from behind the bins. The men softened. But the police whistles were almost upon them. Upon all of them.

"Right, you two…" snapped Bonzo, "…in here."

Chapter Fifty-Four

It was early but the light was already slanting in through the windows, the glass of the roof kissed by the blooming glow of daylight. Not that Finch had slept. He lay close to Annie amid the huddled bodies on the concourse. The concrete was cold beneath.

So fatigued was Annie that she fell into a near narcoleptic unconsciousness as soon as they had lain down, his jacket pulled over her, partly for warmth, partly for cover. It had since slipped off. Finch wrested it up over her shoulders and continued to scan his surrounds, his sore eyes dry and prickly from tiredness.

The Cape Town railway station was the safest place they could think of, hiding amid the hundreds dossing down for the night – the human flotsam waiting for trains or connections amid the 24-hour transport circus, around them the great wall of khaki as soldiers embarked for the Front or were delivered battered and broken from it.

The great fug of steam and Woodbines was rent by the shriek of a whistle, the clank of couplings and a hiss of steam as another locomotive was dispatched. Finch watched an ambulance and its RAMC personnel loitering, waiting for the wounded. He was reminded of his true purpose.

Annie stirred. He saw her take the few seconds necessary to come to, and watched the awareness of her environment settle. Though she tried not to betray it, the concern was etched into her face.

"We're still alive then," came her attempted quip.

The rows of the sleeping and stirring stretched off right across the concourse. There must have been 200–300 people, Finch estimated. Human nature being what it was, they had arranged themselves in rows with haphazard walkways in between, some erecting little makeshift dividers with their suitcases.

A few bodies along, a mother was trying to comfort a restless babe of about six months. It, too, put Finch in mind of the poor souls at

Camp Eureka. He thought about the white mother and daughter, the natives who had sheltered them and their epic trek, of the proud black man who had protected them so.

Saviours came in many guises. The bruising bouncers of the Gaiety Theatre had proven unlikely ones – shielding them as much for their own benefit; keeping the police at bay, waiting till the coast was clear, then leaving them to their own devices.

It was while huddled in that backstage corridor, beneath the gaslight – the very same one into which he had sneaked to see Vesta Lane – that they had opened the envelope and read its contents, that superficially innocuous yet ultimately ominous sheaf of papers, the pair of them slowly absorbing the information in stunned silence.

"How long do we stay?" Annie asked.

"Don't know."

"I'm afraid I'm going to complicate things… I need to use the ladies' room."

The public washrooms were about 20 yards away, Finch saw, the entrance partially obscured by the newspaper kiosk. Above it, hanging from the ceiling, the big station clock said eight minutes to six. Time meant nothing here. Barking NCOs had already worked their way up into full voice.

On the departure board, local trains were still listed as running normally around the city suburbs and the branch lines of the Western Cape. The line remained open further along the coast, east to Port Elizabeth. But the rest of the destinations – the ones heading north on what would have been the route to Kimberley, or veering off to Bloemfontein and on to Johannesburg and Pretoria – had been blacked out.

The main line and its rolling stock had been commandeered for military purposes, the armada of troop transports heading on to Beaufort West, De Aar and then Hopetown, now the railhead for the Front.

"Okay, you see where the WCs are?"

She nodded.

"Straight in. Straight out. Don't talk to anyone."

She handed the jacket back and he slid his hand in the pocket, ensuring that he could withdraw the revolver this time, should he need it.

"Got you covered. Now go!"

"Just one thing. And I hate to ask."

"What?"

"Do you have a penny?"

"Again?"

He smiled, fumbled in a pocket and pulled one out. The copper was old and worn. Queen Victoria still had ringlets. He flipped it towards her. She caught it mid-air.

Finch turned to lay on his front, propped on his elbows, and watched Annie move briskly away. He glanced up at the clock. He would allow her five minutes before deciding on any action. Ten minutes and he would send someone in to find her.

He was lost in thought about the options before them; how they might extricate themselves from this almighty pickle.

Then he felt it, a tap, a light kick, delivered to the sole of his right boot. His insides contracted. Discreetly, he slid his hand onto the grip of his pistol.

"You're proving a tricky bugger to find," came a familiar voice.

Finch rolled over and sighed. That warm wave of relief; Brookman was staring down at him.

The detective crouched down. He spoke in a forceful hush, his dark eyes darting this way and that. He put his arm on Finch's.

"Come on, we need to hurry... Before the MFPs spot us."

He nodded over to the entrance. Now Finch saw it. There were military police moving in.

"Where's Nurse Jones?"

"The lavatory," said Finch.

He pointed in its direction.

Brookman nodded again, a signal to an unseen someone across the concourse.

"Okay. We've got her covered," he assured. "Better you leave here separately anyhow. Let's go."

Brookman stood and walked towards the side entrance to the station and bade Finch follow but keep a few yards behind. They moved indirectly, using the cover of pillars, assembled soldiers, an army mess wagon.

Finch threw a glance over this shoulder. The MFPs, about eight of them, were combing through the crowd.

"Down here," he said, motioning Finch towards the street.

They descended a few steps to the pavement. Immediately, a sporty one-horse buggy trotted out. Its roof was up. Finch recognised the driver as Corporal Pienaar, only this time in plainclothes. He was beckoning for them to get on board as fast as possible. They climbed in, he twitched a whip and the lean, high-stepper trotted off at speed.

Brookman waited till they had moved clear, satisfied that they weren't being followed.

"Sorry to have put you through all this," he said, keeping watch continually. "It was for your own protection. It's been a crazed 24 hours. Some significant developments."

"Developments?"

Brookman cleared his throat.

"Well Rideau's dead, for one."

"*Dead?*"

He shook his head sombrely.

"Found strangled. Last night. In his apartment… or that's what I'm being informed. Bit out of the game at the moment."

Finch exhaled a whistle.

He had forgotten that Brookman was now an outsider, an unusual position for him to be in, probably.

"But you'll already know by now that Rideau was involved in this whole Cox business," the detective said. "And not for the good. Not the great friend he proclaimed."

"Sadly I do. And it wouldn't take a wild guess to nail Payne as Rideau's killer either."

"Payne?"

"The red-haired man, the one—"

"So his name's Payne now, is it?" Brookman scoffed. "How sickly appropriate."

"Not his real one?"

"One of several aliases. Though the person remains unchanged. Hired muscle. A killer. Clinical."

"They were in it together somehow, the pair of them. Rideau and Payne."

Brookman sighed.

"Rideau may have believed that to be the case. But Payne… if that's what we're now going to call him… doesn't operate that way."

"You know the cabbie was confused," said Finch. "It wasn't Kilfoyle returning to get into the cab with Cox that night. Most likely it was Rideau."

Brookman nodded. Finch looked out. The streets of downtown were coming to life, the docks absorbed by hustle and bustle, trams disgorging workers along the quaysides.

Finch remembered Brookman's interrogation of Kilfoyle and his absolute certainty at the time that he was Cox's murderer. He knew the error would have stung Brookman deeply.

"Everything pointed to Kilfoyle," consoled Finch. "It made perfect sense."

Brookman said nothing.

The buggy wound away from the docks. Ahead lay the sprawling makeshift khaki city at Green Point and, to their left, Signal Hill, down whose slopes they had scrambled not hours before.

They were heading straight into the rising sun. It was difficult to pick out details. To their right, the breakers crashed hard on the windswept beach, great swirls of luminescent foam beating down on the shore. The boom of the waves and the swish of the shingle was visceral.

"Where are we going?" Finch asked.

"There's a judge… Justice Dood," Brookman explained. "Has been quite vociferous about maintaining the integrity of civil law during the Emergency. Has been helpful to me in the past. I can trust him."

He returned to look Finch in the eye.

"The plan is this: we go to his place – you, me, Nurse Jones – we tell him everything we know. *Everything*. He has a stenographer waiting to put it on record. Discreet and safe. Key thing is he's friends with the Governor, Sir Alfred Milner. Has his confidence. With authority like that – especially amongst people keen to avoid political scandal – one hopes we can straighten this whole thing out and, crucially… get you off the hook. *Both* of you."

"And you?"

"Don't you worry about me. I've been in this game a long time. In and out of favour as circumstances dictate. I'm a survivor."

He yelled an instruction up to Pienaar. The buggy took a left turn.

"Where is he, this judge?"

"Not far, past the Point. The Twelve Apostles. In the shadow of them."

He smiled.

"Actually that sounds rather apocalyptic, doesn't it…?"

Brookman looked behind them again, through the oblong in the canvas cut for a rear window, making sure they were not being tailed.

"Nurse Jones will be on her way. The plan's for her to take the inland route, just in case. My regret at your getting caught up in all this, Captain Finch, is only exceeded by my embarrassment at Nurse Jones' entrapment in it. It's most unfortunate for her. I'm truly sorry."

He barked another order to Pienaar.

"Come on. Faster!"

Finch saw the craggy coastal range of the Apostles loom ahead to the left.

"Look, we haven't got much time so we'd better pool what we know," said Brookman. "Here's the situation as I see it – and this is absolutely privileged. You understand?"

Finch nodded. Brookman took a deep breath.

"So, here goes… As we have already established, the Military Foot Police arrested you for the battery of Lady Verity. She was roughed up. That was true. Though in terms of all this, she seems somewhat untouchable. Not expendable like everyone else. Whoever did it didn't have long. Just a couple of minutes. From what witnesses were saying he was seeking information. They put two and two together and assumed it be you, just like we thought."

"It was Payne?"

"Most likely. She, of course, is keeping absolutely *shtum*. Afraid to say anything."

"*Shtum?*"

"Quiet."

"Oh."

"Payne was there or thereabouts that night, after all. And is in the hunt. But what the Military Foot Police really wanted was to find out was about the hunt itself… just what you knew about…"

"Moriarty."

"Exactly. This bloody Moriarty. Now here's where it gets complicated…"

He paused, assembling his thoughts.

"…The Military Foot Police don't like the fact that us Cape Police picked up the Cox murder case in the first place. The fact that we know there's some chicanery going on, something involving restricted information, state secrets even, has got them riled up... don't want some bumbling colonial bobbies in charge of the investigation. The key to Cox's murder, and whatever motive is behind it, lies with finding this Moriarty, we're all clear on that. But it's not just us in the chase now. As you well know, certain other parties have been on the case, only pursuing this Moriarty far more ruthlessly... and lethally."

"Like Payne?"

"Like Payne."

It was Finch's turn. He explained the events of the past 24 hours – of their visit to Cox's RAMC office, about the Cape Town Races, Shawcroft, the chemist's shop, about Pinkie Coetzee and, most of all, what had happened at Rideau's.

Brookman listened attentively, grunting a 'yes' of punctuation here and there. Save for Finch's mention of their visit to Sammy's Bar, there was no overt display of surprise by the detective, no eyebrows raised. Finch deduced that it concurred with what he already knew. Brookman seldom asked a question to which he didn't already know the answer. He had probably had men shadowing them the whole time.

"Did you know that Rideau had been dishonourably discharged from the army in India and had served time for fraud?" Brookman added.

"I didn't but, given what I know now, it wouldn't come as a surprise. Sad actually. I quite liked him."

"Threw a damned good lunch... Seems his involvement in all this was purely for personal gain... the fool."

He paused again, choosing his words.

"Captain, what if I told you that Payne is on the payroll of the Secret Service... brought in by Military Intelligence, as and when, to make certain 'problems' go away."

"Like Cox?"

"Like Kilfoyle, like Shawcroft, like Rideau, possibly like Cox. And not just because Cox was running around getting his jollies with Lady Verity, scandalous as that may be, but because the pair of them, our star-crossed lovers, were on to something. Something *big*."

"Yes, but what?"

"Look, it's always risky making idle speculation in front of a judge. They're bigger sticklers for facts than me. But I detect a lack of lateral thinking here on the part of those in the hunt."

"Meaning?"

"How can I put it...? They're all working on a certain assumption about this mysterious Moriarty – who he is, what he's holding. But here's the thing, Captain. There's not been one single reference to a 'him'... or a 'her' for that matter. No description, no sighting, no details of movements, nothing on record anywhere. Which leads me to a conclusion... I don't think Moriarty – whether it be a code-word or whatever – is a person at all."

Finch smiled. Brookman's instincts were second to none.

"I congratulate you on your powers of perception, Inspector. What if I told you Moriarty was, indeed, not a person but..."

"But what?"

"A King Charles spaniel."

"A *dog*?" he spluttered.

"And a badly carved one at that... Moriarty is in fact an ornament – a quite hideous wooden statue, sitting cross-eyed in the hallway of Ans Du Plessis's guest house."

"Yes, yes. I know the one you mean! On the dresser!" Brookman yelped. "Ugly bugger. Remarked on it myself."

"Well this 'ugly bugger' dog is also hollow and has a flap in the back. That key I showed you—?"

"I'll be damned," said Brookman. He exhaled a whistle and rubbed the back of his neck.

Finch reached into his tunic, pulled out the manilla envelope and handed it over.

"Here."

The detective took it.

"It's what Moriarty was sitting on. What everyone's been after," said Finch.

There was a twinkle in the detective's eye as he fondled the sheathed documents in his grasp.

"Bloody hell, Finch. You beauty! You bloody beauty!"

Finch turned mournful.

"I'm afraid what's in here represents anything other than beauty," he sighed. "Documents, mimeograph copies of cables between the Cape and Whitehall, all stamped 'Classified'. I've read them. They refer to papers from Military Intelligence... This here... South Africa... They're fighting the good fight all right, but it's also seen as a test, a rehearsal for a conflict that will feature battlefield horrors as yet unimaginable. It's all in there, alongside references to meetings between members of military high command, the cabinet, the War Office—"

"What could be more horrific than what has already occurred?" asked Brookman.

"A new weapon," replied Finch. "Poison gas. Nerve gas. Gas that, when inhaled, can kill and blind and cripple. Vapours that can be wafted into an enemy's trench and fell him without a shot being fired. A kind of warfare by chemical, if you will. And it's already being tested right here in South Africa."

Brookman looked sceptical.

"Come, come, Captain Finch. If the Boers had been attacked with this gas you describe, this magic weapon, they surely would have reported it. It would be to their political advantage… playing the victim and all that. They've got huge sympathy internationally."

"That's the point. It wasn't used in combat. Not according to what's in here…"

He jabbed a finger at the envelope.

"…It was tested… on civilians."

"Civilians?"

"And prisoners of war… There's a remote area of the Northern Cape where a series of villages has been systematically cordoned off and gassed; POWs and natives used as guinea pigs – maimed, blinded and dying excruciating deaths, men, women, children. The results were recorded coldly and scientifically… and indeed, according to the documentation, most favourably. Anyone who escaped was eliminated."

Brookman waved the envelope.

"And that's all in here…? You *sure*?"

"Believe me, Inspector. My eyes are the first to glaze over when it comes to reading official documentation, but any fool can see what is meant. The way they're thinking, a war – and no one's making bones about it not being Germany – it's seen as inevitable. Within ten years maybe."

"Not exactly a revelation. The Kaiser seems to be agitating for a confrontation. We've got Germans right here on the border in Southwest Africa, remember? And elsewhere… Tanganyika, Kamerun. Like to blow their bugles, stamp their jackboots every now and then. That's just the way they are."

"But not in the way hinted at here, Inspector. Generals may talk of swift victories and quick offensives – Lord knows there's been enough hot air in this bloody show – but those in the know, those *really* in the know, are talking of a more realistic scenario, of a long, slow battle of attrition right across Europe, with conflict spreading across the associated Empires, the likes of which we've never seen. New ways of war. Entire generations in arms."

"That's just conjecture. It counts for nothing."

"Maybe. Only there's another thing, Inspector. Three days ago, at a refugee camp near Paarl, I met villagers... Nama... who'd escaped from the north, the Karoo. Some of them had been blinded. What they described, the way they described it, it matches exactly what military intelligence claims to have done."

"You sure?"

"Yes. There was a black man, and a white mother and daughter, the family of a missionary. What they told me at the time, about the slaughter, about the 'green mist' that had killed everyone, I hadn't understood; thought it was superstitious claptrap. But it makes sense now. The Bantu man, he had been there. Had seen a mass grave. He showed me the headgear that the soldiers who had carried out the attacks had worn. It was a covering, a kind of a mask with a breathing filter... He gave it to me. Should have kept it."

It was the first time Finch had seen Brookman truly flummoxed. The detective sat in silence for a moment. He even stopped his habitual scanning of the road behind him.

"This information... So Lady Verity, and then, by association, Cox, had come into possession of it somehow? They were going to reveal it? Expose it? To the press?"

"Shawcroft's involvement suggests something of that order. Quite how they were going to do it, I don't know and to what specific end, I'm not sure. But I'm positive they were going to leak it. Lady Verity was privy to information that came and went from Government House, after all. It's not unrealistic for her to have come across it, or to have heard something else which led her to taking it to a newspaper. She struck me as a principled sort of woman. Maybe she was blowing the whistle for moral reasons. I like to think it was more than cocking a snook at her husband. Although as for Cox, God only knows. Hate to say, but I think he saw it as an opportunity to make a few quid – 'sell' rather than 'give'. Journalism by cheque book."

Brookman, a man who seemed generally unruffled, appeared anxious to Finch now.

"This is dangerous stuff. Incendiary stuff!" he said, his tone turning purposeful. "And certainly too much for one man... one woman to sit on, by God."

He urged Pienaar on faster.

"Look, who else knows?" he added. "Has either of you told anyone... speculated with anyone?"

"Absolutely not."

"Good."

Brookman patted his jacket. He'd remembered something.

"Listen, my revolver. You still have it?"

Finch delved in his pocket and produced the inspector's Webley. Brookman took it.

It happened so quickly that Finch had no time to register. The gun's stock hit him hard and true across the side of the neck, delivered with an expert, whipped blow.

Chapter Fifty-Five

It was dark and wet. Somewhere up high, off to the side was a chink of light. Finch could not see clearly, his vision blurred. Through the congested blood and mucus he could smell the sea, the salt air, the seaweed and, with it, damp rock.

Lying on his side on the hard wet stone, granules of sand and shingle were embedded sharp in his cheek. There was the trickle and dripping of water. He could sense splashes and ripples around him. The acoustics, the reverberation, suggested height and breadth.

Finch tried to move but there was a stab of pain up the left side of his neck from shoulder to ear. It made him feel nauseous.

He felt the suffocating wad of cloth forced into his mouth – not tied at the back but rammed in roughly. Then he realised – his hands had been bound tightly behind him, as had his ankles. The gag was stifling, his inhalation laboured. He began to panic, forcing his breath into small, involuntary gulps.

He tried to focus on the light. He heard the squawk of a seagull, then a boom as a breaker pounded outside. He tried not to splutter and to keep his breathing calm, measured – to concentrate on his surroundings.

He was in a cave, a sea cave.

There was more squawking, more gulls and then another boom. Though this time it was distant, different, out to sea. He heard a high-pitched whistle…

Magersfontein.

…And then…

CRASH!

…felt the almighty crack as something – a shell, yes, a shell – exploded, so loud, so concussive on its impact that stones rained down, jolted free from the nooks and crannies up above.

It was not safe, in any sense.

He detected a faint groaning. Another person. Female. He called as best he could. The word was muffled.

"Annie?!"

He thought he heard a 'yes'. As his eyes grew accustomed to the darkness, he could make it out now – her shape, the long dress. Like him, she was lying on her side, bound.

He wriggled his chin, working his jaw round in circles. He pushed hard with his tongue. There was leeway in the gag but not much – the cloth, a kerchief, had been rammed in deep, right to the back of his throat. He managed to dislodge it a little.

"Are you hurt?" he tried this time.

A muted cry came back.

"Okay," he thought it went. "I'm okay."

BOOM!

The rumble was louder, like a vicious thunderstorm, the accompanying whistle more demonic. And then...

CRASH!

...Another almighty explosion, more seismic than the first. He ducked his head in vain to deflect the falling debris which showered down hard. Small stones danced on his skull.

Cape Point. They must be at Cape Point.

At Christmas dinner the naval officer had told him about it. The warships testing their guns, shooting at tugs or at land targets, perfecting the art of a shore bombardment.

This cave. No one ever comes here. No one would ever hear them, probably ever discover them.

He tried to shift himself, to roll over to Annie. She was 10ft away.

But then came a flicker of orange from the side. The sound of leather soles on rock, the crunch and splash of pool and shingle as men strode towards them. A lantern was swinging.

With a thud, it was deposited on the ground next to Finch's face – so close the light blinded him. The heat hurt his eyeballs. He caught a brief and distorted glimpse of himself in the nickel plating. It was not someone he recognised.

He was jerked from behind, by the elbows, up into a kneeling position. He winced as he was forced to bend his damaged leg.

His gag was yanked out roughly. He choked and coughed. He mustered what little moisture he could to spit out the aftertaste and could hear Annie doing the same. They both gasped, swallowing in the air.

Before them stood three men – Brookman and two others he did not recognise. One – older, fatter and bespectacled – wore a tweed suit and had a walrus moustache; a watch chain hung on his waistcoat. His bowler hat seemed too small for his head. The other man was younger, leaner, better tailored.

The first one introduced himself.

"Agent Soames," he offered, flashing some kind of badge in a leather wallet, as if the circumstances were entirely cordial.

"Rutherford," nodded the second.

And then, there he was, a fourth man, stepping out of the shadows, loitering at the back.

…Payne.

Annie shrieked, thrown into a panic, as yet unaware of the detective's duplicity, complicity.

"It's him, it's him…! Inspector, it's HIM!"

"Now, now, Miss," Brookman soothed. "Let's not make this any more difficult than it has to be."

And now Finch understood – Brookman's 'regret', his 'sorrow' about Annie getting caught up in this. And 'Dood'… Was that last bit really necessary? In Afrikaans, Finch knew this much, 'dood' meant 'death'. That was with whom they had their appointment. Their final judgement.

Payne remained impassive, disinterested. It was the first time Finch had been able to get a good look at him. And now the penny dropped. The mud… Magersfontein… It was him, the wounded lieutenant who, in his delirium, had whispered 'Moriarty'.

But how… why…? What on *earth*?

"Seems my colleague Mr Payne owes you a debt of gratitude, Captain Finch," pronounced Soames, like a grandee at a prize-giving. "It was thanks to you that he got through the lines that day. The late Major Cox had been uncharacteristically smart in anticipating his own tormentor's arrival. Knew we wouldn't stay bottled up in Kimberley for long. There *are* ways and means of getting out."

Kimberley?

"Cox was unbelievably fortuitous in having you deliver Payne to him broken and incapacitated," he added. "Putting him under lock and key. What Cox hadn't gambled upon was our man's resourcefulness; that he would escape his guard and continue pursuit."

Rutherford, chuckled.

"Though retrieving the documents proved more difficult than we'd expected," Soames continued. "Our fault for trusting that fool Rideau."

It was Brookman's turn.

"Rideau had convinced us that Cox's papers were in his possession, or at least available to us via an associate... this Moriarty... and that he could procure them for us for a fee."

Said Rutherford: "In which case, Captain, we are grateful – and with no small amount of irony – that it should have been you, too, who delivered the goods to us... And absolutely for free."

Soames turned to Brookman. For all the horror of their predicament, he really did sound like he was on stage at a village fête.

"And it is thanks to the professionalism of our friends in the Cape Police here," he beamed, extending his palm to indicate the detective, "that we have also managed to restrict access to this vital information. The situation has thus been contained."

Nodding his appreciation, Brookman reached inside his jacket and pulled out the manilla envelope. Like the scroll of an honorary doctorate, he presented it to Rutherford.

"Inspector," nodded the agent in thanks.

What happened next occurred so swiftly and without suggestion that Finch could barely comprehend it, his head echoing with the disbelieving scream of Annie.

In the blink of an eye Payne stepped forward, nonchalantly raised his pistol and with such devastating violence and volume – the percussive echo ringing in their ears – shot Brookman through the chest.

He crumpled to the floor, life extinguished.

"Most unfortunate," muttered Soames. "But a case of what you might call covering our tracks."

Finch could hear Annie sobbing now. He couldn't see her face properly. It was shrouded in a veil of untamed dark hair. But he felt her presence, her tired, scared, confused presence. He yearned to hold her.

Annie, I am truly sorry.

And for a moment he understood Ans Du Plessis's need for all those Bibles.

"Cowards!" she was yelling now, the fight not over. "Pathetic cowards!"

"Nurse Jones," admonished Soames. "Might I ask you to keep control of your emotions. This is no time for hysterics."

If Brookman could be eliminated in the pursuit of Cox's documents, there was little hope, Finch knew, that they would spared.

"They got Rideau, too, Annie," said Finch. "Last night."

Brookman lay there in front of them. On his back, he looked as serene as if he'd just taken pause after a heavy Sunday picnic on a glorious sunny riverbank, his black eyes twinkling up in silent post-prandial contemplation.

You miserable two-faced bastard, Brookman.

"Not one of the Chosen People, after all," mused Rutherford. "Unlike yourself. As you've probably guessed, you weren't selected at random. The Inspector proved an expert fisherman. You were a juicy bait for us to dangle."

'*Were*' a juicy bait. He already existed in the past tense.

"You even gave up Lady Verity's letters," Soames added. "Fortunately we've managed to nip that scandal in the bud."

"I don't get it," snarled Finch. "Why run round chasing after documents… after Moriarty… offing people left, right and centre when you had Cox right there. He could have led you anywhere you wanted."

"Because that idiot Rideau went and killed him," Rutherford snapped.

"Rideau?"

"Cox's error was that he'd entrusted some of what he knew to Rideau, including that the document had been passed on to someone… or as we now know some*thing*… called Moriarty. Rideau, pathetic little addict, thought he could extract some reward out of the situation – blackmailing Cox for pharmaceuticals in return for not spilling the beans about it… or the Lady Verity affair for that matter… then trying to extort cash left right and centre from those in the hunt, on the basis that he was the gatekeeper to the information."

"Got to hand it to Cox," conceded Soames. "He threw everyone off the scent with that Moriarty trick."

It was starting to fall into place for Finch. It was Rideau who had got wind of Cox revealing the documents to the press. Cox had genuinely been planning to expose the story about gas warfare and in an entirely proper manner, but then Rideau popped up, queering the pitch, offering Shawcroft money for the same information, once it came his way – '*Your man... a big price.*'

Presumably Rideau was doing so to save his own neck, to procure the documents then deliver them to the secret service as he'd promised... though, again, for a fee.

Cox, you were acting honourably all along.

"Cox had been harassed by Rideau in the months before the war," said Rutherford. "But this time, when Cox arrived back on leave and Rideau immediately got up to his old antics, Cox had had enough. He called his bluff by procuring some laudanum for Rideau, as requested, but then withholding it. He'd hoped to bring Rideau to heel but instead it provoked him into a rage."

The row outside the chemist's shop.

"That night Rideau took advantage of Cox's inebriation at the Officers' Club," explained Soames. "Saw that Kilfoyle had put him in a cab, drunk, then hopped in himself. Started rooting around in Cox's pockets for the laudanum bottle, but couldn't find it. Then, in a fit of pique, he killed him by stuffing his own handkerchief down his throat."

Rutherford gave another derisive snort.

"The bloody bottle was right there in Cox's coat all along. He'd missed it. At the Somerset Road Cemetery our friend Payne sneaks on board, too. Had been following behind and was alarmed to see that Rideau had not only got into the cab but had killed Cox to boot."

"Thought he'd teach Rideau a lesson," said Soames. "Pulled out the kerchief, whipped out the laudanum and poured the whole damn bottle down the dead Cox's throat, right in front of his very eyes... before replacing the kerchief again. Showed Rideau who was boss... we still needed him at this point as our lead to Moriarty, of course. Payne then threw the coat with the bottle in the pocket out of the cab just for good measure, just to spite Rideau."

"Of course Rideau was then forced to jump out and root around in the dirt for it like a pig," described Rutherford. "Poor bloody cabbie meanwhile is so bloody drunk himself, he doesn't know what the hell's going on under the canvas."

Finch spluttered, too inaudibly for his inquisitors.

"You what?" asked Rutherford. "Spit it out, man."

"Cox's coat. How did it end up with Shawcroft?'"

"Aha. Didn't crack that did you? Originally, unbeknown to everyone else, Cox wasn't meant to go straight home. Had a clandestine two o'clock rendezvous with Shawcroft at the cemetery gates. Our intrepid reporter had become particularly exercised, what with this Rideau suddenly turning up and trying to put in advance order for the Moriarty merchandise, so to speak. Needed to find out from Cox what was going on."

Said Soames: "Unfortunately Cox got so sauced that when Kilfoyle put him in the cab and wrote down the address to the guest house, the cab went sailing on past. Shawcroft didn't like the look of what was going on, so stepped back into the shadows. Cox's coat came flying out and landed in the mud nearby. He grabbed it."

BOOM!

Another shell. A devastating roar. And…

CRASH!

There was more debris showering. None of them, not even Payne, could escape flinching. This time there was little interval between the sound of the guns and the shell's arrival – like the diminishing pause between thunder and lightning. The shells were exploding closer.

Soames examined his pocket watch and harrumphed.

"We haven't much time."

He cleared his throat.

"This is not a pleasant business. But sometimes such things are necessary to preserve the security of Queen and Country. You find the trial of poison gas revolting? We all do. But the Germans are already working on it themselves. They've conducted wholesale massacres of natives up in South West Africa. We are merely keeping up. Freedom, and the means to protect it, comes at a cost, usually, regrettably, human."

"You find something honourable in slaughtering innocent people?" Finch protested.

"Come, come, Captain. There were ten million Indians killed in the Mutiny; 30,000 Sudanese perished in a single afternoon at Omdurman. Today, in Tasmania, they shoot Aborigines for sport. Why only when victims are white and Christian do you do-gooders get so high and mighty?"

It was true, no one would had given a damn about the native villagers had it not been for the Suttons.

BOOM!

The naval guns rumbled again, louder still. This time, even from within, they could hear the shell shriek through the air.

CRASH!

The explosion was so close, so loud, so jarring, it nearly threw those standing off their feet. The blast rocked the cave, the stones rained down harder, painfully harder. The flame in the lamp almost flickered out.

Soames wanted it wrapped up.

"We'll not delay," he assured. "You will be recorded as having died in battle. We'll see to that. But first…"

He nodded to Rutherford, who took the envelope, ripped it open and slid out the sheaf within.

His face turned to thunder.

"What the—?"

He flung the contents straight into Finch's face – 27 blank white pieces of foolscap paper.

"Very funny," he growled. "We can make this as painful as you wish. Now where are they?"

He nodded to Payne, who stepped forward and slapped Finch hard, open-handed across the cheek.

Finch, blood pouring from his mouth, grinned maniacally. If they were going to kill him, to kill poor Annie, he would make it as unpleasant for them as possible.

"This morning, on my instruction, the papers were delivered by a station bellboy to the Central Post Office," he crowed. "They are now on their way via steam packet to Southampton where they will proceed to an address in London. More precisely, they will be delivered to an attorney colleague who has strict instructions only to open the envelope on the untimely death of myself, Captain Ingo Finch…"

Payne went to strike Annie.

"…or Nurse Annie Jones of the New South Wales Army Nursing Service Reserve."

Payne stopped.

The two agents looked at each other. Finch sensed confusion… doubt.

"Then we'll have to take our chances," said Soames.

Rutherford nodded at Payne.

"Ladies first."

At which Payne went to stand behind Annie and placed the barrel of his revolver to the nape of her neck.

Annie, I am so sorry.

She said nothing. He could see now. There was a look of defiance on her face. She wouldn't give them the satisfaction. Finch loved her for it.

Payne cocked the hammer. The click was the worst sound Finch had ever heard.

BOOM!

Another naval gun. The banshee wail of the incoming missile distorted Finch's eardrums. And then...

CRASH!

...Amid the flash of phosphorous white light, they were in a cauldron, a swirling whirlpool of stones and sea and rocks. From on high, large jagged slabs rained down.

"ANNIE!"

There was smoke. As it cleared Finch could see she was alive but knocked for six, lying dazed on her side, beside her now... *Rutherford?* He had been flung there, face down, motionless, his body horribly contorted, twisted under a cairn of limestone.

He called to Annie but could not hear himself above the ringing in his ears. In the other direction Soames, now a pathetic old man, hatless, covered in grime and dust, was staggering, trying to gather his senses, his watch dangling on its chain. He fumbled vainly for his spectacles in the light of the lantern, its glass broken, lying on its side.

Finch rose. His ankles were bound, his arms behind his back. But with every ounce of strength he could muster he charged at him. His head butted into the man's chest, knocking him over, spilling the lantern again.

In the flicker of it, the man looked petrified.

There was no sympathy. Finch jumped hard, with both feet, and brought both sets of hobnails down on Soames' face. There was a sickening crack. Finch, on his backside, shovelled the feet with his body, rolling it over, face down into a rock pool. It didn't move.

But elsewhere the water was rising, whirling. As his hearing returned he could hear it roar. White foam crashed in through a gap which hadn't existed before. With tied limbs Finch tried to get up, but he had poor balance. He toppled over.

"SIR!" he heard. A cry of warning.

"Annie, get out of here."

"SIR!"

Payne tumbled right past him.

On the ground. His gun.

Finch had staggered against a rock and used it to work his way upright. He looped his bound hands under his feet and brought them to the front of his body. He, too, sprang towards the weapon. The men rolled over on one another. Finch took a sharp elbow to the bridge of the nose as Payne attempted to beat him back.

Using the only weapon he had at his disposal, Finch bit down on Payne's good hand, hard… so hard he could taste the other man's blood. Payne merely kicked him off. Just feet away, Payne dived, arms outstretched and got his hand to the pistol's grip.

Slowly he raised it, raised himself.

Finch was on his side, fully in its sight, completely helpless.

There was the thin smile of satisfaction on Payne's lips as he began to squeeze the trigger…

BANG!

…But, with the expression of man who'd been jilted at the altar, Payne froze for a moment, before toppling forward, his legs buckling under him and crashed down into the shingle.

Both Finch and Annie turned.

Brookman, his own gun arm shaking uncontrollably, was propped on an elbow.

He dropped his Webley and collapsed onto his back.

Finch shuffled over; Annie followed.

He was barely alive, his face bluey-white, blood trickling from the corner of his mouth. He groaned.

"I… I… I'm so sorry."

They could hardly hear him, they leaned closer.

"Finch… Miss… I'm so terribly sorry."

"You know Brookman, of all the people, you were the last—"

But Finch couldn't find adequate words.

"Goddamnit man, I believed you, *trusted* you."

Brookman was trying to say something again. Finch looked down at his chest. The wound was massive.

Finch turned to Annie. She had moved away to retrieve the shattered lantern and now sat with her back to it, holding her rope bindings over the flame.

She winced as it burnt her. Then she tugged her hands apart and the rope shredded.

"My pocketknife," said Finch.

She reached in his tunic pocket, then set to work on his own hands then both their ankles.

BOOM!

The naval guns fired again. But this time it was quieter. There was no whistle. They heard the crash of the shell a distance away. Brookman was still alive. Barely. Finch cradled his head.

"Was working… for British Intelligence," he rasped. "Was told you were a spy. Had to keep close tabs… Said you'd double-crossed us… Stolen state secrets… passed them to our enemies… Lives at stake… But they tricked me, *used* me… I never imagined—"

There was fluid gurgling in his throat.

"It's all right, Inspector," soothed Finch. "It's all right."

"I mucked it up, Captain. I *assumed*—"

His face was motionless, the sparkle now gone forever from the eyes. Finch let him go.

There was a swirl and a rush. The water was rising fast, the sea flooding in. Lower down, Rutherford's body was completely submerged now, save for the back of his head and the knuckles of his hands floating out to either side. Soames' body was bobbing against the rocks. Payne's would soon be carried off. Brookman would then be swept up.

"Come on," Annie said.

This time it was she who took the lead. She grabbed Finch's hand and pulled him to his feet.

"See, up there…"

There was more daylight.

"We go up, this way…"

Five minutes later they had squeezed through the gap. The sun and the light sea breeze caressing them like a doting mother.

Out to sea the grey naval warships sat. There was a muzzle flash and a muted crack. But this time the guns were aiming away from the shore. There was an old barge two or three miles out. A great white geyser of water shot up next to it.

The coast was rocky, windswept, tree-less, the coarse grass of the slopes strewn with boulders. In the distance, a pack of baboons charged down the bank, behind them Signal Hill, Cape Town and, beyond, great Table Mountain, its summit shrouded in a fine mist, its 'tablecloth'.

To sea again, on the Cape of Good Hope, the breakers crashed, the gulls squawked and the great mass of ocean rolled – nothing between them and the Antarctic, the very end of the Continent.

They drank in the air and stood in silence.

"You know what today is?" said Finch eventually.

She shrugged.

"Happy New Year," he offered.

"No," she corrected. "Happy New Century."

Epilogue

In the main square, across from the great, deep hole of the Kimberley Mine, the regimental band of the Royal Garrison Artillery gave its recital.

Mbutu recognised the tune. He had heard it many times – *Rule Britannia*, a jolly imperial jingle. The whites always enjoyed it, discreetly clapping along while the cheery conductor waved his baton, throwing a smile of appreciation over his shoulder.

Lining the thoroughfares they were a fine sight, these masters and mistresses, you could not deny it – silks, satins, bows, white gloves; servants to hoist frilled parasols and protect the ladies in their high Parisian fashion; men preening in their well-cut morning suits, with starched collars and hats – toppers and homburgs.

The streets were thronged. People ecstatic. Paper Union Jacks fluttered everywhere, folks waved them frantically on wooden sticks, pushing and jostling to see the approaching parade.

"He's coming," said someone, and the buzz spread.

And then there he was, up high, on his charger, leading the column, a king in all his vainglory.

"God bless you, Mr Rhodes," he heard someone yell, a man almost in tears with admiration.

The crowd swelled, the cheers rose, the soldiers marched on – the Kimberley Regiment, the Lancashires, Royal Engineers, then the Royal Artillery, their field guns creaking and lumbering on their great heavy carriages.

"It's Roberts! It's Roberts!" went the cry. And then there he was, too, in his khakis and pith helmet on his impressive chestnut horse – his face red, moustache bushy and white, nodding acceptance of the plaudits.

The Major-General... French... the one whose cavalry had entered five days ago, was now in hot pursuit of the retreating Boers, it was understood. His force had already pushed on into the Orange Free State. It was only a matter of time...

Then, at the back, the dignitaries, hastened up from Cape Town – pale men in dark suits, civil servants and mandarins, accompanied by their wives following in their landaus, looking uncomfortable in the great outdoors, embarrassed at being there.

—

With Annie called back to the Kimberley Hospital, Finch watched alone. In Sir Alfred Milner's absence, Sir Frederick Hancock's coach passed by. Lady Verity sat next to him, gazing out under the ostrich feathers of an oversized hat.

"Enjoying the show?" came a voice.

"Officially or truthfully?" Finch replied.

Jenkins smiled.

"See the report exonerated that chap," added the Welshman.

"As a matter of fact that's why I'm here."

Finch had been looking up and down but knew he'd find him eventually. And there he was, in the shade of a jacaranda... set back from the crowd, smoking and watching – in a state, Finch fancied, of reluctant acceptance.

Standing proudly, he had on a pale blue corduroy suit, riding boots and a slouch hat pinned up on one side with the stub of a red feather in it – loitering near him two MFPs, the Boer officers having been granted a privileged status over the ordinary POWs, paroled in the daytime upon their honour, though on this auspicious occasion with minders hovering just in case.

"Excuse me, sir," Finch emphasised, turning to Jenkins.

"Now, now, Ingo," Jenkins admonished. "No need for that in private."

But Finch was gone, striding over.

"I believe it's written in our stars," he declared.

The man looked up, extinguished his cigarette and smiled. He extended a hand to shake, the MFPs began to move in, but Finch signalled that it was okay.

"Swanepoel, I want to thank you," said Finch. "The casualties reached Bloemfontein just as you promised. They have been well cared

401

for. I understand several have been repatriated. Some spoke up for you personally."

"As did you."

"I'm just sorry that—"

Swanepoel waved a hand in dismissal.

"It was an unscrupulous trick, a stunt by a superior of which I thoroughly disapproved. Designed to antagonise. It did its trick."

"Look, if there's anything I can do… your family, any letters, please don't hesitate."

Swanepoel nodded his thanks.

"Oh, and there's this…"

Finch reached into the side pocket of his tunic… a full, sealed quart bottle. He handed it to him. Swanepoel admired the label.

"Talisker," he sighed. "Twelve years old."

"I believe I also made a promise," said Finch. "When you drink it you will think of me."

Both men smiled.

"Good luck Swanepoel."

"Good luck, Captain Finch."

–

Mbutu sat on the wooden steps of the veranda of the general store. On the flat roof of the warehouse opposite was a small man in a yellow suit. He had two colleagues with him, hunched over a big box camera on a tripod – unlike anything Mbutu had seen – one of them cranking a handle.

"Perfect," the man was enthusing, his accent unfamiliar, his manner most excitable. "Beautiful. Now get the guy on the horse… No, the guy on the horse!"

Below, on the dusty road, played children, a knot of them running, shrieking with joy – girls in pinafore dresses, boys cavorting despite their uncomfortable suits and knickerbockers. They had grown bored with the parade and were chasing after a wooden hoop which one girl, a blonde girl with big blue eyes, propelled with a stick.

She saw Mbutu and waved, nearly losing control. Mbutu waved back. Then he hugged his own son, blissfully asleep on his lap.